A DOOR IN THE DARK

Also by Scott Reintgen

A Whisper in the Walls

A
DOOR
IN THE
DARK

SCOTT REINTGEN

Margaret K. McElderry Books

New York London Toronto Sydney New Delhi

MARGARET K. McELDERRY BOOKS
An imprint of Simon & Schuster Children's Publishing Division
1230 Avenue of the Americas, New York, New York 10020

MARGARET K. McELDERRY BOOKS is a trademark of Simon & Schuster, LLC.
Simon & Schuster: Celebrating 100 Years of Publishing in 2024
For information about special discounts for bulk purchases, please contact Simon & Schuster Special Sales at 1-866-506-1949 or business@simonandschuster.com.
The Simon & Schuster Speakers Bureau can bring authors to your live event. For more information or to book an event, contact the Simon & Schuster Speakers Bureau at 1-866-248-3049 or visit our website at www.simonspeakers.com.
Also available in a Margaret K. McElderry Books hardcover edition
Interior design by Irene Metaxatos
The text for this book was set in ITC Veljovic Std.
Manufactured in the United States of America
First Margaret K. McElderry Books paperback edition March 2024
10 9 8 7 6 5 4 3 2 1
The Library of Congress has cataloged the hardcover edition as follows:
Names: Reintgen, Scott, author. Title: A door in the dark / Scott Reintgen.
Description: First edition. | New York : Margaret K. McElderry Books, [2023] | Audience: Ages 14 up. | Audience: Grades 10–12. | Summary: Follows six teenage wizards as they fight to make it home alive after a malfunctioning spell leaves them stranded in the wilderness. | Identifiers: LCCN 2022016792 (print) | LCCN 2022016793 (ebook) | ISBN 9781665918688 (hardcover) | ISBN 9781665918695 (paperback) | ISBN 9781665918701 (ebook) | Subjects: CYAC: Wizards—Fiction. | Magic—Fiction. | Survival—Fiction. | Forests and forestry—Fiction. | Fantasy. | LCGFT: Fantasy fiction. | Novels. | Classification: LCC PZ7.1.R4554 Do 2023 (print) | LCC PZ7.1.R4554 (ebook) | DDC [Fic]—dc23 | LC record available at https://lccn.loc.gov/2022016792 | LC ebook record available at https://lccn.loc.gov/2022016793

For my wife, Katie, who heard twenty different versions
of this story, all with different character names,
and patiently listened every time I came in the room
and said, "Hey. Can I read you something?"

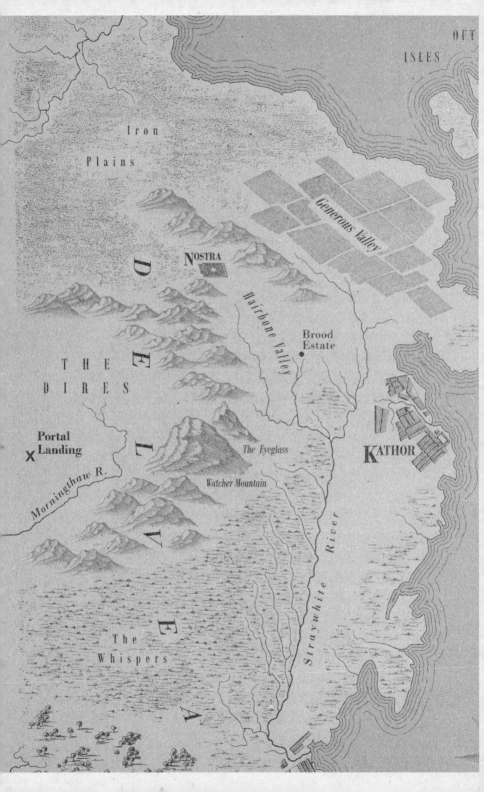

PROLOGUE

For a few seconds Ren stood there, bent over, her chest heaving. Even the smallest motion threatened to rock her stomach. She waited until she was certain she wasn't going to throw up again. Then she pulled her scarf up over her nose and turned back to face the dark scene.

Timmons looked like a dying flower. She was kneeling in the dirt, face buried in her hands, her entire body shaking uncontrollably. Theo stood with one hand pressed to the base of a giant tree, struggling to keep his feet. He'd turned his back to them. Anything to avoid looking at what was lying on the forest floor between them. Ren's eyes skipped over that same spot.

She looked at Avy instead. He was on his back, staring up at the thick canopy. His chest rose and fell, and she remembered he'd been hit by a stunner before the portal spell activated. Likely its effect had amplified. She suspected the magic felt like a two-ton anvil now.

Only Cora remained calm. Of course. The medical student

would know what to do when everyone else was panicking. Ren watched her navigate through the maze of bone-thick roots. She knelt down to take vitals and announced unhelpfully, "He's dead."

Those words finally brought the image back into focus. Ren couldn't ignore it now. Clyde Winters was sprawled at a strange angle on the forest floor—and he looked very, very dead. Cora was fishing through her bag. She unpacked a small medical kit. The sound of her tools clinking together finally forced Theo to turn around. He wiped his mouth with one sleeve.

"Knock it off. That's an heir of House Winters. He's not a test cadaver."

Cora paused in the middle of her preparations. Even though the forest was thick with shadows, Ren saw the girl's expression clearly. She looked like she wanted to tell Theo that was exactly what Clyde was now. Instead she offered a begrudging nod.

"You're right. It's just . . . unlike any death I've ever seen . . . knowing the cause. . . ."

Ren saw the sharpness in Theo's expression. She decided to intervene.

"Not now, Cora. We need to figure out where we are first."

Avy finally sat up. He blinked a few times. When he saw Clyde's body on the ground, both hands went up defensively. "I . . . I didn't do that. I swear! There's no way. . . ."

For some reason his denial dragged Timmons back into the conversation.

"I *told* you not to do magic in there. Look at that. Look what happened to him!"

Avy shook his head. "I didn't even cast a spell. That's what I'm saying. It couldn't have been me. I didn't use any magic. . . ."

There was a moment of silence. No retching or heaving or sobbing. It was just long enough for the forest to press in around them like a shadow. A sharp breeze stirred the branches, clacking them together like spears. Ren heard dying birdsong and the distant shuffling of larger creatures. The group looked around, unnerved. The quiet was a reminder that this place—wherever they were—was also a threat to them. She'd never felt so exposed. It didn't help that one of them was already dead. That thought was followed by a darker one.

And one of us killed him.

BEFORE

1

Wind prowled wolflike through the waiting crowd, sinking its teeth into exposed necks and bare ankles. Ren kept her hood up and her eyes down. Still, it found every threadbare hole and feasted. There was an unspoken camaraderie to how everyone in line huddled closer together as it howled. On the first day of every month, Ren left her dormitory on Balmerick's campus and traveled down to wait in line in the Lower Quarter.

She knew the place by memory now. The patterns on the stone walkway. How decades of passing boots had rounded its edges. The rows of windows that were always boarded shut. Even the other people who waited in line with her, assigned to this particular magic-house.

Sunlight might have warded off the chill, but there wasn't sunlight in this section of the Lower Quarter. Not at this hour. Not in her lifetime. Ren couldn't resist looking up.

The Heights hovered magically overhead. When she was a child, it had been a marvel to her. An awe that only grew when she studied the actual magical theories involved. It was no small task for the Proctor family to create an entire neighborhood of glinting buildings in the clouds. Her favorite part had been the relocation of Balmerick University. The building's foundations had proven rather tricky. Decades of residual magic had made the walls more or less sentient. It turned out they liked where they'd settled down in the Lower Quarter. A team of wizards had used veracity alteration spells to convince each individual rock that the sky was actually the earth. Ren liked to imagine them spending hours underground, lying to the stones.

"Eyes ahead, dear."

Ren startled. She'd allowed a gap to form in the line. Two strides brought her back into position. She glanced at the woman who'd spoken, an apology ready, before recognizing her.

"Aunt Sloan."

Not her real aunt. Her mother was an only child, just as Ren was an only child. But every woman who lived in their building was an aunt. Every man an uncle. The other kids were all cousins, until they were old enough to start flirting and figuring out where they could sneak kisses without being seen. Aunt Sloan lived up on the third floor. She worked on the wharf.

"Little Monroe," she said. "How's your mother?"

"Doing well. Strong and happy and willful."

Sloan laughed. "Of course. I hate that our shifts changed. It's been too long since she and I sat down to play a few hands of barons together. About four years now. Agnes was always such a good time, too. It's a shame she's all alone these days."

Barons was a rotating card game that Ren's mother loved. It involved seven suits, and the winner was usually the one who got away with the most cheating. Ren quietly took note of the other implications hidden beneath Aunt Sloan's words. She kept her tone neutral, polite.

"I will tell her you said hello."

Sloan nodded. "It's kind of you to stand in line for her."

Her aunt gestured to the bracelet hanging on Ren's wrist. It was a memorable piece. A little loop of dragon-forged iron. Smoke black except for the rivulets of flickering fire that boiled in the metal's depths. Ren's father had bought it for her mother as a wedding gift. It was for the woman, he'd said, who bent to the will of no one. And a nod to the fire she brought out in him.

Sloan kept prattling on. ". . . my boys. Too busy to stand in for me. Both of them landed jobs in Peckering's workshop. Making ends meet. You know how it all goes, dear. Or you did. Before you went off to live in the clouds and do your . . . studies."

There it was. The neighborhood's favorite slice of gossip. Ren knew the others always wondered how she'd gotten into a private school like Balmerick. What trick did the Monroes have up their sleeves? They always praised the achievement to her face, but she knew exactly what they said behind her and her mother's backs. *Reaching for the stars, isn't she? Bound to come back empty-handed.*

The line moved. Ren used it as an excuse to drop the conversation. She kept her eyes forward and waited patiently until it was her turn. A pair of doors were propped open. The building to which they belonged was hunched and industrious, singular in its purpose. A government official sat at a table. His hair was slicked back, eyes narrowed in meticulous calculation. He offered the barest of nods when Ren stepped forward.

"Vessel?"

"I have two that need to be refilled, sir. One is mine. One belongs to my mother."

She slid off her mother's bracelet and set it on the table. Next she reached for the wand hanging from the loop on her belt. Her own was shaped like a horseshoe. Both ends curved to sharpened points, but the central section offered a crude handle for her grip. She preferred this style to the aim-and-point wands. She'd found it far easier to control the range of her spells.

The government accountant briefly appraised both items.

"Listed under Agnes Monroe and Ren Monroe."

He ran a finger down the list of names. She saw him pause and knew the question he'd ask before his lips even moved. "And what about Roland Monroe?"

The name shivered down her spine the way it always did when a stranger spoke it so casually. Ren saw a brief vision of his body, bent in all the wrong ways. Every time she came to collect her monthly allotment, they would say his name before tracing the line across to see the explanation for his absence. Ren spoke the word before the man could. The smallest of victories.

"Deceased."

He tapped the notation in front of him and nodded. They never showed sympathy. Never whispered a condolence. It was just a status that determined how the rest of the transaction should go. This particular arbiter didn't even bother to make eye contact.

"Very well. I've got you listed for an allowance of one hundred ockleys per vessel. The law requires I inform you that another magical stipend will be avail—"

Ren cleared her throat. "I've got coin to add more. If that's okay?"

"How much?"

"Just twenty mids. I earned a few tips this week."

He hunched back over his list to make another notation. Ren had learned never to add too much. A big down payment could earn unwanted attention. Sometimes the government would investigate. Cut off your welfare entirely. She couldn't afford for that to happen.

"Twenty mids convert to about two hundred more ockleys."

If you want to be precise, it's 201.32. But Ren only nodded at the approximation. An ockley was the exact amount of magic it took to use a single-step spell. Named for Reverend Ockley, who Ren knew had come up with the original and very incorrect equation. His math had been honed by far cleverer wizards, but he was the one in the history books. Sometimes, being first was all that mattered. Ren looked up and realized the accountant was staring at her. He repeated himself.

"Which item do you want them added to?"

"The bracelet," she answered. "My mother could use the extra spells."

A well-worn lie. It fit like an old shoe at this point. Her mother hadn't used any of their magical allowance in years. The man didn't ask any questions, though. He simply turned and handed the two vessels to a hired runner. The young girl slipped inside the warehouse through an interior door. Ren caught a glimpse of the factory-like rows. Discolored gases churned in the enclosed space. It was still strange to think the city's entire magical supply came from underground. Ren knew the histories. She'd memorized all the dates for her exams back in undergrad. She could recite the year that her people—the Delveans—first landed on this continent. She knew the name of the woman who'd cast the first recorded spell in their people's history, and the group of wizards who'd invented the conversion process that refined raw magic into a form that could be dispensed to the masses. Like every other primary school student, she'd memorized the names of the four ships that had sailed up the eastern seaboard to land in what would one day become Kathor.

She'd also read through all the modern theories and conspiracies about magic refineries. One author claimed there was infinite magic underneath their city and that the five wealthiest houses had created a scarcity model to keep the rest of the population underfoot. Another claimed that the city's supply was nearly depleted, and when it ran out, society would completely collapse. After spending time with the scions and heirs at Balmerick, Ren suspected the former was far more likely to be true.

As the interior door shut with a thump, Ren watched the girl vanish with the two most valuable items she possessed. She wondered how the accountant—who'd barely even looked at her—might react if he knew all the spellwork written into the veins of each of those vessels. All the time she'd spent hammering perfection into her stances and her enunciations.

All he sees is another welfare wizard.

"You can step to the side. She'll return shortly."

Ren complied. She felt an itch at the back of her neck. A whisper of an echo of a curse. This was where she always stood as she waited for her items. She knew that the alley over her right shoulder ran straight and narrow, down to the place where her life had changed forever. Every time she stood here, she tried to resist looking. And every time she failed. As Aunt Sloan stepped up to speak with the accountant, Ren looked down that arrow of an alleyway.

It pointed to the distant canal bridge. Unfinished back then, it was the place where her father had turned to wave back at her. Ren's eyes found the wooden bench where she'd sat down to wait for him. Sometimes she couldn't believe it was still there. Like a relic that she'd summoned from her own memories. And then she imagined hearing the sound of the earth grinding beneath their feet as it had that day. The way her father had looked back one final time before he fell. Her entire life, changed in less than a breath.

"Your things?"

The girl was back, standing with both vessels held out. Ren liked to imagine she saw a new glow in them, but the truth was they looked exactly the same. She accepted both vessels, and the runner slipped back to her position behind the table. Ren glanced at the line one more time.

Everyone was waiting. She knew they'd refill their vessels and use spells that unwound the knots in their backs. Spells that added strength to get them through another grueling day. Aunt Sloan liked to spice her soups with a little magic. Others entertained grandchildren with clever charms. She almost envied the thought. Using magic to touch up their days. Meanwhile, she would spend the next few weeks try-ing to create entirely new spells with her meager allotment. Doing her best to impress people who seemed to find nothing so impressive as their own lives.

Ren took a final look, tucked her wand into a waiting belt loop, and started to walk.

2

The Lower Quarter divided into a dozen smaller neighborhoods.

Ren had grown up on Stepfast Street, north of the busier markets. It would always be home, even if she'd lived on Balmerick's campus for the last four years. She skirted the growing crowds and took the road that led to the building where her mother lived. It was a drab, square structure with only brightly painted doors to mark it as more than abandoned stone. She aimed for the pearl-blue door at the far end of the building. It swung on groaning hinges, and somehow the sound was even worse than she remembered. She took the stairs on her right and found her mother's second-floor entry unlocked and unwarded.

"Well, that's just incredibly safe of you, Mother. . . ."

It was silent inside. The kitchen was the dining room was the living room. One wall boasted open shelving and a half-rusted stove. It cornered into a fold-out table where every single Monroe family meal had taken place. A hop and a skip would set a person firmly in the living room. There was the knee-high table her father had built, surrounded by cushions her mother had sewn. Ren saw three teacups abandoned there. Not a sign of company, she knew, but more a measurement of the passage of time. The color variations of the stained tea bags in each cup marked how long they'd mulled there in silence.

Ren set to work. Arranging the cushions. Washing the cups. There were abandoned clothes that she folded in a neat stack. Next, the magic. It was a delicate balance of improving her mother's quality of life but keeping enough to get in the practice reps she needed for her graduate work. She'd learned all about continuous spells during junior year and had been using them to save a few precious ockleys ever since.

A cleansing enchantment kept back the mold common in the Lower Quarter's poorly lit living spaces. Magical sealants along the frames of every door and window warded against infestations. Each spell already sat in the air—thick and stagnant from when she'd last cast it—though each one faded to uselessness by the time the first of the month came around again.

Refreshing them was like scrubbing out an old canteen and filling it back up with fresh water. Once she finished the normal spellwork, she took the threaded edges of all that magic and layered a longevity spell of her own invention through them. It took, binding invisibly through everything like a braid. Ren was wiping sweat from her forehead when one of the two doors at the far end of the room opened. Her mother emerged, not from her own bedroom, but from Ren's.

"First of the month," she said without preamble. "Almost forgot. Tea?"

Agnes Monroe was a spitefully beautiful woman. Life had given her physical body every reason to surrender, but she wore the years and suffering like armor. Her skin was a shade darker than Ren's, deeply tan. Shifts down on the wharf had drawn out the constellations of freckles running down her neck. She hauled crates of fish sometimes, and her arms were lean and muscular from the work. The deep creases around her mouth spoke of a woman who laughed often and loud. Or at least, a woman who had once had plenty of reasons to smile.

"No thanks," Ren said. "I'll be late for class. How's work?"

"It's work. What about you? Interviews going well? Any prospects?"

Her mother slid around her to fetch the tea, pausing only long enough to kiss Ren lightly on one cheek. Her stomach churned as she watched her mother get the stove going. The decision to attend Balmerick had centered on the hope of finding favor with one of the five great houses.

The city of Kathor was a distinct hierarchy, and Ren needed to earn a position with them if she ever wanted to do anything of consequence. The second semester of her first year as a graduate student should have been full of interviews, recruiters eager to learn how she'd gotten such high marks on all her tests, but only the lesser houses had shown any interest.

Until yesterday.

Her advisor had left a note outside her dormitory. Ren had an interview with House Shiverian this morning. She also had no plans of sharing that news with her mother until she'd secured a position. False hope was a fuel that Agnes Monroe already knew too well.

"Nothing worth mentioning."

Her mother set out a mug. "I don't get it. You're the top of your class."

"I'm technically fifth."

"Fifth," her mother repeated. "Out of hundreds. And with none of the resources their families could offer them."

Ren knew the numbers. She always hated being reminded of the numbers, even if her mother's claim was true. The oldest houses had been in Kathor for six generations. Her mother and father had left southern Delvea when they were only about Ren's age. Like many others, they were lured by the bright possibilities of a sprawling new age city. Kathor had replaced the original settlements and become the epi-center of trade and magic. Her father used to describe the day they'd first landed in the city's harbor. A pair of dream-ers, her father used to say, but she knew her parents' dreams were eventually reduced to backbreaking shifts and poor liv-ing conditions. The one time her father had demanded more from the world, he'd been killed for it.

"I'm working on it, Mother."

"Oh, honey, I know. I'm not mad at you. I'm mad at _them_. The unfairness of it all. See, this is why I gave magic up. We talk about this in our meetings, you know. It's called vol-untary dependence. Every time we use magic, we're leaning into the system _they_ built for us. . . ."

Ren had heard all of this before. Any discussion that focused on "they" was a dangerous road to let Agnes Monroe walk down at such an early hour. A road that always led back to her father's death. Ren never questioned her mother's deci-sion to give up magic, and she shared her mother's distaste for the city's elite, but she preferred a more rational approach to dealing with those inequalities. Her mother favored conspiracies and wild speculation.

"I have proven myself for four years. It will work out. I am not concerned."

The steadiness of her voice acted as a salve. She saw the tension riding her mother's shoulders shake loose. She turned back around, fussing over her cup of tea. Ren needed to go. She wanted to have at least an hour to go over her notes on House Shiverian and their various business concerns, but she hated the idea of leaving her mother here in the lonely morning light. It helped to remember she'd be returning with Timmons for break in a few days.

"Why were you sleeping in my room?"

Her mother glanced back. "I don't know." The two of them looked at each other, quiet for a moment. Then her mother spoke the begrudging truth. "There's less of his ghost in there, I guess."

In the first few years after his death, Ren would have walked over and cupped her mother's face. She would have pulled her close and whispered what her mother had always whispered to her when she'd had nightmares as a child. *No darkness lasts for long.* But now they stood ten years in the shadow of Roland Monroe's passing. The clouds still hung thick over both of them. Ren knew this darkness would exist until she dragged them out from beneath it.

When her mother turned back to her tea, Ren strode over and wrapped her in a hug from behind. Her mother's hand settled half on her wrist, half on the iron bracelet that she'd once worn.

"I am a Monroe," Ren whispered her father's words. "And a Monroe stands tall."

Her mother squeezed her forearm. Ren left her there, sipping tea.

Outside, the city of Kathor was stretching tired limbs, rising to the glittering invitation of another day. It wasn't until she reached the public waxway portal that she felt sunlight on her neck. Ren savored the warmth before tucking her shirt into her trousers and turning her bracelet over. She traded the plain brown cardigan for a fashionable plaid jacket, then she removed a forest-green tie from her bag and knotted it artfully under her shirt's collar. All the minor adjustments that would have made her look like a snob down in the Lower Quarter, but without which she'd look out of place up at Balmerick. After glancing at herself in a storefront window, Ren turned.

Her eyes drifted once more to the Heights. How bright the buildings looked in that empty sky. It helped to see it from down here. Sometimes as she walked around campus, talking with friends or sitting in on lectures, it was easy to feel like Balmerick was actually her home. The school had that effect. Slowly luring a person into comfort. But from below it was easier to see the truth of where she belonged, even after four years of navigating their politics and climbing up their ranks.

It didn't matter how calmly she went about her business. No mantra or meditation could fully tamp down the panic she felt whenever she thought about her true situation at the school.

She was a mouse.

Balmerick, the hawk.

3

Ren's classmates could hire charmed chariots to take them up to the Heights. Others had personal portals built into their high-rise villas. A few families even owned wyverns. The people who were waiting in line with Ren for the public waxways were far more industrious. Shop runners making special deliveries and hired hands attending to less glamorous tasks.

The inner room of the waxway station divided into four sections. There were stone recesses—each one about twice as wide as an average person—with identical paintings nailed into the mortar at eye level. Each painting was of the great fountain in the main square of the Heights, just outside Balmerick's front gates.

For visualization. If you cannot see yourself somewhere, you cannot possibly travel there.

Ren knew the safest method for travel magic involved carrying a physical piece of the location. As a nervous sophomore, she had collected blades of grass from the main quad just to make sure she didn't end up becoming a story of warning for the rest of the Lower Quarter. It turned out that repetition and familiarity were more than enough to shield her from the negative consequences of teleportation. Ren had taken this portal a hundred times now.

Beneath each painting sat a row of waxway candles. All of them flickered with ready flame, running lowest to highest. The thickness of the candle determined how far a person could travel. Long-distance traveling might call for a candle to burn for two or three hours. A jump to the Heights required no more than a few minutes of dancing flame and focused meditation.

The priestess tasked with refreshing the travel stations stood on the other side of the room, helping an elderly gentleman. A box of extra candles had been abandoned on the floor beside Ren. She glanced over a shoulder—no one was there—and let a hand reach down. The borrowed candle vanished into her satchel. Some supplies weren't covered by her scholarship. Every little bit helped.

Ren refocused. In the recess there was a half-burned match. She raised it to the wick of the second-shortest candle, mimicking the priestess who had lit it in the first place. The preferred method was to light the candle herself, but Ren—and most modern wizards—knew the echoed motion was more than enough to establish a magical link.

Next she looked at the painting. Traveling required visualization. Her eyes combed the bright streams of the fountain and the perfect circle of stones and all those flanking trees.

The final step to the spell had always been her favorite part. With that image fixed in her mind, Ren calmly set her forefingers to the chosen candle. Some people preferred to let the candle burn itself out—which was the safest way to initiate the spell. Others liked to lean down and blow it out with a quick breath. But Ren's father had done it this way, so she did it this way.

Her fingers pinched together. She felt that brief and satisfying burn, then the flame vanished. Before the scent of that curling smoke could even reach her nostrils, Ren was snatched into the waiting nothing. She could never get fully used to the sudden *absence*. Traveling the waxways always made her feel small, as if she were standing at the mouth of a cave with no end.

Her mind shoved into darkness, through the sprawling labyrinths. Plenty of wizards had vanished as they traveled the waxways over the centuries. Some had attempted to travel too far. Others had been distracted in the moment before the spell began. Ren knew it was best to empty her mind completely. Best to allow the magic to forge its own path.

After all, it knew the way.

Her feet set down in the square. There was a wide lane flanked by narrow villas in the distance. The Heights wasn't completely unlike the city below. Here, the buildings pressed together, tall and lean, each spaced the exact same distance from the next. The main difference was that, up here, an entire building belonged to one family. Ren still remembered the first time she'd visited a friend's home for a study session. Learning the entire place belonged to the same family—and that they used the place only *occasionally*—had been the second shock to her system.

Balmerick had been the first.

A series of coal-black castles sliced through the clouds on her right, their slanting spires unadorned. Perfectly manicured lawns separated the scattered buildings. Imported oaks cast shade over the crisscrossing paths. Pockets of students drifted between classes. She'd been here for four years now and still felt like she was entering contested territory every time she stood at these gates.

Ren settled into the version of herself that Balmerick wanted to see. When she felt mentally ready, she started through the yawning gates and headed to her interview.

Her advisor was Professor Agora. He conducted Magical Ethics in a circular lecture hall. It fell on his shoulders to keep the young elites of Kathor from becoming tyrants. Ren enjoyed him, even if she felt he was fighting a battle that had been lost a few generations ago.

When she arrived, Agora was busy at the back of the room. Steam clouded up as he poured three teas. He liked to make the room feel like a coffeehouse. They were just citizens of the city, discussing matters of great import. He was a slender man, olive skinned, balding around the crown of his head. He kept his beard trimmed artfully and never missed an opportunity to show off his fashionable collection of buttoned vests. Today's mimicked blue-green dragon scales. The window light fractured in dazzling patterns any time it caught the gossamer material.

"Ren. You're here. Good. How are you feeling?"

She took her seat. "Ready. I have a few more notes to study, but I feel prepared."

"Very good. The meeting will be with Lucas Shiverian. I

sent your resume, my recommendation letter, all of the normal paperwork. They expressed interest in your research on a new version of the standard coil spell."

Ren thought back through her notes. Lucas was the youngest of the current ruling generation in House Shiverian. Likely the least powerful of the siblings, but that didn't matter. Being hired by anyone in the primary family line would make for a brilliant starting point.

Each of the five houses had played a distinct role in the founding of Kathor. Some had even taken on new surnames to reflect their family's position on that new frontier. The Broods were gifted in tactical warfare. The Proctors oversaw the building and organization of the city itself. The Winters family were the first doctors and priests. And the Graylantian farmers grew the crops that eventually fed the entire population.

But the Shiverian family had always been known for their prowess with magic. Many scholars argued they were the deciding factor that transformed Kathor from fledgling harbor town into the greatest economic power of the modern age. Half the spells in the current magical system had been invented by the Shiverian family, but Ren knew that some of their most complex magic was kept under lock and key. Their secrecy offered Kathor a constant edge in world affairs—and the Shiverians worked hard to maintain that advantage. Not only would they provide Ren the perfect foothold for her larger goals, but she might actually enjoy the work she'd get to do with them.

Her optimism stumbled only upon hearing Agora's final point.

The coil spell she was working on was very promising. The standard version fell into the larger category of binding spells. Coils were the most popular method for linking one magic with another magic—effectively combining their separate purposes into something more uniform. It allowed the user to create clever, cross-purpose magic.

The limitation with the current version was that, once bound, the magic remained tangled. In fact, the bond grew stronger as time passed, and it often took years for small-level bindings to loosen or break. Her version provided a coil that bound entities or magics briefly. The breakthrough had come when she'd braided a temporal charm through the other two spells. It would be a huge advancement if she could get it to work, but that was precisely the problem.

"My coil spell research isn't complete. I'm still in the early testing phases. I haven't ruled out side effects or calculated the impact of the spell when dealing with high-level magic. It'll be months before I even have a proper proposal in order."

"Don't tell Lucas Shiverian that," Agora replied. "Tell him you're making progress. This is an elder heir in one of the great houses. You cannot use words like 'testing' or 'incomplete.' Creatures like him bore easily. Always give a sense of momentum. You are on the verge of something *new* and *groundbreaking*. It doesn't matter if it takes you another five years to figure out the magic. They just want to feel like they're recruiting someone who can add a new angle to what they already do."

Ren nodded. "Lie to him. Sure. What else?"

Agora offered her a hesitant look.

"What? What is it?"

"Wield your knowledge with precision. You are one of the most intelligent students I've ever taught, but Lucas Shiverian isn't one of your classmates. He is not your peer. He believes that he is your superior. You must shine without causing a glare. Do you understand?"

"Be excellent, but on his terms. Understood."

"Precisely. Go ahead and study. I'll keep an eye on the hallway and let you know when he's coming. You can do this, Ren. I'll be right back."

She turned through the pages of her research. The ancestral chart offered details on her potential interviewer. His age, spouse, children. Ren quietly studied those notes before cross-referencing his name with the court-reported business filings. Public records that walked through who in the family had been responsible for signing off on which projects. His name appeared on any record connected to the family's coastal trading. She saw that he did a lot of work with the northern ports that had larger Tusk populations. There was even a note about the fact that he observed some of their religious customs, which would make him unique amongst the more agnostic Delveans. She was weighing the appropriateness of bringing up religion in an interview when the door creaked.

Ren glanced up to see Agora peeking inside.

"He should be here any minute."

Ren took a deep breath, eyeing the notes. She continued studying until the wait became unbearable. She closed her folders and crossed the room. There was a single pane of glass looking out into the hallway. Agora was alone. And he was pacing. She quietly returned to her seat.

There were theories about how time slowed or quickened, depending on the perspective of the beholder. Certain dragons, it was said, once existed outside of time. Some claimed to live in their favorite moments permanently, offering only a begrudging awareness of the present. Ren felt a kinship with them now. It was as if a grain of sand were stuck to the roof of the hourglass, unwilling to fall, and nothing outside the room was moving. That illusion broke when Agora returned again. Alone.

"He's late, but I'm certain he'll be here shortly. More tea?"

Ren shook her head. She could hear the nervous clinking of Agora's spoon as he mixed honey into his drink. A clock in the corner kept the time, the second hand gliding mercilessly around the circular frame. Ren sat straight backed and ready. She refused to allow herself to believe that the interview might not happen.

The door finally opened. It wasn't a middle-aged man with sloped shoulders and a stark jaw. It was Percie James, slight and wispy, peering in at them. "Am I too early?"

Ren hid shaking hands under her desk. A glance at the clock showed it was nearly time for class. Lucas Shiverian was more than an hour late. *He isn't coming.* Agora glided forward.

"Come on in, Percie. I've got more of that darkthyme tea you liked. There are a few bags of summer lily left from last time as well. . . ."

A few other students filed in behind her. Agora went about the business of setting out everything. There was a great fuss over mugs and seats as the rest of the class settled in. Ren's advisor paused briefly beside her and his voice was lower than a whisper.

"It has to be some mistake. I'll check after class. We'll get it rescheduled. Chin up, Ren."

Ren said nothing. She was used to this by now. It did not matter how brilliantly she performed. It did not matter that her grades were the best in her class. All they saw was a girl who'd come from the Lower Quarter. Dirty or dull or worse. She'd have to prove them wrong. Somehow.

4

The rest of her peers took their seats. Some of them already wore the coats of arms from the various houses, all freshly sewn into their school jackets. It was like they belonged to a club for which Ren couldn't find the address.

"Let us begin with a story," Agora was saying. "You're all familiar with Marcus."

As he spoke, he turned in slow circles, considering each student. Ren noticed the way that he avoided eye contact with her. Was he embarrassed that his contact had failed him? Or embarrassed that he'd championed the cause of a student they found unworthy of meeting?

"Marcus was one of the greatest blade makers in history, yes? Each of his weapons is more famous than the last. Honed to perfection. He took on many students over the years, but his most famous is Rowan. Do you know that name?"

Ren nodded but was saved from answering as Agora plunged on.

"He studied under Marcus for nearly a decade. Improved

so much at his craft that he started to think he was better than his teacher. To prove this, he challenged Marcus. 'Let us each make a sword. We will bring them to the river. The sharpest blade wins.' Marcus agreed.

"Both of them took time to make their swords. On the appointed date they met along the banks of the Straywhite River. A neutral judge joined them. Rowan went first. He plunged his creation blade-first into the river. There was nothing it failed to cut. The passing leaves split in two. Great logs were severed. Even the river itself began to part ways at its touch."

Agora's strangest and most charming quality was how lost he got in his stories. He'd bellow and whisper and move his hands in great sweeping motions. Sweat always trickled down his forehead. In the longer lectures he'd have great patches showing under his arms. His passion was a buffer, Ren thought. It was one way to ignore Percie half-asleep in the front row or Clyde Winters snorting about something with Mat Tully whenever his back was turned.

"Satisfied, Rowan withdrew his blade. He knew he'd won. How could any blade match the sharpness he'd just displayed? Marcus went next. He plunged his own sword into the river. Drifting leaves came, but at the very last moment they'd dart to the left or right of the blade. The same was true of passing logs and debris. Every time they reached the place where his sword waited, they'd skirt the blade at the last second. Rowan watched and waited. The judge came forward."

Agora smiled to himself.

"Twenty lines on who won. Begin."

He used a spotted handkerchief to wipe the sweat from

his forehead. There was a shuffle of materials moving from satchels to desks. A few eyes rolled. Percie leaned over to her neighbor, asking what the story had been about. Ren hadn't noticed which coat of arms the girl was wearing. A hawk clutching a string of pearls between its talons: House Shiverian.

How did you get recruited when I can't even get an interview?

Annoyed, Ren set to work. She knew the answer to Agora's question because she'd read the entire historical account. Now she needed to reframe it through some other principle. That's what her ethics professor enjoyed most. A small shift in perspective earned high marks every time. Thirty minutes later Agora descended once more into the teaching circle.

"Well, who won?"

Ren had learned not to answer first. It was always easier to impress by correcting someone else's almost-right answer. Clyde Winters opened things up with a lazy hand in the air. Ren knew he was second in line to a massive empire. His family had a monopoly on every medical sector in the city. Not to mention, they also ran most of the cathedrals. Those were the benefits of having ancestors who'd been the only doctors aboard the first ships to sail to Kathor.

"Rowan won," Clyde said. "The challenge was the sharpest blade. The Pyras theory argues the simplest answer is most often the right answer. Rowan met the challenge, on its simplest terms."

Agora nodded before signaling for the rest of them to join in. Percie leapt at the chance, all too eager to correct Clyde's answer. Her being recruited by House Shiverian made them rivals of a sort.

"But that's not how it goes. Marcus was the winner. After all, his sword would not cut that which was innocent. It's not enough to be the best at something. If the weapon or the advancement doesn't take the greater good into account, that just moves society in the wrong direction."

"Very nearly a direct quote from *Age of Reason*," Agora replied. "Anyone else?"

Ren finally raised her hand. Her teacher nodded.

"While Percie's is the well-worn answer, I think it's interesting to see how this problem relies on the Beneficent Effect. One agreeable result causes the judge to assume all future results will be agreeable. He believes the sword will always protect the innocent. Which sounds wonderful, but that's a naive assumption. The problem is that the sword's moral system can extend only as far as Marcus's moral system. The leaves floating by in the river were innocent, and thus his sword would not cut them. No one's going to argue against the moral innocence of a leaf.

"But what happens when the wielder of the sword attempts to kill an enemy soldier? Murder is immoral. Unless you're defending yourself in battle. But what if the battle you're fighting is based on an immoral cause? Or the person you're dueling is your own child? There are so many scenarios in which the sword would be forced to make decisions that our own moral system hasn't fully categorized as innocent or guilty. It would inevitably fail, because it relies on the morality of the wielder. I'd rather have Rowan's blade. It's a tool, and it's not pretending to be anything else."

Silence followed her answer. Agora sipped his tea while Percie looked as if she was still trying to figure out if Ren had insulted her. For once, Ren didn't care what any of them thought. Until now she'd handled her reputation in class with surgical precision. Impress enough that she couldn't be ignored, but not so much that she became a target. Maybe she'd gotten it wrong. Maybe she'd done just enough to get snubbed. Not enough to force them to take notice.

The wealthiest scions had begun building their entourages, and Ren was quietly being left behind. Percie's coat of arms was evidence of that. Soon all the good spots would be gone. Rising to power from one of the minor houses would take far too long for what Ren was hoping to accomplish. She needed the attention of the people who mattered.

"Onward," Agora said, raising a finger. "The focus of this week will be on the correlation between increasing power and moral imperatives. Let's turn to page seventy-three. . . ."

It was past time to do something bold.

5

When class ended, Agora promised to follow up and get to the bottom of the heir's absence. "I'll circle back with the Shiverians. And while I do that, what about the Broods? They offered an interview early on in your recruitment process. A low-level cousin of the family, but it would be a start. That's all you really need, Ren. A starting point. There are no limits once you're in the door."

Ren was already shaking her head, though. "Thank you, Professor, but no. Any other house but House Brood."

Agora apologized one more time as Ren left the room. It was a mercy that the end of Magical Ethics at least coincided with the day's first glimpse of Devlin Albright.

The two of them had been dating for a few months now. Nothing too serious, but certainly a welcome distraction. Devlin was the youngest son of a merchant. Not only was he handsome, but he was also a potential backup option if none of the superior houses pursued her contract.

His family was as rich as the rest of their peers', but their wealth was newly earned. His father's trade had elevated their status in less than a decade. The only reason Ren could stomach dating him was that there wasn't a hallway of gaudy portraits hanging anywhere in the Albright household. It also didn't hurt that Devlin looked like he'd been carved out of stone.

He had dark hair, trimmed high and tight on the sides. His green eyes were deep set, like they'd been hammered into his light brown face by a Citadel jeweler. Today Devlin wore a navy wool cardigan over a too-tight collared shirt. She liked the way he always buttoned things all the way up to his throat.

Devlin was looking particularly broody this morning. Combat training with the Brightsword Legion had been more demanding than expected. She'd tried to warn him. Brightsword was the military arm of the government. A city guard supported by city taxes. Unlike the armies recruited and retained by the wealthy houses, they didn't have enough money to hire all their recruits. Which meant they tried to force out as many applicants as possible during the training process. He'd still applied, because he thought Brightsword was the most noble place to serve. She hadn't bothered to mention that their legion hadn't been in a proper battle for decades.

Ren and Devlin had spent far less time together ever since training started. She hadn't minded because the other result of his training was equally rewarding. She set a hand on one of those rewards—his finely carved chest—as she kissed him hello.

"Good morning. You're looking well."

He nodded. "Finally got my divinity shield sorted out. How was Ethics?"

They started walking toward the back of the building, where a set of double doors led to the main quad. Ren hadn't told him about the interview, and now she was glad that only Agora had known. It meant there were fewer people to pity her. She despised pity.

"Oh, you know, discussing the moral implications of enchanted swords."

"The Marcus and Rowan debate?"

Devlin was a year older and had been through several of the same classes she was taking now. Another advantage of their relationship. He'd been reluctant to pass on his actual notes. A side effect of training to be a paladin was upright-ness. Her request to borrow his papers had been viewed as cheating, but a little convincing had drawn out plenty of helpful advice since then.

"A tale as old as time," Ren confirmed.

"And who did you think won the challenge?"

"I used the Beneficent Effect to argue that Marcus's sword is more problematic than the story suggests. Full marks from Agora. Naturally."

She expected Devlin to grin but caught a flicker of some other emotion on his face.

"What?"

He shrugged. "Nothing. It's clever."

She knew it was clever, but she didn't know why he was being so odd about it. There was no point dragging him into a debate, though. Devlin had been stressed over the past few weeks. His divinity shield had cracked during a training session. Divinity shields were delightfully complex magic. A shield spell, looped into an ongoing growth spell, woven through with a favorability charm. As long as the wielder treated others "with noble intention," the spell would grow more and more powerful over time. Devlin was embarrassed by an early crack in his shield, even if it was incredibly common for trainees.

Outside, sunlight greeted them. The fair weather had lured a sprawling scene onto Balmerick's open quad. Underclassmen on blankets, their scarves set aside to sun their necks. Brief flashes of practiced magic. Ren even spied a pair of hellhound puppies being paraded around near the school's memorial statues, their bifurcated tongues lolling happily. It was a shame that she intended to spend the rest of the day practicing spells in an archive room.

"It's nice out," she noted.

Devlin shrugged again.

Another downside to dating a paladin in training. Broody often meant enigmatic. And enigmatic was a slippery slope toward boring. She was about to ask if he wanted to come over to study later when Devlin turned to her. He could not have looked more uncomfortable. It was like he was trying to escape from his own body in order to avoid the coming moment.

"Look, Ren, we need to talk."

She raised a knife-sharp eyebrow. "We are talking."

"It . . . this . . . look. It's been fun, but it doesn't . . ."

He trailed off as a pair of younger girls passed. Both of them snuck glances at Devlin, though he pretended not to notice. Their boldness helped Ren find her own voice.

"Are *you* really about to break up with *me*?"

"Look. It isn't anything you've done—"

"I'm well aware of the fact that I haven't done anything wrong, Devlin."

His lips quirked. It was the same distasteful look he'd given in response to her earlier answer.

"Go on," Ren said, unable to keep the bite out of her voice. "I'd hate to part ways without whatever . . . wisdom you have to offer. That is the Brightsword Legion motto, isn't it? Leave them better than how you found them?"

Devlin's jaw tightened. "Fine, Ren. You want the truth? You're too much of a temptation for me. We've—I've been uncomfortable. With . . . the things we've been doing. I sought advice from my training general. She believed our activities might have been what caused the crack in my divinity shield. There's some anecdotal evidence that—"

Ren couldn't believe what she was hearing. She'd never expected to marry Devlin, but for him to try to end their relationship with some holier-than-thou speech was beyond absurd.

"Evidence of *what*, Devlin? I've never read an account that suggested a heavy make-out session broke a paladin's divinity shield. Oh, and I'm trying to recall the part where our *activities* made you *uncomfortable*. Because from what I can recall, you looked *pretty* comfortable with everything that was happening at the time."

Devlin's teeth actually clacked together with force. "Keep your voice down."

"Sorry. I could barely hear anything over the *smugness* ringing in my ears. How did you think this was going to go?

You're breaking up with me to protect *your* purity? I hate to break it to you, Devlin, but I wasn't getting horizontal with myself for the last few months."

He swung from embarrassed to angry with predictable speed.

"And I have repented for my part in all of this. I highly doubt you feel bad about what you've done. That's the difference between us, Ren. Do you want to know what happened when I decided to break up with you?"

Her hands were shaking. First, she'd been stood up by House Shiverian. And now even a basic creature like Devlin was abandoning her? Ren had rehearsed what she might say if they broke up a hundred times, but practice was different from the real thing. She tried to ignore the people sitting nearby, their conversations gone quiet for the sake of eavesdropping.

"Let me take an educated guess," she finally said. "I'd imagine your divinity shield healed itself. And you falsely correlated that occurrence with some . . . arbitrary decision you'd made, even though it actually lines up with a far more conclusive study that Thurman did in *Golden Years* that shows definitive timelines for healing are about a fortnight with young paladins. That book also explains shield cracks are common in new trainees. Which is the *entire* reason I gave you that book in the first place. Guessing you didn't get around to reading it? But, you know, I'm glad you think your change of heart is what made everything better."

Devlin made the face a third time. Ren waited for him to speak and knew she was about to hear the real reason for all of this. "You're always right," he said. "No matter what. You just *have* to be right. It's exhausting."

Those final two words struck Ren like a blow. She could suffer judgments on her purity, but she would not be made to feel small for being well read. Good research was not a sin.

"You know what, Devlin? May the magic's light be with you."

She brushed past him.

"Marcus," he called after her. "The right answer is Marcus. He was doing what's right by making the sword that he did. Everyone knows that's the right answer."

Ren couldn't resist turning back.

"Yeah? Well, in the real story Marcus kills Rowan, because his sword *was* better. But I'm sure you'll believe whatever fairy tale makes you feel less guilty about being a sanctimonious prick."

She left him there, bells tolling in the distance, desperate to believe she'd won the exchange.

6

R en needed a proper target for her fury.

   She went straight to the archive room. There were seven scattered around Balmerick, but she always booked the same one. It was in the northeastern corner of campus, hidden in a grove of speckled pines that had been translocated from the southern plains to provide a better atmosphere for the Heights. Their great limbs bent overhead like the arches of a cathedral. An appropriate image, as time in the tower room was the closest Ren came to worshipping anything.

   The cellar door was set diagonally into a hillside. A stone staircase descended into the dark. As she reached the bottom, the passage narrowed. There were no torches to guide her steps. This far down, the darkness became a living thing. She shivered against the cellar's chill until the first lights stirred in reaction to her movement.

   Bright tendrils reached out from the stone walls. As Ren walked forward, the entire room filled with their gentle glow. A low hum of energy buzzed to life. She still remembered the first time she stepped foot in an archive room. Her teacher had explained that the rooms were designed to make magic visible in the air around them, offering wizards a safe environment to practice their spellwork. It was here that wizards could learn—and archive—new spells for their arsenals. Ren reached out now, as she had then, and let her fingertips graze the almost-solid wisps.

Before coming to this continent, Ren's ancestors—the Delveans—had no magic at all. Neither did the Tusk people, for that matter. It was only in sailing here—to the land where dragons once lived—that both groups discovered a new power. Every time Ren stepped into an archive room, she could not help tracing back through history. If she'd been born three centuries ago, she'd have lived a magicless life. Two centuries ago, and only the most fledgling spells would have been in use. One century, and she'd have been practicing wild magic as she waited for the impending discoveries that would form the cornerstone of the modern, structured magic system.

But she hadn't been born in any of those eras. She existed in a time when she could walk into a room made *by* and *for* magic—a time when anyone could build up their arsenal, one spell at a time. Even if society did its best to limit people in her position, Ren was always grateful for that small gift of fate. After all, she could not imagine a life without her favorite spells.

The narrow passage widened into a single room. Two small towers waited at the very heart of the space. One stood about waist height, the other up to her shoulders. Neither tower was wider than a stack of books. A parade of facts marched traitorously through Ren's mind. She knew the number of attempts it took the average person to master a new spell, and how many spells the greatest wizards in history had in their possession when they died.

She knew . . . she knew . . . she knew . . .

You just have *to be right. It's exhausting.*

Devlin's words struck her again. Harder this time. She might have shrugged off a breakup for any other reason, but his words cut deeper than expected. They breathed life into other suspicions. If Devlin found her intelligence exhausting, maybe others did too. She pictured that empty hallway outside Agora's room. Maybe whispers about her had reached the Shiverians. Maybe everyone thought of her as a know-it-all without any real substance. Maybe she'd never get recruited.

Ren angrily shrugged off the strap of her satchel. She crossed the room and opened the front panel of the taller tower. Inside was a lone candle. She lit the wick and stared intently at the flame. The point of this particular candle was meditation. An effort to quiet all other thoughts except for the steps of the spell she intended to master. When she'd visualized the entirety of the magic, she shut the compartment. Turning, she set her mother's bracelet on top of the second tower. If she succeeded, the new spell would write itself into the memory of her vessel and become a permanent part of Ren's already-impressive arsenal.

You just have *to be right. It's exhausting.*

"Shut up. Just shut up."

Ren took a deep breath.

The Tusk people believed that magic was a question. The wizard asked and the magic gave an answer. Most Delveans thought of it as a matter of willpower. A strong mind could shape the invisible world into whatever form it desired. Ren thought that magic felt more like the first steps of a dance. Almost like she was holding out her hand, waiting for an invisible partner to accept that first inviting touch.

"Energy distribution spell," she announced to the empty room. "Attempt thirteen."

The surrounding magic took form. Ren set her feet, thinking back through the complicated steps of her altered spell. In the vague and distant light she saw a projectile shape itself in the air. The spearlike object rotated until it was aimed directly at her chest, then it cut through the dark with speed. Ren's right hand shot up instinctually.

The first layer is a catch-point for the tip of the projectile.

Her palm flexed, fingers splaying.

The second layer dispenses energy. Instead of one direct path, give it hundreds.

She twisted her wrist in a quick rotation.

Third layer forces that momentum to circle, and then the fourth—

But Ren's motions were a step too slow. The projectile hit her summoned wall of magic. Its force dispersed outward, harnessed by the circle she'd built, but she'd failed to summon the fourth and final layer of the spell. The one that redirected the weapon harmlessly into the ground behind her.

"Well, I guess I'm dead," a voice said in the dark.

Ren couldn't help smiling. Timmons Devine was striding forward. Her best friend and only trustworthy ally at Balmerick. The fake spear was lodged just below her right shoulder. She brushed at the magic with an idle hand, and the light dissolved back into the rest of the swirls in the room. Timmons approached with a look of pity on her face. Ren scowled.

"Seriously? You've already heard?"

Timmons smiled. "You called him a sanctimonious prick in the middle of the quad."

She made a face and they both started laughing. Timmons came forward to wrap Ren in a hug. Her best friend was nearly a head taller and always smelled like a walk through a garden. Her silver-white hair looked fine enough to string a harp with. Ren felt the knotted anger in her chest unravel, if only for a moment. Timmons pulled away to get a good look at her.

"Paladins. All that light just makes it easier to see the rot underneath. You can do better."

Ren nodded. "I know. I've already decided to marry this archive room. A far better suitor."

"And likely a more engaging conversationalist than Devlin."

Ren laughed again. Her friend was watching her closely.

"It's not just Devlin," she said. "I had an interview today."

Timmons raised an eyebrow. "With which house?"

"Shiverian."

"Gods, Ren. Why didn't you tell me? We talked about this last week. All you needed was a chance to show them who you are. This is what we've been waiting for. How did it go?"

"It didn't go. I was snubbed. No one showed."

Timmons looked shocked. She pulled Ren into another hug. "Their loss, dear. When you invent the next *brilliant* spell, it will be even more their loss. Go on. I'll help you with whatever you're working on. Just this once."

Her friend retreated to the back wall and took a seat. Turning, Ren prepared the practice magic again. She and

Timmons had been best friends since sophomore year. Their paths had crossed in a few classes, as well as while taking the school's waxway portal home. Both of them attended on scholarship. Ren had been plucked out of the public schools down in Kathor for her exam scores. Timmons had been chosen because she possessed one of the rarest and most sought-after genetic traits in the world.

She was an enhancer.

Enhancers were born with the natural ability to increase the potency of magic. Every great house courted people like her and barely managed to keep from drooling in the process. Timmons had been pursued since her first day on campus. None of the houses wanted to appear too publicly desperate, because the founders of the city would not stoop so low as to beg, but secretly they all left her gifts. High-end dresses made of specialized weaver's thread. Small trinkets wrought from gold. Marriage proposals to their second- or third-born sons. Anything within reason to lure a powerful commodity like Timmons into their family. It was also why the two of them rarely discussed Ren's recruitment. The chasm between their experiences was too large for her to stomach at times.

As Ren settled into her stance again, she could feel the power waiting in her friend's veins. The magic re-formed into another projectile in the distance. It took aim. Timmons acted like a funnel. Whatever magic Ren might have wasted alone, Timmons gathered and honed to a fine point. Her presence made executing the spell impossibly easy.

Ren completed all four steps before the spear was halfway through the air. The weapon's tip caught. Its momentum circled in a tight sphere. And then the imagined spear planted in the ground directly behind her. Just as intended.

"Flawless," Timmons announced. "Though, I'd recruit you on looks alone."

Ren laughed at that, dabbing the sweat on her forehead with a sleeve.

"I won't always have you to amplify my magic."

"No, but it's easier to use a spell than it is to learn the spell in the first place. All you have to do now is practice."

"Very true. Which will mean more time down in this archive room, to which I am recently wed. We will live a very happy life together, I think."

"That is . . . pitiful," Timmons replied. "Speaking of pitiful, I think the best way to get you out of the societal basement is to attend a festivity."

Ren rounded on her friend. "No."

"And there happens to be a festivity *tonight*."

"Timmons, come on. . . ."

"And considering the favor I just extended to you, I think it only fair that you return said favor by coming to a party I am practically obligated to attend."

"I have homework."

"Actually, I checked the itinerary board. You don't have any assignments."

"Exams—"

"Just finished. The next round are nearly five weeks away, Ren! We're about to be on break."

"Devlin might be there."

"I daresay he considers himself above such debauchery."

She had a point. Ren groaned. "Do I have to go?"

"Ren Monroe. Did we not recently discuss your prospects?

Did we not discuss the idea that you have, until now, failed to properly kiss the rings and asses of the city's elite? Are you not down here bemoaning the cowardly ignorance of House Shiverian? This is your chance to shake a few hands and remind people that you are more than a walking textbook."

"Ouch," Ren replied. "A walking textbook? Really? Is that how you see me?"

"I know better, but they don't. Come to the party. Smile and drink and prove them wrong. I am not going to let the smartest girl in our grade go belly-up in graduate school. You deserve a spot in one of the big five houses. It is time to dig in and fight for it."

Ren snorted. "I'm confused. Is this about making me feel better? Or finding me a job?"

"Both," Timmons replied. "Two wyverns with one stone, as they say."

Deep down Ren wanted to disappear into the comfort of her bedroom and be alone. Timmons had come through plenty of times for her, though. And she was right about making some social strides. Even if she didn't land a job tonight, it'd be nice to get out and have a proper drink.

"Fine."

Timmons let out a squeal. "All right. I'll leave you alone. Practice away. Oh, and perhaps hit the baths before tonight? Just a thought."

"Do I smell?"

"Like sweat and hatred."

Ren laughed. "I'll see you later. And thanks for the help."

Timmons waved over one shoulder, vanishing back up the stairs. Ren turned to find the fire in her mother's bracelet was glowing. A sign that the new spell had been stored inside. She slid the metal onto her wrist, resetting her feet.

"Energy distribution spell," she enunciated. "Alteration attempt one."

It was Ren's favorite moment. Idea on the verge of substance.

Knowledge—pushed and prodded—into magic.

7

Theo Brood had promised to throw the party of the century. It was an enticing invitation from the lips of the university's most spoiled creature. Enticing for everyone but Ren. She could not have dreaded anything more. She'd never met Theo because she'd intentionally avoided anyone with the last name Brood during her time at Balmerick. His family was known and notorious. Ren had her reasons for despising them, but Timmons would not hear any protests as they wound through the pristine streets of the Heights.

"It's just a party, Ren."

"You didn't say it was Theo Brood's party."

"How could you not know that?" Timmons replied. "It's all anyone has talked about for *weeks*. That's just another sign that you're in the right place. If no one mentioned this party to you, then you are sorely lacking on the very connections we intend to make tonight."

Ren felt a cold sweat forming at her temples as she followed Timmons up a lovely stone staircase that led to the front entrance. Her friend was drawn by the music and the noise, a creature returning to its most comfortable habitat. Ren preferred the upper stacks of the library.

"What's your issue with the Broods, anyway?"

"I don't have an *issue* with them."

"Oh, really? Then why does your entire face curdle every time I say the name Brood?"

Ren scowled at her.

"See? That right there. That face. What's so wrong with them?"

Everything, Ren thought. *If only you knew all the many things that are wrong with them.* She altered her answer into something more rational. The kind of answer Timmons might expect from her.

"Their business practices have been predatory for centuries. They took more prisoners in the Expedition Wars than the other four houses *combined*. Their family tree is basically a who's who of the worst tyrants in Kathorian history. And it's not like all their worst offenses are ancient history. Landwin Brood forged contracts to seize land from Lower Quarter tenants literally a decade ago. And then he balked on his promise to hire all of those people to work in the resulting canal's shipping yards. I just . . . I don't like the Broods. I never will."

Timmons nodded. "Gods, Ren. If morality is the centerpiece of your search for a house, I'm not sure you'll find one worth joining. Every one of the founding families has a few skeletons. Why do you think they're the most powerful people in the most powerful city in the world? Hint: it isn't because they're all super generous or something."

Ren knew that was true. All the founding families were corrupt; she just had very personal reasons to dislike the Broods. Reasons she'd never spoken out loud to anyone else. Ren kept quiet as they reached an overcrowded entryway. Everyone had a drink in hand. They were skirting the first crowd of bodies, moving deeper into the villa, when Clyde Winters snagged Timmons by the arm.

"Hey! I've got something for you! It'll take just a second."

Her friend shot an apologetic look over one shoulder. "I'll be right back," she said. Ren started to respond, then watched in disbelief as Timmons vanished down the nearest hallway with Clyde. Freshly abandoned, Ren sought the only other comfort in sight—an open bar staffed with attendants. It was a bit over the top, but at least she'd have something to sip.

Ren avoided the larger crowds and was drawn almost immediately into a more dimly lit study. It was far quieter there. Ren took a seat in the most remote corner she could find and began counting the Brood family's sins. She'd never thought it a sin to be rich, but Ren knew how their family earned their money. They sacrificed men like her father to improve their financial bottom line. All without consequence. Everything she knew—all the research she'd done—threw a harsh light over the wealthy flourishes of their home.

Every bookshelf was lined with first editions. She flipped a few open just to check. She sensed cleaning enchantments layered over every piece of furniture. A comfort charm had been cast over the scattered cushions. Through the door to the study she saw an ice sculpture of Balmerick. Its slanting roofs had been converted into frozen pathways for various beverages. Spirited chants rose and fell from that corner as the various heirs of Kathor entertained one another. Ren took a sip of her drink, but even that was annoying.

The servant had placed three cubes in her glass. Now she watched as they transformed, twisting to take on the appearance of miniature ballerinas. She held her glass up to the light of the nearest lamp. Her drink was fizzing but was clear enough for her to see the enchantment begin anew. The three miniatures tiptoed in circles across the bottom of the glass, twirling here and there. Ren admired their timed leaps. It was annoying only because she knew an enchantment like this would cost half of her monthly allotment of magic to perform.

She was nursing her drink when she accidentally caught the eye of someone in the nearest group. A red-faced Mat Tully grinned over at her, blinked once, and broke away from the others.

"Ren Monroe? Out at a party? What an honor. Cheers! And cheers to break!"

She tilted her glass to meet his. "Cheers. Do you have plans?"

He stumbled his way into sitting next to her on the couch. She saw from the angle of his body that it was not a permanent decision, which was a relief. Ren was thinking of ways to remove herself from the conversation quickly when she remembered the whole point of being here was to try to make connections.

"I'll be busy over break," Mat answered, tapping a freshly sewn emblem on his chest. "The Winters family officially hired me today. I'll be an acquisition specialist. Magical artifacts. They're interested in developing new medicinal techniques based on the more religious Tusk practices."

Her eyes landed on the coat of arms. It shouldn't have surprised her. Mat Tully sat with Clyde Winters every day in Magical Ethics. She'd seen him following the heir around campus like a trained lapdog. But Ren couldn't separate that from the fact that this was *Mat Tully*. Ranked 130th in their class. A boy whose test scores couldn't sit at the same table as her test scores. He'd been recruited and hired by one of the great houses on the same day she'd been snubbed for an introductory interview? Her hands were starting to shake just thinking about it.

She mumbled, "Congratulations."

"It's a decent entry point." Mat shrugged. "How about you? Prospects?"

"I am keeping my options open."

She'd grown tired of saying that to her fellow students, and her mother. Teachers inquired often as well. How were interviews? Which house had the best proposal for her? Any exciting contract incentives? They always looked so surprised to learn she'd not been recruited. At the end of each discussion they'd offer to pull what strings they could. Promises had proven a rather cheap commodity at Balmerick. Words were wind. As she eyed Mat Tully's new coat of arms, she forced herself to do the unthinkable: impress him.

"You know, I've always found Tusk religious practices interesting." She was digging back through memories of undergrad papers she'd written. "It's a really unique twist on the Delvean belief system. The whole concept of transubstantiation? I find it pretty fascinating."

Mat Tully took a nervous sip of his drink. "Oh yeah? Transubstantiation?"

"Well, yeah. Delveans, we have the whole 'God created everything and left it for us to figure out' concept as our central religious thesis. But most Tusk people believe that God is literally the world around us. The oceans and the mountains and all of it—they refer to the whole world as God's Body. Which is also why they call this continent the Hearthland. Not Delvea, like we do."

Mat Tully looked more than prepared to drown himself in his drink. It was clear that he'd never studied any of this. Which was quite a starting point for someone who was about to begin professional research on how Tusk religious practices could influence modern medical magic. Ren's tongue was all but tripping over itself to go on. The other related research was crowding forward in her mind. Hearthland. The Tusk called it that because they believed this place was their god's actual heart, in part because it was the only location where they'd discovered any magic. Their people also believed it to be the very center of the known worlds. . . .

But Mat's expression was an echo of the one she'd seen on Devlin's face earlier that day. *You just* have *to be right.* She bit down slightly on her tongue, swallowed back all those hard-earned facts, and forced a smile instead.

"Anyways. It's pretty fascinating. I'd love to talk with you more about it sometime. If you hear of any openings in House Winters, I'd love the opportunity."

Mat took another sip of his drink. "Right, yeah, of course. I mean, I'm sure you're going to find a good fit before I'd have any strings worth pulling. You're obviously really book smart. Solid exam scores. Aren't you top fifteen in our class or something? If you just keep pulling on the connections you've made along the way, what's there to worry about?"

There is everything to worry about. Literally everything. And I'm fifth, thank you very much.

Clearly, her attempt to impress had failed. When Ren only nodded, the pause in conversation was enough for Mat to extract himself from the couch. He tipped his glass to hers one more time, wishing her a good break.

"I'll keep an eye out for any openings and let you know if something comes up."

She could tell from his voice that it was a dead end. She thanked him, though, and quietly finished the rest of her drink as other classmates swirled about the room. Ren considered searching for Timmons. She was the only reason Ren had come to this party in the first place. Without her, the voices were too loud, the laughter was too hollow, the lights were too bright.

She would rather have been anywhere else in the world.

8

Ren was on her third drink, seated on the same couch, watching small packs of other students drift in and out of sight. She knew their faces, their names, their exam scores. It felt like the entire graduate program was jammed inside the villa. The place was stuffy and insufferable.

At least there was music.

Gentle notes drifted in from the balcony on her right. A seventeen-string stood against a backsplash of stars. Three musicians had taken up the standard positions around the instrument's sinuous frame. One played the arms, another the neck, and the last was seated by the stringed legs. As they played, they sang, their falsettos flitting in and out of the melody. It gave Ren the sensation of floating down a river. A part of her desperately wished to float away.

She was saved by the only reason she'd agreed to come to the party in the first place. Timmons finally appeared in the entryway. Every step she took across the room turned a different head. Ren's best friend had always been fashionable. Tonight she wore a white collared shirt tucked into a high-waisted black skirt. In place of a belt, the skirt attached to a decorative outer corset. The reinforced black fabric was slatted, so that the white shirt was visible beneath it, running in a checkered pattern around Timmons's waist. It was not a look that Ren had seen around campus—and she suspected the outfit had been designed specifically for her. Timmons plunked down unceremoniously on the couch, crinkling her nose at Ren.

"Why do you smell like lavender?"

Ren nudged a throw pillow. "There are pressed flowers in the lining."

"Naturally. I can tell you're annoyed. Sorry again. Clyde insisted. Also, best if you don't use the bathroom. You'll be *really* annoyed then. There's a livestone attendant. It offered me a towel when I was finished."

"A livestone attendant?" Ren asked, incredulous. "Isn't there an edict about their usage?"

Rare stone, enchanted to life by magic. Ren knew the best blacksmiths in the city needed at least a year of constant work to make one successfully. And she also knew only one in every thirty statues actually came to life. The rest were discarded. Using a priceless statue to dispense towels felt like blasphemy.

Timmons nodded a confirmation. "Statues can only be activated 'in defense of the city, or the city's interests.' I suppose we cannot risk Theo Brood leaving tonight without his ass properly wiped."

Ren snorted. The sharpness of the sound earned a few glances, but she didn't care. She could always count on

Timmons to help her quietly eviscerate the nobility, even if she was destined to join their ranks before long. "Are you packed?" Ren asked. "The Monroe home will be a step down from this place."

Timmons waved a dismissive hand. "What is there to pack? The whole point of coming to your house for the holiday is that I can wear the same comfortable clothes the entire time."

"Are you pretending not to care about fashion while wearing a tailored outfit?"

"I was," Timmons laughed. "Thanks for calling me out, you sack. It was a gift from the Winters family. Perfect for interviews. And the occasional dance party."

Ren messed with the frills at the shoulder. "It suits you."

"I should hope so," Timmons replied before falling abruptly silent.

Her gaze fixed on something over Ren's shoulder. A glance showed no one was there, but her friend's eyes grew wider and wider. It took a moment to notice the tiny red streaks coloring her irises. Like dying flames. So that's what she'd gone into a back room to do.

"Seriously, Timmons? How much did you take?"

She offered a lazy smile. "Just a little. There's a gremlin on your shoulder."

"Lovely. Tell him I said hello."

Timmons lowered her voice to a whisper. "She says *hello*."

And then she cackled to herself, eyes roaming about the rest of the room. It was clearly a dose of dragon's breath, or the breath. Ren had taken a hit one time, her sophomore year. It was an unpleasant experience. The breath illuminated the unseen world around them. Magical streaks and creatures from other dimensions. It allowed the imbiber to see the world the way dragons had once seen it. Although there was some contention on that subject. A few experts believed users were seeing the illusions that dragons would have wielded as a mechanism to distract their prey. No one knew for sure because the dragons—who were the true first inhabitants of this continent—had long been extinct.

"If you knew how it was made," Ren said, "you'd never take it again."

The hallucinogen was created from the corpses of buried dragons. Their decay gave off noxious fumes that could be harvested and refined into inhalable smoke. It was like sipping extinction. Timmons just smiled, though. "The bookshelf is on fire."

"That'd be a pity. Those are first editions."

The silence stretched as both of them looked around the room. It was just quiet enough that Devlin's voice snaked back into Ren's head. *You just have to be right. It's exhausting.* The emotions she'd been keeping carefully bottled must have broken through in her expression, because Timmons slid an unexpected arm around her.

"Let's dance."

Even intoxicated, her friend proved rather convincing. Ren took a final swig of her drink before giving in to the summoning. The musicians were picking faster rhythms now as the night pushed on and the crowd of dancers grew. Timmons forged a path, catching glances as she went. Once they'd carved out a space for themselves on the balcony, her friend turned in tight circles, black skirt swishing and catching the moon's light.

Ren smiled, two-stepping in time with the rhythm. She wasn't going to turn any heads like her friend, but there was a certain satisfaction in letting her feet pound the floor. She swung Timmons around a few times, laughing merrily, forgetting everything except the music.

It didn't take long for the crowd to double. Bodies pressed around them. Timmons was quick to sink her teeth into the extra attention, lifting her hands overhead. Ren was about to suggest taking a break when the music stopped. Everyone turned to look.

Theo Brood was making his entrance.

He looked properly smashed already. His collar had been loosened, though Ren guessed not by his own hands. He lifted his glass unsteadily, sloshing liquid onto the nearest scion. Bright hair curled down a pale forehead. Ren didn't think he looked that handsome, but that didn't stop Brood from grinning like the world had fallen neatly into his back pocket.

"Everyone!" He shouted the word. "It is—it is past time for my yearly party trick. Remember last year? We gave Kingston those exquisite wyvern wings?"

That was greeted with obnoxious laughter. Ren could never tell if it was forced or not. Did they actually find each other humorous? Or did they laugh to keep up appearances with their future employers? A few students slapped the shoulder of another boy she recognized from her anatomical magic class.

"Tonight I will showcase magic so clever that we'll have the viceroy's investigators knocking on the door!"

Theo stumbled forward. Ren couldn't believe how quickly the crowd parted to make way for him. The sight clawed through her own memories, linking with a moment that could very well have been this moment's twin. Ren had been much younger then. Another crowd had parted to make way for another Brood. Theo's father—Landwin. She could still picture his proud strides, the broad shoulders, the self-importance. He'd joined her at the railing of the canal, eyed the wreckage and the bodies below, then called for medics with that gilded voice of his. . . .

Ren shoved that memory aside before her stomach turned. She swallowed back bile as Theo Brood reached the balcony's edge and gestured to the waiting musicians.

"Away from there! Come now! Out of the way!"

The trio exchanged glances before obeying. They undid support straps and slid out of their seats, clearing away from the massive instrument. All of them exited in silence. Ren watched the way the oldest musician kept glancing back, and guessed the seventeen-string belonged to them.

Until now.

Theo Brood ran his pale fingers down the polished wood. Ren knew his ancestors had made a name for themselves through warfare. During the Expansion Age hundreds of magic-barons set out in search of priceless underground veins. The Broods just happened to be aboard one of the four ships that landed on the shores of what would one day become Kathor. It was pure luck that they—and the other founding families—discovered the most valuable vein of magic in the world.

All the families played their part. As the others extracted the magic and built the actual city, the Broods bloodied the noses of anyone bold enough to knock at their door. Theo's grandfather notoriously doubled Kathor's territory in his lifetime, though his methods for dismantling the northern farming tribes earned him a war tribunal. Later his father would design the canal system that displaced thousands of people from their homes. Theo had clearly inherited the same talent for claiming things that did not belong to him.

"A favorite song?" he called, turning around. "Anyone?"

Ren's jaw tightened. She didn't know what Theo was planning, but she sensed it would be far more obnoxious than the rest of the party had already been. A few boys were shouting for him to play "Beatrice's Ballad." Theo laughed with good humor, but a princeling like him would never stoop so low for his grand act. He let the moment breathe, happy to tease the crowd.

"'The Winter Retreat'!" someone called.

He seized on that. "A perfect song before the break. Come! Let's listen!"

The crowd watched as Theo rolled back his sleeves. The seventeen-string stood nearly as tall as him, and twice as wide. A bit larger than a traditional piano. He set his flattened palms against the wood and magic surged to life. There was a drunken cheer as the other students felt the first wave hit them. Ren was the only one sober enough to take note of how it formed.

She'd always been good at sensing magic. It was a matter of familiarity and pattern. If you repeated a spell enough times in an archive room, you could memorize the shape of it in the air. The senses of a gifted wizard started to adapt to those patterns. And no one on the balcony had logged more practice hours than Ren. Theo was using a memory spell. It had a nuance she didn't recognize—and could not study further—as he layered a second spell over the first.

Tethering magic? She could barely trace the connection as he drew a line between the instrument and the building. Then a third and final layer. At first she thought it was a simple levitation spell, but the traces had a telling curve to them. . . .

"He combined it with orbiting magic," Ren whispered.

She sucked in a breath as she realized what he intended to do. The music came first. Theo turned a smile back on his expectant crowd, motioning with his hands like a conductor. There were a few gasps as the instrument began playing itself. Ren saw it now. A memory spell—adjusted for an object rather than a person. It recalled its own movements from the last time it had played "The Winter Retreat." Such a clever and beautiful and useless spell.

But that was only the beginning. As it reached the chorus, the seventeen-string floated into the air. Up first, over the railing, and then out into the night. Ren tore her gaze from the magic just long enough to look at the musicians, still standing at the back of the crowd, matching expressions of horror written on their faces.

She turned back. Theo was leading the crowd in song now. He sang off-key, changing the lyrics as he liked, and Ren felt her disgust growing with each passing second. The instrument continued floating away until the drop would no longer be a few stories. It had passed the small, well-manicured lawn in the back. Now its path carried it beyond the edge of the Heights.

If the instrument fell, it would plummet down to the city below.

Ren watched the seventeen-string follow an expected path. She guessed that it would orbit around until it touched back down where Theo had first started the spell. Clever magic.

Except . . .

She retraced the fissures in the air. Magic always left a trail. Her mental hands found the thread she was looking for. As the booming chorus grew louder, she traced the connection and finally saw his mistake. Theo had not tethered the seventeen-string to the actual building. He'd missed his mark by a matter of inches. That bond would have held. It would have worked. His aim had been clumsy and drunken, though. The actual thread attached instead to a metal frame that was purely for aesthetic purposes. And the frame was already starting to bend.

Ren's eyes swung back out to the instrument. The farther it traveled, the stronger the pull. Logic and mathematics dictated what would happen next. She reached for Timmons. Her friend was clapping in rhythm with everyone else. "Get down!"

Her cry was the only warning. There was a massive snap of metal as the frame behind them finally gave way. The glass on either side shattered against an invisible punch of force. Screams echoed. Most of the crowd ducked just as the metallic frame ripped free of the building entirely. It came snarling overhead. Theo watched with drowning eyes as his magic failed. The frame missed him by less than a breath. And the seventeen-string fell. Everyone stumbled to the edge of the balcony to watch. Ren's mind raced through possible spells.

Levitation? No, too much momentum.

A blast of force? No, that would create a wider radius of potential damage.

By the time she thought of the third spell—a featherweight reversal charm—the seventeen-string had vanished into the clouds. Ren's entire body went still. She imagined the Lower Quarter. The streets she'd walked through just that morning. Would the instrument land on Peckering's workshop? A building like the one her mother lived in? Dropping an apple from this height could smash someone's skull. An instrument the size of a seventeen-string . . .

They were too far up to hear a crash, but Ren stood there at the railing, quietly praying no one would be killed. She was desperate to go down and find out what kind of damage had been done. She expected the same of everyone else. A mad rush to the doors. Instead Theo Brood turned back to those gathered in silence. He shrugged those gilded shoulders and raised his glass for a toast.

It was the first time Ren had ever wanted to murder another person.

"To picking a better song next year!"

And the rest of the crowd shouted the same.

Morning light whispered across Balmerick's campus.

After seeing Timmons safely home, Ren had spent the rest of the night pacing in her dorm room. The public waxways were closed for the holiday, and Balmerick's private port station—the one Ren normally took to get home—wouldn't be active until later that morning. There was no way for her to go down to the Lower Quarter and check on what damage Brood had done.

Now she crossed the pristine lawns at the heart of campus, not bothering with the stone walkways. It had taken her two years at Balmerick to learn that the morning dew speckling the quad was enchanted. It couldn't soak her socks because the guiding charm was aesthetic, not functional. All the weather in the Heights filtered through protective spells. If it ever rained on the finely cloaked shoulders of Balmerick students, it was only because the headmasters had seen fit to allow it.

Ren wished she had an exam to study for. Anything to

keep her mind preoccupied. Normally, she'd walk straight to the library at this hour. Instead she joined a small crowd at the heart of the quad. There was a brass box there where the morning paper was always delivered. A shipment of the *Kathorian* had already appeared. She took her place in line and spent a mid to get her own copy.

The disastrous story was front and center.

Ren found a bench near the library to read the article. There was no mention of Theo Brood at all. At least fifty witnesses had watched him enchant the seventeen-string out over the edge of the villa's raised magical barriers. She couldn't imagine that the journalist who wrote the article had failed to discover the guilty party. That thought had Ren seething. It was not the first time the Broods had spent money to avoid scandal. In fact, the Heights were barely mentioned, as if an instrument might have fallen out of a passing cloud. No one had died.

At least according to this article, which Ren did not fully trust. It did claim the seventeen-string had fallen through the roof of a teahouse. Twelve were injured. Two in critical condition. The article spun a fine focus on the response times of the local hospital. It also cast doubts on the infrastructure of the building, as if the roof should have been able to withstand a wooden meteor being cast down from the heavens. Ren felt sick to her stomach as she finished reading the article. She was tempted to write "Theo Brood is guilty" all along the stone walkways of the school.

Instead she stowed the paper inside her satchel. Ever the dutiful student, Ren went to check her schedule outside the library. The master itinerary towered on the wall there. A black backdrop with gold-framed letters. Students were already gathered, hoping to see their final classes cancelled and confirmation of break starting early. The names of professors ran down the left side of the board. The next column listed their classes, and a final column displayed updates. Cancellations, homework, meeting venues, and more.

As Ren eyed the board, the names rearranged. Her current professors all rotated up to the very top. The relevant classes swung into waiting slots. It was a lovely version of a reflection spell. Every student standing there would see a different arrangement, based on their schedules. Three of Ren's courses were cancelled, each with minor notes about what to study from the professor. She scribbled down the assignments before letting out an involuntary groan at her fourth and final class.

Agora – Magical Ethics – Normal hours.

The update was written in her professor's handwriting. A binding spell linked his personal chalkboard with the section visible on the itinerary board. The spell had been modified slightly a few years back when a group of unruly students edited one entry to suggest that one of their professors was part kobold. Ren wished she could alter Agora's update. She'd spent too long garnering perfect attendance to ruin it by skipping a class, but the last place she wanted to be was in a room discussing the moral failings of her peers.

As other students checked their schedules, Ren heard the tale from last night sliding in and out of their whispered conversations.

"Did you hear . . ."

". . . lucky it didn't."

". . . no harm done, really."

She knew the whole day would be like that. Most of Balmerick would smirk at the idea of Theo Brood's party foul. There'd be no consideration for those he'd nearly killed. Knowing she didn't have it in her to skip class—and knowing Timmons wouldn't wake up for the first scheduled waxway portal anyway—Ren headed inside the library.

She spent the next few hours reading the same paragraphs over and over, retaining nothing. Outside there was a departure happening. One wyvern had been summoned. Chariots were turning in slow loops overhead until someone flagged one down for a ride. Ren watched their spinning wheels catch the sun's early rays before vanishing over the shoulders of Balmerick's dark buildings.

It was a mercy when the hour arrived for class to begin.

She took her customary seat. Agora wasn't whistling this morning. He set out the teas quietly, distracted. Their class was far from full when he began. Percie and a number of others had elected to skip. Only eight students were present.

"All right. Our final session before break."

He circled, handing out materials as he went. Ren tried to hide her annoyance as he set down a sketch pad with some coloring sticks in front of her. These were the materials she'd have been given to pass the time back in primary school.

"Today we have a very simple assignment. Not to mention freshly relevant."

Ren's stomach tightened. There was a surprising amount of bite in Agora's tone.

"Draw me a monster."

Clyde Winters muttered under his breath. Mat Tully rolled

his bloodshot eyes. Ren shifted uncomfortably. One face came to mind. Could she just draw his portrait and be done with it?

"Get creative," Agora said. "Surely, you've read a book or two. Maybe taken a taxonomy class? Or walked through the art exhibits over in Quarry Hall? Go on. Draw me a monster."

Ren flipped to a blank page. The coloring sticks made the task feel childish. She considered a number of starting points. A clawed creature with Theo Brood's face. A great dragon, twist-toothed and scaled. Eventually she set to work on something imagined. An animal with curling horns, sharp fangs, and claws like shadowed blades. She deliberately colored its fur the closest approximation to Theo's golden curls that she could find in her set. It was satisfying to sneak in that cheap shot, even if no one else would make the connection.

Ren stole glances at the others but couldn't tell if they were taking the task seriously or just trying to look busy. Her animal ended up more lopsided than scary. But Ren kept working. She took her time coloring each scale, shading the claws. Every head was studiously down. She traced back over the edges of her monster until Agora set down his tea and walked to the center circle.

"Let's see them."

Everyone held up their drawings. It was a wide range of artistic talents and results. Mat Tully's picture looked like a blob with eyes. Clyde Winters surprised her with a neatly drawn hawk, wings spread as it swept down for a kill. *He would be classically trained in sketch work.*

The rest were a mixture of claws and twisted visages. Several had gone with humanlike creatures from myth. Ren waited for Agora to explain why they were all still here, drawing sketches, while most of the school had departed for break.

"Step two is simple. Why is it a monster?"

He looked around the room, hands out and inviting. Clyde jumped in first.

"Claws. Teeth. Fangs."

Agora nodded. "Seeing a lot of that. Let's take Ren's creature. It has claws. Sharp teeth. But what if this creature was domesticated? Looks like a sturdy animal, doesn't it? Maybe it pulls wagons for farmers. Would it really be a monster then? Just because it has claws?"

Clyde answered, "If it used those claws to shred the farmer's child, sure."

"Interesting. Thus, it is not simply the *presence* of claws. It's the use. I doubt we'd be upset if Ren's monster dug irrigation trenches or used those scythelike fingers to clear fields. What else?"

Ren looked around at the other drawings.

"Predators," she said. "We associate the word 'monster' with something that preys on other species. We're especially aware of anything that preys on us as a species."

"A common starting point for this discussion, but that definition relies on perspective. We're quite monstrous to chickens, no? We raise them. Butcher them. Eat them. And chickens must seem like giant monsters to the bugs and flies they peck at. And bugs . . . well, you see the pattern. If 'predator' is our only definition, it relies on who starts the conversation. Very interpretive results."

Mat Tully raised his hand. "I thought being a monster meant you were scary."

Agora considered the drawings again.

"And there's evidence of that concept in your drawings. The misshapen nature of the creatures. One too many eyes. Oversized teeth. It's a curious trend, because the apex predators in our world are known for their symmetry and beauty. The dragons supposedly looked like great gemstones brought to life. Nymphs lure passing sailors with songs and swaying. Have you ever seen a vayan's eyes? They look like small galaxies. Very few predators are so crude as what we've drawn today. Most predators use their beauty to lure."

Ren saw the line that might be drawn to Theo. A gilded boy who'd likely face no consequences for his actions. Agora stood there for a moment, encouraging other responses with his silence. It annoyed Ren to realize she'd never dare speak Brood's name aloud. If word got out, she'd burn bridges she couldn't afford to burn. It would all but ruin her chance at finding a position in a proper house. But that was where metaphors could be useful. She raised her hand.

"'Predator' is too simple a definition. But what about creatures that act beyond their assigned role in nature? Clyde's hawk is a good example. If it snatched a mouse from a field, we wouldn't think twice. But if we were in the forest one day and saw it *torturing* a mouse? Picking it up. Letting it go. Catching it again. Dropping it on the stones for fun. What if it was not simply hunting, but glorying in the pain it caused? That would be monstrous."

Agora's eyes glinted. "Expand on that."

"Maybe 'monster' is our definition for something acting outside the parameters of its design. Hawks hunt to survive. Acceptable. A hawk who tortures its food? Monstrous. We could apply that same principle to people. It's one thing for a warrior to kill his opponent in battle. Quite another thing for him to smash an innocent child's head with a stone. 'Monster' could apply to anything that's self-aware of its purpose in the world and chooses to act in a fashion ill-fitting to its calling."

Like dropping a two-ton instrument on a teahouse for a party trick.

An understanding passed between her and Agora. They were both talking about the same person today. And neither of them was brave enough to say his name. Ren didn't blame her professor. It was how their world worked. Instead her teacher wrapped up the discussion with some theoretical connections to the text they'd been reading.

"Essays after break," Agora concluded. "You may choose one of two arguments. The first is that there are no monsters in our world. The second is that everything in our world is a monster. Cite your sources. At least three scrolls' worth. Due after break. You're dismissed."

She watched the rest of the class file out before following, feeling the guilt of her silence weighing down on her shoulders. As she left, Ren wasn't certain if she lacked the power to speak up or if she simply lacked the will to do so. The line separating those two notions seemed rather thin. The exercise had her mind racing, though. She'd spent most of her time at Balmerick weighing every action and word with such care. Always she chose the least risky option. Perhaps it was time to take a more direct role in her future.

Some monsters are quieter than others.

Outside, the tolling of bells announced another hour.

10

B almerick's public waxway room would be available soon. Ren headed in that direction, while everyone else on campus walked toward the main quad, their fancy chariots ready and waiting. Brood's mistake already seemed like old news. Every conversation she heard focused on break:

"Where are you sailing?"

"The Oft Isles again?"

"We're going to the northern foothills. Father's just . . ."

All the anger churning in Ren's chest burned cold by the time she reached the grove of trees fronting the school's private waxway system. It was nestled within a squat building, dark shouldered and hidden amongst the sprawling limbs. She took a seat in the shade and waited for Timmons. This portal was unlike the public access she'd taken to come up to the Heights. Instead of individual candles, the waxway room had a spell that activated at regular intervals so that as many as twenty people could travel using the same wave of magic. It mimicked all the usual steps—visualizing a destination, lighting a candle, dousing the flame—but with a guiding spell to make everything more convenient for Balmerick's students. Not that most of the other students ever bothered with the place. There were only two other classmates who regularly joined Ren and Timmons in using the room.

The first passed by as Ren waited. Cora Marrin was short enough and quiet enough to be missed in any crowd. Ren thought that was a part of why she never saw the girl around campus. She kept her dark hair trimmed tight, except for a set of artful bangs that ran unevenly down her forehead, slightly longer on one side than the other. Ren spied a new piercing on the girl's exposed eyebrow, inset with a lovely little amber stone. Her skin was a faded olive color. Ren knew she spent quite a bit of time underground in the school's mortuary. That also explained why the girl looked dressed for the dead of winter. A pair of thick trousers, the curling wool scarf, and a plaid forest-green coat that ran down to her calves. Ren supposed it always felt like winter in the rooms where they stored the cadavers.

Over the years she'd learned that Cora had grown up in a farming town north of the city. Most of her surgical practice had come from dissecting animals in the woods near their house. Now she was a medical student, here on scholarship like Ren, because she'd proven incredibly adept at anatomical magic. The girl offered her typically shy wave before slipping inside the waxway room.

The fourth member of their occasional crew was Cora's obnoxious opposite. Avy Williams came swaggering around the corner, trademark grin already stretching his wide face. His skin was bright and tan and always seemed to have a glow to it. In the sunlight it almost looked bronze. Ren knew the glimmer was partially from the oil he applied before wrestling matches. It was legal to slick the skin, which offered the slightest advantage when wrestling in the arena, even if Avy already possessed every advantage imaginable for a fight.

He was the youngest person ever to place in the Games. The performance had earned him a full scholarship to compete for Balmerick, which prided itself on dominating Kathor's other universities in athletics and dueling. He wore the traditional buttoned cardigan that most of the athletes wore, with Balmerick's symbolic towers stitched into the right breast pocket. She didn't follow any of the sports very closely, but she knew Avy was undefeated this year. That was no surprise. Even a statue like Devlin looked like a toy soldier by comparison.

Before Avy became a famous wrestler, Ren had always thought of him as the younger and far less morally centered brother of Pree Williams, her first boyfriend. She had known Avy since they were little, and knew he was prone to mood swings. One moment laughing at a joke, the next ready to slam someone's head into a wall. It was difficult to say if he preferred magical duels or fistfights more, as he got into plenty of both.

Balmerick tried to keep that side of their prized athlete hidden. Anything to avoid expelling him. It was hard to veil, though. His right eye had been destroyed by an illegal spell last year, which left him with a dark scar and a melted socket set in the middle of an otherwise boyish face.

"Ren Monroe. Tell me something I don't know."

He always said those words to her in the same singsong

voice. She smiled back as he threw his hands on his hips and waited for her to spin out a new fact. It was a game they'd played over the years, and Ren always had a few hidden up her sleeve for the occasion.

"Did you know that the first vessel in recorded history was a nipple ring?"

Avy's dark eyebrows soared. "No way."

"A man named Pryor was using the ring for alternative activities when he realized the pain was channeling his magic into and through the metal. He started storing spells inside, mostly for the purpose of further enjoying those alternative activities."

Avy grinned at that. "I'm surprised he told anyone."

"He didn't. The information died with him, and vessels were *discovered* about a decade later, but once the guiding theories were in place, a historian backtracked to other instances of channeled magic and discovered Pryor's story written in a book for people who enjoyed . . ."

"Alternative activities." Avy grinned again. "Maybe I should read more often."

Ren smiled back. This was the point where their friendship always faltered. Avy did not care for the finer points of magic. He was not the kind of person who enjoyed in-depth discussions. And she didn't care about his workout routines or the results of his latest city tournament. They shared a home neighborhood and all the memories that came with growing down in the Lower Quarter. Footraces through the canal district and sneaking pies from market stalls. Other than that, they had very little in common. So it was a surprise when he stepped closer, his voice kept deliberately low.

"Anyone you know get hurt?"

She shook her head. "No way to know, but I doubt it. My mother gave up going to teahouses years ago. She would have been at home. Asleep. You?"

"Pree sent a note. One of our cousins was in the wreckage. A few stitches, but nothing life-threatening. There's one person who still might not make it."

Ren frowned. "The article said recoveries were expected."

"There was a lot that article didn't say," Avy replied coolly. "She was impaled by a piece of shrapnel. City's best doctors are working on her, but it's grim."

She could only shake her head. When the silence stretched, Avy threw that big grin back on his face. Ren wasn't sure if it was a sign that he possessed a rare ability to compartmentalize, or if it was a defense mechanism Balmerick had built into him. Smile long enough and all the injustice would feel like it weighed a little less.

"Catch you inside," he said.

Ren's eyes swept the quad for any sign of Timmons. This was about the time that they liked to enter the portal room together. It always helped to settle in early before using the waxways. Calm nerves meant smooth travel. She was starting to grow restless when two figures turned the corner. Ren's breath caught. Theo Brood was walking toward her with Clyde Winters.

For a brief moment she thought Clyde had informed Theo of what had happened in Agora's class. Maybe he'd interpreted her comments as the criticism she'd intended them to be. Theo was coming to confront her. Ren mentally fumbled for an explanation, but the two boys barely glanced at her.

That anger flickered back to life inside of her. Here were two of the most influential scions in the school. The people she needed to impress if she ever wanted to achieve her true goals. Like Lucas Shiverian, they hadn't even bothered to look in her direction.

Theo seemed properly hungover. His eyes sunken, his skin pale. He'd managed to comb his hair and straighten his tie and that was about it. Clyde, on the other hand, was lively and grinning.

"Can't believe he confiscated all of them," he was saying. "Brutal, man."

Theo snorted. "The best part is I'm not even sure *when* he took them. How do you sneak out three chariots in the middle of the night? The old man is efficient, I'll give him that much."

"I've never . . . taken . . . before . . ." The wind whistled through gaps in the trees, stealing every other word Clyde spoke. ". . . know . . . it works?"

Theo shrugged. "You just light a candle."

Ren's stomach tightened. She watched as their feet carried them to the entrance of the waxway room. Her mind traced the possibilities, all the cause and effect. She linked what had happened the night before to what she'd just heard Theo say about missing chariots. There was only one person who'd dare to take something so valuable from a spoiled princeling like him. His own father.

And this was his punishment. Taking the Balmerick waxway portal home. The spoiled prat would learn his lesson by traveling with the school's welfare students. Ren's chest pumped. She idly pulled strands of grass from the mossy stones beside her and tucked the blades into a coat pocket. Her pulse was still running fast when Timmons finally arrived, breathless and disheveled. She'd abandoned her school jacket in favor of a white-and-gray-striped shirt with a dramatically large collar. There were clever brass buttons pinching both sleeves, and Timmons wore a slender brass necklace to match them. Disheveled, for her, simply meant that her shirttail had come untucked from her trousers as she crossed campus. Ren circled around to help her fix it.

"Sorry I'm late."

Ren nodded. "No worries. We've got guests."

Timmons frowned. "At your home?"

"No. In the portal room."

"Who?"

"Two of Balmerick's best boys. Come on. Let's go say hello."

Ren walked through that door into the dark, her mind turning and turning.

11

The group waxway room was one of Ren's favorite places on campus.

Balmerick was not the public transportation authority. They would never offer their students a plain travel candle and send them off without pageantry. Instead they'd designed their portal room with exquisite beauty. The result was a perfectly scaled wax model of Kathor, as well as the surrounding regions. It looked like a sprawling dollhouse castle and took up nearly the entire room. Wicks peeked out from neighborhoods and market squares. The whole room functioned as a group portal. Individuals lit the location that was closest to their home before waiting for the time-appointed wave of magic to douse all the flames and sweep them away.

Wooden chairs circled the display. Ren had spent over four years sitting in this room with Timmons, Cora, and Avy. There were other guests from time to time, but those were the four mainstays. Sometimes they'd wait in silence, studying between exams. On other occasions they'd discuss their least favorite professors. The four of them were friends of circumstance, bound by the fact that they'd never quite be the same as everyone else at Balmerick.

As she entered, Ren saw their usual comfort had been shattered by the two interlopers. Avy and Cora had already lit their candles. Cora's glowed at the very edge of the map. Avy lived at the south end of Kathor, close to the wharf where Ren's mother worked. He sat in his chair, massive arms crossed. If glares could kill, Theo Brood's neck would already be slit from end to end.

A glance showed Cora trying to process this new development. She was one of the least likely people on campus to have shown up at last night's party. It was possible the girl had no idea the accident had happened. She was smart enough, though, to sense the tension. Ren saw that she was chewing on her fingernails.

Theo and Clyde talked as if they were alone in the room. It was so typical, the assumption that something became theirs as soon as they sat down. Theo even had his feet kicked up, those fashionably worn boots digging their heels into the wax-made miniature canal. The two boys had lit candles in the same neighborhood. Their houses were nestled in the Upper Quarter. She'd found that name annoying ever since the first time she researched its origins. It wasn't north of the Lower Quarter, and it wasn't physically higher than it either. It had been named that simply because the people who lived there had more money, because it was considered superior. She saw that both boys lived in the Safe Harbor area—the wealthiest of those wealthy neighborhoods. During her time at Balmerick, no one using the public portal had ever lit a candle to travel to that section of the city.

Ren circled around the wax display in the opposite direction and snatched one of the lighting rods. She touched the extending flame to her usual candle, which bordered one of the markets near Stepfast Street. Timmons mimicked the motion to establish her own connection with the location, relighting the exact same wick. It was clear she was trying to make quick work of it so she wouldn't be noticed, but discretion was not one of her talents. Clyde's eyes flicked up. He smirked when he saw her seated across from him.

"Timmons. Have fun last night? Quality product, no?"

Her cheeks colored. "It was fine. Thanks."

Ren had forgotten it was Clyde who'd pulled her friend into the back room. Which meant it was Clyde who'd given her a hit of breath at the party. He wasn't a surprise source. The Winters family had made its fortune on the more legal and traditional medicines. It wasn't hard to imagine their posh son having access to the auxiliary branches of their trade.

"I was still seeing sparks this morning," Clyde said. "Consider it an open invitation."

Theo watched the exchange with hooded eyes. Ren couldn't tell if he disliked a topic that was tied so closely to his recent mistake or if his disdain had some other source. When he caught Ren staring, he made a quick appraisal of her in return. The ease with which he dismissed her as uninteresting struck like an arrow. That anger pulsed in her chest again. She was trying to figure out what she could say—how she could get their attention—when Avy interrupted.

"Could you take your feet off the wax?" he asked, arms still crossed.

Theo glanced that way. Avy was well known. Famous even. That didn't mean they ran in the same circles. "Pretty sure the portal will still work just fine," Theo replied. "Boots or not."

Avy straightened in his seat. "It's disrespectful."

Theo smiled, and the expression was so smug that Ren considered the best spell for wiping the look off his face.

"Disrespectful of who? The wax worker who built the display? His name is Gothen. Family friend. I can assure you he'd take no offense. Besides, it's not like I can actually scuff the wax. It's enchanted."

"It's disrespectful to us," Avy corrected. "The toe of your boot. It's touching the mill my father still works in every day. I'd appreciate it if you took your feet off the display."

Ren saw that flash of privileged annoyance in Theo's eyes. He was not accustomed to someone ordering him to do anything. She also realized Theo wasn't afraid of Avy. Not because he was guaranteed to beat the other boy in a duel, but because if Avy so much as breathed on him, the Brood family would bury the other boy's future with a snap of their golden fingers.

After a moment Theo adjusted his footing. The toe of his boot shifted slightly to the left. His heel settled down in the middle of the canal. Ren went utterly still. It was coincidence. Pure coincidence. But she knew the location that his heel was digging into. Yesterday morning she'd stared down an alleyway and seen that very spot. The bridge that spanned the canal. The place where she'd stood as a little girl on the darkest day of her life. She was about to speak when Theo nodded in Avy's direction. His eyes glittered.

"There. Now my feet are in the canal. Which my father

built. Hopefully, you have no complaints about me dipping my toes in an area that belongs to me."

And he turned back to Clyde, as if that settled matters. Ren instinctually slid one hand to her waist, fingers settling on the grip of her wand. She could see the veins along Avy's temples pulsing. Cora leaned over, urgently whispering something. Ren guessed that she was begging for him to stay calm. Don't take the bait. It wasn't worth it.

But Avy Williams had already been pushed too far. He was a champion wrestler. He broke other fighters for a living. He was likely being trained to crash through enemy lines at full force. Boys like him didn't brook such trespasses. He took his feet.

"I bet you always talk that way. I bet no one's ever slapped your hand for it. And I'd bet good money you'll get away with what you did last night too."

They all watched as he started walking around the circle. The boys were a half-moon apart, twelve paces at most. Theo stood. Ren saw both of his hands slide to different vessels. One was a delicate, stylish-looking wand. Another was a speckled chain hanging from a loop at his hip.

Overhead, the light of the room fluttered. It was a signal from the waxway portal. Ren knew it meant the magic would engage sometime in the next few minutes. Everyone was supposed to take their seats and begin the process of calming down. Center themselves on an image of the place they wanted to go before the wave of magic swept through and extinguished the wicks they'd lit.

"I don't want to hurt you," Theo said, his wand raised.

Avy pointed a finger at his dead eye. "What could someone

like you do to someone like me? I've ground fools like you beneath my heel before. . . ."

Clyde edged protectively around Theo.

"Seriously, Avy? Do you really want to lose your scholarship?"

It was the only thing that could have halted his steady progress around that circle. He stood there, massive chest heaving, on the verge of fighting two of the most powerful heirs at their school. Ren knew the other boys likely possessed powerful magic, but in a tight space like this? It wasn't unthinkable that Avy could reach them. It wasn't hard to imagine what would happen if he did.

And Ren knew that the rest of his life would be over.

"Avy," she called across the room. "It's not worth it."

All eyes swung to her. She ignored the others. Her eyes were locked on Avy Williams. She could see that pulsing fury, a twin to the feeling she always kept locked away in her own chest. The anger was in his eyes and the flex of his hands. He wanted to paint the walls with blood, and Ren didn't blame him. After a brief hesitation Avy thrust a finger in Theo's direction. He breathed out the words.

"You could have killed them. My cousin was there. In that teahouse. One day you'll have to answer for all the—"

A blast of red light gave his sentence a new ending. Avy was lifted from his feet and slammed into the back wall. Cora barely ducked to one side to avoid getting crushed. Clyde's wand tip glowed with a matching light. Timmons shouted at him.

"Are you out of your mind? Doing magic in a waxway chamber?"

"Tell that to him." Clyde scowled. "This brute really thinks—"

There was a roar as Avy thundered back to his feet. Ren saw the lights flutter overhead again, faster this time. It was a final warning. The waxway spell was about to activate amidst all the chaos. Timmons was shouting again. Cora was shaking her head. Theo and Clyde both raised their wands as Ren's mind raced through calculations. She took a deep breath and started to lift her own wand.

A god-sized punch of force slammed through the room.

Magic—greedy and sharp and clutching—pulled her into darkness.

AFTER

12

The portal spell set Ren Monroe down in the same way a child would discard a toy. She came gasping back into the world on all fours. There was pain. Far more pain than normal. She reached up and used two fingers to loosen the collar of her shirt, because it felt like she was choking. Opening her eyes brought on a wave of vertigo. It took a moment to get her bearings.

A forest. Great trees with sprawling roots. The air was notably cooler than on campus. She tried to push up to her feet and stumbled back to her knees. Her mind and body were struggling to reconnect. Ren realized she wasn't alone.

Dark shapes were scattered around the forest floor. As she squinted, they became people. Ren heard one of them groan. Someone else started heaving for air on her left. Ren's own breathing came in shocked gasps. Five other figures were in the forest clearing.

That's not possible.

Everyone who'd been in the portal room was here. That

meant something had gone terribly wrong. They should have appeared at their own destinations. In their own neighborhoods. But this wasn't the Lower Quarter. It wasn't Kathor. Looking around, Ren wasn't even sure if these were the same trees that marked the bordering forests of their city.

"Where are we?"

Her words came out as rust. No one answered. Another groan nearby. Ren recognized the beautiful silver-white hair, streaming ghostlike down slender shoulders. The fashionable shirt was now covered in dirty streaks. Timmons was here too. *No, no, no . . .*

Ren started crawling toward her best friend. As she did, she noted the group was in the same pattern they'd been in back in the portal room. Exact distances and relative positioning. Her fogged mind struggled to process that fact. Avy Williams was flat on his back, breathing in thick and slow. Poor Cora was trapped beneath him, working to pry herself free. Ren's eyes circled to the right.

The two heirs were there: Clyde Winters and Theo Brood.

"What the . . ."

She watched Theo shove to his feet, curses rattling out as he stumbled sideways into the nearest tree. He pointed down at Clyde before retching on the ground. Ren stood, her head still spinning, and saw the reason for Theo's reaction.

Clyde Winters was a husk.

There was no other word for him. It looked like he'd been cooked from the inside out. Every vein had burst. His eyes bulged and popped. She saw blackened scorches underneath the skin. Almost as if the magic flowing through his body had boiled, hard and hot. Even his clothing looked burned. There were dark streaks across his cardigan and his trousers. Ren thought she could handle it. Cadavers had never bothered her before, but then the scent of burning flesh hit her nostrils with full force. She turned in time to retch on Timmons's shoes.

"Hey! That's disgusting, Ren! Why . . ."

And then her friend saw the body. She let loose a scream.

For a few seconds Ren stood there, bent over, her chest heaving. Even the smallest motion threatened to rock her stomach. She waited until she was certain she wasn't going to throw up again. Then she pulled her scarf up over her nose and turned back to face the dark scene.

Timmons looked like a dying flower. She was kneeling in the dirt, face buried in her hands, her entire body shaking uncontrollably. Theo stood with one hand pressed to the base of a giant tree, struggling to keep his feet. He'd turned his back to them. Anything to avoid looking at what was lying on the forest floor between them. Ren's eyes skipped over that same spot.

She looked at Avy instead. He was on his back, staring up at the thick canopy. His chest rose and fell, and she remembered he'd been hit by a stunner before the portal spell activated. Likely its effect had amplified. She suspected the magic felt like a two-ton anvil now.

Only Cora remained calm. Of course. The medical student would know what to do when everyone else was panicking. Ren watched her navigate through the maze of bone-thick roots. She knelt down to take vitals and announced unhelpfully, "He's dead."

Those words finally brought the image back into focus. Ren

couldn't ignore it now. Clyde Winters was sprawled at a strange angle on the forest floor—and he looked very, very dead. Cora was fishing through her bag. She unpacked a small medical kit. The sound of her tools clinking together finally forced Theo to turn around. He wiped his mouth with one sleeve.

"Knock it off. That's an heir of House Winters. He's not a test cadaver."

Cora paused in the middle of her preparations. Even though the forest was thick with shadows, Ren saw the girl's expression clearly. She looked like she wanted to tell Theo that was exactly what Clyde was now. Instead she offered a begrudging nod.

"You're right. It's just . . . unlike any death I've ever seen . . . knowing the cause. . . ."

Ren saw the sharpness in Theo's expression. She decided to intervene.

"Not now, Cora. We need to figure out where we are first."

Avy finally sat up. He blinked a few times. When he saw Clyde's body on the ground, both hands went up defensively. "I . . . I didn't do that. I swear! There's no way. . . ."

For some reason his denial dragged Timmons back into the conversation.

"I *told* you not to do magic in there. Look at that. Look what happened to him!"

Avy shook his head. "I didn't even cast a spell. That's what I'm saying. It couldn't have been me. I didn't use any magic. . . ."

There was a moment of silence. No retching or heaving or sobbing. It was just long enough for the forest to press in around them like a shadow. A sharp breeze stirred the branches, clacking them together like spears. Ren heard dying birdsong and the distant shuffling of larger creatures. The group looked around, unnerved. The quiet was a reminder that this place—wherever they were—was also a threat to them. She'd never felt so exposed. It didn't help that one of them was already dead. That thought was followed by a darker one.

And one of us killed him.

She tried to trace back through the steps that had led to this moment. The chaos in the portal room. The fight that had broken out just before the waxway spell had activated. Somehow they'd *all* been transported to this forest full of shadows. Ren tried to refocus on the present. Theo had removed his cardigan and was attempting to cover Clyde's body with it.

He's dead. I can't believe he's actually dead.

The others were in varying states of shock, but as Ren watched, Theo straightened. His hands reached up, almost on their own, and adjusted the tie at his throat. She saw his facial features smooth out. It was a quick clearing of the head. That polished facade slipped back on like a mask. This was the son of a family who built and conquered cities. She should have expected this kind of poise from him. When he spoke, his voice didn't even shake.

"There's nothing in transportation magic that would have caused a death like this. The magics don't just mix. That's not how it works. Balmerick's portal spell is an established magic. It's been in place for a decade. Clyde brandishing his wand and casting a few stunners wouldn't be enough for him to tap into a preexisting spell of that magnitude. It doesn't work like that."

He was cleverer than he looked. Ren had concluded the same thing.

"Tell that to Clyde," Timmons shot back. "He's . . . gods. He's actually . . ."

She turned around and burst into tears again. Cora was still kneeling by the body, clearly hoping for permission to continue with her inspection. Avy paced back and forth like a massive wounded animal. Ren felt the need to defend him.

"There's no spell Avy could have cast that would have killed Clyde."

Avy shook his head. "I *didn't* cast anything. He's the one who hit me."

Theo ignored him. "You're right. It was something else. . . ."

Ren knew he wasn't asking her for an answer, but she'd considered all the details. There were some inevitable conclusions that needed to be drawn. "We're all in the same place, right?"

Nods from the others.

"That means our destinations merged. Instead of porting to our assigned locations . . ." She gestured to Clyde's body and her stomach threatened to turn again. "Something went wrong. We got ported to the same spot. If our destinations merged, it's possible that our *distances* merged. I'm pretty sure the magic took our individual bearings and combined them into a single route. One straight line. We're lucky that it wasn't aimed out to sea. We all would have drowned."

Theo shook his head. "That doesn't explain what happened to Clyde."

"Magic," Ren answered. "He performed a spell. And he was in the middle of performing another one. You were aiming your wand, but did you actually cast anything?"

"No, I didn't."

"Avy?" Ren asked. "You swear you didn't cast anything?"

He shook his head. "I was too angry to think of a spell to use."

Ren gestured to the body. "Look at those burn marks. He got boiled from the inside. The only identifiable difference is that he was using magic when the portal malfunctioned. The waxways aren't predictable. We're basically using a system that the dragons left behind. There's so much we don't know about how they work or who created them in the first place. It's possible that the active magic Clyde was using was seen as a threat. Which means . . ."

"The waxways eliminated the threat," Theo said, arriving at the same dark conclusion.

Cora ran a finger over Clyde's blackened nails. It almost looked like he'd been electrocuted.

"Cut that out," Theo said. "Don't touch him."

Avy's voice rumbled out in warning. "Hey. Don't talk to her like that. It's your fault we're out here."

"My fault?" Theo shot back. "You're the one who pitched a fit about a wax-model building. What kind of child—"

"Hey!" Ren shouted. "Calm down. Can we just focus for a second? We need to get our bearings. We have no idea how far we went. Where's the nearest overlook?"

For a heated moment Theo and Avy continued staring at each other. The massive wrestler broke off first, obediently turning to search. Cora was absently scratching at her eyebrow piercing. She stood up and joined them, but Theo turned his back on the rest of the group. Ren couldn't tell if he was refusing to take orders or still reeling from Clyde's death. She kept her nose covered as Avy pointed through a gap in the tree line.

"There. There's a rise right there. Might take ten minutes to climb."

"I'll go with you," Ren said. "I've got most of the map of Kathor's surrounding regions memorized. We might be able to figure out exactly where we are if I can see the landmarks."

Theo glanced back now. She knew he'd spent his entire time at Balmerick calling the shots and leading a dedicated crew. Friends had likely sat around waiting to agree with his plans. The idea of watching someone else take the lead of their search party clearly dug under his skin.

"I'll come too. I've spent a lot of time at our home in the foothills. I might recognize the location."

Timmons looked up. "I'm not staying here with . . . with the body."

All eyes went to Cora. She was still hovering near Clyde, eyeing the corpse every few seconds. It wasn't hard to guess what she was thinking. She answered in a quiet voice.

"I can stay behind. It would be sensible to perform even a cursory autopsy."

"No way," Theo shot back. "Clyde's family is religious. There are certain rites they'd want performed. No one touches him. Not yet. Let's all go. Up to the rise and back. Avy said it won't take long. We get our bearings and then we come back for Clyde. All of us."

Ren nodded. "Fine. Let's get moving."

Theo leaned down, tugging the edges of his cardigan to better cover Clyde. Ren knew he would want to transport the body. Especially after the comment about Clyde's family. She was trying not to scoff internally at that. Most of the major houses only worshipped themselves and their own power. There were nods in wedding ceremonies or prayers to the Old Delvean god, but she highly doubted the Winters family put any true stock in the faith they sold to the masses.

Besides, transporting a body would be difficult. They could use levitation magic, but it relied on relatively small changes in undulation. If the path became too treacherous, it would be very difficult to maintain the integrity of the spell. They could always make the body lighter, but too light and they'd risk letting him float up into the clouds like a balloon. Their best bet would be a featherweight spell with some kind of tethering magic. . . .

Ren was so lost in her mental calculations that she didn't realize Timmons was sobbing, walking a few steps behind her. She paused long enough to hook an arm through her friend's. The two of them trekked up the hill together. Avy marched well ahead. She could see that he was still fuming a little after his second showdown with Theo. His prime physical condition made the uphill climb look easy. The others struggled through the trees, skirting undergrowth. Sunlight guided their ascent. Cora lagged behind, muttering under her breath about wasted opportunities.

"Almost there," Avy called.

Ren was starting to sweat by the time she and Timmons plunged through a final curtain of branches, out onto a barren hillside. A few more strides brought them to the top of the same perch where Avy and Theo stood. It offered a decent view. Valleys swept from multiple directions toward a peak they all recognized. Ren's eyes found the Watcher. Fog draped its passes and foothills. The mountain was one of the highest and most recognizable landmarks outside Kathor, and the second-tallest mountain on the entire continent. Ren was still eyeing the distant peaks when Avy spoke.

"We're not too high up. Somewhere in the foothills. It shouldn't be a long hike. I'm not sure we can make it by sundown, but at least we're closer to Kathor than we are to the Watcher."

Cora arrived, breathless. Theo's entire face was drained of color. He considered the distant mountains and ignored Avy's assessment. "Kathor should be that way." He pointed. "Doubt there are any paths this far up, but we'll eventually find hiking trails farther down. We can get to a safe spot to sleep tonight and get back home by tomorrow."

It was his effort to take control of the group. Timmons squeezed Ren's arm in relief. Just one night out here, and they'd be home. None of the others noticed the detail Ren had.

The distant fog was churning and shifting. She knew there were two notable peaks visible from their city. The first was Watcher Mountain, but the second and slightly smaller peak was the Eyeglass. She'd finally spotted its blade-sharp top. The old tale was that the Watcher used the Eyeglass to spy on the valleys below. Ren considered the position of the two mountains.

That's not possible.

Still, she spoke the words. "The Eyeglass is on the wrong side."

"What?" Theo shook his head. "No, it's . . . right there. . . ."

Ren recited the poem they'd all learned as children. "'The Watcher was watching at half past two. He was watching and watching, waiting for you. Fog in his left hand, eyeglass in his right, he'll watch and wait from dawn till night.' The Eyeglass should be on the right side. It's on the left."

All of them stared into the distance, maybe hoping if they looked long enough, the mountains would shuffle positions and it would all turn out to be some cruel joke. Timmons hissed a curse. Ren felt the truth knife into her gut. She'd imagined a few days of hiking at the most. But those distant mountains confirmed they were not in the tamer forests outside Kathor.

"We're in the Dires," Ren said. "We're lost."

13

The Dires had earned and defended its reputation over nearly two centuries.

When the dragon population vanished from the Northern Sea, two groups set sail in search of their home continent. Both believed it would be valuable to find the land that the only magical creatures in existence called home. Both succeeded. In fact, historians often noted that the groups landed within a fortnight of each other—though few could agree on which group landed first.

The Tusk people settled on the western seaboard, while Ren's ancestors—the Delveans—claimed the south. Cities blossomed. The absence of dragons offered mankind a chance to rise. Magic was discovered and developed for the first time in recorded history. As populations swelled, both groups naturally expanded their territories. But neither the Tusk nor the Delveans found success in the very heart of their new continent.

The Dires was home to the very last dragons. There were

hundreds of stories, mostly found in abandoned journals, about explorations gone wrong. Entire caravans that went missing. Later, when the dragons finally became extinct, the efforts to settle the Dires were renewed. Bold kings promised unimaginable riches to anyone who could establish a foothold in those territories, believing that there had to be priceless magical deposits in that land as well.

The result was ghost town after ghost town. No settlement ever lasted for long, because other creatures still thrived in that wild, desolate place. The Dires proved its name over the centuries, a land so dangerous that no one had ever produced a proper map charting its entirety.

And this was where the portal had taken them.

It was an effort not to completely panic.

How could we possibly have traveled this far? Even if our distances combined, there's no way we'd get ported across an entire mountain chain. How could the calculations be so far off? What is the missing factor? Maybe something about the waxways being an unstable source of magic? Or are the mountains themselves permeable?

" . . . anyone have a way candle?"

The specificity of that question dragged Ren out of her own thoughts. She looked up sharply at Theo, who glanced back in surprise.

"Wait. Do you actually have a way candle? Who carries a way candle?"

"It's in my bag," Ren said. "A standard-sized candle. I always have an extra."

Avy was nodding. "Finally, some good luck. One of us can port back. Bring help. We'll just have to pick a fixed location to head toward, so the rescue party can meet us halfway. . . ."

Theo shook his head. "It doesn't work like that."

"Oh, now you're an expert on rescue parties?" Avy threw back.

"He means the candle," Ren said. "It can take me about two days' travel. Maybe two and a half if I push it? Willard's theorem calculates the average distance for a standard candle at thirty-four thousand fifty-two paces. A wizard's focus and willpower can stretch that distance fractionally, but I'm assuming we're a lot farther from the city than two days, right? If we're all the way out here?"

Avy nodded. "I'd guess we're closer to eight or nine."

"Which means if someone used the candle, they'd just port a few days ahead of everyone else. And they'd be alone, with no one to watch their back. Not the best plan. We need to save the way candle for when we're on the right side of the mountain. When we're close enough to Kathor to have someone actually make it back to Balmerick to get help."

"What if I boost the jump?" Timmons asked. Her eyes were red from crying, but the idea of usefulness had lured her into the conversation. "I could enhance the magic for more distance."

Her words hit Ren like a strike of lightning. It was an answer to the other question Ren had been thinking about. *That* was the reason they'd traveled so far. Timmons had unintentionally amplified their tangled routes and distances. Ren almost blurted the realization out to the others before biting her tongue. Her friend hadn't stopped crying since they arrived. Knowing her own role in how far they'd traveled would drain what little fight she had left. But at least Ren knew the missing factor in the equation. Timmons's innate power had multiplied how far they traveled.

"If you're really strong, it might triple the distance?" Theo answered. "The person who travels would still be on this side of the mountain. That's a lot of terrain to cover."

"What's the worst that would happen?" Timmons asked. "If one of us tried to push past the limitations of the candle. Travel as far as we can."

"A big part of the function of the candle is protection," Ren answered, recalling a section she'd read in *Wax and Way*. "Think about it like a cocoon. Something pungent that covers up our real scent. Remember, the waxways were left behind by the dragons. Like everything else on this continent. It's how *they* traveled. We're just tapping into an old system. It's kind of like running water through another civilization's pipes. Most of the time it works flawlessly. But every now and again you run into whatever has grown in the dark all this time. Traveling past the limitations of the candle means exposing yourself. Trying to travel too far is the reason some wizards don't come back."

She glanced around and realized that wasn't the most positive framing. She probably could have just said *It won't work* and left it at that. Most of the faces around the circle had fallen. Only Avy still wore a determined expression.

"My grandfather was full Tusk. I never met him, but he was a true pioneer. Never stopped traveling. Always going on exploration treks. My father—he learned some pioneering from him. And he taught some of that to me and Pree. I know enough to get us through terrain like this. The mountain passes . . ." He trailed off, eyeing those distant peaks.

"I'm not going to lie. They'll be a lot harder than this. But if we all stay together? We can survive them."

Theo scowled. "Good pioneers die in those passes all the time."

"Alone," Avy threw back. "Testing their own physical limits. Most of them don't use any magic because they're survivalists. We're not trying to set records or anything. We're just trying to get back to Kathor alive."

Ren saw that it was going to fall to her to keep the two of them away from each other's throats. "Let's focus on right here, right now. We can't use the way candle until we get back on the other side of the mountain. So how do we survive, Avy? What's the first step?"

He nodded, thinking. "Find a heading. Establish our landmarks. Keep moving."

Those simple tasks brought a renewed focus to the group. Avy picked out the pass he thought had the lowest elevation, and they all memorized the landmarks they'd need to follow to get there. Having a firm plan—and a little sun shining in from the west—was almost enough to buoy their spirits. Until the conversation returned to the shadowed wood and the body they'd left behind. "We should go back," Theo said. "We need to get Clyde."

Ren was already mentally preparing an argument against bringing Clyde with them. Their new situation was dangerous on a number of levels. There were far more deadly predators in the Dires. This had once been a hunting ground for dragons. Only the most dangerous creatures had survived them and now flourished in their absence. It would be difficult to walk through territory like this with a 170-pound piece of bait in tow.

The other danger was in running out of magic. Their vessels stored only so many ockleys. Refreshing a levitation spell every few hours would have a cost. And the odds of successfully carrying a corpse through the mountain passes were slim. She'd have to frame the suggestion to make it sound like the obvious course, because she knew bringing Clyde was the kind of mistake that might get them killed. Better to give him a grave out here and be done with it.

"We'll have to do a resource check before we get moving," Ren suggested as they descended into the growing shadows. "Go through our satchels. Carry only what we need. It'll be good to know how much food we have. Calculate our combined magic, too."

Everyone stiffened at the last comment. She saw the way Theo chewed on his lip. It wasn't exactly taboo, but much like politics, magical accommodations weren't discussed at the dinner table. Everyone knew the wealthier houses received the largest magical allowances. It was supposedly a meritocracy. The more your businesses benefited the city—or the more citizens you employed—the larger your magical allocation. Which meant that families like Ren's received the lowest stipends. She knew the entire system was designed to maintain the established hierarchy, especially since the public wasn't actually allowed to know how much each of the houses received each month.

When the silence stretched on, Timmons finally chimed in. "I've got some textbooks I'd gladly leave behind."

This had always been her way of dealing with stress. Dry humor could help her weather any storm. Ren offered a grateful nod. They'd survived junior and senior year by acting as each other's armor. Offering their strength whenever the other felt too weak to go on. Timmons picked up on Ren's signal and kept trying to lighten the mood.

"Quentin's *The Wizard and the Kingdom* is practically begging to be abandoned in a forest, never to be read again. The first eighty pages are just him slobbering over Malfa's charmwork."

"Oh. I liked that one," Ren replied.

"You like them all, dear."

Avy glanced back. "We'll want to keep pages for tinder, but all the bindings can go. Did anyone else pack any food? I'm pretty sure I—"

Theo's voice cut through their discussion.

"Where's Clyde?"

They'd reached the hollow where his body had been covered. Everyone saw that Theo's cardigan had been thrown aside. There were dark streaks, disturbed branches. The forest glade was empty now, though. No one spoke because no one knew what to say.

Clyde's body was gone.

14

The missing body made the surrounding shadows even more unnerving.

Up on the overlook it had been bright and sunny. Late afternoon. Down here the canopy was thick enough to draw on their darkest imaginings. It would be night before long, and anything could be hiding just out of sight.

"Defensive spells at the ready," Ren whispered. "Avy? What's out here?"

He struggled to keep his booming voice quiet.

"Depends how deep into the Dires we traveled. I'm hoping we're on the very edges of the wilder territories. Hard to say. Wyverns usually stick to higher elevations. If we're unlucky, maybe there's a vayan matron nearby? They usually only hunt at night, but we . . . we left Clyde out in the open. A scent like that could have lured anything. If I'd known we were on this side of the mountains, I would have made sure we posted a guard. There are wild hellhound packs out here too, but they probably would have . . . fought over him."

That was pretty grim. Ren saw paling faces and heaving chests, but Avy kept talking, unmindful of the effect his words were having on the others. "A lot of bear species. Way bigger and faster than the ones in our forests. Oh, and there are slipsnakes that might be strong enough to pull him up—"

"You can stop," Ren said. "A few seconds ago."

Timmons muttered under her breath, "A snake. That can lift a body. Wonderful."

"Let's stay together. Keep quiet and look for clues."

Even Theo obeyed Ren's order this time. They started forward, and she didn't doubt that each of them held a mental image of their least favorite creature on Avy's list. There were more snapped branches. Several natural pathways led away from where the body had been, but there weren't any signs of animal markings. Ren glanced up—the slipsnake idea still fresh in her mind—but the canopy was empty. The group circled back to where their satchels waited in a scattered pile.

"We have to keep looking for him," Theo insisted. "He deserves a proper burial."

Ren heard the tremor in his voice. He was saying what he thought was the right thing to say and hoping they would disagree. She decided to give him an out.

"Anything big enough to carry him away is big enough to come back and cause damage to us. You heard Avy. It will be hard enough to survive on our own. Even harder if something picks up our trail. We need to get moving and hope it doesn't follow."

"What about our stuff?" Timmons whispered.

"Bring everything," Avy answered. "We should hike as far as we can before it gets dark. Find a more defensible location.

It will be easier to go through our packs when we know we're safe."

There was a silent assent from the others. She was surprised that, once more, Theo made no objections. It took a moment to understand the reason for his hesitation. He was now the outsider in their group. Clyde had been his friend. The rest of them were strangers to him and possessed a kinship he could never share. She watched him reach for Clyde's bag like it was a lifeline, then throw the extra weight over one shoulder.

Everyone followed Avy out of the clearing. He chose a path that brought them up into sunlight. It was the only warmth the day had offered them. She kept searching for signs of Clyde as they walked, but as they put that shadowed forest behind them, she secretly hoped they'd never see Clyde's body or whatever had taken him ever again.

For a while there was an almost-pleasant silence. Everyone trudged on. One foot after the other. Survival mechanisms were activating. One of their friends was already dead. It would require all their skill not to lose anyone else. Some luck, too. Ren silently promised that she'd do everything in her power to make sure no one else died. She waited a long time before edging into the first conversation she knew they needed to have. There were two important commodities out here.

Food and magic.

At night their camp would require defensive spells. The mountain passes would be particularly demanding on their magic. Other than Cora, no one was wearing proper clothing for the temperatures at that elevation. Ren had a thin coat while Theo and Avy wore cardigans. Timmons had only a long-sleeved shirt. At least they'd all worn trousers. If anyone had chosen a skirt that morning, there would have been numerous other problems to worry about.

Ren assumed the elevations they'd eventually need to climb would drop the temperature below freezing. They'd have to cast warming boons every few hours. Foot-steadying charms and magical anchors would be used in place of the climbing gear a normal pioneer would have. Every day would significantly drain their stores.

Magic could help them survive the trek, but only if they knew their starting point and made a plan. Use too much now and they'd be left exposed in the most dangerous part of the journey. Use too little and they'd struggle to reach that section alive and whole. As they wound past a patch of wildflowers, Ren decided to broach the subject.

"I've got three hundred and fifty ockleys," she announced.

There was a shift in the group. Hands drifting unconsciously to vessels. Acting the part of dutiful friend, Timmons went next. "I've got the standard two hundred. But keep in mind that my enhancement magic is free. I'll be able to add my strength to your spells as long as I'm not exhausted."

Cora Marrin nodded. "Two hundred and fifty ockleys. We should try to save my magic for injuries. Mending cuts won't cost much, but if someone tears a ligament or breaks a bone, I'll need most of what I have to help them."

Avy looked embarrassed. "Sorry, everyone. I didn't have time to get my vessel refilled. I'm sitting at seventy ockleys. We were about to go on break. Didn't think I'd need them."

Ren saw him exchange a quick glance with Cora, but the girl said nothing.

"Don't apologize," Ren said, even though she was struggling with the concept that anyone might miss their assigned refill for the month. "You couldn't have known this would happen."

Between the four of them, they had 870 ockleys. That would have sounded like a fortune to Ren when she first arrived at Balmerick, but she'd learned over the years that the more complicated the spell, the more ockleys it burned. Very few single-step spells would actually be of service to them out here. Most of what they'd need to cast would fall into a slightly more complex range. An average of 4 to 5 ockleys, if they were lucky. There were a few high-level weather reversal charms that could burn through 20 ockleys in a single casting. It really just depended on how severe conditions got—and what other threats they would face. Considering it was the Dires, they'd have to plan around the assumption that there would be numerous obstacles. After a quick calculation Ren guessed that they had about 140 spells at their disposal.

Would that be enough? Certain protective magic would have to be cast each night. Any encounter with wildlife would demand defensive magic. Feeding themselves would require traps. The passes would be particularly exhausting on their supply. Her attention—and the attention of everyone else—swung to Theo Brood. He hadn't announced his total yet. When he noticed that everyone was staring, he scowled.

"This discussion is untoward."

"Seriously?" Ren asked. "Just say the number and get it over with."

His jaw tightened. "Clyde Winters is dead. It is untoward to discuss another topic right now. There's a time and a place for these discussions. He died less than an hour ago. His body is out there. Right now. Something took him."

"Just say the number," Avy replied. "Quit whining."

There was a stuttering of footsteps. Ren looked back and saw that Theo had pulled up short, his wand raised and his eyes narrowed. "How about you try that again in a different tone?"

Avy turned, warming to the thought of violence. He slid his own crooked wand from a belt loop. Ren couldn't help thinking it felt like less of a threat with just seventy ockleys stored inside, but she knew Avy didn't care about that. She suspected he was the kind of boy who liked to end fights quickly. He backtracked toward Theo with a hungry look.

"How's this for a different tone?" he asked.

The air above them crackled with magic.

15

Ren's spell shoved forward—bold and bright—separating the two boys. Like a sharp wind, the magic knocked them back several steps. Looks of surprise appeared on both of their faces.

"Pull it together," she snapped. "We're lost out here. Clyde is dead. We don't have time for chest-thumping. Put your wands away."

Theo's jaw tightened. "Fine. But I've got thirteen hundred ockleys. Keep that in mind the next time you aim a wand in my direction. If you lose me, you lose all of those spells, too."

He stalked on without another word. Timmons caught Ren's eye and mouthed the number. Ren could feel that anger building in her chest again. Thirteen hundred. She'd been expecting a large number, but the truth still stunned her. Everyone walked on in awkward silence. Ren ran a quick calculation. Theo was casually walking around with 200 spells on his person.

More than the rest of them combined.

It increased their odds of survival, but she hadn't missed the other implication in Theo's revelation. *If you lose me, you lose all those spells, too.* The balance of power swung in his direction now. They couldn't simply tie him up in the woods and leave him there. Nor could they afford to piss him off too much. Those vessels were attuned to him. The stored magic was not something they could thieve or borrow or coerce. They needed him to help willingly. Ren focused on the silver lining.

"That's a strong starting total. We'll want to conserve as much as we can for the mountains."

No one replied because what else was there to say? The sting of heels and muscles intensified as the sun finished its descent. Avy took it all in stride, but everyone else was clearly lagging. Timmons was wearing a particularly unreasonable pair of heeled boots.

"We could modify them," Ren suggested. The others were walking ahead of them. "There's no way you can make it through the mountain passes in those. I'm surprised you made it across campus in them."

Timmons shrugged. "I know a few spells that will cushion the heels."

"You do?"

"I'm always having to jam my feet into these for galas and all that. I learned a few cushioning spells just to make life more reasonable." There was a long pause before Timmons lowered her voice. "Can you believe it? That much magic every month?"

Ren nodded. "I read that the Brood family was granted the second-largest allotment of all the major houses. And, of course, they're given full oversight by the viceroy to dispense it amongst their family and hired hands. Never knew how much it really was . . ."

Timmons's expression darkened. "You know, Avy isn't going to forget about what happened just because we're lost out here. He'll keep poking at Theo until he finds a weak spot."

"I'll talk to him. We need Theo. We don't have enough magic to get home safely on our own. It will run out in the mountain passes."

Timmons shook her head. "Even out here we need to kiss the rings of that prat."

"Even out here."

They were all caught off guard by how quickly the temperature dropped. As the sun slipped below the shoulders of the distant mountains, Ren's plaid coat was no longer a proper defense against the chill. Theo sported a fashionable but thin cardigan. Avy's was no better-suited to the cold. Only Cora wore something with enough lining to be called warm. Her calf-length coat was the most functional piece of clothing in the entire group.

"It's cold down in the mortuary," she explained. "I wear all these layers so my hands won't shake."

The growing darkness forced their group to a halt. Avy found a spot where the trees grew tight and thick, forming a protective half-moon to set their backs against. He cleared the ground in a circle before asking the rest of them to look for firewood. As Ren paired up with Timmons, she noticed that silent tears were once again streaking her friend's face.

"I can't stop seeing him," Timmons said. "The way he looked. Burned like that."

Ren nodded. Clyde's death had been weighing on her, too. It wasn't the first time she'd seen a corpse. Several of her senior-level courses had required studies in decomposition and corporeal magic. But it had been easy to distance herself from those bodies—already guided on by the gentle hand of a mortician—with the idea that they were no more than test subjects. The mind sorted them into the same category as any other study material.

It was impossible to think of Clyde in that way. She'd been in class with him earlier that day. He'd been so very alive in the portal room. What a waste that he'd spent his final moments acting like a pompous brat. She'd only ever witnessed one other death, and even if Clyde didn't deserve to be mentioned in the same breath, Ren knew Timmons needed some comfort, however imperfect.

"When my father died, it was an open-casket visitation. I remember standing there and looking down at him. The details were all wrong. His lips were too colorful. His body too thin. It took me the entire funeral to realize that it wasn't him. It was a body. My father was the one who told bedtime stories and took me on walks through the Lower Quarter. He was always pointing out the little details about everything. He never stopped moving. I wanted to remember him that way."

Ren set a firm hand on Timmons's shoulder.

"We keep them alive by remembering *those* things."

Her friend nodded. She wiped away the tears and collected more firewood before the two of them returned to camp. Theo and Cora were piling up their own stacks. Avy had traced a circle on the ground and was carefully turning the rocky soil with a sharp branch. Ren watched him work at the task for a few minutes, building the dirt up into a solid mound. When he finished, he turned to look at what they'd gathered.

"'Start small, sticks and all,'" he recited. "We need more tinder. Dry leaves, needles, smaller twigs. Easier to get the fire going that way."

Everyone turned and started a second round of gathering. Ren watched closely as Avy stacked the largest logs at the base. He set out the next logs in a crosshatch pattern and went on like that until the firewood was about four or five solid rows high. Then he took their gathered kindling and tinder to place on top of the makeshift pyramid he'd built.

"Now we need fire," Avy said. "Theo?"

"Can't you start it without magic?"

Ren couldn't believe how petulant he made everything sound. Avy shook his head.

"Without a piece of flint? I could sit here for an hour trying to get this to light. Or you could open up your precious bankroll of magic and get the fire started. Up to you. We'll just sit here in the cold until you make up your mind."

Theo seemed ready to object, but as he looked around, Ren knew how pitiful they appeared. She and Timmons stood there hunched and shivering. He offered a begrudging nod before crossing over to the stacked pile. In spite of everything—the malfunctioning spell and Clyde's death and their chances of survival—Ren hadn't forgotten that this was a chance to impress a high-ranking member of House Brood. If she could help them survive, it was possible he'd recruit her. The coming week was like one long interview, and Ren could do more out here than she'd ever been able to display in a classroom with her nose in a textbook.

She cleared her throat. "You can use Aria's spell—"

Theo scowled. "I know the spell."

His feet shifted slightly. She watched him invert his hand, bringing his fingers into a clawlike grip that resembled a torch. Magic whispered through the air. A flickering flame appeared in his palm. He held it out to the tinder long enough to let it catch. Smoke curled to life. He turned a satisfied look back at Ren. She was used to this kind of challenge from other students. They liked showing up the smart girl in class. Usually her best move was to let them think that they'd won.

Not this time. Not today.

"I was going to say you could use Aria's spell for temperature change. It's the more basic version. Your spell costs three ockleys. That costs one. I know you don't normally have to think about how much something costs, but out here it might end up mattering."

Theo shook his head in annoyance. Ren was ready to dig into him even more, but Timmons waved a tired hand to cut her off. "It's too late to fight. We need to sleep. What kind of spells do we need to cast around the camp? Please tell me there's a snake-repellent charm."

Begrudgingly, Ren turned her attention to the new subject. The crew walked through all the potential wards that might be useful. A tripwire spell to alert them to movement. A warding line that would discourage the interest of larger creatures. Lastly, a weather spell that would keep out rain without trapping the smoke of their fire, thereby torturing all their lungs in the process.

She quietly counted the cost: seventeen ockleys. The spells would need to be cast three times a night, which added up to fifty-one. And that was assuming no fizzled spells or wasted magic. Her best guess was that they'd be out here for at least seven nights, which multiplied the number up over four hundred. About one fifth of their supply would be used on evening wards alone.

Theo agreed to cast the barricades tonight, but what happened if he cracked his skull in the mountains? Ren knew they'd never survive without him. She was thinking through all the possible options when Theo approached her with a look of mild embarrassment on his face.

"The weather spell's not working."

He gestured. Ren's eyes trailed upward. The smoke was gathering in dark swirls along the invisible barrier he'd summoned. She drank in this brief taste of humility, letting it roll around on her tongue like honey, before nodding.

"It's how you've layered them. You've got the ventilation spell above the weather ward. The smoke is hitting the weather barrier first. It's obeying that magic before it can reach the second layer of the spell. Just reverse them."

He chewed his lip for a second and nodded. "Thanks."

She resisted telling him how much magic he'd just wasted. At least he'd muttered a thank-you this time. Ren felt like that was a step in the right direction. He'd come to her for information. Trusted her to have the answer. It was a starting point.

Everyone took a few minutes to settle in. Cora was already snoring. Avy had his head cradled in those massive hands, lying with his back to the ground, eyes tracing the stars above.

Theo eventually returned to the fire, choosing a spot that was carefully separated from the rest of them. He sat leaned back, legs stretched, his arms behind him to prop up his upper body. She was finally able to look at him closely for the first time.

A tapered jaw, sharp cheekbones. He had the body of a runner, tight with corded muscle. He was more handsome when he wasn't smashed drunk, his golden hair falling imperfectly down a pale forehead. But when he looked her way, she saw that he had his father's pitted eyes. They looked out on the rest of the world as if it were already in his possession. Ren tucked back beneath her jacket, nestling in next to Timmons. Her friend curled a little closer before whispering good night. Exhaustion tugged at Ren's tired limbs. It didn't take long for her to drift off to sleep.

16

A bell tolled.

Ren sat up straight, briefly thinking she was back on Balmerick's campus, late for some forgotten class. The sound reverberated as she took in her surroundings. At this hour the dark forest had a far more sinister appearance. The fire cast its dying light on the curtain of surrounding branches. Everything beyond the first red-tipped leaves sat in shadow. That strange bell continued tolling as the others stirred. Theo stood nearby with his wand raised.

"What is that?" Timmons hissed.

He didn't look back. His eyes kept searching the tree line. "It's the tripwire spell. Something crossed into camp."

"Did you have to make it so loud?"

He scowled. "It's useless if it doesn't wake us up."

Ren was standing now too. Her eyes found movement. A branch trembled slightly. In its shadow she saw a dark-furred hare. The light of their fire reflected in the creature's glassy eye.

"Did you set a size threshold on the tripwire spell?"

Theo shook his head. "No. I didn't—I assumed some of the predators out here might be smaller."

Ren was too tired to laugh. At least he could pull an explanation out of thin air. "Well, there's your dangerous predator," she said, pointing. "A blackthatch rabbit. Make sure it doesn't bite you. I hear they're rather poisonous. Adjust the spell. I'm going back to—"

Her sentence was cut off by a slash of movement. The rabbit planted its back legs to leap before a second shadow pinned it to the earth. Momentum brought the hunter sliding briefly free of tree cover. All of them saw the slouched shoulders. Eyes like the speckled streaks of a red sky. The great cat was about Ren's size, all bone and thin-layered muscle. The creature shook its prey in a clamped jaw until the rabbit went limp. Only then did it look up at them. A lip curled instinctively. Ren heard a noise of warning rattle out of the creature's throat.

Theo unleashed a bolt of magic that briefly illuminated the night, blinding the rest of them. She was blinking away the afterimage as Theo took a few bold steps forward in his search.

"Gone," he announced. "Scared it off."

"I hate it here," Timmons whispered. "I hate it all."

"It was just a slink cat," Avy said. "Wicked quick, but too small to go after us. It's honestly a good sign. They're pretty common on our side of the mountain too. Might mean we didn't go too far into the Dires after all."

"Yes," Timmons replied dryly. "Those claws were reassuringly small. Not sharp at all."

Avy was already repositioning his satchel for sleep, though, as if he hadn't just watched one creature kill another creature less than ten paces from where they'd set up camp. A glance showed that Cora hadn't even woken up. Ren tried to nestle back in next to Timmons, who she could tell was crying again. Theo circled their camp and refreshed the wards.

Sleep never came. Timmons eventually drifted off, but about an hour later another sound shivered through the air. Distant, but too clear. A low moan. Theo had finished altering the spell, and now he stood a few paces away from Ren, eyes tracing the cloud-thick dark around their camp. He glanced back and their eyes met. The moan sounded again. No closer, but that was hardly a comfort. Ren slid free of Timmons. She pushed up to her feet to stand beside Theo.

"What do you think that is?" he asked.

It sounded a third time.

"I don't know. I don't want to know."

They stood for a time, listening. The low moans continued. Ren thought the source of the noise was moving south, away from them. It was hard to tell.

"Surprised there's anything you don't know," he remarked.

Ren could tell from his tone exactly what he was doing. Trying to charm his way back into her good graces. Trying to find some comfort in this group of strangers. It was another good sign that he recognized her abilities. She could work with that foundation. Continue to impress. Survive this place. She'd never considered how her true goals could be accomplished from *within* House Brood. It would be strange to wear their emblem on her chest, but as Ren thought through the details, she saw how it might work. What other option did she have? Clyde was dead. She looked back at Theo.

"Animal noises are not the focus of my studies."

"It might be whatever took Clyde."

She shook her head. "It might be a loud frog. Or the slink cat we saw earlier, worried that we're in its territory. There's nothing we can do until it tries to cross the barrier. Go get some sleep. I'll stay up a little longer. We're going to have to do shifts like this eventually."

He nodded. There was a brief pause where he looked like he might say something else, but then he settled back into his spot by the fire. Ren rolled over the thickest log she could find and took a seat. She'd much rather be sleeping, but the silence gave her time to think. And that was nearly as valuable as rest. She traced through spells, thought through possible scenarios they might face, and by the time light crept through the valley, she felt prepared for whatever might come.

Morning offered light but not warmth.

Avy was turning the remains of the fire with a boot, making sure the embers were properly buried. Theo caught Ren's eye and raised an eyebrow. It was a silent question. She shook her head to say that no, the noise had never manifested into more. She hoped whatever had taken Clyde's body wasn't tracking them. She didn't have any spells to hide their scent, not from real predators.

"I'm hungry," Avy announced. "Anyone else have food?"

Ren unbuckled her satchel. "Let's dump out everything. Sort through what we should bring and what we should leave. It'll give us a baseline for resources."

No one objected. Ren pulled out textbooks one by one,

deliberately placing her possessions where everyone could see them. Her pile consisted of seven books, five apples, the stolen waxway candle, a newspaper, and several journals of rigorous notes. Ren went ahead and started ripping out pages from the books, which felt sacrilegious, but there was no way she'd be able to carry their weight the whole way. When she picked up the newspaper, she noticed Theo watching her carefully, no doubt aware there was an article in there that should have had his name written within it.

Timmons had the oddest assortment of possessions. A consequence of all the random gifts she'd been courted with over the years, some of which never made it back to her dorm. An enchanted paperweight bearing the sigil of some minor house. A small crystal chalice. Three different sets of ivory-plated hair combs. Timmons was quietly crying as she separated out the useless items. Ren knelt down beside her.

"You've been carrying all this around campus? No wonder your shoulders are so broad."

Timmons sniffed. "Those are inherited."

Ren smiled. She considered the scattered objects again before reaching down to pick up a set of earrings. They were shaped like humming-sword birds, no bigger than a fingernail.

"These are small enough to bring with us."

"Small . . . and sad," Timmons replied. "They were a gift from Clyde's family. They're enchanted. You can hear the music playing in their family's tavern. The Minstrel. I used to put them on at night and listen to the musicians before falling asleep. Guess we're too far for the spell to work now."

"Keep them," Ren said. "As a reminder."

Timmons sniffed again. Ren watched her friend tuck the earrings away in a side pouch. It took a moment, but Timmons straightened her shoulders and stood. Her silver-white hair hung loose, almost gossamer in the morning light. *You shouldn't be here,* Ren thought. *People like you aren't meant for places like this. I promise I'm going to get you home, Timmons.*

A glance showed Theo had already categorized his items into two piles. One he intended to leave behind, and the other he intended to keep. There were several books, but Ren was surprised to find the majority weren't textbooks. He was reading adventure novels. In the stack he planned to keep Ren saw a worn journal, several writing instruments, and an almost life-sized statue of a hawk.

"Are you sure you want to carry a statue over a mountain?"

He offered that charming scowl. His wrist twisted slightly. The statue's wings uncurled on command. She stared as the stone creature ruffled its feathers, head swiveling to take in the rest of them. Theo offered a triumphant smile as the bird launched into the air and circled overhead.

"Don't worry. Vega can pull her own weight."

Avy was watching the bird's flight like a delighted child. "You're carrying a livestone statue. In your bag. Like that's a normal thing. To carry in a bag. I've got salted nuts."

The sight of the bird winging in the sky got Timmons's attention. Her eyes widened.

"Wait. You have something that can *fly*. We can send it back to Kathor. It can bring a rescue party to us. What the hell have you been waiting for?"

Theo bit his lip. Ren had noticed this tell before. There was something he didn't want to discuss, even though she thought the answer to this particular complaint was obvious.

"Attunement limitations," Ren supplied. "The livestone statues are designed for city defense systems. Most of their attunement spells are limited to a specific radius. I assume the statue is attuned to Theo. If he sends her flying away, she'll reach the limit of the spell and the magic will force her to turn back around."

Theo was appraising her again. It was like he didn't know that people could read all this information in books. Maybe he assumed the only knowledge that existed was what his father had taught him growing up.

"Exactly," he said. "Vega only goes where I go."

Avy made an awkward show of his own pile. There were hand wraps for his boxing training, a huge canteen, and a sealed pouch full of nuts. She noted that he'd been heading home for break without a single textbook. Cora went next. It was hard to reveal anything that could rival a livestone bird, but her medical kit was a fine addition out in the wilderness. She'd already removed a few tools she thought would be unnecessary weight on their journey.

"It's more of a surgical kit," she explained. "I'm short on gauze and bandages, but if someone really gets hurt, I'll need these. They're imbued with spells that took years to get right. I would not part with them, even if my back is a little sore already."

Ren nodded her understanding. Cora had also set out a loaf of bread and neatly divided it into slices for each of them. The last item in her bag caught Ren's attention. An amber orb. Historically, the handheld stones were alternative vessels to wands. Modern practice had transformed them into safe houses for a wizard's emotions. It was the equivalent of carrying around a giant stress ball. Ren was about to ask what she used her orb for when she noticed Cora half hiding the item with her boot. They locked eyes and Ren finally pieced together the detail that had been bothering her. The orb matched the amber stone in Cora's eyebrow piercing. And judging from her expression, Ren knew there was an intensely personal reason for that.

"Bread?" she asked instead. "Should we save any for later?"

Cora passed the slices around. "It's already stale. We should eat it now before it goes bad." Her cheeks colored slightly. "I . . . I can hunt some. Especially out here. The Dires should have plenty of wild game."

Ren nodded. "Avy. How much paper should we keep?"

He shrugged his broad shoulders. "A bagful? We won't find tinder in the upper passes."

Everyone ate the offered bread, which was delicious. Ren heard Cora shyly tell Avy that she'd baked it herself. They held off on divvying up the apples and nuts for later on. Cora's promise of meat and fish had Ren dreaming of a fire-cooked meal. She wasn't that hungry now but knew the day would be far worse if they didn't have energy at the start.

One more matter needed to be addressed before beginning the hike.

"We need to go through Clyde's bag," she said.

Theo looked at her like she was a lowly thing. "He's dead. It's untoward."

"We're alive. It's necessary."

"I'd prefer not to look through a dead man's things," Avy said, making the Tusk sign of warding. "But Ren's right.

Survival is all that matters. We can't make a plan if we don't know what we have to help us survive."

Theo realized he was going to lose this particular battle. When Ren reached for the bag, though, he pulled it back and undid the buckles himself. His way of maintaining control. They all watched as he began setting out the contents. A few books. An extra sweater, which would be useful. He hesitated briefly before removing a small pipe and matching canister.

Avy snorted. "Is that what I think it is?"

"Breath," Timmons confirmed. "A decent amount of it too."

Cora chimed in. "That could be useful. It's the closest thing we have to a sedative."

"It also has recreational benefits," Timmons said.

Theo rolled his eyes. "Getting high won't help our survival chances."

"For medical purposes, then," Ren said. "Pack it and let's get moving."

Final arrangements were made. Ren agreed to carry the torn pages from their books. She watched as Theo finished going through Clyde's things. The image of the hawk he'd drawn in Magical Ethics fell out of a notebook. Theo looked at it for a moment, one finger tracing the charcoal-colored lines. Ren watched as he folded it carefully and slid the sketch inside his own journal. A keepsake. She looked away before he could catch her studying him.

The others were packed and ready and fed. There was nothing else to do but begin.

"Keep track of your magic usage," Ren said. "We don't want to lose count of what we have left and end up doing guess-work once we're in the mountains."

As they started their journey, a crisp caw drew her eyes upward. Vega dutifully swooped overhead. Theo hadn't looked too embarrassed by the revelation. That didn't stop Ren from being embarrassed on his behalf. There were only fifty active livestone statues in all of Kathor. Now he was directly linked to two of them. There was the one he'd used as a bathroom attendant at his recent party and this one—which seemed more like a personal pet. Most of the known statues were contracted to the city's defense. They patrolled during peacetime and converted into active soldiers when it was under attack. Casually owning one was like casually sleeping with a princess. Impressive in the worst way.

If not for Clyde's death—and the uncertainty of what waited ahead—the day might have been perfect. Enough sunlight to warm them but enough of a breeze to keep them cool. Every now and again the surrounding forest would break, offering undeniably gorgeous glimpses of the mountains and valleys. Even the company was pleasant. Ren was almost lured in by it all.

Until she remembered she was in one of the most dangerous places in their world. A land that had turned away settlers for generations. It was a small comfort that they had no plans of staying, but eventually her thoughts circled back to Clyde. His body dragged off through the woods. And that image merged with the dead rabbit from the night before.

This place was bright and beautiful.

It was also hunting them.

17

Ren had never regretted her lack of wildlife training until now.

The limitations of her knowledge on that subject—and the spells associated with that knowledge—meant relying entirely on what Avy had learned on hiking trips as a boy. Ren could tell that he was thrilled to be their resident expert. He bounded ahead of their group like a child.

"Those are poisonous. 'The dark tips of the leaves, ignored by the bees, always in threes.' The rash is hideous, too. Pree got it when we were kids. Not that it mattered. I was always the more handsome of the two of us. Right, Ren?"

He grinned back at her.

"Out here? With nothing else to look at? Sure, you're plenty handsome out here."

He laughed at that. She noticed the way Theo glanced between them, uncomfortable with the exchange. She imagined him saying it was "untoward" and wanted to roll her eyes. Timmons seized on the conversation, all too eager to focus on anything that was a reminder of normal life at home.

"Ren went on a date with your brother?"

Avy nodded. "It was his first date. He even had someone shine his shoes, the prat."

"I'm just trying to imagine what it's like to go on a date with Ren," Timmons said. "She probably gave historical accounts for various items on the menu. 'Oh, hermitage soup? Well, did you know . . .'"

That earned a snort from Avy. Ren reached out and gave Timmons's ponytail a small tug.

"Hermitage soup *does* have an interesting origin story."

"Gods help us," Timmons replied. "If you tell me who invented it, I'm going to ask Avy to help me tie you to a tree. Especially when we have a far more interesting topic available to us. Avy, are you courting anyone? Someone mentioned the other day that you and Rosh were a possibility."

He snorted again. "Rosh? Have you seen her? Have you seen me? Our children would come out eighty hands tall and made of iron. Pretty sure we'd give birth to an entirely new species. Besides, I turned down the Brightsword Legion. They don't see much action these days, and the pay is nothing compared to the private armies. I'd rather wait and see which house hires me before starting a courtship. There's no point getting entangled with someone only to find out they're committed to an opponent."

"There are plenty of reasons to get entangled," Timmons threw back. She swung a look over her other shoulder, bright hair catching and throwing the light. "What about you, Cora?"

Cora's cheeks flushed a slightly darker color. Clearly, she'd been anticipating the question eventually being asked of her.

The girl answered by tapping the satchel bouncing against her hip.

"I'm wedded to my scalpel."

Ren smiled. "Good for you. I recently married an archive room."

"Besides," Cora said. "There are very few anatomically appealing candidates at Balmerick. Too much inbreeding amongst the upper classes."

That brought out even more laughter. Theo, who'd quietly attended to every word, was the only one who took offense. "There is not *inbreeding* amongst the upper classes."

Cora shrugged. "No offense intended, but the propensity for arranged marriages at that stratum of our society does lead to a narrow breeding pool. There were only so many families involved in the initial settlement of Kathor. It helped when the Shiverians founded Balmerick. They invited every child in the surrounding region to attend. It was actually pretty clever of them. The wealthy families used the school to determine who had the most magical talent, and then they had their children marry the most capable wizards from the lower classes. That actually explains why the next generation made so many famous advancements. There was a much larger talent pool.

"Oh, and your family helped, Theo, when they intermarried with the Graylantians in the north. It probably would have helped more if they'd committed fully to their promise to arrange marriages with some of the other northern rebels too. But one is better than none! Ever since, the breeding pool has started narrowing again. Heirs matched to heirs. Alliances that call for cousins to end up bound to other cousins. I wrote an entire study on the bloodlines and their overall medical impact. . . ." She trailed off, finally realizing she'd gone on a rather long rant. She looked back at Theo, completely earnest. "I can let you borrow a copy when we get back to Kathor."

Theo scowled. Ren wasn't sure if he was scowling at the idea that such a study existed or the idea that he'd ever be asked to read such a condemning text. It might also have been the natural expression his face reverted to regardless of circumstance. That thought had her grinning. She was just glad that someone else had studied those histories and found them as interesting as she had. But that wasn't the part that Timmons found interesting.

"Out of curiosity, who are these anatomically appealing candidates at Balmerick? I've got my own ideas, but who meets the high standards of our resident surgeon?"

Cora was consciously avoiding eye contact. It took a moment for Ren to figure out that someone in their present company must have been on her short list. The girl was the kind of shy that inspired protection. Ren rarely saw her around school, but if she ever came across someone picking on Cora, she would gladly step in and bloody a few noses. She was trying to think of some way to change the subject and spare the girl when Cora plunged on with her answer.

"You have an incredible bone structure," she said, eyes darting over to Timmons. "Easily one of the most beautiful people on our campus. I'd put you on the same tier as Jude Shiverian and Briar Holdaway. There's an argument to be made for Ash Proctor, but I noticed recently that he has abnormally small hands. It's hard to imagine walking through a park and holding . . . such small hands."

Timmons looked like she'd been hit by a drop spell. Avy was laughing obnoxiously at the front of their group. "What about that one girl?" Ren asked. "The one who was the inspiration for that new statue outside Viceroy's Square?"

"Narvin Farrow," Cora answered. "She had a very high rating, but I believe she is now bound in marriage to one of the Rask siblings. Not simple, spoken vows either. The two of them used bond magic at the ceremony. I do not assess the unavailable. Not worth my time."

Theo was shaking his head at all of this. "Attraction is more than just physical beauty."

"Agree to disagree," Cora replied. "I have a scientific scale that measures physical appeal based on the components that make up the intended, pristine human form. You're a six point three."

Now he looked mortified. "Out of what?"

Cora was clearly enjoying stringing him along. Ren found herself utterly surprised. She'd always thought of the girl as impossibly shy, but maybe she'd just never asked enough questions. Before Cora could answer, though, Avy stopped dead in his tracks. Ren collided with him and would have stumbled off the trail if Timmons hadn't seized her by the scarf. All of them crowded forward to see what was wrong.

Daylight made the scene grotesque.

A slink cat lay on its side, gutted from neck to navel. One rust-faded eye stared unblinking at them as flies circled the great rips in its flesh. It was impossible to know if this was the same cat they'd encountered the night before or another one. Ren pulled her shirt up over her nose to avoid retching. Timmons quietly whispered, "This place is the worst."

There was a silent and mutual agreement not to discuss the details. Something bigger and faster had killed this creature. Something they didn't care to encounter. Wands were out and Avy led them on. The brief light of their previous conversation faded. Everything from that point on was utilitarian. They crossed small creeks and paused to refill the canteen with water. No one wasted breath on things as unnecessary as laughter. Avy passed out portions of his mixed nuts when they finally stopped for rest at the end of the first day.

"Our team physician always has us eating these during the longer tournaments," he explained. "Good for maintaining energy and strength. We'll need something more substantial before heading into the mountain passes, but these will have to do for now."

Another fire was built. Theo cast the spells he had the night before. At Ren's urging, he doubled the spell that would ward off larger predators. She watched him properly layer everything this time, and even sensed the slight alteration he made to make sure nothing too small set off their tripwire. Everyone curled up to sleep in the dying light, doing their best to get comfortable. She strained to hear the noise they'd heard the night before. Any sign that what had taken Clyde— or what had killed the slink cat—was nearby. But no sound ever came.

Before she could drift off, her eyes roamed in Theo's direction. His back was to her, but the angle offered a view of what he was holding. She craned her neck just a little. It was Clyde's hawk sketch. She saw him tracing the lines with a finger before folding it again, setting it back inside of his notebook. As she watched, he turned to a new page and scribbled a few more notes. She saw him sketching something, writing out numbers and angles.

It was her suggested spellwork.

There was very little reason to smile out here, but Ren sensed a momentum between them. He'd clearly taken note of her talent. It offered an unexpected path forward. Her goal—for nearly a decade now—had been to join one of the other major houses. The Shiverians had been her top choice, given their focus on spellwork. She would happily have settled with the Winterses, the Proctors, or the Graylantians, though. Earning a spot had always been the first step. She needed a position that would allow her to acquire influence and power if she wanted to pursue her *real* goal. A secret that she'd kept even from her mother.

She'd avoided the Broods, but now one was sharing her fire. Depending on her. Assessing her value. Maybe this was the path she'd been waiting for all along. A scion of one of the wealthiest houses in the world was watching her every move. All she needed to do was shine.

Bright enough that he wouldn't see what lurked beneath.

18

The next day in the wild was particularly brutal.

A long parade of clouds warded off the sunlight and had the group shivering in their too-thin clothing. Theo offered Clyde's extra sweater. It was too small for Avy, so Ren and Timmons took turns wearing the extra layer as they walked. She took little comfort in wearing a dead boy's clothes, but out here they had no other options.

Avy became their anchor. His barreling voice picked them up every time they felt low. His strides were a goal for the rest of them to match. Sometimes he'd come back and jog alongside them as they walked, offering idle conversation to get their minds off the task of surviving. Partnered with his tapered haircut, it was as if they'd hired their own Brightsword drill commander.

At some point he ranged ahead, and Cora eased in beside Ren.

"He's bonded, you know."

Ren frowned. "Bonded?"

"To his mother," Cora explained. "It's not typical in Delvea. More common in Tusk, where communal magic is normalized. They performed the ceremony a few years ago. It's the reason his ockley count is low. Not because he didn't get his vessel refilled, he always does, but because his mother siphons magic from him to stay alive. She drains his count every month. I saw the face you made when he said his number. I didn't want you to think less of him. His strength has been keeping her alive for a few years now. He doesn't talk about it because some recruiters would consider the relationship a liability. And he's . . . humble. Well, sometimes."

There was so much to unpack that Ren walked on in silence for a moment. She remembered Pree mentioning that his mother's health was delicate. Some kind of blood disease. A bond between mother and son was certainly atypical. Family members often linked a vessel—as she did with her mother—but it was very rare to bond directly with kin. That was an intimacy that was usually reserved for romantic partners. Her eyes found Avy up ahead. No wonder he kept himself in such great physical shape. A magical siphon would leave anyone else exhausted.

"Oh, and don't tell him I said anything. He doesn't like people to know."

Ren nodded. "I promise I won't."

Her mind turned back to the other detail that Cora's comment revealed. *I saw the face you made.* Ren had assumed her expressions and thoughts were well guarded, but Cora had seen right through her. What else had she noticed? Ren would need to be more cautious going forward.

Sunlight broke through during their lunch break. All of

them unwound scarves or unbuttoned sweaters or jackets to allow the light to soak their skin. It was well-timed restoration.

"I'm starting to get hungry," Avy said. "You said you hunt, Cora?"

She nodded. "I can set traps tonight."

Theo stood. He looked up to the branch where Vega had settled, forgotten for most of the day as she winged above them. He snapped his fingers and the bird took flight. They all watched her sweep the sky in quick circles before darting down with true velocity. There were a few smaller birds unsettled by the swooping shadow. When Vega appeared again, she had a rabbit clutched in her stone talons. It all seemed so effortless.

"She rarely gets one on the first try," Theo admitted. "Got lucky."

Her wings spanned out as she fluttered to a near halt. Everyone laughed when she dumped the dead rabbit directly on Theo's shoulder. He jumped, muttering under his breath.

"Looks like she didn't appreciate the insult," Ren said with a smile.

She knew they should keep moving, but the prospect of actual meat was too good to delay. Theo sent Vega winging up in search of more prey while Cora found a large rock nearby and set to work. Ren would normally have thought skinning a creature to be a bit brutal, but the girl was surgical and quick. An artist returning to a favorite craft. Ren saw the pleasure she took in extracting as much meat as possible. Avy built a quick fire and had the smaller chunks of meat spitted and roasting in no time. No one complained about the lack of seasoning or the small portions. Their hunger more than made up for that.

"I might marry you, Cora," Avy said. "Even if you don't find my anatomy sound."

The girl finished swallowing a large bite. "You're handsome in a roguish way."

Avy grinned at that. Hearty food, however meager, turned out to be the restorative they'd needed. After washing their hands in the nearest creek, they picked up their satchels and pressed on.

Ren was still tracking their spells carefully, but as they settled in for the night, she allowed herself to believe they'd actually get home. Surely, they were capable enough to survive. Cora always fell asleep first. Her skin had taken on a deeper olive color. Maybe the slightest of burns from all the extra sunlight out here. Ren knew this was a far cry from the mortuary.

They'd been out here for only a few days, but that was enough time for Avy's beard to come in. It was a dark brown that verged on black, with a random splotch of white near one dimple. It was hard not to think of his brother, Pree. He'd been growing a beard when the two of them dated. She still remembered the way it scraped and snagged during their first kiss. She felt a long way away from first kisses.

Ren was imagining being back in Kathor when Timmons nudged her. She'd assumed her friend was asleep. She turned so they were face-to-face.

"The night before the accident . . . at the party."

Ren sighed, thinking her friend was going to apologize for abandoning her.

"It doesn't matter now, Timmons."

"I hooked up with Clyde."

There was no way for Ren to hide her reaction at this distance. She should have known. The way Clyde had tried to catch her attention in the portal room. How flushed she'd been at the party. It was hard to comprehend that someone like Timmons would ever settle for someone like Clyde Winters.

"He was there. And I was there. We were both high. I don't know. His family's been secretly courting me. Harder than anyone else. They recently offered his hand in marriage. I knew I didn't have to decide right away, but it was the best prospect I'd been given so far. The second-born son of one of the wealthiest houses. He was my age and decently handsome . . . or he was. Before . . ."

Ren decided not to point out what a prat he'd been in the waxway room. Or the fact that he'd hit Avy with a full-fledged combat spell. Timmons didn't need criticism. Ren thought she understood, having no prospects herself. It must have been devastating for Timmons to lose her best chance at a future. Seeing Clyde dead on that forest floor changed everything.

"We will survive this. You'll have other suitors. I promise."

Timmons offered Ren a strange look.

"I'm not worried about my prospects. Clyde is dead. It's not like I was in love with him or anything, but he's dead, Ren. And it wasn't an easy death. It wasn't quick. He was burned from the inside out. I don't know how long it went on. I have no idea how much pain he felt. But I know the screams we heard were his. I guess I'm just glad that he had one good thing. Before it ended."

Ren nodded. "I'm sorry, Timmons. No darkness lasts for long."

Her mother's words. The two of them nestled together, silent for a time. There were night sounds. A few evening birds, singing their sad songs. Ren's mind started to drift back to that first sighting of Clyde's body, fouled by unspeakable magic. She needed to think of anything else.

"Remember the day we met?"

Timmons offered a pitiful snort. "How could I forget? You rescued me."

It had been in an entry-level magical history class. The professor had called on Timmons, and she'd offered up a very incorrect answer about the Expansion. It was one of Ren's favorite historical eras. Her Delvean ancestors had built up their citadels to the south. The Tusk were entrenched in the west. The rest of the continent felt too dangerous to explore. There were still a handful of dragons then. Other predators too. No one wanted to push the boundaries of the map.

Until the true nature of magic was discovered. One Delvean family had risen in power, their sons and daughters all particularly gifted with magic. The matriarch claimed it was hereditary. They were simply born with a talent for it. The lie was disproven only because a boy snuck onto their farm as a dare. He fell through a hidden door in one of the barns and landed in the very first magic-harvesting room that ever existed.

When others learned that magic came from the ground—and that anyone could dig down and find it—a quarter of the city's population set out like explorers in a fairy tale, all in search of buried treasure. There were two particularly famous groups. The first sailed too far north, landing in fertile farm country but finding no magical veins. The second group of magic-barons were the ones who landed in what would one day become Kathor. It was pure guesswork, but fate rewarded them with a bounty that had lasted for generations.

"You said the barons were religious zealots," Ren recalled.

That earned another snort. "I don't know why I said that. Maybe I got them confused with that one Tusk group that eventually sailed around the northern tip of the continent? I don't know! I was nervous! Why the hell did they have to call on me first?"

Ren smiled at the memory. "Eryn Shiverian was the one who corrected you."

"Oh, I remember. That rhyming-named, uptight brat. She was so *smug* about it too. 'Actually, the *motivation* was purely monetary.' Blah, blah, 'there was only one priest on board,' blah, blah."

It was true. The Expansion was very much about money. That era was also referred to as the Age of Man. It represented the greatest decline of religious interest in Delvean history. It hadn't been easy to summon a reasonable defense of Timmons's answer, but Ren had attempted it anyway.

"Eryn never saw you coming," Timmons whispered. "Did she? I still remember you raising your hand. I thought—I don't know. I thought you might pile it on. But you were the only one in that room who wasn't laughing at me. You looked so . . . angry."

"I was angry," Ren whispered back.

"And you spun the most outlandish argument I've ever heard to defend me."

Ren laughed. "It shut up Eryn Shiverian, though, didn't it?"

Timmons had no idea that Eryn had bullied Ren for the rest of the semester. Eventually she'd grown bored—but Ren had learned then what it meant to wield her knowledge against someone with one of those five famous last names. She'd never told Timmons because she hadn't wanted to taint the memory of the moment they'd become best friends.

"It was nice," Ren whispered. "Knowing you weren't one of them."

Timmons nodded. "It was nice knowing the smartest person in the room had my back."

"Always. You know, we're going to get home, Timmons. Together."

The two of them fell silent. Ren found it difficult to believe her own words. The surrounding darkness offered no comfort. The shadowed mountains promised no easy passage. Deep down she knew the only true relief would come when they walked through the front gates of Kathor again. They had to survive what had killed one of them already. It was the only way out.

19

t's all the same after a certain point. Chain spells and out-lawed magic. I'll probably get a taste of all of it on the front lines."

Avy had been going on for a while now. Ren couldn't even remember who'd started the conversation. A classic under-grad question about what everyone was majoring in. Cora's focus was on anatomical magic. A clear-cut surgeon who par-ticularly liked the brain.

"We know so little about it," she'd said, quiet and hungry-sounding.

Timmons was an enhancer who was majoring in magical law. Ren had talked through that decision a hundred times with her. It was a clever investment for any girl whose rare talent would cast her as the natural pawn of the city's elite. Never hurt to understand magical jurisdiction when you were asked to perform nebulous tasks on their behalf.

Avy's pursuits were no surprise. He was training to be a reaver. Modern armies wanted warriors with specialized magic. There were paladins—Ren tried not to think of Devlin—who focused on protective magic. In a proper battle they would form up the front ranks. Reavers were trained to break through those ranks. Avy would be focused on learning aggressive, offensive spells that relied on physical prowess in close quarters. And Ren knew a boy like Avy would receive plenty of interest. He'd already mentioned turning down an offer from Brightsword—the city's official guard. She thought that was smart. Contracts with the private houses would be far more lucrative. Each one maintained its own personal army. After all, they were more afraid of one another than any of the armies in the surrounding regions. There hadn't been a true rival to Kathor in decades.

"What about you, Theo?"

He'd kept quiet. Ren knew scions like him were sent to Balmerick to better their parents' businesses. What vital role could they play in the future expansion of an already industrious oligarchy? Some children were trained to rule. Others encouraged to innovate. A few were simply smudged from the family records, embarrassments to their lineage.

"My primary focus is in tactical defense and city planning."

It sounded boring on the surface, but Ren knew his father's magic was focused on city planning as well. He'd helped the Proctors map out the Heights. Not to mention he'd designed the majority of Kathor's canal system. It was the tactical defense part that snagged her attention. Theo was a far cry from the typical frontline warrior, but maybe he had his sights on commanding armies? Field generals required mastery of magic and perspective and quick thinking. Ren glanced up at Vega winging overhead. She had a few other guesses about what a boy like Theo Brood might be groomed to do in their city.

"And you, Ren?"

The question came from Theo. His eyes always narrowed slightly when he was genuinely curious about something. She met his gaze and tried to pretend as if the scion of one of the wealthiest houses in Kathor wasn't showing direct interest in her. How many times had she prepared her responses to interviews that had never come? Now, lost in the woods, she had her chance.

"I'm advanced magical theory."

"Which branch?"

"Research and development."

Timmons hooked an arm through hers. "She's a *spellmaker*."

"I'm open to several possibilities, but yes, I have an eye for creating new magic." Ren hesitated before adding, "The Shiverians were interested in my research on energy distribution spells. Just one of many breakthroughs I plan on making."

Theo raised one of those knife-sharp eyebrows, but he was impossible to read otherwise. Did that impress him? Did he find it vain or foolish? She knew the big houses had large appetites for new magic, but she also knew spellmakers were like authors. Frowned upon as hobbyists until they created something that merited actual attention.

"Ren also has a knack for magical tracing," Timmons went on. "It's not a full synesthetic gift, but she can sense most magic as it takes shape. My girl is talented. . . ."

That earned another look from Theo. Ren was hoping he'd ask something, show a little curiosity, but any chance of a response was cut off by Avy. He thrust a single fist into the air. A hiss for silence. The group went quiet, fearing the worst, but the only sound was a faint rumble.

"No way," Avy muttered. "We can't be that unlucky."

As the group pressed on, the noise grew louder and louder. Gaps in the trees confirmed the obvious. A river swept across their intended path. Wide enough that Ren couldn't make out the features on the other side. Avy picked his way forward, leading them to an elevated bank.

"This is the Morningthaw River. I knew it was out here, but I didn't think . . . we're on the wrong side. You've got to be kidding me."

"Do you think there's a bridge?" Timmons asked. "Maybe to the southwest?"

"Built by who?" he replied. "This territory has never been occupied by anyone."

"There might be a ford?" Ren asked hopefully.

Avy scratched his beard. "We'd have to hike pretty far up the mountain to find something crossable. And that will have us backtracking in the direction of far more difficult passes. Besides, the river will flow faster where it narrows." He glanced downstream. "And it looks like it gets wider to the south. Bet it's freezing up here too."

"We have magic," Theo pointed out. "There are spells for all of those problems."

Avy snorted. "Have you ever done magic while crossing a river?"

Theo chewed on his lip but said nothing. Avy was right. Magic required concentration. It was possible they could summon a few boons to help them, but just as possible that those spells would slip through their grasp the first time their heads were dunked underwater. The river wasn't running particularly fast, but even the slightest tug of a current could do serious damage. Ren's mind was racing on to other possibilities, having long dismissed a spell-aided swim.

"What about a raft?" Timmons asked.

"Sure," Avy replied. "Do you know how to build one?"

"Don't you?"

He rumbled a laugh. "I went hiking with my father as a kid. We never sat down and built boats together. Besides, you're talking about ferrying one or two people across at a time. There's a ton that can go wrong, even with magic helping us."

"The way candle." Theo's eyes swung to Ren. "You have a way candle. We can use Cora's knife to slice it into equal pieces. Everyone lights their own and we port across."

Ren nodded. It wasn't a bad idea, but it was one she'd already thought of and dismissed.

"We don't have a full visual of the opposite bank."

The others squinted, but Ren knew she was right. It was just a vague line of blurred landscape. There was no real sense of their intended target. And she was quite certain none of them had ever visited this particular valley before. They'd have no image of the destination to focus their minds on as they went through the waxways.

"If we can't see where we're going, we can't control where we come out. You never know. It might work. But there's also a chance one of us teleports inside of a tree."

Theo looked annoyed at having his idea so easily dismissed. He eyed the river. "We could port as far across the water as we can, then swim the rest of the way."

Ren sighed. She'd thought of that already too.

"It doesn't account for the standard delay theorem."

That earned a look from the others. Timmons snorted. "Do tell us more, textbook."

Ren answered, "When you use the waxways, your body appears before your mind does. No one usually notices the delay, because we don't see ourselves port. But there's about a three-second span where your body appears in the location you've jumped before you have any conscious ability to command its functionality."

Avy was staring. "And that means . . ."

"It means we'd jump into the river and there'd be three seconds where our mindless bodies are being dunked in the water. What if your mouth is open? What if you happen to hit a rock? It's possible we might drown before our minds and bodies reconnect. Besides, using any portion of the way candle now decreases the distance we can travel when we're on the right side of the mountain. We should be saving it for desperate measures."

"More desperate than a massive river that's cutting us off?" Theo looked properly annoyed now. "All right. What's your genius plan, then?"

"I'm thinking."

Thinking required time. Ren paced back and forth as the others set their satchels down on the sun-warmed stones. Timmons kicked off her boots and rubbed at the backs of her heels while Avy tried to skip stones. Cora actually managed to fall asleep somehow. Ren went through theory after theory as the sun began angling over the trees. She was weighing the merits of levitation spells when she caught a particularly harsh ray of glancing light. She shielded her eyes before looking across the river again. It was a gorgeous blue, colored here and there by white rapids. As Ren stared, she saw that the sun's angle was drawn in a straight line across the water.

Thick and golden and so like . . .

"A bridge."

Theo scowled. "There aren't any bridges out here."

"Not yet." Ren walked to the edge of the bank, squinting to see if the glittering road extended all the way across. Her mind ran through the necessary spells. She turned back to Timmons. "I'm going to need you to pull this off."

Her friend nodded. "I'm all yours."

"Right," Ren said. "We need to move quickly. I don't know how fast the angles will change, and any huge shifts will loosen the grasp of my spell. We're going to make our own bridge. Out of sunlight."

She pointed. The others looked out and saw what she'd noticed. The golden light speckling the surface was thick and rich. It extended in a flawless line across the water. Not an *actual* bridge, Ren knew, but nothing a little magic couldn't solve.

"I'm going to use a binding spell. From one bank to the other, with the sunlight as the fixture. Once I've bound them, the sunlight will be drawn into a single, functional unit. Which means the next spell can alter the entirety of the bridge, rather than individual particles."

"What spell will you use?" Theo asked.

It was the second time he'd sounded more curious than pompous. She called that progress.

"Well, the reflection we're seeing is due to the angle. It's coming in shallow enough that the surface of the water redirects its path. And as you know, redirection is a change in function."

Theo was nodding. "Ockley's tertiary principle. Change is a doorway for magic."

"I can alter the alteration."

"And make the particles solid." Theo actually smiled. "That's clever."

Ren tried not to show how much Theo's interest pleased her. She had his attention. All she had to do now was pull this off. Pull off *this* spell, here and now, and she'd take the first necessary step into her future. Lost in thought, Ren didn't notice that the rest of the group was staring at the two of them. Timmons grinned. "Describe it as you would to a child."

"The light becomes a bridge."

She pointed to the opposite bank.

"And we walk across it."

20

Once more Ren imagined the magic as the first, nervous steps in a dance.

She took a deep breath and drew on her knowledge of the spell. The bracelet flashed as magic chased through her veins. She carefully attached her first anchor to the solid earth beneath their feet. She made sure it wasn't a single stone that might be ripped free as her spell extended. She would not make the mistake Theo had on the night of the party. Once she'd anchored the first half of the binding spell, she took another steadying breath.

"Timmons."

A hand fell on Ren's shoulder. The answering churn—the depth that Timmons rendered in Ren's magic—was unmistakable. *No wonder they all want you.* Ren allowed that adrenaline to pump through her veins, chasing all the way to her fingertips.

Then she made a gathering motion in the air. It was like raking a hand across the surface of the water. The threads of sunlight pooled in her grasp. Once she'd gathered them all, she cast the next step of her binding spell. The threads grew taut in her mental palm. When they were as tight as she could draw them, she flexed Timmons's power along that line.

A visual ripple raced across the water.

She knew it was real because the others gasped. The golden road tightened and straightened. It had looked fickle before. Something they had to pretend was a road. Ren's binding spell solidified every particle into a single entity. Pretense became actuality. She felt the first resistance farther down the line. She was asking a great deal of the magic, but the power Timmons was offering helped her stay the course. It was a relief when her mental touch finally landed on the other bank.

Ren carefully twisted her wrist. A circular motion to tie off the second anchor. As soon as it was set, her entire body felt the relief. All the tension vanished. The sunlight was bound now between the two banks. It had worked. The magic held. Now for the second part in the spell.

She raised her horseshoe wand in the opposite hand. Some wizards liked using the same vessel when layering their magic, but Ren had found it easier to use two. It kept the magic from merging in unexpected ways. With Timmons's hand on her shoulder, Ren reached out mentally for the sunlight she'd just bound together. It wiggled at her touch, new and joyous and slippery. Ren hunted for that moment when the sunlight from above became the sunlight reflected back.

Alter the alteration.

It was a moment as brief as a grain of sand, but she set her fingers on its pulse and unleashed the final wave of magic.

The golden light shivered into more. It coalesced into something like paved gold. There was a sound like a thousand fingers all snapping at once as every piece slid perfectly into place. A bridge. She'd made an actual bridge.

Ren's chest heaved. "It worked."

I can't believe that it actually worked.

In her breathless excitement Ren almost forgot about Timmons. She took a step forward, but her friend hooked her by the arm, careful to maintain physical contact.

"Can't invite a girl to the dance, then leave her behind," Timmons whispered.

"You literally did that four days ago," Ren reminded her.

Her friend laughed. Avy let out a whoop from behind them. When Ren glanced back, Cora offered a salutatory nod. Theo's face was priceless. Ren knew this was breathless magic. The entire reason she studied and worked as hard as she did. For moments where a wizard could do the unthinkable. And now a member of House Brood knew exactly what she was capable of doing. Survive the journey home, and everything would change.

She and Timmons took the first testing steps. A little jolt of shock ran down her spine when the road actually held. Water was splashing over the sides, slickening everything, but her magic was clearly working. She'd made a bridge out of sunlight. Ren briefly savored that triumph before remembering to give instructions.

"Go ahead of us," she called over one shoulder. "Try not to block my line of sight to the other bank. It's safest if you go in front. As we cross, I'm not sure how well the bridge behind us will hold, since it's not directly in my vision. Go on."

Avy slid around them first. "Pree always said you were a genius."

Theo and Cora followed. Vega winged above. Ren was still trying to fully grasp the moment. She'd performed magic before. She knew that feeling, but this was magic as solution. Not magical theory she'd created for some manufactured problem summoned by a professor. Not a practice duel against a friend. It was achingly real, this magic.

They needed to reach the other side before she'd begin celebrations, though. Cora slipped once and Theo caught her by the arm. They shared a nervous laugh before pressing on. Ren had to tell Avy three separate times not to stand directly in front of her. She could feel the magic trembling underfoot. One of the great paradoxes in magical theory was that unbound magic enjoyed order. It liked direction. But as soon as it was shaped into a spell, that same magic wanted nothing more than to be free, so that it might dissipate back into the ether. It was why spells around Kathor always needed to be refreshed and maintained. Very few magics lasted forever.

She felt that tension in the threads beneath her feet. The bridge would hold, but it would not hold for long. Ren was well past the halfway point when she heard the noise. It grated against the even, continuous churn of water all around them. A familiar moan.

The hairs on her neck stood on end. She knew she shouldn't look back. It would endanger the bridge, but thankfully, Theo heard the noise too. He'd spent a small part of that first night listening to the sound with her. It had likely made him more attuned to it than the others. He turned to look and his face instantly paled.

There was terror and dread and anger and fear written there. He opened his mouth to speak, but no words came. Cora finally noticed that he'd stopped walking. She turned, and the same haunted expression echoed onto her face. The moan sounded again—a little closer—as Ren and Timmons maintained their slow but steady pace. *Keep walking,* she thought. *Get to the other side.*

It was so tempting to look over her shoulder. How close was the creature? How big? Was it a wyvern or a bear or a wolf? She quickened her steps as much as she dared. If she slipped, though, the entire spell would flicker out. All of them would drop into the water, and there was no telling if the creature pursuing them would have the advantage then or not. She could think of several predators that would be more suited to the water than they were.

Avy finally noticed the others had stopped. When he turned back, his good eye widened like a moon. "What the hell is that?"

Theo still hadn't moved. Ren and Timmons were approaching his position. She was trying to stay calm, trying to keep her eyes on the golden road ahead. "Theo. Start walking. Now."

His mouth hung open. Sweat trickled down his forehead.

"But it's Clyde."

Those were the only words that could have made Ren turn. There was no logic to them. Clyde? What was Clyde? A dark curiosity forced her to look back.

There was the golden road, and the pearl-blue river, and him.

Clyde was seventy paces back, making his shambling way

forward. He looked like something that had crawled out of the morass. Something from a cruel fairy tale. His entire body was a giant scorch pattern. It had bubbled up on his skin. There was color only in places where the magic had failed to fully burn it away. His left eye was still blue. One bone-pale button glistened near the center of his chest. Checkered fabric slashed across his stomach like the tattered remnants of a flag.

He raised a burned hand. Ren felt magic flick against her senses like a whip.

Nothing physical manifested. Instead she felt her mind briefly plunge into darkness. There was a slight rip at the back of her conscience. Like something too large was trying to force its way through a narrow door. A second later her vision of the world returned.

She was on the river. And she saw the others had been hit by that wave of magic as well. Hands were pressed to temples. Eyes squinted in pain. A glance back showed Clyde closing the distance. Their only advantage was the physical weakness of his body. All the corporeal damage forced him into a graceless shamble. Still, he was coming.

Ren solidified her grasp on that golden light, pinned her eyes to the waiting bank, and started walking. Timmons stumbled once before picking up the rhythm. Theo looked frozen in place until Ren kicked him in the shin. He let out a cry, but it worked. His eyes locked on hers.

"Get moving," she snapped. "We need to get to the other bank *now*."

He started to backpedal. Cora was already putting distance between herself and the monster pursuing them. *Clyde*, Ren thought. *The monster chasing us is Clyde.* The waiting river-bank wasn't steep. Water-slick stones formed a gentle slope. Avy took Cora's hand, pulling her to safety and urging her to start climbing. Theo maneuvered past him without a word. Ren and Timmons had fifty paces left when Avy began back-tracking to help them.

"Keep moving," he whispered. "Just keep moving."

The next moan transformed into a growl. Avy's reaction made it clear the creature was close enough to charge them. He settled into a wrestler's stance and slid protectively around them, intentionally placing himself in Clyde's path. Ren had no idea how her magic would react, but she was forced to turn sideways. It took every ounce of her mental energy to keep the golden bridge on both sides steady and intact.

One hand was aimed at the bank they'd left behind. The other was aimed at the bank ahead. Timmons was well trained. She ducked in time with Ren's movements, keeping both hands touching Ren's shoulders, never once breaking contact. The two of them continued sidestepping toward the safety of the waiting bank as Avy called out a warning to Clyde.

"Last chance to go back before I break you into a hundred pieces. I don't know what the hell you are, but you're not wel-come here. Turn around now or I'll . . ."

As Ren reached the riverbank, she heard a voice. Not echo-ing out over the water, but whispering through her mind. It was dark and rasping.

I am hungry and you are food.

Avy was still crouched in a wrestler's stance with his hands out. The bright sunlight glinted over his bronzed skin. Every muscle was flexed and ready, a body prepared to do what it had spent years training to do: violence. But as Ren watched, Avy straightened unnaturally. All the bravado vanished. He stood there in silence. The creature leapt on him. Charred legs wrapped around the bigger boy's waist. Clyde's arms circled Avy's thick neck, interlocking so that they were chest to chest. Avy didn't resist. He didn't cry out. He just stood there as Clyde draped around him like a lover.

The creature stared over Avy's shoulder, watching them with that lonely blue eye.

Theo and Cora were there, dragging Ren and Timmons safely up onto the bank. The golden light of the bridge trembled in earnest now. Clyde stared with that hungry expression before adjusting his position. He set a blackened hand on each side of Avy's motionless head. All the others could do was watch as the creature snapped his neck with a sharp twist.

The bridge vanished. Solid gold became sunlight again. The two figures plummeted into the river below. The last thing Ren saw was the creature, riding Avy's body downstream.

21

A vy Williams was dead.

It's all my fault. He's dead and it's all my fault.

In his absence every forest sound became more ominous. Ren heard Timmons cursing every five steps. They had no idea how far behind the creature was—or how quickly he was pursuing—and so they pushed themselves to their physical limits. Half running through a landscape that they were utterly unprepared to face. Cora had been crying silently to herself for the better part of an hour. Theo's face looked like it would never fully regain its color. It wasn't every day that your resurrected best friend hunted you through the wilderness.

Worse, Avy's death exposed them. None of them were the sons or daughters of pioneers. Clyde had destroyed their most valuable source of wilderness knowledge. It reduced them to what they'd likely been all along: vulnerable survivors, hanging on by less than a thread.

It's all my fault.

Ren tried to focus on logic. The creature was undoubtedly

pursuing them. Based on the grunts she'd heard the other night, it had been tracking them for a while. Which meant that it could find them again. For now, all they could do was hope to put as much distance as possible between themselves and their hunter. She hoped his physical form was a limitation. On the bridge he'd been moving at a slow pace. She guessed their deliberations on how to cross the river had given him a chance to catch up.

It was nearly an hour into their flight when everyone silently agreed to stop and rest. There were great heaving gasps from everyone. Ren hated that she couldn't hear anything beyond their breathing. There was no way to sense what else was around them, blocked as they were by branches and brush. A glance showed that Cora looked downright wretched. Fresh tears were following newly formed paths down both cheeks. She kept scratching at the skin near her amber eyebrow piercing.

Her eyes were pinned on the trail they'd taken. As if she was hoping that Avy might still appear. For all of this to be a nightmare that she might wake up from. Ren knew how close the two of them had been. A sibling-type relationship that had existed in those brief hours they'd spent together in the waxways over the years. It was Theo who finally broke their silence.

"Are we not going to talk about what just happened? I've got a few questions for our medical trainee back there. Like, for example, how could you *not* know that Clyde was still alive when you took his pulse back in the clearing? Aren't you supposed to be the lead surgeon in your class? What happened?"

Cora burst into tears again. It was so unexpected, so unlike the person Ren had gotten to know over the years. She'd always seen Cora as a kindred spirit. A cerebral girl who'd earned her way into Balmerick through a combination of will and talent. She'd never once seen her express emotion like this. Timmons thumped Theo's shoulder with a backhand.

"Look . . . ," he said, clearly uncertain how to console another person. "I just . . . I'm not blaming you. I'm just trying to figure out what happened back there. I'm sorry."

Cora wiped her tears with a sleeve. She spoke in a hollow voice.

"He was dead."

Theo raised an eyebrow. "Looked pretty alive to me . . ."

"His return is unnatural," Cora answered in that toneless voice. "I didn't miss a pulse. Clyde is dead. Your friend? He's dead. That *thing* that chased us across the river . . ."

Tears slid down both cheeks again. Ren watched Cora's jaw quiver.

"That *monster* that killed my friend isn't Clyde."

Theo fell silent as they continued to try to catch their breath. Every shadow felt dark with possibility. It had been hard enough when Ren had imagined normal creatures lurking in the forest's depths. Now a monster out of the worst fairy tales pursued them. She tried to refocus their attention.

"What was that, Cora? What do you think happened?"

She was hoping to tug at her medical knowledge. Make her feel useful, and maybe that would soften the pain of Avy's loss. "It's hard to say. I wasn't allowed to inspect Clyde's body. Even the most routine autopsy would have given us answers."

"I wasn't going to let you cut out his organs, all right? It's untoward."

Cora shot Theo a withering look. "What do you think happens when you die? It might not be performed in the middle of a forest, but we take your bodies and cut out your organs, Theo. You made such a fuss about Clyde's family being religious, as if they might look down on having their son's body examined. Who do you think *invented* most of the modern spells for autopsies?"

She let that question hang in the air long enough for Theo to figure out the answer.

"The Winters family owns every medical clinic in Kathor. Including the one I work in on campus. We do research on everyone. Even the damn heirs and scions. The second your life expires, you're one of their test subjects. And for good reason. The more we look at bodies, the more we understand them. The more we understand them, the better job we can do of keeping people . . . alive."

Her voice fell off at that last word. She looked on the verge of tears again.

Ren wanted to keep them focused. "Guesses, Cora."

The girl nodded. "Guesses. Right. I'd *guess* that we're dealing with a revenant."

A shiver ran down Ren's spine. Timmons muttered a curse. There were no good stories about revenants. No lighthearted tales. Revenants were haunted things, dreadful creatures. Ren's mind was flipping through the pages of textbooks, trying to remember all she'd read on them.

"They're drawn back to the land of the living by two things: magic and unrest." She looked to Cora for confirmation and received a nod. "And the whole walking-corpse part fits."

"Your initial suggestion," Cora replied, "was that magic had been burned out of his body. I should have critiqued that theory more closely. It's very difficult to fully destroy magic. In hindsight, I believe the burns we saw were a form of corrupted magic."

Ren nodded. "And the unrest part is obvious. We all saw what happened in the waxway room. The argument. The fight that broke out. Even if I think Clyde was wrong to act the way he did, it's not hard to see that his soul wasn't restful when the portal spell activated. The textbook I read said revenants are driven back to life by designs of vengeance. They . . . they hunt the people who caused their death."

That earned another curse from Timmons. Theo was listening closely to everything.

"It's done, then," he said. "Clyde was upset with Avy. His revenge is satisfied. Why would he keep hunting us? We didn't do anything wrong."

"That doesn't matter," Cora answered. "Revenants are creatures of consumption. I told you: he's not your friend anymore. He's a predator. You are prey. End of story. Besides, don't you think Clyde was conflicted about defending you? Or upset that none of us intervened? Magic is pettier than you'd imagine. Ren's right. We're all tied to his death. Clyde will hunt everyone who was in that room." She looked around. "Which means we're next."

"But now we know that he's coming," Ren said. "No more surprises. We'll be ready to face him next time. What else, Cora? I know the basics from Arlo's *The Principal Bestiary*, but that mostly covers the broader definitions of magical creatures. Are there any case studies on them?"

Cora briefly buried her face in her hands, rubbing at her

eyes, before looking back up. Ren knew this would be important. Knowing what they were facing could change everything.

"Well," Cora began. "We know he can use magic."

Theo frowned. "How do we know that?"

"Because of Avy. He approached Clyde as a purely physical creature. Like it was a wrestling match. You saw what happened. One of the strongest fighters in Kathor didn't even put up a fight. Clyde incapacitated him with magic. We'll need to figure out what kind of spell he used to do that."

"And how to ward ourselves against it," Ren added. "That's smart. What else?"

Cora was drumming two fingers against her lips, deep in thought.

"Most of the knowledge is based in mythology. From what I remember, revenants get more powerful as they seek revenge. It's possible that the next time we encounter Clyde, he will be more . . . whole. It's like feeding a baby. Except . . . we're the food. We can expect him to be physically sturdier. Magically stronger." Cora shook her head. "Some myths suggest revenants are driven by the promise of returning to the living."

That caught Theo's attention. "Clyde can come back to life?"

"Yes, but in order to come back, he'd have to consume all of us."

The brief spark in Theo's expression died away. Ren saw despair settling over the group like a cloak and decided they'd reached their limit on hard truths for the day. Time to focus on a new subject. "Let's get moving again," she said. "Pick up the pace. We got a head start on him. If we push hard enough, it's possible he'll never catch up."

Cora looked doubtful, but Timmons and Theo were glad to cling to even the smallest hope. Ren had always found hope impractical. She cared more about pressing their advantage. She wanted to focus on what was within their control. They needed to walk as far and as fast as they could while the sun hung overhead. But no matter how demanding a pace they set, she could not stop thinking about the monster that now pursued them.

Or the night to come.

22

It didn't take long for Avy's absence to translate into mistakes.

At least three times they found their chosen trail leading into unpassable brush. It forced them afield. Ren thought it was a product of the changing landscape around them, but it quickly became clear that Avy had been guiding them away from similar choke points during the first few days of the hike.

Their path also started to undulate. A few downhills at first, but each one was always followed by a difficult incline. No one complained. Ren thought that had to do with knowing what pursued them and the consequences of slowing down. The group considered pressing on through the night but eventually agreed that their progress in the dark would be minimal. Not to mention, they'd be making a great deal of noise that might attract nocturnal predators. It was safer to make camp and post a rotating guard.

Ren built the fire up the same way she'd seen Avy do it. Everyone helped gather firewood and kindling, doing their best not to stray too far from one another. Ren was making one last pile of smaller sticks when she spied Cora staring off into the woods. She thought there might be something out there—a predator that had forced her to stillness—but when she maneuvered to where Cora was standing, she saw the girl was simply lost in thought.

"I can't believe he's dead," Cora whispered to Ren. "My grandmother was part Tusk. When I was little, one of my cousins died. Just . . . the kind of death that should never have happened. Not to someone that young. My grandmother tried to comfort me. She explained that the Tusk believe that God *is* the land, and dying simply means returning to God. It sounded nice then. . . ."

Ren stood in silence, unsure of what to say. The afterlife was not her best subject.

"I'm just not sure I really believe in any of that. I've spent a lot of time with dead bodies. They never seem to be communing with God. They just seem to be bodies. And I—I don't know what that means for Avy. He's not coming back. He'll never . . ." Cora shook her head. "He was my only friend."

"I don't have any answers. Except for the last thing you mentioned. He wasn't your only friend, Cora."

Cora let out a pathetic snort. Ren set a firm hand on the girl's shoulder.

"You are not alone, Cora. Not out here. Not when we get back to Balmerick."

Cora's expression steeled when she heard that. All they could do out here was offer each other what little strength they still possessed. Ren nodded once before returning to the fire. Everyone settled in, doing their best to take in the warmth of the flickering flames. Theo finished up with the wards.

"I adjusted the tripwire spell. Cast it out wider. Hopefully it gives us more time to react."

Ren nodded. "Smart."

"I've set a few traps," Cora added. "If we catch something, we can cook it tomorrow. Avy had all the nuts in his bag. It might help if we can forage as we go. He mentioned trying to eat a big meal before hitting the actual mountain passes. I agree with that assessment. Food will be scarce up there."

"That makes sense. Let's get some rest."

It was easier to say the words than it was to achieve the goal itself. Ren tossed and turned that night. She had always kept her mind organized and tidy. There was a place for every detail and every fact. But something had been altered. Every time she traced back for the source of that feeling, it felt like touching her tongue to a broken tooth. She'd wince at the pain, resettle her mind, and try to figure it out again. Eventually a begrudging sleep came.

And Ren found herself being dragged into dream, into memory. . . .

She maneuvered through a small market in the Merchant Quarter. She had her father's lunch, a tavana roll with cream, wrapped in delicately thin paper and tucked under one arm. Her mother had started trusting her with small tasks like this. It gave Ren a chance to see more of the city. The delight of it was twofold. First, it felt rather adult to walk all on her own, with no one to watch or check on her. She felt she could have walked wherever she wanted. But there was also unexpected joy in completing a task.

She loved trying to find the fastest route to wherever her father happened to be working. Ren walked and tried to ignore the tingle down her spine. The sense that someone was following her, tracing her footsteps.

Today she was headed for the canal site. There'd been tension at home the last few months. Ren knew that her parents' arguments always had to do with work. She caught snatches of their conversations. Poor conditions at their current job. Her father had taken it upon himself to spearhead an effort against their employer. Apparently, it had worked. She'd heard him singing that morning as he helped her mother wash clothes. It was the happiest she'd seen him in months.

She found him waiting by the bridge. It was a pretty thing, stretching halfway across to its intended partner on the other side of the canal. Her father was always busy, always moving, always talking. She loved the way he stopped dead in his tracks, though, the moment he spied her waiting. The way he set down everything in his arms to sweep her into a hug. She handed him the roll. He winked down at her. She saw the quiet pride that he felt in simply standing beside his daughter in front of all the other workers. Her final glimpse was of him walking across that bridge with the others. He held his head high. He kept his shoulders straight.

A king without a crown.

Her vision of him flickered. She felt it again. A presence. This time a shadowed hand settled on her shoulder. The grip sank into her skin like sharpened teeth. She was forced to walk to the edge. Forced to witness it all over again. The shadowed figure placed her hands on the railing. He arranged her stance like a doll. Ren was forced to watch the part of this memory that her mind had worked so hard to block for so long.

A violent rumble. The stones of the bridge giving way. How their screams tangled in the dust-thick air. She could only stand there and watch as the blood spread. Her father's body was easy to find, bent wrongways in the belly of the canal. She felt the grip on her shoulder tighten again, but before she could turn . . .

Ren gasped awake. The fire was low. The forest around them shadowed but motionless. She shook herself, blinking rapidly. A dream. It was just a dream. She turned onto her other side and closed her eyes, trying to put up those old barriers in her mind. Anything to keep the worst memory of her life behind the mental bars of its cage.

She never fell asleep fully after that. Her only comfort was in the restless turning of the others. A shifting of bodies. A rustle of clothing. A cleared throat.

Reminders that she wasn't alone.

23

Morning offered a false brightness.

A sunrise that would have been beautiful if they hadn't just watched a creature from myth murder one of their friends the day before. Ren tried her best to remain focused on surviving.

"That bridge spell cost forty-five ockleys," Ren announced. "I'm down to three-hundred and five. Approximately."

She couldn't help adding that last word. Even out here she felt the need to give the most correct answer—as if this were a test and the others were grading her responses. It was true, though. No wizard could perfectly track their magical usage. Not even Ren. She always kept count. Force of habit for someone with such a limited supply. But a professor had demonstrated the limitations of their system in class. Four students with an equal supply of magic were tasked with casting the same sequence of spells. They all ran out at different points on the list. It was proof that even the slightest details—a person's stance or focus or rhythm—could cause more or less magic to burn. Even so, Ren knew their group needed to keep the general range of their supply in mind.

Cora held up two rabbits she'd strung together. "My traps brought me down to two thirty."

"I'm somewhere around one ninety," Timmons said. "We can blame my bad choice in footwear."

"I've already used two hundred or so." Theo's tone made it clear that he wanted recognition for the sacrifice he'd made thus far. No one offered him more than a nod, though. "Mostly for the camp protections each night."

"And now we're without Avy's supply," Ren added. "Which means we're right around eighteen hundred. We're going to be using warming spells from here on out, I think. Alford's conversion is the easiest. The colder it gets, the warmer we'll feel. Everyone know that one?"

Theo and Cora nodded, but Timmons shook her head.

"Never stored it."

"I can cast it on you," Theo offered. "Don't I just use an extension charm?"

This was directed to Ren. Again she noted his casual reliance on her knowledge. The bridge incident was likely to live on in his memory for different reasons than she'd anticipated, but he hadn't forgotten the cleverness of her magic, in spite of what had happened. Ren nodded in return.

"Just don't forget to set a clear radius limitation, or you'll end up trying to warm the entire forest. It'll kill the spell's longevity."

In rare cases that mistake also killed the caster of the spell. The most famous example was a wizard named Henri Carver. He mishandled a warming spell in the middle of winter that resulted in the hottest day in Kathor's recorded history. Everyone enjoyed the unexpected weather except for Carver, who was found melted into the stones of his own apothecary shop.

Their version of the spell would last for a few hours. They'd refresh it at least three times a day. About ten ockleys per person, per hike. At least losing Avy hadn't meant losing much magic. It was a dark thought, and Ren felt awful for quantifying him that way. But he was the one who'd said that survival was the motto of the day.

"What do you think about strength spells?" she asked. "Today will be mostly uphill."

"Let's wait until it hurts," Theo replied. "Until we feel like we can't keep going."

They didn't have to wait long. Ren's calves were throbbing halfway through the morning hike. Avy's absence was proving to have a mental cost too. No one aimed them like an arrow at their target. No one drove them on with encouraging words. Ren tried at first but quickly ran out of lung capacity. It was difficult enough to keep walking and breathing.

Their warming spells performed admirably, not waning until lunch. Everyone made an effort to forage. Timmons returned with berries that no one could identify. Cora had managed to find a handful of rootstalks. She passed them out, and everyone chewed as they trudged on.

"Getting more nutrients stuck in my teeth than in my stomach," Timmons complained.

The elevation did provide some small sense of safety. The paths were tightening and the trees grew sparse. Great rocks punched out of the earth, providing footing and leverage. Down in the valley there had been shadows and places to hide. It had felt like Clyde—or another predator—might attack from any direction at any time. Up here there were only a few paths by which they could be pursued. If Clyde came, they'd see him well before he arrived.

Camp that night required a bit more searching for firewood. They built the fire higher than normal so that Cora could roast the rabbits. She set a few more traps, then carved up both animals. Everyone looked spent, and tomorrow would only require more from them. After rations were passed around and the night's watch settled, Ren fell into an exhausted and fitful sleep.

She maneuvered through a small market in the Merchant Quarter. She had her father's lunch, a tavana roll with cream, wrapped in delicately thin paper and tucked under one arm. Her mother had started trusting her with small tasks like this. It gave Ren a chance to see more of the city. The delight of it was twofold. First, it felt rather adult to walk all on her own, with no one to watch or check on her. She felt she could have walked wherever she wanted. But there was also unexpected joy in completing a task. She loved trying to find the fastest route to wherever her father happened to be working. . . .

But the dream lurched forward. Past the normal moments. Past the point where the bridge collapsed. It was guided on by an unseen hand. Ren felt like a passenger in her own memory. Light and color swirled, and then she was standing at the railing. The crowd was parting to allow someone through.

Landwin Brood.

Hatred stirred in the depths of Ren's heart. The feeling didn't belong in the actual memory. At nine years old, Ren hadn't known the truth that day. When Landwin Brood had come forward, she'd thought of him as a rescuer. Everyone else in the crowd had been so painfully still and quiet. All of them had looked down, their mouths covered to hide their horror. She'd never understood. Why didn't any of them help her father?

But Landwin had taken action. She heard him shout, a gilded echo in her memory.

"Medics! Get a medical team down there!"

It was easy to hear the truth in his voice now. The playacted concern written into the lines of his face. The way it touched everything but his eyes. Ren watched in the memory and hated him even more, because she saw the way he searched the canal below. It was like watching a murderer who'd returned to witness the final breath.

Those feelings of hatred consumed her.

And that was when she felt the claws—razor sharp—sink into her shoulder. Something latched on to her with unexpected strength. The grip was so tight that she couldn't turn. All she could see in her periphery was shadow.

"I am hungry," it breathed. "You are food."

Timmons's hand was on Ren's shoulder. Her grip merged in Ren's mind with the claws in the dream. Ren shook herself free, almost violently. It was dark enough that Timmons didn't notice.

"Sorry to wake you, but you were snoring like a goat. Good night."

Ren's mouth had gone dry. A glance showed Theo was on watch. Ren could feel that spot in the back of her mind, frayed and raw. She'd mistaken the feeling of disorder the other night for an absence. Now she understood. It was a presence. She'd had the same dream two nights in a row. Both times she'd encountered something that didn't belong in the memory. Both times she'd been forced back to that specific place and memory.

She lay there in silence, staring up at the stars, her mind racing. She tossed restlessly until it was her turn to take the final watch. And it was in the bare-bones light of the morning that she figured it out. She resisted waking the others. When they finally stirred, she wasn't sure what the polite amount of time was to wait before launching questions at them. She waited about thirty seconds.

"Dreams," she said. "Who had dreams?"

Timmons rubbed her face. "Everyone. Literally everyone has dreams, Ren."

"Sorry. Nightmares. Who has had the exact same nightmare the last two nights?"

The others exchanged uncomfortable glances.

"So . . . that means everyone?"

There were nods all around. Her guess was looking solid.

"And it's not just any nightmare, correct? It's one of your worst memories."

Before it had been uncomfortable. Now the others looked suspicious.

"How could you know that?" Theo asked.

"Because I had a dream of the day my father died. Twice now. And both times the dream was . . . wrong. Something was off about it. There's a shadow there. In the real memory I was alone that day. Sitting on a bench. My father . . . he was . . ." She couldn't help glancing at Theo. His face was so similar to the one she'd seen pretending to help her in that memory. "It was an accident. No one else was standing with me. I'd gone alone. But in both of the dreams I've had out here, someone's hand is on my shoulder. They . . . move me around in the memory. It's like they want me to get closer to the accident. They want me to really *see* the moment he died again. . . ."

As Ren trailed off, she realized her hands were shaking. It felt like she was completely alone—maybe even losing her mind—until Cora spoke up.

"My memory was altered too. It's exactly how you described. There's someone lurking in the shadows."

"You're sure?" Ren asked.

"Yes, because I was alone when my memory happened too. There was no one else. Everyone had left for the day. They'd left me behind and there was no one to help me. But it's like you said. These last two nights someone's with me in the dream. Damn. That's terrifying."

Ren's eyes swung to Timmons. Her friend nodded.

"I didn't notice. I'm sorry. It's a horrible memory. I hate everything about it. So I wasn't, like, trying to look for the details or anything. I'll pay attention. If it happens again."

Theo shook his head. "I had the nightmares, but nothing like that. There wasn't anything strange about it at all. It was just a memory."

"Of what?" Ren asked without thinking.

That earned her sideways glances from the rest of the group. Theo lifted his chin ever so slightly before answering. "I must have missed the part where everyone else talked about what happened in their worst, most personal memories. Would you like to go first?"

She considered sniping back at him but realized from the look that Timmons was giving that she'd gone too far already. "I'm sorry. You're right. Let's talk about what matters. Cora: This has to be Clyde, right?"

Cora nodded. "The timing aligns with his attack the other day. It also links to another mythological understanding of revenants. I've read that they feed off fear. I didn't mention it the other day because . . ." She shrugged. "You were all so panicked already. But that's one of the basic tenets from all the old stories. They enjoy fear, guilt, pain. It tastes good to them. Which means it would make sense that Clyde wants our minds preoccupied with nightmares."

Now Theo objected. "Actually, none of that makes sense. Your theory is that he's forcing us to dream something? I mean . . . he'd have to be outside camp each night, hitting us each with individual spells. Why not just attack us if that was the case? What you're describing is a passive, ongoing spell. Magic that doesn't even require proximity to maintain? That's nearly impossible. Not to mention, the mind is guarded by some really strong, innate magic. It isn't easy to force your will on someone else. There are trained manipulators who spend years trying to plant a single thought in someone's mind. I don't see how Clyde could tamper with our dreams. Let alone be *in* the dreams."

Cora had an answer ready. "Think about Clyde's genesis. The moment of creation is very significant for a revenant. All of us were present when he was born. Inside the waxways."

That was a detail Ren hadn't considered. A monster born in an instable environment, surrounded by untapped power. It had been easy to dismiss him as a creature of baser instincts.

Terrifying, of course, but one that could be beaten if they'd simply been prepared the first time around. Maybe she'd been underestimating him. And that was always a dangerous thing to do.

". . . the waxway passages are a tool that our people use but don't fully understand," Cora was saying. "It's like a hammer that decides it wants to hit back sometimes. I find it very likely that our minds were particularly vulnerable. Drawn in by the maelstrom of power that was devouring Clyde. It's quite possible that we are linked to him. Beyond the fact that we're his prey."

"Which is my next point," Ren said, trying not to sound too excited. "I know what happened to Avy. I figured out how Clyde's magic works."

Theo almost rolled his eyes. "There's no way you could know that."

"It's a reversal of the theory of functional opposition."

Ren found it rather pleasing to watch Theo open his mouth, an objection on his tongue, only to snap it shut again when he realized how far out of his depth he really was. Cora nodded slowly. Timmons made the gesture she always made when Ren baited information. A little wave of the hand that meant, *out with the rest of it.*

"The theory states that mind-based spells can limit, if not completely halt, the functionality of the physical body. Manipulators are a great example. They're completely motion-less while casting. We had one visit as a guest speaker for our Logistical Physics class; it's really creepy. They don't move, they don't breathe, they don't blink. Because the entirety of the *mind* is engaged in the spell."

Timmons sighed. "Is this the part where I ask you what it all means?"

"Yes, please."

Another sigh. "What does it all mean?"

"It means that Clyde reversed that process. He pulled Avy *into* his worst memory. It's clever magic, really. If Avy was fully *there*, he couldn't be *here*. His mind was so engaged by the dream that his physical body was left completely incapacitated. Which explains why he didn't resist. He didn't fight back, because his mind was elsewhere."

Theo nodded. "I guess that makes sense."

Ren considered kicking him in the shin again. "Yeah, I know it makes sense. Seriously? I don't need you to tell me that it makes sense."

Timmons smacked Ren's arm. "Calm down, textbook. None of us have coffee or tea out here. It's still a little early for magical theory. How about we eat? And then you can tell us how we beat . . . a reverse version . . ."

". . . of functional opposition theory," Ren finished. "And you're right. Sorry. I was just excited that I figured it out. There are a few wards that should work if we encounter him again. Maybe focal point shields? Or a layered retreating ward? That's probably our best bet. I've got a few ideas, but let's eat first. Today's hike might be a little harder than yesterday's."

She eyed the distant hills, hoping she was wrong.

24

She *was* wrong.

It wasn't just a little harder; the second day of pure incline broke them. Every new tier rewarded them with an even steeper road ahead. She'd heard pioneers talk about the thrill of summiting Watcher Mountain. How it built character. She had a few choice words for all those guest speakers who'd visited Balmerick over the years. Clearly, they'd left a few details out of the grand stories they'd told. There was nothing particularly charming about having to use the bathroom while buffeted by high winds.

Overhead, Vega was no longer the only bird circling the sky. Ren saw a variety of hawks and falcons. A few of the birds tested her, darting in and probing at her defenses. When the unnatural caw echoed out of her stone throat, they'd retreat, unsure of this new predator's place in their food chain.

The mountains weren't without beauty. As the forest thinned, they saw wider glimpses of the surrounding peaks. Bulky slate bodies, dusted with snow. Like giants cursed to an endless sleep. Ren was grateful they'd found a worn path of sorts. She knew the higher elevations would not have such generous footing. The group was making a hairpin turn up their chosen trail when Cora stopped dead in her tracks.

"That isn't good," she whispered.

Ren turned the corner and saw the same problem. On either side of their chosen path the stone barriers ran higher and thinner now. Shelves that started at head height and boasted steep drops along the edges. Those rises narrowed ahead, choking the path, so that only one person could walk it at a time. The worst part, however, was that the path dead-ended into a stone wall about one hundred paces in the distance. It was three times taller than any of them, and it wasn't a natural formation.

It had been built.

"Kobolds," Theo whispered, spitting on the ground.

Eight of the creatures sat like wardens atop the wall, their clawed feet dangling down. All of them were furred like bears with great potbellies. The rest of their bodies were short and compact, thick with muscle. It made for an odd sight, because they were no bigger than toddlers.

It was common knowledge that kobolds were builders and diggers. Nature's odd architects. Wizards used to study their cavernous homes, hoping to take concepts back to their own cities. The creatures were cunning, but more like insects than humanoids. As Ren's party approached, the leader grunted out a guttural sound, patting the construction in their way.

"They saw us coming," Theo explained. "And built this. They'll demand payment."

Another few grunts sounded. Ren heard something like

laughter as several of the kobolds rubbed their bellies. Their diamond-shaped eyes blinked sideways. Ren kept her voice low.

"Payment? Where'd you learn that?"

"*The Tale of Peck and Pearl*. Bunch of other stories. That's how kobolds work."

"We're basing our tactics off your adventure novels?"

He shrugged. "Unless you know something about them that I don't? In the story the hero tried to trick the kobolds with a false jewel. But they knew a lot more about stones than he did. Pretty sure they tried to eat him after they found out the gem was worthless."

"Oh. That's good. Very useful information."

Ren was trying to remember what she'd read about kobolds, all while filtering out Theo's unproven knowledge. *The kobold species adapts, more than any other creature, to their environment. Evolutionary cycles run quickly. A mountainous . . .* One of the creatures reached down, dragging its nails along the top of the wall. It was a horrible sound. The others fell silent as the creature double-tapped that same fingernail against the wall, then held out one hand. The gesture was clear. Theo's guess was actually right.

"I told you. He wants payment."

Ren kept her voice low. "How do we know they'll let us through?"

Theo shrugged. "We don't, but unless you want to blast your way through with a few spells . . ."

There was a quiet hiss. All the creatures perked up at Theo's words. That same hiss echoed from all sides. Ren could hear other kobolds, hidden in the stones around and below them, answering their leader. *Kobolds are similar to ants. Their hives can number over three hundred.* She looked sideways at Theo, who held up both hands in a show of innocence.

"Don't worry. We'll pay." He nodded to Timmons. "Tell me you kept something."

She bit one lip as she reached into her bag. Silence loomed as she dug inside and removed the pair of earrings she'd kept. One of the few gifts from Clyde that remained. Ren watched her hold one of the earrings out for the kobolds to see. Their leader let out another grunt before shoving off the wall. He plunged fast but landed with a delicate roll. They all watched him scuttle up to Timmons to inspect the offering.

"It's an earring," Timmons was saying. "Like this."

She held the other up to her own ear. The kobold repeated the motion, then slapped his belly, laughing at how it looked. His sentries up on the wall laughed as well. He turned back to Timmons, wagged the gift in the air, and grunted his satisfaction. Ren admired the speed with which he made the earring disappear. She also noticed Timmons was sliding the other, matching piece into her own ear, clearly surprised to be allowed to keep it. There was a second grunt as the leader trundled back to the wall. A sharp knock was all it took.

Ren marveled as a door opened. She hadn't even seen a break in the stone before, but now it slid away on perfect hinges. A few kobolds on the other side waved them through. Ren and the others were forced to duck. They walked on with a makeshift escort, various creatures poking their heads out of tunnels or scuttling along beside their party. She wondered if it was a novelty, seeing a human in this section of the mountain. A trio of kobold younglings came chittering forward, surprising Timmons by climbing straight up her side and fussing over her silver-white hair. They were surprisingly adorable.

A run of entrances opened now on both sides of the path. Ren watched little faces peer out from dark tunnels. Some were wide enough to drive a wagon down. Others looked far too narrow for the potbellied creatures to actually fit through. One wall boasted a series of stone shelves packed with pine needles and small twigs like nests. Maybe for sleeping? Ren noted that a female kobold had taken an interest in Cora's piercing. The creature tapped the same spot on her own forehead before producing a glittering collection of gathered stones, all threaded into some kind of moss vest.

Cora smiled. "I like mine, but thank you."

Ren was enjoying the procession until she noticed most of their guests starting to shrink back. The leader kept gesturing, leading them up the path like they'd agreed to have him as a guide for the rest of their journey. A few of his sentries marched on with them. Ren was starting to feel a little paranoid when the path opened up, out of the rocky labyrinth the kobolds called home and into a flat, open area. It sprawled as wide and as long and as open as the quad at Balmerick.

Stray feathers covered the field. They were so bright and lovely that they briefly distracted Ren from what was scattered beneath them. She'd initially mistaken the white shapes for sun-paled stones. Now she saw there were hundreds of *bones* decorating the plain.

Ren could feel her stomach knotting. The kobold kept gesturing like the host of an extravagant restaurant. He held up the earring one more time, bowing his thanks, and Ren realized their payment had been for something entirely different than anticipated.

"This is a taming path," she whispered. "We paid a toll to make our approach."

"Taming path?" Timmons echoed. "Taming what?"

The answer cut through the clouds above them. A great sweep of impossible wings. They all watched as the wyvern descended, clawed and cruel in the otherwise empty sky.

25

Ren had seen wyverns in the Heights.

She knew those versions had been wild creatures once, but seeing this one made it clear just how docile wyverns became in service to humans. It was the size of a small carriage. A great mane of red hair tossed in the wind, bunching and curving into a dark V at the creature's neck. The hair ran in a thick line down its spine before forming a whiplike tail that swished as the beast sniffed the air, taking in their scent. Both wings folded neatly into its sides as it began to walk forward.

Scales covered most of its body, alternating between onyx and ivory, a pattern that Ren knew was meant to briefly dizzy its prey. Great talons dragged over the stones as the beast slunk toward them, a menacing growl guttering out of its throat. The eyes were the most startling aspect. Riders in Kathor fitted their mounts with harnesses and ceremonial masks. Even depictions in museums featured such blinders.

Now Ren saw why. Five amber-colored eyes swiveled. Two

on the left, two on the right, and one fixed in the middle of the creature's forehead. It was unnerving to watch each eye spin and rotate separately from the others. It also distracted her attention from the rows of teeth running below them. Ren shook herself. The creature was halfway across the clearing, and she hadn't thought of a single spell. Any chance of recovery was cut off by the sight of Theo Brood.

He was shirtless.

"Do not move," he said quietly. "Do not attempt magic. Do not speak."

Another chest-deep growl. Ren watched as he removed his boots. Pale and exposed, he walked out to meet the creature, skirting bones as he went. Her mind was a flickering pattern of chaotic thoughts. *Look at those teeth. If Theo dies, we're screwed. Look at those teeth. He's not half-bad with his shirt off. Look at those teeth.* She was trying to think of spells as Theo approached the creature.

He set his feet, taking up a stance that made the great wyvern pause. All five eyes were drawn to him. Their flickering attention became flame. And Theo Brood began to dance.

"Well, we're all going to die," Ren whispered.

She briefly wondered if this was something he'd read in one of those ridiculous adventure books. His head slid side to side as the rest of his body remained motionless. She saw his golden hair toss with the motion before he swept both arms wide. His hips moved, rotating in time with a song they couldn't hear. His feet began to shift. She realized the steps weren't improvised. There was a rhythm to how he stood on his tiptoes, then rocked to his heels. A planned pace that his entire body strained to match. She also noted how the steps allowed him to slowly circle the massive creature.

The wyvern was motionless. Only its eyes trailed his progress. There was a practiced art to his movements. The way his back flexed. The way his chest pumped and folded. Every few steps he would dip, swinging one knee toward the other while looping his hands overhead in tight patterns. It was unlike any dance she'd ever seen before. But all that mattered to Ren was that it was working. Theo completed a half circle. The wyvern had slowly turned to watch. The moment its back was to them, Ren felt her mind unlock. Spells came leaping from her memory. A dozen magics that she might use. As she mentally sorted through them, Theo went completely still.

Ren watched closely as the wyvern tilted its head. The only movement was the fog creeping along the crags above them. The wyvern barked twice, deep in its throat. Ren saw the satisfied look on Theo's face. It was clearly an invitation to keep going. He resumed the dance as her mind raced through backup options. She had no idea how much longer Theo would have to keep this up, but she did know there were just seven wyverns in Kathor. The mounts were uncommon because the process of taming them was incredibly difficult. If he failed . . .

She watched him continue to circle, moving easily through the motions now. She couldn't help thinking about how barren he looked. Not a single scrap of armor or cloth stood between him and those waiting claws. If the wyvern struck, muscles would rip and skin would part and blood would paint the stones.

Ren found herself whispering prayers into the empty air as he performed another tight spin. The wyvern's stance changed ever so slightly. Ren noticed the way its front shoulders dipped lower. Its rear end was still raised, tail still swishing, but the rest of its body . . .

"It's falling asleep," she whispered. "It's actually falling asleep."

The air was cold up here, but Ren saw sweat trickling down Theo's chest. His pace was picking up. The increase in speed was not random. She saw him performing the same steps and turns. Just faster now. Ren held her breath as he came around for the final few paces. The wyvern's back end lowered. Its great wings tucked in to its sides. She saw the eyelids growing heavier and heavier. And then the tail stopped swishing.

Theo finished the circle. He stopped his dance by holding the same pose he'd held at the midpoint. The wyvern snorted once, but Ren saw that it was nestling in. It had actually worked.

"Well, that was terrifying," Timmons whispered.

Ren had to pull her scarf over her mouth to keep from laughing in relief. Theo waited a few moments before breaking his pose. He crept quietly back toward them with all the focus of an adult trying to avoid waking a child who'd finally fallen asleep for the night. His body shook with violent tremors. Ren offered him the discarded shirt. All three of them watched as he shrugged his arms back into the sleeves and started buttoning up. He slid his boots back on before looking at them.

"It will sleep for a few hours. We need to get away from the nest and keep moving."

Timmons frowned. "But you tamed it? Can't we fly home now?"

He shook his head. "That dance is just the first step. Riders come up here with all the equipment. The next step is to get a harness around its neck without waking it up. You have to fit a saddle to its back and everything. Then when it wakes up, you have to take it on one ride without dying. Do all of that and you have yourself a tamed wyvern."

Ren realized that she'd never come across any of this in her research. There was a note about the taming paths that fliers used to access wyvern nests, and certainly it was well known that some sort of submission was required. But the dance he'd just done? She'd thought less of him earlier because of his assumption that he knew things she didn't. Now she saw it was actually true. He had a different kind of knowledge, a hoarded sort, that only members of the founding families knew.

"What you just did . . . ," Ren said. "That was incredible."

He wiped sweat from his forehead with a sleeve. "Thanks. But we should get moving. If we're not far enough from its nesting ground, it will wake up and start hunting us. And considering we already have one monster on our trail, it'd be a good idea if we kept going. Come on."

She sensed the slightest shift in their group. A begrudging respect was blooming for Theo. It was not lost on Ren how easily he could have died. It was one of the first selfless acts he'd taken out here. All of them kept quiet, bags tucked to their sides, as they made their way across the graveyard of bones. Most of the remnants looked relatively small. Mountain goats and rock rats and smaller birds of prey. Whatever the wyvern had hunted over the years. Ren tried to ignore the femurs and skulls that looked larger, more human.

There was a single path leading through the mountain

brush ahead. They all edged around the slumbering creature, hoping the rapid beat of their own hearts didn't betray their passage. Theo reached the path first. He held back a few branches for them to pass through, when a sharp crackle cut through the air.

Everyone froze. The wyvern shook its head sleepily, two eyelids lifting in brief flutters. Ren's eyes darted to Timmons. She pointed to her friend's ear. The lonely humming-sword bird dangled there. Timmons scrambled to remove the little keepsake, but her fingers fumbled nervously at the clasp. Another crackle sounded. It was followed by a crooning voice.

"And I've never known a fire like yours. And I've never known desire like yours. And I've . . ."

Timmons ripped the dangling metal out of her ear. Blood spattered the stones. The sound cut out, but as they looked back into the clearing, Ren saw it was too late. The wyvern's great wings were unfolding. Those amber eyes fixed on them. Theo ran forward again, empty-handed this time, straight into danger. Ren was the only one with spells ready. Instinct drowned out fear. She'd practiced this magic a thousand times. She swung her horseshoe wand in the direction of the beast and shouted.

"Everyone down!"

Timmons and Cora hit the ground, but Theo was a step too slow. The spell that barreled out looked like a miniature sun. It struck the wyvern right before it could slash Theo's chest. Ren shielded her own eyes as the light exploded. She heard the grating screech as the creature reared back on its hind legs, blinded by the magical blast. Theo dropped to his knees with a sharp cry.

Ren hit the wyvern with a second spell before yanking Theo by the arm.

"I can't see! I can't see!"

"Shut up," she hissed. "Stay quiet!"

The wyvern scratched at its own eyes before unleashing another roar. Lacking the main sense it had always used to hunt, the creature charged forward with reckless, brutish strength. Ren barely pulled Theo clear of its chosen path. Another roar sounded as the creature raced past them, on the verge of running straight over the edge of the cliff.

Ren was guiding Theo toward Cora and Timmons, who were already safely hidden in the brush, when the creature's armored tail whipped back around at the last second.

"No!"

It raked a brutal path across Theo's stomach. Blood gushed instantly. His scream had the creature's head swiveling. Claws dragged against stone to bring the wyvern to a stop. It was trying to follow the sound. Ren slapped one hand over Theo's mouth, hissing for quiet, as she stumbled through the gap in the bushes with him. Cora was there. She pressed a spare cloth to his stomach, trying to staunch the flow of blood. All of them fought forward, through the overgrowth, ducking under scrub trees and around bushes. There was another roar as the wyvern took flight, blinded but on the hunt.

No one made a sound. The creature's flapping wings helped them. Each gust of wind covered their smaller footfalls. Ren was trying to figure out how far they should run before stopping to take care of Theo. He was losing a lot of blood. Cora had his other side. Ren saw her starting to sag beneath the extra weight.

"It hurts. . . ." Theo's face was growing paler. "Please. It hurts."

They kept moving until he passed out. Then the weight was unbearable. Timmons turned just in time to catch his forward fall. All three of them struggled before Cora hissed in frustration, "Set him down. Levitation spell."

Ren and Timmons backed up as she performed the magic. His unconscious form floated up, suddenly weightless. Cora snagged him by a sleeve and spun him around so that his stomach was facing the sky. The gashes there were massive, still gushing blood.

"Find a safe spot," Cora said. "I need to start working on him. Now."

Everything was laced with fog. Ren thought the wyvern had given up the chase, but a moment later there was a piercing cry overhead. They finally found an offshoot trail. Ren saw why Cora had chosen it as they ferried Theo along. Rock curled overhead to form a makeshift shelter. The trail led to a covered ledge that looked out over the western valley. Ren saw a normal-sized nest tucked into one corner, but knew the space was too tight for any large creatures to reach. It was the best they could have hoped for.

"I'll ward everything," she said. "Get to work on him."

Timmons helped with his buttons as Cora undid her levitation charm. Ren wasn't sure if any magic could really keep them safe once the wyvern recovered fully, but for now she layered the air with every ward she knew. It cost her precious ockleys, but if they didn't save Theo Brood, they'd have nowhere near enough magic to survive the passes. Once the wards were in place, she settled in beside Cora. The girl had unrolled her medical kit and was quietly muttering under her breath.

"Tore through the muscle. Damn. That's going to require . . ."

Ren watched as she exchanged tools, making quick but precise decisions. Magic churned in the small space. Each of her surgical implements was thick with enchantments. Ren sensed traces of spells that made them sharper and cleaner and steadier. She was thankful the girl was so prepared. It took less than an hour to seal Theo's three wounds. The puckering slits were barely visible when Cora had finished her work.

"Bound the layers of muscles back together," she said, wiping her hands. "He'll be sore, but a little rest and we'll have him back to normal in a few days. Lucky it wasn't worse. Two inches higher and that strike slits an artery. He'd have bled out in minutes."

"Great work, Cora."

Timmons nodded. "All class. You were steady as a stone."

In response Cora sagged back, putting all her weight on hands still stained with blood. She heaved a massive sigh. "What happened? What was that noise?"

Timmons showed Cora her earring. "It's enchanted. If you put it on, you can hear the music that's being played at the Minstrel. We've been too far for the spell to work."

"Until now?" Cora asked. "That's bad luck."

Timmons stood. "No more bad luck. I'm pitching this off the side of the mountain."

"Wait!" Ren grabbed her friend's elbow before she could wind up and throw it. "That might be useful. It's our only measure of proximity to Kathor. We could hear the music, but it was a weak connection. The closer we get to the city, the stronger it will sound. We might need that earring if we're going to use my waxway candle to portal back."

Timmons nodded but tossed the earring on the ground next to Ren.

"You keep it. I can't stand the thought that I almost got him killed."

Ren nodded her understanding. She slid the earring into a small pocket on the front of her satchel. The three of them sat in silence for a moment. Theo was groaning a little in his sleep.

"I'll sit with him," Ren offered. "Do you think it's safe to build a fire?"

Timmons nodded. "I'll gather wood."

"We should eat," Cora said, still breathing thick and slow. "I'm exhausted."

"I'm not sure we should go hunting out there. Not with the wyvern nearby."

But the girl nodded to the nest in the corner of the cliff they'd chosen. "Eggs. Rich in protein. I count four."

Ren lifted an eyebrow. "Don't you think that will piss off the mother?"

"So? This time we're higher in the food chain." Cora started walking over to collect the eggs. "And besides, we have magic."

26

The mother bird wasn't happy, but the eggs were delicious. Ren wiped her mouth, watching as the falcon winged in frantic circles outside their wards. She let out a mournful call. Ren would have felt guilty if they hadn't needed every advantage to make it through the next few days alive. Theo's surgery had cost Cora more than half of her magic. Ren was draining her own ockleys to create the wards and keep them all safe and comfortable. All while Theo tossed and turned, too fever-ridden to do more than occasionally sip from Avy's canteen.

Their panicked departure had felt like the course of an hour. As the fog lifted, Ren saw they'd cleared the wyvern's nest by only a thousand paces or so. Still well within its hunting range. She just had to hope that the spell she'd hit it with had caused enough damage to weaken it for a few more days. Otherwise, they'd be hunted before long.

"Should we try to start the next leg with him like this?" Ren asked the following morning. "We could use a levitation spell again."

"As we climb, the air will get thinner," Cora pointed out. "Corporeal magic at that height is subject to a lot of variance. You might end up launching him into the sky."

Ren nodded. "You're right. I forgot about Veeley's atmospheric proof. One wrong step and we lose him. How long before you think he'll be ready?"

Cora shrugged. "A day. The magic exacts a price. If he isn't going to feel pain, it will make him feel something else. Exhaustion is demanded. At least he won't be climbing a mountain with a shredded abdomen. We'd never make it through the pass with him in that state."

They encouraged one another to catch up on rest and sleep. Ren sat with Theo on the first watch. Several times he'd whisper and turn, but it was never more than muttering.

Cora risked setting a trap outside their cave and got lucky. Rabbit meat was spitted and cooked over the fire—seasoned by some mountain flowers that Cora had salvaged. The girl had even roasted some roots into a far more palatable form. It was by far the best meal they'd had, and Theo managed to choke down a few bites before slipping back into a fitful sleep. Ren found the way he curled up against her boot pathetic, though she did begrudgingly admit that he had made two separate efforts to save them from the wyvern, even if the last had been tragically foolish.

"What were you going to do?" she whispered to him. "Punch the thing?"

He shifted restlessly in his sleep. When they were awake, Timmons and Cora got along well. That didn't surprise Ren. Timmons got on well with everyone. It was approaching night when Timmons nudged Theo's bag with her foot.

"I've held out for a while, but I've got to take the edge off."

Ren laughed. "Seriously? We're sleeping on the edge of a cliff and you want to get high?"

"Right," Timmons said. "As if you haven't warded the whole ledge?"

She snatched Ren's bag and tossed it into thin air. Cora gasped, but the bag hit the invisible barrier and rebounded safely back into the cave. The same spell that kept the mother bird away from her nest was also keeping them sealed safely within. Ren grinned at Timmons.

"Awfully trusting of you."

"Please," Timmons said. "I've known you for four years, Ren Monroe. You think of everything. Do you remember that time we went stargazing with our astronomy class? Everyone left early because there was a bunch of cloud cover. You told me to stay, because you'd researched the weather patterns and knew the window of visibility. Who even does that?"

"But we saw the stars, didn't we?"

Timmons grinned. "That we did, textbook. But you're just proving my point. If I'm going to take a little bit of breath to calm my nerves, I couldn't think of anywhere safer to do it. I'm with the best-trained surgeon in the city *and* my best friend, who is always three spells ahead of the rest of the world."

Ren laughed. "Can you smoke some without using the whole batch?"

Timmons was already rooting through Theo's bag. She held up the canister.

"This is enough for a month. Clyde . . ."

Her friend fell briefly quiet, biting her lip, before shaking her head at some unspoken thought. Having a classmate hunt them was bad enough, but Ren knew it was hitting Timmons the hardest. She distracted herself by focusing on the latch mechanism to release the breath.

"Do you want some, Ren?"

"No thanks." She tapped her temple. "I will not blunt the one useful tool I have in this world."

Timmons smirked. She'd heard Ren say that exact quote many times now.

"Cora?"

Ren rolled her eyes as Timmons turned her charm on their travel mate. It was like watching the sun pick a single flower on which to shine. She twirled a lock of silver-white hair and shook the pipe invitingly. Cora eventually grinned back. "It would help to learn more about the impact breath has on the brain by having firsthand experience. . . ."

Timmons laughed at that. "Well, consider me your lab assistant."

Cora nodded shyly as Timmons arranged everything. The poor girl never stood a chance. Ren considered intervening but realized it was the first time she'd seen any shine in their expressions since Clyde's death. So much had happened since then. They deserved a break.

"Breathe in lightly at first," Timmons said, handing the pipe to Cora. "Quick exhalations."

Theo stirred a little before continuing to sleep. Ren watched as the girls traded the pipe back and forth. It didn't take long for their smiles to stretch. Timmons pointed at Cora.

"This one, right? This one."

Cora grinned. "Your hair has unicorn dust in it."

Timmons held one finger to her forehead, and both of them fell to giggling. Ren could only smile and shake her head. She was about to say something when Timmons pointed again.

"Gods! Look at her magic. It's *pretty*. Look at that. Six layers. I've known a few boys at school with less than six layers to their entire existence. Right? Right?"

Cora was tracing her fingers through the air, plucking at the unseen threads of Ren's magic.

"Why is it gold?"

"Because she's kindhearted," Timmons said, glancing back at Ren. "Actually, she called Devlin a sanctimonious prick the other day. Maybe that's not it."

Ren smiled. "It's because the magic is *pure*."

Cora frowned back. "Huh?"

"Oh, dear gods," Timmons said. "Here we go. I hear a thesis incoming."

"A century ago there was a theory about magical purity," Ren supplied. "Everyone thought it had to do with bloodlines, because the wealthiest houses told them that was how it worked. Powerful wizards marrying other powerful wizards. But about three decades ago a man named Silas Cross figured out that it had nothing to do with birth or blood. The purity of the magic's appearance has to do with how perfectly it's cast. The hand motions and the tone of voice and the command of the magic itself." She squinted at the invisible wall. "Is mine really gold?"

Cora giggled. "It looks like sunshine."

Ren nodded to herself. "Then you know it was done right."

Timmons giggled. "Speaking of *doing* something right. Dancer over there was impressive with that wyvern. I wouldn't mind being put to sleep like that myself."

"7.1," Cora said. "Let it be known. I've adjusted his rating. Although he still loses a few points for his airy demeanor."

Timmons lifted her chin and put on a mocking face. "Such discussions are *untoward*. You don't mean to say that Mr. Brood is *uppity*? Surely, you wouldn't, Cora. Surely . . ."

They both fell into bubbling laughter again. "Uppity," Cora repeated. "Who wouldn't be? His father owns half the city. I'd have my head up my ass too."

Timmons laughed again. "And that is not the best place to keep one's head, if I say so myself. Very poor storage units."

She adjusted to inspect her own. Ren couldn't help laughing at the way Cora craned her neck to get a look as well. Timmons caught the girl at it and reached over to bop her on the nose.

"Do you know the story about the boy and the silver belly button?"

Ren snorted. "You always tell that story when you're like this."

Timmons scowled at her. "Fine. Didn't want to tell you it again anyways, you prat."

She covered her mouth but soon was giggling again, tracing the air with a finger. "I'm trying not to tell the story, but it's coming out all on its own! Look!"

Ren looked up to where she was pointing. There was nothing on the walls, but Cora leaned in next to Timmons and squinted up as if she was reading the hidden text as well.

"That's sad," she said. "That they made fun of his belly button. People make fun of me all the time. Too quiet. Too weird. They'd rather have a doctor who smiles. Like any of that matters. Most of them just hate that I'm better than they are. . . ."

She trailed off. Ren watched as both girls continued to read a story that was apparently projecting from Timmons's thoughts onto the walls. Ren knew the breath was powerful and strange and unpredictable. A vision of the world from the long-extinct dragons. She always claimed she didn't want to blunt her mind. That was one part of why she didn't imbibe. The bigger reason, though, was that she didn't want to see her deepest secrets exposed through lack of control. She feared what might slip out if she ever unlocked those carefully sealed vaults, even for a moment.

Lost in thought, she almost didn't notice Timmons rooting through Theo's bag again.

"Hey. No more breath tonight. We can't waste it."

But her friend pulled out Theo's notebook instead. She waved it in the air like a prize before flipping through the pages. A little hiccuping laugh sounded. "Oh! How delightful. It's a *journal*."

Ren shot her a look as she continued to peruse.

"'I will have a new weight on my shoulders. A new duty. A new responsibility . . .'"

"Timmons. Stop. Now."

She didn't mean for the tone to sound so sharp. Her friend blinked a little before tossing the journal to the ground. Ren leaned down to place the notebook back in his bag.

"You wouldn't want someone going through your things."

Timmons held up both hands innocently. She wiggled her fingers a bit, which caught her attention. She held out her right hand to Cora, plucking at her thumb. "This little dragon went to the market. And *this* little dragon started a furniture company. And *this* little dragon . . ."

The two of them went on like that for another hour. All the obnoxious laughter at least served to lighten Ren's spirit. There was one rather serious debate about the choice between a lifetime of cheese and a lifetime of handsome suitors. Cheese emerged victorious.

Cora eventually fell asleep midsentence. Ren watched Timmons tuck the girl in like a doll before lying down herself. It was quiet for long enough that she thought her friend had fallen asleep. Then she heard her whisper.

"I talked to Clyde."

The hairs on the back of Ren's neck stood up. Talked to Clyde? A million questions were born from those words. They tangled with a heavy dose of fear. Did this have to do with taking the breath? Could she somehow sense his presence nearby?

"That night," Timmons clarified. "The night we hooked up. I convinced him to give you a position within House Winters. It was . . . the least I could do. Clyde was in love with me. He would have done anything for me. Anything. He told me he'd find you a spot. I'm sorry, Ren. . . ." Her voice fell to something less than a whisper. "Because he's dead now. He's gone."

And with that, she drifted off to sleep.

27

R en sat in that dimly lit cave, struggling to breathe.

Timmons had gotten her a position. An actual position. A promised path forward from the lips of a dead boy. She couldn't believe her bad luck. The idea that she might have landed a sponsorship with House Winters if only the accident in the waxway chamber had never happened . . .

"Why didn't you tell me?" she whispered. "Why didn't you tell me?"

Ren quietly tucked her friend in next to Cora, then set to the task of refreshing the wards. When she took her seat again, she saw Theo's eyes flutter open. "You're awake."

His voice was all rust. "Food?"

She pushed to her feet. The fire was dying, but the cuts of rabbit meat had kept warm enough. She gathered a few of the strips before sitting back down. It took effort for him to wedge up into a sitting position beside her. His hands shook as he reached out.

"Here. Let me help." She ripped off a smaller portion and

held it out, the same way you'd feed a hound. The look he offered in response had her smiling. "What? Too proud to accept help?"

He nearly rolled his eyes before leaning back and accepting the offered portion. She fed him like that, bite after bite. He was quiet at first, working his jaw, one hand set over his bandaged stomach. The wounds were still healing. She'd had a small surgery as a girl, and she knew how he must feel. That strange tightrope of fatigue that left a person standing between the dreaming and waking worlds.

"Where'd you learn that dance?"

His eyes found hers. "It's a mating dance. The Delveans first learned it from the Tusk sailors who settled with the farming tribes north of Kathor. It was one of the largest exchanges of information between our two magical systems in history. Until the Shiverians did the same a few decades later."

Ren knew the stories. The first Delvean expedition that sailed up the eastern coast in search of magic never found any. Instead they chanced upon fertile farmland. It kept them alive as they hunted in vain for magic. When the second expedition—sent by the same Delvean monarch—discovered Kathor's vast deposits, the first crew traveled south to share in the discovery.

They were turned away. It began a decade of battles in that region, most of which the Broods won decisively for Kathor. But the northern group was strengthened by Tusk sailors who sailed around the very northern tip of the continent. The two groups eventually merged into one people, and it was only through the Accords that the Kathorian houses avoided a costly war with them. It was no surprise

Theo knew all the details. After all, it was his family's legacy.

"There's a good amount of Tusk in my family line," Theo said. "But that didn't matter to my father. He forbid me from seeking a wyvern for myself. The reward wasn't worth the risk, in his opinion. I tried to prove him wrong by learning all the steps. When I finally performed the dance for him, he nodded once. 'Next time, put that same effort and dedication into something more useful.'"

Theo took another bite. She knew the story was meant to draw empathy from her. He, too, was denied things. He, too, was a dedicated student. She smiled the way she knew she was supposed to smile. If only he knew what his father had denied her.

"The mating dance is some kind of bond magic, right?"

He nodded. "The completed ceremony acts like a bonding spell, yes."

She raised her eyebrows. "I'm surprised a boy like you would consider bonding to anything or anyone. But I'm glad that you were stubborn enough to learn it. It saved us. Without that dance, I imagine one of us would have died."

"And without your magic, I would have died. I can't believe we survived waking up a sleeping wyvern. What spell did you use?"

She smiled again. "Why do you care?"

"Because every time I think I know what spell I would use in the same situation, you end up using one that's far cleverer. I am open to a continued education. Even out here."

"And I am to teach you?" Ren said, lifting one eyebrow. "Free of charge?"

He snorted. "What do you want? Coin? Can't exactly spend it out here."

"What do I want?"

Ren had been calculating this risk ever since the river, waiting for even the slightest opening. Theo had been so impressed with her magic. At first she'd thought the quick glances were purely a response to her spells. A newly earned trust. But she'd wondered if there was more. If they survived out here, his interest in her magic might be enough. At the very least he'd vouch for her talent to his father. But all it would take was Landwin Brood's disregard for Ren's potential position to go up in smoke. There were other ways to solidify the connection. Ways to intensify Theo's attention. Timmons had just given Ren a fine example of what a little flirting could do. Now she just had to follow suit.

Her eyes drifted down. Cora had put Theo in Clyde's other shirt, but she'd not bothered to button the top three buttons. It was likely she'd left it open so his wounds could breathe. Ren thought touching his chest might be too forward, so she let her eyes fall to his hand. She bravely reached out and slid her own into his. The way Theo shocked to stillness was utterly satisfying. He didn't pull away. Instead, as she used her thumb to trace the lines of his palm, his throat bobbed.

"I could think of an exchange," Ren said softly. "Several, in fact."

His chest rose and fell. She kept waiting for him to say this was *untoward*, but he didn't. It was a risk because Ren didn't know how often a boy like Theo faced such advances. Had other girls, hoping to lure him into a match, done the same back at Balmerick? Would he think that she was desperate?

She watched as he shifted his weight. They were facing each other properly now. Theo's eyes darted from Ren's lips to her hand and back to her eyes. She bit her lip, like this was all new to her.

The truth was that Devlin Albright—for all his faults—had imparted a certain confidence. He'd written bad poetry about the rich brown of her eyes. He'd whispered about how soft her lips and skin were. Ironic that a boy dedicated to protection had sharpened and honed Ren's idea of herself into a far better weapon. Quietly she wielded that knowledge now.

Ren knew to wait. Hunger was pooling in Theo's eyes as he traced the lines of her palm in return. She could not be the first to make a move. Patience had its rewards. He tugged, ever so slightly, on her hand. Pulled it up to his lips. She let him graze the spot with a kiss, and another. She responded by running that hand down his jaw. Letting it settle on his chest as the distance between them grew narrower. The whole room smelled like ashes.

"And I said to him, put *that* in your vessel!"

Ren and Theo both froze. Timmons was sitting up in her sleep, eyes still closed. She laughed at her own words before nestling back in beside Cora. The intrusion ruined the moment, drawing out all the awkwardness. Ren and Theo pulled away from each other, all hesitant smiles. Every nerve in Ren's body was firing. She said what girls were expected to say in these moments.

"Sorry," she muttered. "I didn't mean to . . ."

"Don't apologize. Not for that."

He winced a little as he propped himself back against the cave wall.

"Maybe another time," Ren said. "We can continue our exchange."

He smiled before taking another bite of his food. Ren glanced sideways at him.

"And don't get all haughty now. Just because I held your hand."

That familiar scowl surfaced, but it didn't hold for long.

"You still haven't said what spell you used."

"Now that I know what I can extract from you, I was considering withholding the information for later." Another scowl. She smiled at him. "It was a brightening cantrip."

Theo shook his head. "I've never seen a brightening cantrip that looked like that. What'd you combine it with?"

Ren grinned. At least he was smart. "I concentrated the cantrip into a sphere, increased its velocity, and then used the impact exclusivity charm to direct—"

"The brightness at whatever the spell struck. That's clever. Really clever."

She pretended to be pleased by the compliment, though she'd have preferred if he stopped being so surprised by her skill. At least Ren had him right where she wanted him. If they survived, Theo would be a fool not to see her usefulness. Agora's words about the city's elite came back to her. *Creatures like him bore easily.* A little flirting along the way would make sure that Theo didn't lose interest by the time they made it back to Kathor. But he'd be suspicious if Ren came on too strong too fast. What did a boy with the world at his fingertips—with friends who acted more like servants— really want? Ren's guess had been proven correct. He wanted someone who wasn't afraid to challenge him. Someone who wasn't there to agree with everything he said and every plan he made. She knew she could give him that.

"You've got this crease," he said. "Right here."

He tapped the spot between his eyebrows.

"It's settled in permanently, because you always make the same face when you're thinking."

She threw him a scowl of her own. He laughed.

"Don't worry. It's cute."

She pretended to be embarrassed before offering a response.

"I have to think twenty steps ahead of everyone else. It's the only way to survive when you come to Balmerick with nothing, when you've been through what I've been through in life." She caught and held his gaze. "I've earned that crease, however cute you may think it looks. Good night, Theo."

She settled in, turning so that her back was to him. *Let him think about that one for a while. Let it roll around in his mind and fester.* Ren fell asleep easily, the smell of ashes still hanging in the air.

28

Ren dreamed of her father's death again. Only this time she was led by that shadow—by some version of Clyde—into the aftermath. Those memories were just as gutting. . . .

The constable was explaining what had happened with the bridge. No one was at fault, he said. An accident. It was coincidence, he told Ren's mother, that all the men who'd organized the canal strike had been in the same place at the same time. No, they couldn't confirm that a meeting had been arranged in their honor. There was no record of such an appointment on any of the official itineraries of Landwin Brood. Press charges? On whom? The bridge? Hadn't they been the ones who were responsible for building it in the first place? It would be like prosecuting the dead. No, there was no point in pursuing such a case. Ren had listened from her room. She'd never forget the younger constable standing outside their window, down in the alley, crying silently when he thought no one was watching. . . .

Ren stumbled out of their cave. Everyone was still sleeping as she dry-heaved into the bushes. Her hands were shaking. She'd carefully buried all these memories. She'd set them aside, converted her fury into fuel. And she hated how easily Clyde's power drew the worst moments of her life back to the forefront. It was threatening the balances she'd worked so hard to create and maintain. All the safeguards that veiled her biggest secret.

Her stomach churned uncomfortably as she thought about what had happened in the cave. The feel of her hand in Theo's. The way his rose-pale lips brushed her knuckles. But as her mind replayed that moment, Theo's face blurred and widened. It was Landwin Brood smiling at her. His lips were the ones pressed to her skin. Ren dry-heaved again.

No darkness lasts for long.

She heard her mother's constant refrain, their only comfort since her father's passing. Ren had accepted those words, until one day she realized that their family's darkness had a name. It was a person, and people could be destroyed. Her despair became anger. Anger breathed purpose. It had been ten long years since her father's death. Ren had spent every waking moment in service to a single goal. One that even her mother did not know about.

On the surface Ren was a smart girl who worked hard. Her mother believed a fine job with a good salary would change their luck. Ren knew that was simply a means to an end. She needed money and she needed power and she needed a position because the larger goal demanded it. Her eyes flicked back to the mouth of the cave. It looked like a door into the dark.

Ren took a moment to center herself. It felt good to remember her larger purpose. When the contents of her mind were carefully rearranged, all set in their proper order, she walked back into the cave. She nestled underneath her jacket and listened. Next to her, the son of the man she hated most in the world was breathing. One staggered breath after the next. Ren felt her own breathing matching that rhythm. When she slept, she did not dream.

In the morning Cora and Timmons were slightly hungover but otherwise ready for the next treacherous leg in their climb. Theo appeared mostly healed. Ren found that the majority of her aches from the previous climbs had finally faded. Rest came with other consequences, though. They were now blind to the progress and location of their hunters. Time inside the cave had obscured any movements outside it. Had the wyvern recovered? Would it target them as soon as they left the safety of the cave?

And then there was Clyde. It was difficult to imagine him taking the same path they had. Ren wasn't sure what a revenant could offer a group of greedy kobolds, or how he might navigate the nesting grounds of a full-grown wyvern. It was possible there were other paths that intersected with where they were heading. All Ren knew was that they didn't know. And that lack of control had her grinding her teeth as they pulled straps over shoulders and set off once more.

The sun was out, but its warmth was barely felt as bitter-cold winds bit through their clothing. Everyone cast warming spells. Cora suggested adding calf-strengthening boons as well. All of it cost precious magic, but as they set out, the group looked as fresh as they'd been since the wax-way room. Ren made sure to remind everyone of the wards they could use if they encountered Clyde, and a plan was made for another wyvern attack as well.

The first half of the hike demanded caution. They never walked out in the open for long, choosing instead to tuck against ridges and duck beneath branches. Anything to avoid attracting unwanted attention. Thankfully, there were no signs of their hunter in the sky.

As they climbed, snow appeared. Thin patches that puddled in the shadiest spots of the mountainside. Nothing too tricky, but Ren knew each mound of snow was a sign of what waited for them in the higher passes. It was well past noon when they reached a flattened sweep of highlands.

There was a pearl-blue lake, good for refilling their canteen and washing their hands. Huge knuckling rocks punched up from the ground like the shoulders of buried giants. Every-thing else was covered in knee-high grass as far as the eye could see. There weren't any proper paths, which Ren took as a sign that no one had come this way before.

"This might be the last flat stretch before we hit the pass," Theo said. "Should we try to stock up on food? Doubt we'll find anything at the higher elevations."

He tried to make the suggestion sound casual. Only Ren saw the slight shift in his mannerisms. One act of selflessness and he fancied himself the leader. She allowed it for now.

"Cora. Do you have enough magic to spare for traps?"

She nodded. "I'm down to ninety ockleys. If I go below fifty, I won't have enough to mend bones or heal ligaments. I'll set a few traps, but we should conserve the rest."

"Let's collect firewood," Theo said. "Scavenge roots and nuts. Anything edible."

Timmons smiled. "Always such a bountiful feast out here."

Before they could split up and start their search, a sharp bleat sounded. Everyone looked up. On the nearest crest, a family of goats watched them. Ren saw three adults and one kid. They'd come over to inspect what was likely the first human entourage they'd ever had in this highland.

"They're so cute," Timmons whispered.

"Food," Cora breathed back. "Get them!"

The girl darted forward. Somehow she already had one of her surgical knives in hand. Ren let out a surprised laugh as the animals shot in the direction of the nearest cliffs. Cora came to her senses as they started to break away from her, far too agile to be run down on foot. She pulled up short and brandished her wand in a tight, whiplike circle. The back leg of the eldest goat caught in an invisible rope. It was the clearest evidence yet that she'd grown up on a farm.

The other goats scrambled away to safety. Cora threw up both hands in triumph before stalking over to finish her dark work.

"Hate to eat something that cute," Timmons remarked. "Unless we properly season him, I suppose."

She set out in search of herbs. Ren laughed a little at the look Theo gave in response to that. They both went searching in different directions. She threw him a deliberate glance over one shoulder, though, and was pleased to see him trying to catch her eye as well.

There wasn't a great deal to harvest at this elevation. Cora returned with slabs of meat, ready to be spitted and cooked.

Theo had a stack of limbs and branches. He was working to snap them into smaller pieces so they could fit in one of their satchels. More fuel for the eventual fires they'd need to light in the more barren passes.

Timmons dramatically unveiled a huge handful of honey-berries. Not fully ripened yet, but none of them complained that they didn't taste market-fresh. Out here anything that wasn't a tuber was delicious. A fire was built. A meal was had.

All of them felt full and happy as the light faded from the foothills.

29

All right," Timmons said, nudging a log back into place with her boot. "Time for bed. Put us to sleep, Theo. One dance should do."

He snorted. "You are unlikely to ever see that again."

"A pity," she replied. "But if that means I'm unlikely to see a wyvern ever again, I'm willing to make the trade. Sorry, by the way. About the earring."

"Not your fault." Theo shrugged. "It was just bad luck."

Every time he spoke now, his eyes would briefly dart over to Ren. It was like he was checking in, trying to see how he sounded in the mirror of her attention. She didn't mind that. Cora was the first one to tuck in for the night. The corners of her lips were stained from their meal.

"Sleep is as important as a full belly. Night."

Timmons saluted her with a meatless thigh bone. "Good night, you deadly little thing."

Ren added another log to the fire. Theo looked lost in the flames. Timmons tossed the morsel into a pouch. Cora had instructed them to save their bones, just in case they needed to boil them for nutrients higher up in the mountains.

Overhead, stars glittered, countless in number. They'd chosen an elevated clearing that offered a view of the small lake below. The light of the stars was mirrored on the glass-still surface. Theo broke the silence with the last thing Ren ever expected him to say.

"I'm long overdue for an apology."

Ren and Timmons exchanged a glance.

"For the party. The incident with the seventeen-string was . . . incredibly reckless. You asked me before what I've been dreaming about. My worst memory. And that's the answer. I've been dreaming about what I did at that party. I know . . . what you must think of me. I just wanted you to know that I'm sorry for what I did."

Ren remembered him spotting the newspaper—with the article about the incident—when she'd emptied her satchel. She guessed that he'd been waiting to explain himself for some time now.

"I wanted to visit the hospital where the injured were taken, but my father had our chariots removed. I also demanded to be put on trial for any damages or crimes, but the presiding judges were already bribed to keep matters quiet. I'm very aware of how all of that makes me look."

His eyes were on Ren. She felt that anger pulsing to life inside her chest. She was grateful that she'd taken a moment last night to settle her mind. Otherwise, she might not have held it all together. Some of that anger must have slipped into her expression, though, because Theo didn't meet her eyes for longer than a moment.

"I know we must seem obscene to you. My father's wealth. Our way of life. I grew up wanting to be a wyvern rider because it felt like a way out. An escape from all the expectations. All the greed. I wanted to fly up to a place where my father wasn't the first thing people saw in me."

Ren didn't know what to say. She glanced at Timmons, who looked speechless as well. The two of them sat in uncomfortable silence as Theo went on.

"I am not asking for your sympathy or your forgiveness," he said. "I made a grave error. People could have died. . . ."

The weight of that word finally freed Ren to speak. "Then why did you do it?"

His face fell again. "There's a pressure that comes with my name and my title. A pressure that I have, at times, allowed to shatter my will to change our family's legacy. And that *is* my will. I do not want to be one of the Broods of old. I have no designs on living as a bloodstained magnate, turning one coin into two by holding a blade to society's throat. That's never—I've never wanted to be like *him*."

The emphasis on that word made it clear. He didn't want to be Landwin Brood. But Ren wasn't satisfied with that answer. Not even close. "Peer pressure? That's why you dangled a seventeen-string out over the heads of the people in the Lower Quarter's poorest neighborhoods? For the sake of *popularity*?"

He shook his head. "Pressure is why I sometimes feel the need to . . . perform. I wanted to show off my magic that night. And that's what the incident was. Not a failure in pride, but a failure in magic."

Ren bit her tongue. She felt it was a failure of both.

"As I said, I'm very aware of how you see me. I'm very

aware that the incident doesn't help your opinion of me. I'd understand it if you secretly hated me. I have every intention of making amends for what I did. My life will not look like my father's, or his father's before him. I will be a servant to the city of Kathor."

A small piece of the puzzle that was Theo Brood clicked into place in Ren's mind. She thought back through the details she already knew and finally saw the direction he was heading.

"So you're training to be the city's next warden?"

Theo's eyes widened. "What?"

"Oh, come on. You have your own personal livestone statue," she said. "You're majoring in tactical defense and city planning. Very few jobs use both. And now this speech about living a life in service to others. If I recall correctly, the current city warden is due to retire next year. Your education would conclude at a convenient time to claim the post."

He swallowed. Ren watched him process everything she'd said. He likely realized that denying her guess would lower her opinion of him even more. At this point he knew how smart she was. And now she'd pegged him with the barest of clues.

"Yes," he admitted. "I am training to be the city warden. There aren't many stations that satisfy the demands of the Brood name. My father would fold me into his own plans if I had no direction. Becoming the city warden allows me to serve the people of Kathor, rather than his interests. Rather than the interests of his friends. It has been my goal for years now."

Ren shook her head. She'd reached a breaking point. Her plans of entering House Brood called for her to make nice.

Nod her head at the nobility of his decision. *To hell with that.*

"That's your big sacrifice? Becoming the city's most powerful force of defensive magic? You'll be attuned to fifty of the most expensive statues ever created. You can snap your fingers and summon gargoyles. How damn noble of you."

Theo looked surprised by her interpretation. Of course. He'd never imagined the decision was anything but heroic. It probably felt that way compared to the way the rest of his family operated. It was easy to look innocent in a room full of butchers.

"What? You didn't realize there was privilege in claiming one of the *most* desirable positions in the city, even if it's a step down for your family's reputation? Do you know how many people would get down on their knees and beg for a job like that one?"

The expression on his face made it clear that he'd never considered this angle. Not even once. Now he floundered for an explanation. "But I'll be commanding those statues on behalf of the people, not for the benefit of House Brood. I will be the first warden to truly serve the city—the masses—in decades."

Ren spat back, "How brave of you, to walk away from wealth that we can only dream of having. Should we go ahead and knight you? Timmons, did you bring a sword?"

Her friend sighed. "Ren. Ease up."

She was seething, though. She wanted to tell Theo off, curse him and his entire family to the early graves they deserved. The words burned in her throat. If she spoke now, only smoke would come out. It took her a moment to realize that she was up on her feet, pacing around the fire. Timmons

　　　　　　　　　　　　　SCOTT REINTGEN

watched with a wary expression. Theo looked like he'd been dealt a massive blow.

"Look. I know you're used to people liking you," Ren finally said. "And I do like you. We like you. And we need you to survive out here, but it's not as easy as just forgiving you for what happened at that party. For what happened to the people in that teahouse . . ."

"I know," he said. "It will haunt me forever—"

"Let me finish."

Theo's words tangled. She knew he was not used to holding his tongue. It was a fine moment, to watch him learn how to bow to someone else.

"Do you know Mim's theory of personas?"

He took a steadying breath. "Yes."

She lifted an eyebrow. "Well?"

"What?"

"What's the theory? Go on. Enlighten us."

"It states . . ." He frowned a little. "We're not one person. We're thousands of people. Altered by the contexts in which we briefly exist, minute by minute, hour by hour."

Ren recognized that he'd given the exact definition from the textbook. She held out her right hand like a balancing scale. "Sometimes you are the spoiled fool who nearly murdered people for a party trick. Sometimes you are the son of the man who built canals that killed hundreds of workers, displaced thousands of people, and gutted an entire community all for the sake of filling your family's coffers. You are the grandson of murderers and tyrants. I can't help seeing this version of you." And then she held out her left hand. "But sometimes you're a boy that I like. A wonderful traveling companion with solid magic. You are a steady hand on a road that promises to only get harder in the coming days. You exist as *both* of those things for me."

He stared at her for a long time.

"Solid magic?"

"And there you go, reminding me of the spoiled prat. Look. I'm just trying to give you a chance here. I do like you, Theo. I appreciate the explanation and the context. But it's going to take some time for the second version of you to loom larger than the first. Earn it."

He nodded once. He folded his hands, making the traditional sign of a vow.

"I will. You have my word."

"Good. Then let's get some sleep and pretend this conversation never happened."

Timmons looked surprised by Ren's restraint. She offered a quick nod of approval before adding a few more logs to the dying fire. Theo whispered a "good night" as he settled in for sleep. Ren thought about punishing him, making him feel the weight of that lonely night sky.

Eventually, though, she whispered back, "Good night."

The stars glinted overhead, like teeth in the dark.

30

The next morning Theo was the textbook definition of servitude.

He helped Cora divide the leftover meat into portions for later, wrapping them tight inside the spare newspaper Ren had in her bag. She didn't miss the irony of his earnest efforts brushing right back up against his worst mistake. He doused their fire and gathered more kindling. She'd have been more impressed, but her mother had always taught her that it was easy for someone to live out the first few days of an apology. The true test was whether or not they held their course when the sting of correction faded. How quickly would they revert to who they really were?

He also offered to cast the spells and boons. Cora was down to 70 ockleys. Just a handful of spells, really. They'd agreed to save as much of her magic as possible in case another serious injury occurred. After casting protections over their camp in the cave, Ren possessed only 200 ockleys. Timmons had 170. Theo's number loomed around 900. Ren felt like they were solidly positioned, as long as they didn't lose Theo's cache of magic. And they'd already come pretty close to doing exactly that.

They set out—armored with spells and full bellies—for what Ren knew would be the most difficult leg of the journey. Her guesses at how difficult fell well short of the mark. After getting their bearings, the group started upward again. Snow quickly turned to ice. The footing was devilish at first, playing little tricks that would send them sliding back down a few steps. They'd laugh at one another and press on. It wasn't as funny later in the day, when every foothold was impossibly slick and the wind howled at their backs. Before long the consequences of a fall became far more terrifying too.

Their conversion spells slowly turned into punishments. It was too cold outside the protection of the casting, which meant it grew far too warm within the radius of their spells. Ren was sweating profusely. So were the others. They were eventually forced to switch over to a more costly enhancement spell that made their clothes feel lined with fur. It would deplete their magical stores far faster, even if it felt like a fine solution for the time being.

Each new height exposed them to new dangers. Ren saw birds wheeling in the sky and knew that if the wyvern came for them now, it'd be as easy as plucking oysters off the sides of a dock exposed by a low tide. Theo tasked Vega with flying ahead of them. The bird would set down with a scrape of stone wings, landing on the ledges they needed to reach themselves. It was useful at first to have a guiding beacon, but eventually they came to the point where having something to aim at didn't mean they could actually reach the location in question.

"Too slick," Ren grunted, slipping down a third time. "We need to use rope spells for this."

All four of them were crowded on a slender shelf of stone. There was a nauseating view of the stretching green valley below with stone hilltops scattered throughout. Their view of the surrounding mountains had been reduced and narrowed to their current obstacle—a curving path of ice that led to yet another ledge. Fog curled in and out of everything, obscuring their view beyond that. Vega watched them from above with hooded eyes.

"We'll need to set anchor points." Theo gestured. "There and there and there."

Ren nodded. "Do you know how to do that?"

He'd been an image of humility for the last few hours. Her question finally dragged the haughtiness back to the surface. "Yes, I know how to make anchor points."

She still watched closely as his magic took shape. Checked to make sure each anchor was driven deep in the stone, rather than the surface-level ice. He wove another thread of unseen magic carefully through the invisible anchors before tying everything off with a knotting spell. She wouldn't have done anything differently, except that she could summon each spell much faster. He shot a look in her direction for approval and she nodded.

"Steadfast charms," she said to the others. "Timmons, if you'll amplify, we can use the elementary version to keep our feet steady on the ice. Everyone got it?"

Nods all around. She felt that familiar surge in her magic as

Timmons lent them strength. A steadfast charm didn't offer perfect footing, but it would eliminate minor slips. Theo set his feet, tested out the first chunk of ice, then moved hand over hand up the incline. After he'd gone up a few paces, he looked back and handed off the invisible line to her. Ren reached out. He'd textured the spell to feel like an old sailing rope. She could sense the grainy fibers rubbing against her palm. She got a solid grip and started climbing, trying to ignore the waves of nausea as her body leaned in a perpendicular angle to the ground. Cora came on her heels. She was followed by Timmons, who muttered curses every few steps. Their added weight had the invisible rope flexing taut.

"First anchor is right here," Theo called back. "Just reach around it."

He slid his hand to the right, found the next run of invisible rope, and settled his grip. Ren watched him start moving diagonally to their right, following the icy trail. She repeated his motions. Her stomach lurched as she switched over. Statistically it was the most dangerous part of any climb. They were about fifteen paces above the stone shelf now.

"Well, I'm never going mountain climbing again," Ren whispered.

Timmons snorted. "Reminds me of those inspirational speakers Balmerick is always bringing in. Bloody pioneers climbing mountains just for fun. Teachers were always trying to make a lesson out of it. 'What's *your* Watcher Mountain? What obstacle do you want to overcome this semester?'"

Ren let out a nervous laugh. "Right now, my Watcher Mountain is Watcher Mountain."

Timmons snorted again as Theo finally reached the upper

ledge. Ren was still a few paces behind when she felt *something*. Like a sharp fingernail scratching at the door of her mind. The sound dragged at her senses. She made the mistake of opening that mental door and heard a familiar voice whisper: *I am hungry. You are food.*

Theo was holding out a hand, waiting for her to take it. Ren ignored it, whipping her head around to look. Cora was below her, desperately clinging to the rope. There was fear in her eyes. She'd heard the voice too. Clyde was coming.

"Timmons!" Ren called. "Summon a retreating ward. Now!"

Gravity was tugging her friend's silver-white hair into a bright stream. It pointed back to the ledge they'd left behind. Ren watched her scramble for the wand at her belt. A shadow approached from below. Clyde had transformed. His skin was still a patchwork of burns and scars, but he'd grown unnaturally since they'd last seen him. At least a full head taller. His shoulders broad with muscle. He ignored Theo's rope, climbing from stone to stone with impossible agility. Timmons was still fumbling for her wand. Ren saw she wasn't going to be able to cast the spell in time.

"Cora. Get down!"

The girl pressed her body to the rocky shelf. Ren took aim. Thought, spell, magic. A bolt of fire burst from the tip of her wand. It whipped past Timmons and struck Clyde's shoulder just as he got close enough to swipe at her. His bare feet slid back down the ice, but he lashed out desperately. His hands caught the invisible rope. The entire length shook, jolting all of them. Clyde let out a hissing snarl. Timmons raised her wand at the exact moment he thrust out his hand.

His magic breathed through the air, dark and pulsing and

hungry. Timmons's spell was like a dash of sunlight by comparison. Retreating charms were mental shields. The spell created a false layer—a sort of catch-point—for any magic that attacked it. Ren watched both spells form in the air, on the verge of collision. And then she let out a surprised cry when her friend's spell fizzled. It was a botched summoning.

Timmons's eyes swung back to Ren. "Help me."

And then Clyde's spell struck. Those beautiful eyes fluttered shut. Ren raised her wand, ready to cast another projectile spell, when the magic did the unthinkable. It *leapt* through the air. From Timmons to Cora in a breath.

A chain spell, Ren realized. *It's a chain spell.*

The next logical step happened before Ren could think to summon her own ward. The spell hit her square in the chest, and the world slipped away. . . .

A hand was on her shoulder, the grip sinking in like teeth. She was forced to look down at the sight of her father, bent wrongways in the belly of the canal. But . . . but . . . but . . . Clyde. This was Clyde. He was doing this to her. Think, Ren. Think! The theory of functional opposition. He's using . . . my mind . . . to stop my body. . . .

Ren broke free of the spell just in time to watch Timmons fall.

Her arms spread wide and she fell back with all the grace of an angel. Her body hit the stone ledge with a sickening thud. Clyde leapt down from his position and landed next to her. Ren's mind was still untangling as the monster crouched over her best friend.

A bolt of magic cut through the air. Theo struck true. His spell hit the back of Clyde's shoulder with enough force to send him stumbling toward the edge. The burned arms wheeled. Ren screamed, though, when he reached out for something to steady himself. His hands found the only thing in range: Timmons. Her beautiful silver-white hair.

Momentum took them both over the cliff, rag-dolling out of sight. Ren felt one final slash of Clyde's magic. It plunged knifelike through that spot in the back of her mind. It was so painful that her hands let go of the rope. Gravity snared her. . . .

"Ren. Get up. You're crushing me."

She opened her eyes to immense pain. Her elbow sent shooting vibrations down her entire right side. Something shifted beneath her. It was Cora. She'd fallen from the rope and landed on the other girl. The two of them were all the way back down on the stone shelf.

"Timmons. We have to help her. She fell. . . ."

But Cora grabbed hold of Ren, wrapping her up so that she couldn't start down the ice-laced path. "She's dead. I saw her fall. Ren. No. We can't go back."

"Get off me. We have to go get her."

"Are you two okay? Anything broken?"

It was Theo. He was scaling back down to help them. Cora was stronger than she looked. Ren tried to break free, but exhaustion stole through her entire body. The steadfast charm was completely spent. Every muscle felt even more drained now.

"She's gone, Ren," Cora whispered. "She's gone."

"We have to go after her."

Cora wouldn't let go. "The enhancement magic. Don't you feel it? Her spell is gone."

Those words broke her. It was such a logical conclusion. The truth slicing through a make-believe world where Timmons had survived. Ren slumped down to her knees. There was a scuffle of boots nearby as Theo arrived. Cora was right. The enhancement that had been bolstering their magic was gone. There was only one reason that would happen.

"But she . . . we have to . . ."

Cora still held her tight. "We need to keep moving. He'll come back."

"Let him come." Her anger flared. "I'm ready."

"No. You're not ready, Ren. You're in a heightened emotional state, but you are physically exhausted. We are facing a creature that we do not understand. We're not ready. We need to get as far as we can today and make a plan. If he circles back, none of us stand a chance."

Ren's chest was heaving. She felt something guttural rattle out of her throat. She wanted to pull her hair out. She wanted to burn the world to nothing. Her fingers were bleeding from how hard she was pressing them down into the ice. Theo gently helped her back to her feet.

When she didn't protest, he set his hands on hers, guiding them back to the rope. She followed the trail of his magic with mindless obedience. Her final glimpse of Timmons echoed. Those blackened hands tangled in her bright hair. The way her slender body was drawn like a marionette over the cliff. That memory felt vibrant and knife-sharp compared with the rest of the barren world, which had gone briefly colorless. Ren moved through that void without purpose.

31

U p three more passes.

It's my fault she's dead. It's all my fault.

Theo tried to encourage them, but in truth, Ren didn't listen to a word he said. Cora made no response either. A glance showed the girl scratching nervously at the skin by her eyebrow piercing. She'd clearly been at it a while, because the spot was an angry red compared with the rest of her olive complexion. Ren had no comfort to offer. She'd lost too much to summon any form of hope.

Now their bodies moved out of instinctual preservation. Ren's thoughts returned again and again to that rock wall. She watched the moment Timmons was drawn over the cliff. She couldn't stop replaying it in her mind. The helpless feeling of being dragged into her own memory. The dark shadow that stood at her shoulder. All of it.

She remembered the surprise that had been nestled into Clyde's magic. A chain spell. That was some advanced damn magic. Empty as she felt, her mind ran inexorably back through everything she'd read on the subject. Different spells and strategies for countering one. All the weaknesses and strengths and historical references. Mental research was the only thing keeping her from drowning.

They reached a flat stretch laden with snow. Theo asked if they wanted to stop. The sun would be setting before long. No one replied, so they pressed on. They were high enough now to have some clarity on their aim. The target Avy had chosen, even from the distant valley below, was perfect. A slice of a pass that slipped between Watcher Mountain and the Eyeglass. There were no trails, but the land itself acted as their guide. Ren saw a natural valley running between them. It wouldn't be easy hiking, but finally seeing a path through to the right side of the mountain was the only hopeful offering of the day.

When the sun vanished from the hills, Theo finally convinced them to stop for the night. They had enough logs—and book pages for kindling—to get a proper fire going. The switch from warming spells to clothing enchantments meant cold noses and frostbitten hands. Ren stared at the flames as her fingers thawed. Theo and Cora kept exchanging looks, both silently urging the other to say something. Ren caught the glances and cut them off before they could make the attempt.

"I don't want to talk about it," she said. "I want to talk about how we survive what's chasing us. There's no way to honor Timmons if we die out here. We have to survive. For them."

Another exchanged glance. Theo nodded. "Fair enough."

"The retreating ward should have worked, but her spell fizzled."

Cora nodded. "That was so unlucky."

In truth, her friend had always been a subpar spell caster. That wasn't the strength she offered the world. Ren had watched her falter with any number of spells during under-grad. It was a sign of poor execution—a lack of focus—but there was no point saying that out loud, because it changed nothing about their circumstances now.

"The failed spell left her exposed. And that left *us* exposed. Clyde used a chain spell."

Theo frowned. "Are you sure about that?"

"I could feel the way it spread through the air," she replied. "It hit Timmons first, then leapt to Cora, then struck me. It's not like he was casting new spells for each of us. It was a chain."

"Chain spells are illegal," Theo pointed out.

Ren frowned. "I doubt the revenant is concerned with the codes."

"I just mean they're illegal for a reason. Incredibly difficult to control. They were outlawed because people figured out that if you alter one link in the chain, the entire spell can transform. That's how the Harpy murders happened. It's pos-sible we can figure out how to alter the spell."

Not a bad thought. Those murders were relatively recent. A disgruntled makeup artist realized her boss had gotten lazy, using a chain spell to regularly refresh the mascara of her clients. Harper—nicknamed Harpy—made a slight alteration that poisoned seventy-three women. It was the largest mass murder in Kathor's history. It also offered a potential plan for them. Ren was still sorting through the other pieces of the puzzle, though.

"I was right about the functional opposition theory. The spell he cast back there took me into the same memory I've been dreaming every night. I was immobilized by it."

Cora scratched her eyebrow piercing. "Same."

"I barely felt anything," Theo said. "But that's normal with a chain spell, right? Each iteration would be slightly weaker. Timmons was deep under, but I just blinked once and I was free of the spell, because I was the last link in the chain."

"That's the one silver lining, then," Ren answered. "I wasn't under for more than a second. If the paralytic is weaker in each iteration—and if we use our retreating wards—there's a good chance we can face him on our own terms. That gives us options for beating him."

Theo nodded, but it was Cora's turn to object.

"I'm worried he'll be *much* stronger next time."

"Why?"

"Did you see him?" Cora asked. "The way he looked and moved?"

Ren nodded. "Yes, he was definitely sturdier."

"It was more than just strength. It was Avy."

That dark pronouncement brought silence to the group. Theo was pacing around nervously. Ren had noticed a clear change in Clyde. The broadness of his shoulders. The unexpected height.

"He consumed him?" she asked.

"In a far more literal way than I anticipated," Cora answered. "I've watched Avy's wrestling matches. The way Clyde climbed is a perfect copy of how he moved. It's the way his body worked. Clyde somehow consumed those qualities and made them his own. He also consumed his knowledge. Remember when Avy brought up chain spells the other day? While we were hiking?"

Theo answered, "Which is why the revenant knew what they were. Unbelievable."

Ren's mind leapt ahead to the darker conclusion.

"And now he's consumed Timmons."

"An enhancer," Cora confirmed. "His magic will be distinctly stronger. I'm not even sure a retreating ward will work. It will be like trying to stop an arrow with a piece of paper."

Ren saw a fleeting image of Timmons as she fell. Her silver-white hair flung wide. Her eyes closed. *It's my fault you died. It's my fault you were here in the first place. I'm so sorry, Timmons.* A dark part of her mind wondered if Clyde would adopt some physical quality of her friend, the way he'd taken on aspects of Avy. Would he wear the bright hair? Or the perfect smile? She couldn't bear the thought.

Theo cleared his throat. "So we're facing a creature who won't stop hunting us until he consumes each of us. He uses a spell that temporarily paralyzes his victims, and his magic might be even stronger the next time we face him. How do we fight against that?"

No one had an answer. Ren's mind felt like it had been operating at half capacity ever since losing Timmons. His question hung overhead as the embers of their fire crackled quietly. Cora was the first one to suggest sleep. Theo stood, resetting the wards as snow dusted their shoulders. Ren watched the flames as darkness stole over the mountain. A great veil of clouds cut off the stars and the moon. Nothing outside the glow of their fire was visible. Ren's entire body trembled.

"Get some rest," Theo said. "I'll take first watch."

She rolled onto her other side. Lying there, eyes roaming

the dark, Ren finally felt her friend's absence in full. Timmons had slept beside Ren every night so far. Adding her warmth. Her entire life had been an unconscious improvement on those around her, magical or otherwise. Ren cried now as she stared at the empty stretch of grass beside her.

It's my fault, she thought. *It's all my fault.*

She cried in silence. It was as if a star had been erased from the sky above. No one else would know its light or warmth or beauty ever again. The tears were still sliding down Ren's cheeks when Theo moved his pack over to the ground beside her. He sat down, and a moment later she felt his hand settle on her shoulder. Its weight anchored her back to the earth. She no longer felt like she was drifting off into the unknown. She took a few deep breaths before reaching back to set her hand on top of his.

They sat there for a long time with the starless night bearing down from above. Ren gave the slightest tug. She felt him obey the pull, nestling in behind her. He shifted his weight and held her close. She liked the way his body bent to match hers. She felt his knee resting in the tangle of her own legs. His chest pressed against the blade of her shoulder. She turned so that they were face-to-face in the dark.

"I'm sorry . . . I . . ."

She shut him up with a kiss. Quieted him with the slightest dig of her nails. Buried him there, slowly but surely, beneath the weight of that darkness. The two of them kissed until there was no room for what had happened earlier that day. No need for words at all.

32

The next morning Ren filled the canteen with fresh snow and set it by the fire to melt.

Cora passed out the last of their food—the goat meat they'd salvaged in the pass below—cut in even, precise portions. Ren thought Theo would be embarrassed by their kissing in the light of day. Instead he quietly whispered good morning to her. The softness in his voice was surprising, unexpected. Ren hadn't been thinking last night. She'd simply wanted to feel something. Now, however, she calculated. Now she planned. Theo wasn't embarrassed by the night's events because he wanted them to happen again. The rest of the world felt broken, but at least her path forward was clear. They just had to survive.

He ordered Vega to scout ahead. As she traced the bird's flight, Ren was struck by a new thought. "Why didn't you order Vega to help us?" she asked. "When Clyde attacked?"

She saw the way his throat bobbed. The way his fingers tapped nervously at his side. She knew right away that she'd cut down deep enough to hit some secret vein. He finally answered.

"She's not just a livestone statue."

Ren's eyes narrowed. "She's a vessel."

He smiled. "Do you always figure everything out? I'm glad we weren't in class together."

It was obvious now. The strong link between them was more than just assigned servitude. There was genuine affection because the bird was more than a tool. She was a home for his magic.

"You had to bond to her?"

Another nod. "She's technically alive. It was the only way to make it work."

The bird let out a distant caw. Ren thought it sounded like a protest to the word "technically." She eyed him a moment before pointing to the chain at his hip.

"So that one is fake? Or do you actually have three vessels?"

Another smile. "Fake."

Some wizards famously sported visible chains or bracelets. The intention was to draw the eyes of their enemies to something that was, in fact, valueless. It was the kind of thing a rich kid would do, although she supposed people *were* far more likely to steal from him than from her.

"And just so you know, we did have class together," Ren said. "Second semester of sophomore year. Intro to Physical Magic."

He frowned. "I'd remember that. I'd remember you."

"Don't worry," she replied. "I wasn't as charming back then."

I sat in the back corner and avoided you at all costs, she thought. *Besides, boys like you don't notice girls like me.* The three of them started off across rock and tundra. Their morning path was blessedly flat, but all of them felt the looming absence. Six people had gone into the waxways. Half of them were dead now. Timmons's death was having the most direct impact. Ren hadn't realized how her friend's magic had steadied them thus far. She wasn't sure if the effect had been intentional or passive, but as they started out, she felt aches that she hadn't until now. Sore calves and a throbbing lower back. How much magic had Timmons given each of them simply by walking alongside them?

The biggest challenge in the terrain came with navigating the larger snowdrifts. They couldn't simply go around them when they encountered tighter rock formations. Instead they were forced to trek straight through. Even the best spells couldn't keep all the snow out of their boots. Worse, their pace in those sections slowed to a crawl. Ren wasn't alone in glancing over her shoulder every now and again, searching for signs of pursuit. The idea of a more powerful version of the monster hunting them wasn't a welcome one.

"It was a long drop," Theo noted at one point. "Maybe he didn't survive it either."

Cora shook her head. "A revenant is more spirit than body. It won't feel the pain of a snapped limb or a busted organ. It doesn't rely on blood flow. It's sustained by the magic."

"Very uplifting," Theo replied. "Anything else?"

Cora opened her mouth, ready to explain some other dreadful detail, but caught the look Ren was giving her and fell quiet. As they trudged on in silence, Ren thought of her best friend's final moments. Before her stomach could turn again, she fixed her eyes on the distant peaks and kept walking. The sun started to set and the pass leading between the two mountains was still well in the distance. Ren felt they'd made great progress, even if it seemed like they still had a long way to go. The last stretch had been uphill, which offered a vantage point on the valley they'd traversed.

If Clyde approached tonight, they'd have eyes on him at least.

Their fire was a scant thing. No matter how many book pages they added, it kept threatening to sputter out. Theo finally suggested combining satchels. He volunteered his own bag to the flames, which warmed them for a few hours as night stole over the hills. Much like their physical supplies, Ren knew, their actual magic was starting to run low. Timmons had enabled them to use minor spells, which she'd then enhanced to be more effective. The current conditions forced them to use high-level magic, which wasted more and more ockleys. It was possible that Ren and Cora would run out of magic by the time they reached the other side of the mountain.

A great sprawl of stars winked down on them. Ren took the first watch. Cora fell asleep immediately, while Theo shifted restlessly beneath his cardigan. The emptiness returned. She could feel it yawning in her chest. All the pain and the loss and the nothing. She considered waking Theo up again, just to feel something, but decided against it. There was movement down in the valley. Some kind of mountain cat slinking in the opposite direction. Ren watched for a while, but the lonely passage leading to where they'd set up their camp remained blessedly empty.

In the morning everyone confirmed the return of the same familiar nightmares. Again Ren and Cora could feel Clyde's presence. A shadow, always out of sight, lurking in the backdrop of their memories. For some reason, Theo hadn't experienced anything like that yet. The inconsistency continued to nag at Ren. A riddle she couldn't quite solve.

As Cora went to check on her traps, Theo took a seat next to Ren. His presence was enough to draw out the thoughts that had been rattling inside her mind.

"I met Timmons during our sophomore year. She was so pretty that I just kind of assumed she was one of you. Didn't take long to figure out she was as Lower Quarter as they come."

"Meaning?"

"She cursed the way only someone who grew up on the wharf can curse," Ren replied, a ghost of a smile on her face. "And she possessed the only quality we value. She was *steady*. Folks down in the Lower Quarter could care less about flash. We want fire. We shape the stones that build the city. We forge the weapons that march to war. Timmons never flinched away from our friendship. Not once. She was steady from the very start."

Theo was nodding. "My family didn't want to recruit her."

Ren looked at him in surprise. The words stung a little. What did she—or Timmons—care about the Broods and their damn interests? He saw the look on her face and smiled.

"My father interviewed Timmons himself. It went well until the end. He said she was one of the strongest enhancers he'd ever encountered. But at the end of the interview . . ."

Theo looked embarrassed.

"Oh, please," Ren said, leaning in. "Please tell me what she said."

He grinned now. "Well, he asked if she'd be willing to work with him personally. She eyed him up and down and said, 'There's only so much shine I can bring out in an antique.'"

Ren snorted at that. The idea of Timmons knocking Landwin Brood down a few pegs was the barest of silver linings. It hurt to laugh. It felt good to laugh.

"What a delight."

And what a loss. Ren's good humor vanished as she saw the shadow cast by their remembered light. It was her fault that Timmons was dead. If only she'd been more careful, more focused. She'd let her guard down too many times now. She'd allowed herself to enjoy the conjured fantasy that they were safe. Safe was a distraction out here. Ren knew surviving this would require everything she had. Now her mind was working double. It was time for a more aggressive approach.

"I don't want to wait for the next attack," she said.

Cora was circling back to camp. Theo nodded at Ren's suggestion.

"Meaning?"

"We know what we're up against now. We know how his magic works. Let's set a trap for him. Meet the enemy on our own terms for once."

He nodded again. "What'd you have in mind?"

Her answer was simple.

"Pain."

33

A few hours later they found the perfect spot.

The valley narrowed to a single trail. It was exposed to sunlight, which meant most of the snow had melted away. Having actual, solid stones beneath their feet would be crucial. It was also slightly elevated, with a decent escape route. Ren glanced at her two accomplices.

"Are you sure you're okay being in front?" she asked Theo.

He nodded. "Just don't miss."

She glanced back at Cora. "I'm sorry that you have to be the mindless goat."

"At least I'm a cute goat."

"That you are."

Their plan was straightforward. Ren got the idea from an old textbook. She remembered one of the old rulers of Kathor supposedly wore a specialized ring that would prick his finger every few minutes. It was a specific, intentional design, because the best way to battle mental manipulation was a physical countermeasure. She was doing her best to ignore the part of that story where the king killed himself by accidentally poisoning his own blood.

The group went back through the steps and the spells until there was nothing left to do but wait. The sun traced a path through the clouds overhead. It was the best weather they'd had so far. Still cold at this elevation, but it would have made for a decent day of hiking. Ren hoped their decision to wait was the right one. As the hours passed, however, she felt less certain. Every trace of movement on the landscape drew their attention. The occasional bird wheeling overhead. A sunset-red fox diving into the snow as it hunted. There was no sign of Clyde.

"Can't feel my toes," Cora complained, shifting her footing.

Ren was about to call it off when she heard a distant scrape. Her eyes darted to the mountain shelves on their right. Shadows pooled there. She took a deep breath before whispering to the others, "I'm pretty sure he's here."

The narrowed path they'd chosen extended about one hundred paces in a slight downslope. Ren had made sure there was no natural way around. Clyde would have to learn to levitate if he wanted to take them by surprise, and she was fairly certain Timmons had never mastered that particular skill. A few minutes later she saw his scorched visage peeking around the mouth of the stone passage. That stark blue eye considered them with unblinking intensity. Ren set her feet, but the revenant remained motionless. Minutes passed. On and on like that. The sun was slipping down over the shoulders of the mountains, and the shadows stretched.

Ren hoped their stances and battle formation would draw the revenant's attention away from what they'd buried in the snow. None of their plan would matter if he didn't actually attack them. She was considering cupping her hands and calling a taunt when Clyde started to move. She saw his entire right leg had snapped clean through from the fall. It produced a jarring limp. The rest of him was sturdy and strong, though. He was eighty paces away. Seventy. Ren reached for her magic as something stirred in the space between them.

Clyde went completely still.

She squinted. "Come on. What are you waiting for? . . ."

The air was scented with his foul magic. Was he probing their defenses somehow? Could he sense the trap? She glanced at Theo. Clyde still hadn't moved. He looked more like a wax figurine.

Until he *blinked*.

The shadow on Theo's left changed shape. The revenant had *traveled* from there to here in a terrifying breath. A blackened hand shoved out, and the first slash of his chain spell struck Theo square in the chest. Ren barely recovered in time to cast her own spell. She took aim.

Not at Clyde. Instead her wand tip was pointed at Theo's back.

Timing was everything. Right as the revenant's spell jumped between them, she hit Theo with a pinprick of painfully sharp magic. It would feel like someone stabbing a three-inch needle into his flesh. Hopefully, Cora was about to perform the same spell on her. Ren felt Clyde's magic hit her like a two-ton anvil. He had all of Timmons's strength now. She wasn't just ushered gently into darkness the way she had been all the other times. This time she was dragged head over heels, like being tumbled by a massive wave. . . .

The sight of her father, bent wrongways in the belly of the canal . . .

A sharpness pricked the back of her neck. The pain jolted her free of the mental trap. Theo was standing there, pretending not to move. She knew it had worked, though, because he held one hand behind his back, flashing the signal they'd arranged. Pain had woken both of them up from the memory spell. Clyde was limping forward, thinking he had another helpless victim to devour.

Now they sprung the trap.

The creature's right foot set down in an altered patch of snow. Magical teeth snapped around his good ankle. He let out a wounded snarl as Theo raised his wand to cast the next spell. A half-moon of fire cut off Clyde's retreat. Ren used her own magic to enclose the circle, binding him inside. There was a roar as the revenant realized he was cut off from the rest of the world. She could feel him mentally scraping at the barriers of her spell. His magic was dark and strong and desperate.

He's afraid, she thought. *And he should be.*

Ren and Theo prepared their second wave of spells. They'd carefully curated each set. They mirrored each other's motions. Ren stepped into the casting to put proper force behind the magic. Great blasts of fire struck Clyde in quick succession. His entire right side went up in flames. That arm withered before snapping off entirely.

"Let's finish him," Ren whispered. "Now, Theo!"

They were about to cast their third and final set when Cora barreled into Theo's back. They'd forgotten about her. By necessity, their plan had not involved waking her up from her catatonic state. She'd been trapped inside the memory, and they'd assumed she'd remain standing in place, helpless. Instead she forced Theo's wand hand to the ground, and a bolt of stray magic struck the stones between them. The concussive blast flung Ren sideways. Her grip on the magic prison around Clyde slipped. That was the only opening he needed. She managed to shove back to her feet in time to watch him flee down the stone passage. Fire trailed from his body.

Cora was groaning. "Did it work? Did we get him?"

Theo was blinking up at the stars, dazed by the aftermath of his own wayward magic. Ren spat on the stones as their summoned fire whittled down to smoke. Clyde was a distant speck of light that the shadows were slowly devouring. She reached down to help Cora and Theo back to their feet.

"He escaped. Come on. We need to get moving."

34

Ren's stomach rumbled as they pushed themselves to keep walking.

Their trap had come so close to working. Ren's design was nearly flawless. She hadn't accounted for that last desperate gasp of magic. Somehow Clyde had commanded Cora to do his bidding. In her mindless state she'd tackled Theo before their final round of spells could finish the job. It was yet another clever twist of magic.

Clyde might be wounded, but Ren also suspected he would approach them with an entirely new strategy next time. The same trap would not work again. Rather than delay, the group pressed on by the light of the stars, hoping to keep their advantage.

Theo shouldered their consolidated pack. It was nice for her to walk without the weight tugging at the muscles in her lower back. Vega caught a scrawny rabbit that might serve as a meager dinner. They trudged on through the endless, snow-laced landscape. The Eyeglass cut the star-bright sky on their left, sharp and slender. The higher passes of Watcher Mountain wound like veins in the iron sides of a giant on their right. Ren finally sensed the land starting to wind downward.

"We're almost through," she said. "How much magic do we have for the descent?"

Cora looked over. "I'm down to thirty ockleys after that encounter."

"Six hundred," Theo said. "Give or take."

"I'm under ninety," Ren said. "I wish Avy was still here. I have no idea how many more days of travel we have. Cora and I will run out of spells, but Theo's magic should last until we're in the foothills. The sooner we get out of the cold, the better."

When they finally stopped for rest, their last evening in the pass turned out to be one of the worst. There was nothing dry enough to start a fire with. Theo layered their clothes with enhancement spells, more than willing now to use his cache of magic as their vessels ran out. The hope of eating rabbit dimmed without any way to make a fire. The creature hung on its rope, frozen and uncooked. A harsh wind came sweeping through the valley, pelting the edges of their camp with snow. It wore down Theo's wards faster than normal. And with no fire to warm the enchanted space, they were left to shiver together until dawn.

Clyde made no appearance. There were no signs of any pursuit whatsoever. Ren had been lulled into thinking he was gone before, or that they were well out of his reach. She would not fall into that trap again. The next morning, as they walked, they discussed different strategies for defending against Clyde's inevitable next attempt. She had a few ideas up her sleeve, but it depended on how their next few days went. It also depended on what was waiting on the other side of the pass.

The initial descent turned out to be as difficult as the climb. Maybe worse. Cora slipped coming down one slope and busted her elbow. She couldn't waste magic patching it up, so she used Avy's boxing wraps instead. Several rock faces required rope spells and anchors. Ren could feel the tension growing in the muscles of her neck as they went. Theo's confidence in casting those spells grew, but every needed spell caused a delay. She didn't know if Clyde would suffer through the same pauses. After seeing him leap from one shadow to the next, she suspected he had his own methods for gaining ground on them.

It was a relief when the snow gradually began to vanish. The air grew warm enough during the day that they could drop the enhancement spells lining their clothes. They didn't celebrate, however, until rock gave way to forest. It was like breathing in new hope. Everything from here on out would be downhill.

The pass was finally behind them.

They were navigating another slope when Ren spotted the strange addition to the landscape. Her muscles were so tired and her stomach so empty that she thought that she was seeing a mirage. She stood there on the path, squinting through the trees, pinching the skin at her wrist to confirm it was real. Theo pummeled right into her and nearly sent her sprawling down the hillside.

"Sorry, Ren. What . . ."

His voice trailed off as he saw it too. Cora came up behind them, complaining about the sting of her calves. Her eyes shocked wide. "Is that what I think it is?"

"A farm," Ren said in disbelief. "That's a *farm*."

At first glance it seemed abandoned. There was an ancient-looking stone cabin on one end, with smaller wooden cabins dotting the rest of the property. Her eyes roamed to a larger barn in the western corner. Its paint appeared to be fresh. Really, the whole pasture looked far too well tended to be without residents. Her hopeful guess was confirmed by movement. Behind one of the cabins.

"Those are *cows*."

Cora pointed. "Look."

A figure appeared on the porch of one of the smaller cabins. They were too far away to see a face, but all three of them watched in disbelief as an actual person strode across the field. Ren hadn't even thought to pray for such a thing. They'd stumbled across a farm. All the way out here. Surely, they'd have some food to spare. Directions down the mountain. Ren's mouth was already starting to water when Theo cast a dark cloud over the scene.

"It's a bit dubious, isn't it?"

"What?" Ren asked. "Cows? How can cows be dubious?"

"Well, they're out in the middle of nowhere. This is pretty deep in the mountains. Why come all the way up here to start a farm?"

"For some peace and quiet," Cora whispered. "Fertile soil, too, depending on where you build."

Ren nodded. "You can avoid taxes out here too. Kathor's not sending a census taker up this far. I wouldn't blame anyone for coming out here to avoid the government."

"It could be illegal," Theo said. "Some kind of smuggling operation."

Ren rolled her eyes. "Another slice of knowledge from your adventure books?"

"From my father," Theo corrected, and he'd never sounded quite so golden and pompous than in that moment. He must have realized it, because he shrugged quickly. "I've just heard stories about outfits like this. When bounty hunters track down criminals, it's never a hideout in Kathor. Criminals make their homes in remote places. Like this."

"What do you suggest, then, Theo?"

He bit his lower lip. "Keep moving. We can get down the mountain ourselves."

"No," Cora said. It was the most forceful she'd ever sounded. Just the sight of that distant farm had lured her a few steps closer. Ren knew a place like this would feel more like home than Balmerick ever had. "If there's even a chance they can help, we have to stop. We can't survive without food. I don't have enough magic to set more traps. A farm is our best chance of finding sustenance."

Ren nodded. "And we can get our bearings. Find out how far we are from Kathor."

"Right. And what are we going to tell them?" Theo asked. "Hello. We accidentally took a waxway portal out into the middle of the Dires. Oh, and by the way, we've got a revenant trailing us that's already killed two of our friends. Do you mind if we stay over for the night?"

Cora frowned. "I didn't think about the fact that we might lead Clyde to them."

Ren shook her head. "As long as we move quickly, there's not going to be an issue. We can ask for food and directions, then keep moving. Clyde is after *us*, remember? Not them."

Theo still looked uncomfortable with the idea.

"You can make camp out here in the woods if you want," Ren told him, stowing her mother's bracelet in their shared satchel. She tucked her wand into a belt loop, just out of sight. "But I'm hungry and I'm going down there. Leave Vega if you're that nervous."

Cora nodded. "I want to go too."

Theo bit his lip again. "Fine, but if they're out here harvesting the organs of lost pioneers, I'm going to say I told you so."

"You won't be able to," Ren pointed out with a smirk. "No lungs to speak with."

And with the cheery thought of evisceration on their minds, they started down the hill.

35

A mountain hound spotted them first. He came barking and circling, sniffing the air before barking again. He was oak brown with a running pattern of white spots. Cora knelt down and set out one hand. The gesture lured the massive dog a bit closer. Ren was about to tell her to back up before she lost a finger, when the creature flopped at her feet, tongue lolling.

"There's a good boy," Cora said, scratching his stomach.

Two figures were crossing the pasture. A few other heads poked out of the smaller cabins. Ren couldn't tell if they were relatives or hired hands that worked the farm. The approaching pair were kind looking. Older than Ren's mother by a few years, but in even better shape. Lean and muscular, carved by the demanding work of running a farm. Time was starting to bend the man's shoulders but couldn't dim an easy smile. He waved at them when they were still a ways off. The woman was more reserved, studying each of them in turn. She had the same olive skin tone as Cora—though more burnished, as if she'd spent all morning working in the sun's light. She wore threadbare gloves that still had little clovers clinging to them from her gardening. A sharp whistle from her had the dog darting back to their side. Ren didn't realize they were husband and wife until she saw the comfortable way their shoulders pressed together as they walked.

"Ho there!" the man said. "Come and welcome. I'm Holt. This is my wife, Della. What brings you around our side of the mountain?"

Cora surprised Ren by taking the lead.

"We got lost," she said. "We're from Kathor. My parents have a farm down that way. North of the city. We raise pigs, mostly. Damn, I miss the scent of a proper farm."

Holt smiled at the compliment. "Nothing like it in the world."

"You came from where?" Della asked. "Up from the foot-hills?"

Cora turned and pointed. "From the pass, believe it or not. We were way off course."

Holt whistled. "You're kidding. No one takes the pass. No wonder you look ragged as bones. Come on. Let's get your bags set down on the porch. Are you hoping to stay the night?"

The three of them exchanged glances. They needed to sleep somewhere, but they'd agreed not to delay. For their sake and the sake of anyone who called this place home. Ren already had three deaths weighing on her shoulders. She didn't need any more ghosts trailing them home. There was no reason to endanger these people's lives by luring Clyde onto the property.

"We're just hoping for a meal," Cora answered. "If you can

spare it. And a shove back in the direction of the city, too. We're not sure how far we are."

"From Kathor? About four days," Della answered. She gestured to a hillside of green-stemmed flowers that were on the verge of blooming. "We sell mirror flowers at the Kathorian markets every other year. Beautiful things. One of the few crops that actually enjoy the mountain cold."

Theo eyed the hills. "Mirror flowers? I'd love to see a full field of them."

"The whole field won't bloom," Cora replied, looking to the two farmers for confirmation. Della gave her an approving nod. "They fight for sustenance. Wrapping their stems around one another and choking the weaker plants. Only about a hundred of them will make it, right?"

"Good eye," Della replied with a smile. "We've had about that many every year."

Holt clapped his hands together excitedly. "Come on. Set your things down over there. We'll tour you around a little. Della, let's set out a few more plates for dinner."

Ren hadn't spoken. She'd been too busy looking around the rest of the farm, made nervous by Theo's suggestion that something illegal could be happening. The field hands she saw looked completely at ease, though. One man had his feet kicked up and was reading a book on his porch. Another was washing a shirt to hang on a sagging clothesline. Ren even saw a little girl, thin as a rail, drawing in the dirt with a stick behind one of the cabins. That sight had Ren feeling nervous for an entirely different reason. She couldn't bear the thought of endangering a child.

". . . came out to take over operations of the farm from my

father. I was a historian. Taught primary school in Kathor for a bit. Way back before any of you were so much as a twinkle in your parents' eyes. Della didn't want to come all the way out here. Isn't that right, dear?"

"Of course not." She offered him a slanted smile. It was clear they'd told this story a time or two. "I liked the city. The busy streets and the taverns, all of it. I was young and it was fun. I loved you, dear, but I thought you were dragging me out to a goat track in the middle of nowhere."

As they turned the corner, the vista opened up. There was a sprawling valley, cut through by rivers and creeks and forests. Ren knew families like the Broods spent a lot of money for views just like this one. She was trying to discern the distant landmarks as Holt continued their story.

"We arrived at night," he said. "All the stars were out. Well, you three were up in the pass, so you already know. Out here it's different. None of man's tinkering gets in the way. You can see other worlds up in these mountains. When Della saw that—and saw this view the next morning—I knew she'd never want to go back."

"It's gorgeous," Cora said. "Some people don't know what they're missing."

"Well put," Holt replied. "That is well put. Go on, set your things down."

As Theo placed their lonely backpack on the wraparound porch, Ren finally realized how strange they must look. What kind of pioneers traveled with a single satchel? Their clothes and shoes were odd choices as well. Della's careful appraisal of their group made more sense now. She must have been wondering how a trio like them had ended up out here. Or how they'd survived the pass at all.

"Hope you don't mind a noisy dinner," Della said as she started up the porch. "Most of our hired hands are mountain folk, born and bred. No one ever taught them which spoon to use for which course or anything like that. I tried when I first came. It was a losing battle."

Cora glanced at Theo before smiling. "No worries. I grew up in a family that rolled dice to see who'd get the bone after dinner. Having a spoon for everyone at the table is plenty fancy for us."

Della inclined her head. "I'll ready the dinner. Promise not to bore them, Holt."

He clutched both hands over his heart, pretending to be wounded, before leaning in conspiratorially to the rest of them. "She's heard every story a hundred times. And she knows that's my favorite thing about guests. For guests, my stories are all brand-new. Come on this way. Plenty to see."

He walked across the upper pasture, carefully guiding them around. His love for history hadn't left him. "I salvaged all the wood from the buildings in Little West."

Ren perked up at that. "Little West? Isn't that one of the first ghost towns?"

Her interest managed to churn even more enthusiasm out of him.

"It's one of my favorite stories," he said. "They built it as a retreat for one of Kathor's first kings. Meant it to be solitude from the rigors of ruling. Rumor goes that he came up to inspect the town with a company of soldiers, and he never returned. When explorers found the place, it was just a bunch of empty buildings. None of the people who'd gone to settle the land were there. No graves. No bones. Nothing at all. After that, no one wanted to live there. Which meant a whole lot of free wood for us. And it's high-quality wood too."

Ren nodded. "My mother used to say they were eaten by the last surviving dragon."

"Really?" Holt looked thoughtful. "That's curious. My mother always said they turned *into* dragons. I'd bet that if we traced our lineages back, we'd see that they came from different regions with slightly different religious beliefs. I'd bet my mother's line has some Tusk ancestors. They're always telling stories about magical encounters like that. Honestly, it's why all the best stories have twenty alternative endings. Different folks like to spin their own moral lessons. . . ." He trailed off for a moment and scratched his head. "I was doing it, wasn't I? Boring you all to tears. All right, up ahead here . . ."

They circled the upper pasture and were allowed to pat the great flanks of the cows. A few of the field hands came over to introduce themselves. Ren waved to the little girl, but she was rather shy and went back to focusing even more intently on her straw doll. She noticed Della watching them from the kitchen window as she scrubbed down extra plates. Cora looked ready to move in permanently by the time they'd circled back around to the porch.

"Are you sure you can't stay the night?" Holt asked. "We've got an empty cabin."

Cora hesitated just long enough for Theo to answer for the group.

"We really have to keep moving. We're honored by the offer, however."

Holt raised his eyebrows before winking at Cora. "Honored?

I'm guessing goldenrod here wasn't raised on a farm. Well, we're *honored* to at least have you for dinner."

Theo looked uncertain about whether or not he'd been insulted as Holt thundered up the porch steps. His voice rang out, calling for Della. There was a bell hanging down on the corner of their porch. He started ringing it to call in the field hands for a hearty meal that Ren could already smell through the open window. As it tolled, the three of them had a single moment to themselves.

And all three of them spoke at once.

"I love this place."

"I don't like it."

"That smells *amazing*."

Cora shot a proper scowl in Theo's direction.

"You don't like it because they're not *your* kind of people."

He scowled right back at her, but any chance of a discussion was cut off as Holt came loping back toward them. The older man swung the front door open and gestured inside.

"Go on. Pick good seats or you'll catch elbows from the Mackie brothers."

Inside, the kitchen was the clear centerpiece of their home. It sprawled around a great wooden table that appeared to be two farmhouse doors fashioned and bolted into one longer piece. Finely crafted chairs ran down both sides, and Ren guessed they were handmade. Hooks had been hammered straight into the walls. Any number of cast-iron implements hung like war prizes. Della set out a plate of melted goat cheese, and Ren barely kept the drool from running down her chin.

"Start in," their host said, whirling around to prepare another dish. "The Mackies will eat it all if you don't grab a few bites now."

Holt offered them a *Didn't I tell you?* look as he took his own seat. There was an old-flower scent hidden beneath the smoked cheeses and meats. It reminded Ren of the stores her mother used to frequent when she was a child. Something that, in larger doses, would make her feel a little nauseous. She didn't know the polite amount of cheese to take and was soundly scolded by Holt on her first attempt. "No wonder you're barely bones," he said. "Like this."

He took a stub of bread and smeared four times the amount of cheese on top before offering it to her. She devoured the morsel. Cora and Theo didn't need further invitation. They gathered their own portions and just as quickly made them disappear. Ren realized their challenge might be avoiding eating too much and making themselves sick. She was eating her third slice of bread when a herd of shoulders came shoving through the front entryway.

There was chaos and jostling, and Ren imagined every night was like this. The previously mentioned Mackie brothers were an easy spot. Broad-shouldered boys, faces like flattened stone, their eyes little chips of brown. They plunked into the seats closest to Holt and barely seemed to register that there were guests. A knife of a man sat down on Ren's right. He was at least five or six years older than her, with a burn scar running down his neck.

"Lev," he said, offering his hand. "I'm the crafty one."

She frowned at that. "I'm Ren. Crafty?"

He knocked two scabbed knuckles on the table. "Made this, the chairs, all the rest."

She smiled politely. "It's lovely work."

There were three others who piled into the room. One was an old man with silver-shot hair and a smashed nose. The other two were a young couple. Ren spied a marriage bracelet on the girl's wrist—an old practice that had gone out of style in Kathor. She had the same eyes and nose as the little girl outside, though her husband had gifted their daughter with his dark, tightly curled hair. Both nodded politely when introductions were made.

Della served mountain rice with bright runny eggs on top. There were slabs of a meat that Ren couldn't identify, but watching the Mackie brothers load up their plates with them was convincing enough. Cora's cooking in the mountains had tasted delicious, but Ren realized now it had been a product of their hunger. Here the meats were spiced and the eggs salted. Some kind of butter was melted at the bottom of each bowl, and Ren barely resisted licking her plate.

"Who hikes the northern pass?"

Other conversations were swirling, but Ren heard Della's question to Theo come knifing through the rest. She was sipping mulled wine. Theo shrugged.

"Fools," he answered. "Like I said, we got lost. Lucky to be alive, honestly."

Della raised a curious eyebrow. "Oh?"

"Walked straight through a wyvern's nest. Thankfully, it was out hunting."

"Dangerous creatures," Della confirmed. "Every few years they'll snatch a cow from us. Not their favorite, though. They prefer hunting prey that can actually escape. We learned a while ago not to bother venturing into the pass. Everything on that side of the mountain is a little wilder. It's not the sort of place people are meant to go. . . ."

Ren realized she was eavesdropping, and worse, she'd abandoned the conversation on her side of the table. Lev was spooning his rice without a thought, but the couple across from her were waiting expectantly. She offered a polite smile. "Was that your daughter out there?"

The man nodded. "Talia."

"That's a lovely name. Will she be joining us?"

The couple exchanged a glance. The woman set her fork aside with a grin.

"That girl's like a chicken. Comes when she's hungry, but if she's not, all you'll get for your trouble is a few pecks. She's stubborn like that. All mountain girls are, though."

She elbowed her partner. He spoke up through a mouthful of rice.

"We marry them because everything else up here bites."

Ren laughed. The two of them smiled at what was clearly a well-worn joke. She glanced down the table and caught Della watching her again. She wasn't sure why, but their hostess seemed different from the others gathered around the table. Everyone else fit an expected mold. Della was double edged, though. A coin with two sides. Ren couldn't imagine growing up in Kathor and transitioning permanently to a place like this. There was something in the depths of who she was that made Ren uncomfortable, maybe in part because the woman reminded her a little bit of herself.

Ren took another serving of food before tugging at the discomfort of her collar.

Damn, it's hot in here, she thought.

"What about you?" the woman was asking. "That one is easy on the eyes."

She threw a subtle nod in Theo's direction. Ren supposed she agreed with the assessment. His golden hair was arranged neatly. His lips moved easily as he kept up conversation with Della. Every now and again that effortless smile would appear. Next to him, Cora was giggling as she told a story about pigs from her time growing up. Ren felt beads of sweat running down her forehead.

"Easy on the eyes," Ren agreed. "Sorry, is there a bathroom?"

The couple looked her question toward Della. Their host gestured.

"Right outside, honey."

Ren smiled and offered a polite bow of the head. She wiped sweat away with the back of her hand, a little embarrassed as she stepped out into the lantern light of the porch. The last gasp of sunlight was streaking the mountaintops scarlet. The breeze felt like a fine thing on her skin, cool and refreshing. Ren headed straight for the outhouse. It was a tight fit, and she wondered how the Mackie brothers ever managed. Not that she minded having a proper toilet to use for the first time since the portal incident.

Ren finished up and stumbled back out into the open air. She was feeling a touch light-headed. She eyed the open pasture and saw a moonlit figure. It had her heart pounding until she realized it was little Talia. The girl stood in the doorway of one of the cabins, eyes fixed curiously on Ren. She offered another wave, but the girl ducked back out of sight. Ren was struck by a brief terror that Clyde might come. Might find the girl unprotected. But according to Cora, the magic that had brought him back to life was focused. His hunger was not bent toward random children, like monsters from the stories. It was absorbed entirely with them.

She started back toward the porch, when a glow on the far end of the property caught her eye. Smoke hissed out of something. Maybe a boiler room? She watched the light of the stars and the moon fracture across the spot. It looked green and then blue and then silver. Like an aurora.

A throat cleared. Ren spied Lev on the porch, working to light a pipe. He smiled as she approached. It was the same look older men offered her down by the wharf. A lingering stare that crawled uncomfortably over her skin. *Better to stay away from this one,* she thought.

"Dell is serving up the pie," he said, thumbing toward the entrance. "Go on and get a slice before the Mackie boys shovel it all down. Something sweet for *someone* sweet."

That last line had the hairs on her neck standing up. She couldn't duck back inside fast enough. The warmth of the kitchen washed over her as she did. Ren would just have to resign herself to the fact that she'd be sweating in front of the others. She dabbed her forehead with one sleeve before rounding the corner. Everyone in the room looked up at the same time.

Except for Theo and Cora. Both of them were facedown, heads set delicately on their own used handkerchiefs. Della was humming a little lullaby, running her fingers along Theo's spine. He didn't react at all. Ren felt her head spin again. Her first instinct was flight, but before she could turn, she heard a rustle at the door. Lev stood there with his arms folded.

She reached for her wand and came back empty-handed. It wasn't at her hip.

"Looking for this?" Lev called, waving it in the air.

Ren's wrist was empty too. She'd hidden her mother's bracelet in their satchel. She had no access to either of her vessels. When she turned back, Della offered that slanted smile.

"Careful now, honey. You're properly loaded at this point. Got enough of the breath in you to knock out a horse. Don't beat yourself up for not noticing. It's hard to smell it with all the cooking and whatnot." That old-flower scent. She should have known. Ren's legs threatened to give way. "Working with the substance as much as we do, all of us have an immunity built up to it. Except for Talia, of course. We never risk exposing the children."

Ren stammered the word "why" and it sounded unintelligible even to her own ears. More of a garbled syllable than anything else. Della still answered.

"Let's just say I'm not buying what you're selling. We get lost pioneers coming through plenty. Explorers, hikers. No one comes down from that pass. No one. And look at you three. You don't have the right boots for hiking. None of the right gear with you. A single bag in your possession. You said you're lost?"

Della smiled as the rest of the world began to sway.

"If lost means you're in the wrong place at the wrong time, I'd agree with you. But don't worry. We'll find out exactly who sent you here. And why they sent you. We've got plenty of time to learn all your little secrets, honey. I'll be seeing you again real soon."

The light traded places with the dark as Ren fell.

36

Ren woke to a sharp kick. The room was dark. The right side of her head felt like it had been slammed into stone. She let out an involuntary groan as her eyes tried to adjust. There were shapes, shadows. A voice speaking her name.

"Ren?"

"Theo? Where's Cora?"

"I'm here."

There was a rattle of chains. Ren tried to sit up and finally realized how tightly she'd been bound. The inability to move more than a few inches had her chest heaving. She did not like tight spaces. She didn't like being bound. She didn't like anything that was outside of her control.

"Ren. Calm down. We're here."

But Ren's mind felt as trapped as her body. Her thoughts were sluggish. Her wand and her bracelet were missing. Thinking of a spell to free herself didn't matter, because for the first time in five years, she had no way to use the magic she'd dedicated herself to learning.

Theo's voice cut her thoughts. "Ren. It's going to be okay. Cora has a plan."

Ren pulled again. Her chains rattled. She could feel the metal digging into her wrists and neck. Something feral guttered up her throat. Her entire body felt like it was falling through the earth. She barely heard Cora's voice.

"I've got a *devorium*."

There were very few words that could have broken through Ren's mental barriers. "Devorium" was one of them. She could see that word highlighted in a textbook. The definition floating in the darkness before her. *A devorium is a mass of concentrated time, gathered by illicit means into a singular vessel. The one-time use of this object allows its wielder to travel back as far as two hours, depending on the potency of the time stolen by the object's creator.* Ren read that definition, glowing in the dark air in front of her, over and over. Her breathing finally settled. The cramps in her legs faded. She wanted to believe Cora's claim, but it didn't seem possible.

"How?"

A deep breath. "I made one. For my final exam. Just in case."

There could be no more shocking admission. Ren could hear Cora's guilt written into every syllable. Bringing contraband into a final was the kind of thing that could end someone's career before it ever started, but possessing a devorium? That was infinitely worse.

"They're on the list of unforgivable contraband," Ren said. "Possessing one is a step short of murder in our judicial system. How did you even learn how to make it?"

"It doesn't matter now. I couldn't risk messing up my practical. I worked too hard. There was no way I was going to accidentally slit an artery and lose my place. The exam went well, though, and I didn't have to use it. That's why it was still in my bag."

At least she could understand Cora's reasoning. She'd demanded perfection from herself at Balmerick because even the slightest mistake felt like it might be enough to end her chances. Still, the lengths to which Cora had gone were beyond even her own imagination. Ren knew that devoriums worked on stolen time. And time could only be stolen from other beings who understood their temporal existence. It was a notoriously difficult process, unless you had express permission from the victim. Ren was still too unsettled to piece the riddle together. She focused on what she'd already learned about Cora instead.

"The amber orb," she said. "You hid it with your foot when we were all sorting through what we should bring with us. I wondered what it was, but I didn't want to embarrass you."

"I knew you saw it, but I wasn't sure if you recognized what it was. Devoriums can be stored in a lot of different ways. It's activated—"

"By the gem in your eye piercing. I know. I saw they matched."

She heard Theo sigh. "How do I not notice any of this?"

Because you've never had to really pay attention. It didn't take much for Ren's thoughts to wade into darker currents. She wanted to focus on what they should do next. Make a plan. But another obvious truth was blooming out of the first revelation, like a flower with hidden thorns. Ren gritted her teeth in the dark but couldn't fend off the anger rising in her chest.

"You could have saved Timmons," she said. "Or Avy. All of it, Cora. You could have taken us back to Balmerick when we first got lost out here. . . ."

Those words were met with silence. Her eyes were pinned to the shadow she knew was Cora. She saw the way the girl's head bowed under the weight of all that guilt. Ren had noticed how distracted she'd been after each incident. She'd assumed it was simply because of the horror of what they'd witnessed.

Cora finally answered. "You can't activate a devorium to access the waxways. They are two separate, powerful items that use different temporal theories to power what they do. The results of such an attempt would be catastrophic. Besides, it's not like . . . I wasn't trying to advertise what I had with me. I didn't know how lost we were yet, and I had no personal connection to Clyde Winters. No offense, Theo."

The other shadow shook its head. Ren still wasn't satisfied. "What about Avy and Timmons?"

Cora's voice was a whisper. "When Avy died, we were still running. There was a lot of adrenaline and panic. I forgot what I had until we stopped. Until it was too late. If I'd used it then, I'd have risked wasting it and still not saving him. I felt horrible. If only I'd remembered in time, I could have stopped Clyde. . . . Avy would be alive. Trust me, it's all I've thought about since it happened."

Ren recalled the girl scratching her eyebrow. After both deaths.

"Which means you *chose* not to save Timmons."

A looming silence, and then: "Yes. I could have saved her. The truth is that I was keeping it for myself. I didn't know what we'd face in the mountains. I was afraid to die."

The darkness spared Ren from having to hide her emotions. The thought of Timmons, brought back to life by magic in their possession, was too much. If she'd known, she would have forced Cora to use the devorium. But she also knew that if it had been her secret, she'd have at least considered holding on to the device as well. A fail-safe as they crossed into the dangerous mountain passes. Balmerick had taught them that lesson. They knew what it meant to be chosen, and once they were up in those sunlit heights, surviving was the only instinct that could take root. That didn't mean she would forget this confession. Cora would answer for what she'd done eventually.

For now Ren needed to focus. It was the only way forward. "How far back will it take you?"

"An hour," Cora answered. "But my methods for creating it were likely far from perfect. I have no idea how much time it will actually give us."

"What are you waiting for, then?" Ren asked. "Every second counts."

She imagined Cora traveling back through time to when they'd been standing on the path, looking at the farm from a distance. It would be easy to escape if she could go that far.

"The orb is out of range."

Ren felt the hope in her chest die a second death. Fear crept over its corpse. The chains around her wrists felt like they were getting tighter. Theo's voice barely managed to break through.

"Vega is hunting for the bag," he said. "If she can fly it closer to us, Cora can activate the orb. When she does, we'll all go back in time. Only Cora will know what happened. She's going to do her best to—"

The door opened with a groan of rusted metal. Della was there, framed by the night sky. Her eyes traced the room, flicking from face to face, before settling on Ren.

"Take her first."

The Mackie brothers lumbered forward. Theo tried to kick them. Cora was shouting for them to stop. Ren felt a quiet relief as the chains fell from her wrists, as they stood her up and marched her out into open air. Her skin drank in that coolness before she realized they were guiding her toward another shed. There was a single lantern dangling. It cast shadows across a wall of glinting tools.

"No, wait, please, no . . ."

A bolt of magic struck her neck. It ran down her spine until she couldn't move at all. Ren felt that same panic heaving back to life in her mind. She was going to die out here.

"Set her on the table."

The Mackie brothers laid her down and flipped her over, like they would to prepare any other animal for slaughter. The spell locking Ren in place unraveled a second too late. Her wrists were already bound to the table. The lantern swayed somewhere behind her.

Please, Cora. Please help me. Please.

She heard the sound of a knife sharpening against a whetstone. Her eyes were drawn in that direction. It was the old man from dinner. The one with the smashed nose. He sat in a chair, toothpick rolling along his lips as he worked. "Welcome to my humble dwelling."

The place was just short of decay. Roots shot through cracks in the walls. There was an abandoned cot in one corner with the book she'd seen him reading earlier. The binding and cover had all but unraveled. Della waited in the doorway as the Mackie brothers ghosted back outside. The old man tapped his knife on something metal. The sound echoed.

"Did you hear me? I welcomed you. Are you a rude guest? I've no patience for rude guests."

"I'm not a guest," Ren snapped. "Why are you doing this?"

Please, Cora. Please, please, please.

"You *are* my guest," the man replied. "Until we get the answers we want. Which means that so long as you're on this table in my cabin, I am your host. You can call me that. Call me Host."

He looked over at Della. She was leaning casually against the doorframe.

"We will start the interrogation with easy questions," Della said. "Who sent you?"

Ren licked her lips. "We got lost. I'm telling you. We took a portal. . . ."

Della shook her head. Host put down his whetstone and started across the room. He pulled a chair over that Ren hadn't seen, dragging it across the stone floor so that he could sit comfortably at her side. A small smile played across his face as he started flattening her immobilized left hand, stretching the fingers out. A part of Ren's mind fractured from the rest. She was nothing but the panic. Her words sputtered out.

"I'm telling you the truth. We're students at Balmerick. We were taking the waxways. . . ."

Host glanced to Della. The woman asked again, "Who sent you?"

"No one sent us! It was an accident!"

She signaled. Host brought his knife down with a flash. The

blade caught the extended tip of Ren's middle finger, searing through flesh and spurting out blood. Ren clenched her teeth to stop from crying out. Breath pushed angrily through her nostrils.

"Our guest will answer the questions," Host said, examining his work. "Every time one of us finds your responses are lacking, the fingers get shorter."

Della tried again. "Tell me. Where do you think you are?"

Ren answered through gritted teeth. "A farm."

The knife slashed down. Ren gasped at the pain that shot up her entire right side. Della clicked her tongue. "Specific answers. I know you're smart. Clearly the leader of the group. Where are we?"

"A drug farm."

Della nodded. "Yeah? How'd you know? If you weren't sent here looking for us."

Ren saw a chance to prove her side of the story. The words came rushing out. "Holt steered us away from your eastern field. He had a story about every other crop and building. But not that one? Felt strange. Then there was the scent in the kitchen. Like dying flowers. My friend used the breath at school. The final product didn't smell exactly like that, but it was close."

Della looked impressed. Ren was doing everything she could to ignore the blood.

"What else?"

"Lev's burns. On his neck and knuckles. You were wearing gloves when we first met, but I spotted a burn on your wrist at dinner. Chemical reactions. That kind of thing happens when you're working with noxious fumes. I also saw the exhaust smoke when I used the outhouse. Smoke doesn't usually take on color. Unless it's rising from the corpse of a dragon."

Della signaled. The knife slashed again. This time her entire world briefly reeled. Spots of black. Something sharp and pungent was shoved in her face before she could slip away. Ren's eyes whipped back open as the world, the little details of the room, grew vivid again.

"Can't have our guest passing out," Host said. "Too easy, that. Off into the world of unfeeling. No, no, no. We've far too much to discuss."

Ren's words were mostly spittle. "I answered . . . I answered the question."

"It was a clever answer," Della admitted. "Pretending to simply be an observant girl. The whole bit about being students. That's a nice front. But it doesn't matter how nice your shoes are when you walk through a cow pasture. They're still going to smell like dung. When three 'students' appear at our door without gear or food or anything, I'm going to harbor suspicions."

She nodded to Host again.

"Pain is a road to the truth. Who sent you?"

An odd numbness was spreading through Ren's entire body. She wasn't sure if it was the pain or the fear, or if death itself was coming for her. She felt as if she'd slipped out of her physical body and were watching the scene as an observer. When the Ren on the table didn't answer their question, Host set down the smaller blade. She watched, utterly helpless, as he picked up a massive butcher's sword. It looked crude, effective. She stared as her own blood ran over the table's edge, coloring the dusty floor, and then the entire room went colorless. . . .

". . . good seats or you'll catch elbows from the Mackie brothers."

Inside, the kitchen was the clear centerpiece of their home. It sprawled around a great wooden table that appeared to be two farmhouse doors fashioned and bolted into one longer piece. Finely crafted chairs ran down both sides, and Ren guessed they were handmade. Hooks had been hammered straight into the walls. Any number of cast-iron implements hung like war prizes. Ren thought the room looked oddly familiar. She tried to remember if there was a restaurant down by the wharf that had similar decorations. It was a strange sort of echo.

Della set out a plate of melted goat cheese on the table. Ren could barely keep the drool from running down her chin. "Start in," their host . . .

. . . host . . . host . . . Host grinned down at her, blade in hand. Everything was lightless. . . .

. . . their *host* turned to prepare another dish.

"The Mackies will eat it all if you don't grab a few bites now."

Ren felt that strange flicker of repetition in her mind. What was happening to her? Some image had knifed briefly through her senses. It had her grinding her teeth. Was Clyde nearby? She tried to focus on what Della was saying as Holt took his seat. There was an old-flower scent hidden beneath the smoked cheeses and meats. It reminded Ren of the stores her mother used to frequent when she was a child. Something that, in larger doses, would make her feel a little nauseous.

She was reaching for some bread when movement caught her eye. Cora leaned over and whispered in Theo's ear. Ren frowned, thinking it was a fairly rude and obvious gesture to perform right at the table. Theo blanched at whatever she was saying. That had Ren curious. Holt as well. He was eyeing the two of them and started to ask a question when Cora bolted to her feet.

Aim, whisper, magic.

A punch of force hit the chandelier overhead.

Ren could only watch as it came crashing down.

37

ora and Theo ran, stumbling toward the entrance. Ren was a step slower, but her senses had been unnerved since they arrived. It was easy to be drawn in by Cora's instincts, even if she didn't know what had forced their sudden flight. Muted shouts chased them down the front porch steps. She saw that Cora had already snatched their satchel.

"Hey! What's happening? . . ."

Ren's question was swallowed by the odd pull of time. She saw an outhouse directly ahead. Memories came to her in flickering, colorless glimpses. The stars in the sky above. The little girl—Ren somehow knew that her name was Talia—framed by moonlight. A slender man watching her from the very same porch they'd just run down. An entire roomful of people that she'd never met, staring at her as Cora and Theo slept on their handkerchiefs, frighteningly motionless.

Her senses snapped back to the present as they sprinted around the corner of the building. There were figures in her periphery. She glanced over and saw a small circle of them near one of the cabins, deep in discussion until they finally heard Della's shouts. They were the same people Ren had just seen in that flickering memory. A bolt of magic seared overhead, barely missing.

Cora aimed for the eastern fence. All three of them were sprinting as fast as they could, Ren just a step behind. The field hands were in pursuit. She heard a sharp whistle. In the far corner of the pasture, the hound shot to his feet. He sprinted at an angle to cut off their escape. Whatever friendship had been born in that first meeting was lost now. He let out a menacing growl as he closed in on them.

"Over the fence!"

Cora started pulling herself over. Theo jumped before turning to help Ren. Another spell bent back the fence post on their left. A second later and they were over, vaulting recklessly down an overgrown embankment. Luckily, it ran right into some kind of service path. Cora looked both ways before darting downhill. A sharp pain was digging into Ren's side. She didn't know how long they could outrun their pursuers. Especially on a property they didn't know nearly as well.

The path curled downhill for about three hundred paces. Ren saw hatches built diagonally into the sides of the stone shelf on their left. Far too advanced for a simple farm. It confirmed a truth that had been festering in her mind since they arrived. She knew exactly what kind of place this was. "I'm pretty sure we're . . . this is a . . ."

A figure appeared at the bottom of the path. Ren's breathing was ragged as they all pulled up short. It wasn't one of the field hands. Not Holt or Della. The waiting figure was one all of them knew on sight. A dark whisper filled the air, tugging at the edges of Ren's mind. He was too far away for the magic to fully drag them under.

"It's Clyde."

Voices trailed them. The field hands would arrive at any moment. On their right, the drop was about seventy vertical paces. They could try to jump. Let the upper branches of trees break their fall? As they hesitated, the distant revenant raised both hands. A wave of shadows came roiling up the hillside toward them. This was new magic. Something else entirely. Cora seized Ren by the scarf.

"Come on! This way!"

She'd thrown open the nearest hatch. Great gusts of colored smoke were starting to pour out in waves. Ren's eyes widened. "Cora. I'm pretty sure that's—"

"I know what it is. Move. Now."

They ducked inside the dimly lit chamber before Clyde's magic could reach them. Wisps of colored smoke pooled and eddied in tight curls. There were masks and gloves hanging on the nearest wall. Theo slammed the door shut behind them. She saw him performing a spell that she hoped would actually buy them time. There was no way of gauging how proficient Della's crew was in magic.

Cora wasn't waiting to find out. She snatched the masks from the wall and shoved one into each of their chests. "Tighten the straps. Completely cover your mouth and nose. Cover as much of your skin as you can too. Ren, use your scarf to cover your hair."

"Can someone tell me what the hell is going on?" Theo asked. "What is this place?"

"We're about to run through the burial chamber of a dead dragon," Cora explained calmly. "We're on a drug farm. These are breath harvesters. I should have known. I was distracted by everything. There aren't nearly enough cows in that pasture. Not enough crops to sustain themselves way out here. None if it adds up for a real farm. It's my fault. I should have spotted those inconsistencies sooner. I wanted to believe we'd finally had some good luck."

Ren shook herself. Those other memories were edging in from the corners of her mind. None of what she was seeing in her mind made any sense. How could she be here *and* there?

"They drugged us at the dinner table," Cora announced. "The first time. We sat down to eat dinner with them, and they drugged all three of us. When we woke up, they came for Ren and tortured her to get answers. Della thought we'd been sent here to spy on their operations by someone. It was pretty clear that they were going to kill all three of us, so I used a devorium and reset everything by an hour. This is our only chance to escape. If we don't keep moving, we're as good as dead. Do you understand?"

There were raised voices outside. Ren's mind spun as it tried to set those revelations in their rightful places. The idea that Cora had a devorium was unthinkable. Where would she even get one? But something slammed into the hatch, and her mind shut out those smaller concerns. She hoped the two parties hunting them would slow each other down. She had no idea what would happen if Clyde actually attacked a group of that size. All she knew was they needed to move. Now.

Cora crossed over to the inner door and briefed them.

"This chamber is one of the most toxic places you will ever set foot. Do not expose yourself for any reason. Keep moving. Do not touch the dragon's corpse. No matter what it tells you. Try your best to not even look directly at it. There should be an exhaust pipe somewhere on the opposite end of the chamber. That's where we're heading. Ready?"

"Should we cast wards first?" Theo asked.

Cora and Ren both shook their heads. She was starting to think boys didn't read their textbooks. "Dragons—even dead dragons—feast on magic. It'd be like covering yourself in honey."

Ren knew hospitals and mortuaries ran a yearly census regarding cause of death. Dragons still ranked in the top ten causes every year, even though they'd been extinct for decades. Whatever was waiting in that chamber would be very dangerous to them. A loud thud sounded outside. Something powerful slammed against the locked hatch again and again. They could see the frame starting to bend inward. Ren nodded to them. They had no choice.

"Cora. Lead the way."

The other girl took confidence from that. Ren watched as she unbolted the antechamber door and led them inside. At first there was nothing but smoke. And in the smoke, whispers. Ren heard a distant voice. A lovely baritone broken by scattershot laughter. It was like walking through the dark passages of another entity's mind. She kept tight to Cora. Theo was right on her heels. It was difficult to breathe while wearing the thickly woven mask. All three of them moved in lockstep until their tunnel reached the main chamber.

A prickling sensation ran down her spine. No amount of

research could have prepared Ren for what she saw. The dragon was nearly the same size as the barn outside. A putrid green light backlit its empty eye sockets and broken jaw-line. That arcane fire was the source of all the fumes. The creature's diamond-shaped head lay slack on the stones. A half-rotted neck ran in a sinuous line back to the larger body. Ren saw it was missing a wing, most of its ribs. All the claws had been removed. Likely they'd cut them off and sold them for a great deal of money.

The dragon was well below them, nestled in the heart of a large stone pit. Scaffolds were set up in different locations, half leaning against the dragon's flanks to allow workers a method for climbing up and around the creature. Bright slits glowed wherever they'd cut openings, allowing more of those precious fumes to fill the cavernous space. Installed funnels along the ceiling drew everything into separate chambers overhead. Ren knew that was where they filtered the sub-stance for consumption. Everything in the room felt like vio-lation, like dying.

"Keep moving," Cora said. "Stop looking at it."

Ren realized she and Theo were still on the top platform. Cora was halfway down the ladders but had turned back. Her voice brought Ren back to herself. She followed quickly, paus-ing only when the makeshift ramps wobbled beneath her feet. The closer they got to the corpse, the more incessant the whispers became. Ren had thought them unintelligible. Dragons spoke a different dialect than humans, according to all that she'd read. But when she glanced back toward the sprawled corpse, a presence broke through the barriers around her mind.

I can help you. Give you all. You want the boy? You want the Broods? I can bend them to your will. Look.

Theo let out a clipped shout. Ren turned to see that he was on his knees, chest heaving. He'd been made to bow by the creature's magic. She saw him gritting his teeth in obvious pain.

See? Doesn't it taste delicious? His obeisance? I could allow you to drink from this cup every day, every night. All that he claims would be yours. Come to me, little one. Set a hand on my scales. Taste the power of—

Cora slapped her across the face. Ren cried out as the whispers faded.

"Keep. Moving. Don't. Look."

Theo was back on his feet. The two of them struggled forward, following Cora beneath the outstretched wing. The whispers were back, but unintelligible once again. It felt like it took them an hour to walk around the whole corpse. Ren knew that was impossible. It wasn't that large. But there was something strange and fractious and temporary about this place. She couldn't have felt any more relieved when they put that glowing corpse behind them.

"This way," Cora whispered.

As she'd predicted, there was a narrow pipe at the back of the chamber. It was barely big enough for them to crawl through. Ren had no idea how Cora had known it would be there, but she supposed farms and medicine and bodies were her expertise.

"Great work, Cora."

"Don't celebrate yet," she replied. "The drop is likely to be severe."

All three of them crawled forward on hands and knees. Ren did her best to avoid touching the puddled condensation that had gathered at the bottom of the pipe. It didn't behave like any normal liquid she'd ever seen. The less contact she could make, the better. She had no doubt that it was as toxic as the air around them.

The whispers finally faded as they rounded a final corner. The mouth of the pipe widened. There was a natural landing of stone, eight paces or so, then a drop.

"I told you," Cora said, walking forward. She glanced over the edge. "Oh. Not too bad, actually. It's just a short jump."

Forest awaited them. The distant branches were bent, so that Cora looked like she was standing beneath the arch of some great cathedral. Cora and Theo descended first, turning back long enough to help Ren down. There were about fifty paces between them and the cover of the forest. They started across, keeping as low as they could, when Ren saw two figures emerge from the trees directly ahead of them, their crossbows already raised.

One was her torturer from the dead memories. The other was the thin man from the porch. *Lev,* she remembered. Both of them took aim at different targets. Theo and Cora were a few steps ahead of her. Neither one had slowed. Neither one had noticed that the hunters were in front of them, not behind. Ren had less than a breath to decide who she'd save.

Magic thundered from her fingertips.

38

The steps of the spell flowed perfectly into one another. Barrier, dispersion, redirection.

Timmons wasn't there to power the magic the way she had back in the archive room, but Ren's adrenaline more than made up for her absence. Lev's bolt caught in the air in front of Theo. Briefly frozen, its tail midswirl. The energy ran in a current around the three of them until she harnessed that energy for her own purposes. This was her slight modification to the spell: redirection.

The bolt hit Lev's neck before he could even lower his weapon. She saw him fall, flopping like a fish. The older man was scrambling to fire again when Theo hit him with a well-aimed stunner. It slung him sideways into the nearest tree. They both heard the sickening smack. Ren's heart was in her throat. "We got them. Come on. . . ."

But then she saw Cora. She was on her knees. The other bolt had punched through her chest. Ren dropped down just as Cora sagged sideways, barely catching her.

"Cora. We're here. Stay with us. . . ."

Her eyes were wide and hazel and lifeless. The bolt had cut a path right through her heart. There was no pulse to find, no signs of life. Ren's entire body shook as she set Cora gently down in the grass. Her chest was tight. It was hard to breathe. She reached out to close Cora's eyes, and the girl's body spasmed.

A half-stifled scream guttered out from Ren. It took a few seconds for the body to stop twitching. When it did, Theo leaned down to perform the ritual instead. The two of them looked at each other in a wordless exchange. He nodded a confirmation to the question she couldn't bring herself to ask. There wasn't enough time to bury a body—or to take Cora with them. Not if they wanted to live.

"Let's get the hell out of here," Theo said.

Night complicated their escape.

They didn't dare risk a light cantrip as they descended through the hills. Out in this lifeless place, any lantern or fire would draw attention. The stars served as their only guide. Adrenaline would have been enough to keep them moving, but every now and again they heard extra incentive. The sharp baying of Della's hound. If their hunters did not rest, neither could they.

Cora Marrin is dead. And I'm the one who let her die.

Ren tried to ignore that thought as they pressed on. Three times they crossed over creeks. Whenever they reached an embankment that was too steep, they'd head south—nestling deeper into the waistline of Watcher Mountain—hoping to always be moving in the direction of Kathor, no matter the obstacle. Della had claimed it was a four-day journey to the city. Ren had no idea if the woman had told the truth about that or not. She also knew they didn't have to travel that entire distance. Not with the way candle at their disposal.

Morning dawned, a bright day that did not match how they felt. Ren had never been more exhausted in her life. Every muscle protested. Losing Cora was yet another added burden. There was also the colorless memory, rattling in the corner of her mind, of a cramped shed. Her missing fingers and all that blood. Those events had never actually happened, but Ren could not quite escape from the frightening possibilities of what might have occurred if that timeline had continued on its course. It was noon before they found a place that was tempting enough to stop for rest.

A small waterfall churned into a shallow pool that was so clear they could see the bottom. Ren thought that was what lured them in. Something that contained no possibility of danger. Theo unshouldered the pack and started working at the laces of his boots.

"We shouldn't stop for long," he said. "Wash up, eat, keep moving."

Cora had stolen an entire loaf of bread from the table. Ren hadn't noticed that during their escape, but now she whispered her thanks to their dead friend. It was a complicated feeling, though, as she unraveled all that had happened. Learning about the devorium led to the most disturbing question.

"Why didn't she use it to save them? Timmons or Avy?"

Theo was taking off his shirt and pants to get in the pool for a wash.

"I think she confessed that to us."

"Confessed what?"

"I have a memory of her telling us," he said, tapping the back of his skull. "It's in here somehow, even though it never happened. She confessed to keeping the devorium for herself. She said she didn't know what would happen, so she chose not to use it to save Timmons. I don't agree with her decision, but it doesn't matter now. She died getting us out of there."

She died because I decided to save you instead, Ren thought. Instinct had taken over. She liked Cora more than Theo. Ren respected any girl who was so similar to her, who'd ground her way through Balmerick to earn a brighter future. But Theo was her path forward. It was a selfish decision, prodded on by preservation. How many times would she have to make that decision to keep rising, to keep surviving? The guilt settled on her shoulders like a weighted cloak.

It took a few minutes for Ren to set those feelings aside. Compartmentalize. She needed to place those thoughts in a small box for later, leave them there, and focus on what actually mattered. Survival. She turned her attention back to Theo. He was waist-deep in the pool, using his hands to scrub at bare shoulders and under his arms. They had no soap, but a little water would go a long way to feeling refreshed. They'd been on the move for half a day. Ren waited until she caught his eye.

"What?"

"I was getting brief flashbacks of that dance you did."

He managed to smile. "Pretty sure whatever you're think-ing about involves exerting energy, which we have precious little of."

She raised one eyebrow. "Very well. You win the prize for

most responsible boy. Let's sort through the pack and figure out what to do next."

Ren opened their lonely satchel. Cora's devorium was there. It looked like it had been run over by a carriage. The amber light was gone now, leaving a patterned discoloration. It was still warm to the touch. She shuffled it aside, reaching for the item she'd placed in the bag.

"Well, that's not good."

Her mother's bracelet. She held it up to the light. The dragon-forged veins were a dulled color. Ren slid it onto her wrist and attempted the simplest spell she knew. There was a sharp fizzle as the magic sputtered and failed. That earned Theo's undivided attention.

"Did you just mess up a spell? Did I just bear witness to history?"

"No, you prat." Ren held up the bracelet. "Cora's devorium drained the magic from it. They must have been touching inside the bag when she activated the spell. There's nothing left. All the ockleys I'd stored in there were burned out."

Theo pointed to the wand hanging from her belt loop.

"What about that one?"

"I've got . . . maybe twenty ockleys? I stored most of my allotment in my mother's bracelet. How do things keep getting worse? If we survive, I'll never spend another day in the woods."

She'd been keeping such a close count. If the bracelet hadn't been drained, she'd have had more than enough for a quick duel. Now all they really had were Theo's vessels. At least five hundred ockleys, if her count was right, but she could offer only a few paltry spells. That would be just fine if this ended up being nothing more than an uneventful hike. Not so well if either of their hunters caught them.

Ren dug through the knapsack and pulled out her stolen way candle. In the front pouch she found the earring that Timmons had kept from the start. She slipped her own earring out and replaced it with the humming-sword bird. It dangled for a moment, turning slowly, until a faint voice emanated.

"Welcome, welcome, welcome. This next one is a timeless tune. You'll recognize it. . . ."

Ren looked at Theo before unhooking it. "I think we have two options. Put your clothes back on. I'm not going to mess up details because you're being promiscuous."

That earned another laugh. Ren was trying to keep the mood light. The rest of their day would be gritted teeth and straining muscles and staring death right in the eye. Ren knew they both needed these moments to get them through what was coming. Theo dressed as she washed the dirt from her own hands and feet. As he buttoned up his shirt, she broke down the situation.

"First option is to keep going. At least three full days of hiking. We've got a breath lord trailing us with a tracking hound. We have no idea if they've got other contacts out here or other farmers who are loyal to them. We have no idea if they've got a supply of waxway candles that might let them jump ahead of us to cut off our escape. But one thing we do know is that they'll know all of this territory better than we will. If we keep moving, there's a decent chance we stay ahead of them and Clyde, but it's far from a guarantee."

He nodded. "Three days is a long time to keep up this pace."

"The other option is to walk as far as we can tonight," Ren

explained. "No stopping. No breaks. We find a spot that's defensible. Choke points and wards and all of that. Once we're bunkered in, we light the way candle. It's the standard size. That means it will take at least three hours to burn all the way down. Which also means that all we have to do is stay alive for three hours. That's a lot easier than three full days. And then we port back to Balmerick."

She saw a trace of fear in his eyes. Their last trip through the waxways had been the cause of all of this. Lost in the woods, hunted by a friend-turned-revenant. It took a moment for Theo to steel himself to the possibility that they'd need to travel through those dark passages again.

"You're sure we can port that far?" he asked. "Safely?"

Ren held up the earring. "If this is clear enough and loud enough, I think we'll be in range. And we'll follow the proper methodology. None of the usual shortcuts. No borrowed lights. No early snuffs. We won't take any of those risks this time. We light this candle ourselves. We meditate and focus the entire time it burns down. And we let it burn all the way through, instead of dousing it before its ready. I promise you, Theo, we'll do it the right way. The safe way."

Theo was nodding. It was the affirmation he needed.

"Besides," Ren said, saving her best card for last, "I have a secret I forgot about."

She reached into the small pocket on the front of her plaid jacket. She hadn't mentioned it to the others. It felt like offering a false hope. Her palm spread. Five blades of faded grass. Theo lifted one of those perfect eyebrows.

"Do I have to ask, or are you just going to explain it?"

"It's more fun when you ask."

He sighed. "All right. What are those?"

"Each of these blades of grass came from Balmerick's lower quad. That meadow right outside the portal room? I was sitting there when you walked by. Absently running my hands through the dirt and the grass. I plucked them. And then I found them in my pocket a few nights ago and realized how useful they might be."

Theo was nodding. "An actual piece of our destination. That'll be a lot stronger than the pull of a mental image. Having those will accelerate our passage through the waxways. You're right. It could definitely work."

"So, option two?"

He asked the obvious question. "What happens if they get to us before the candle burns down far enough? What if Clyde reaches us?"

Ren could only shake her head. "You have your vessels. I have a few spells. We'll just have to make sure that we make them count."

Theo looked dissatisfied by that answer. He knew what she knew. In a true duel twenty ockleys were nothing. Silence stretched between them as Theo looked deep in thought. Ren wasn't sure what else she could say. They were winding to the end of this journey. Their options were limited. It was really that simple. Either they'd survive or they wouldn't.

"What if you had more magic?" Theo asked unexpectedly.

Ren stared at him. "Please tell me you're not about to unveil some secret way of acquiring more magic that only the city's elite know about. I mean, I've heard a few theories about that, and it wouldn't even be a huge surprise if it was true, but I've been keeping track of our spells like a professional accountant this whole time. . . ."

"No, there's nothing like that." His finger absently traced the chain at his hip. His fake vessel. "We can't risk you having just three spells. If Clyde comes? Or Della's crew? We can't make a stand like that without your magic helping us."

He shook his head, golden hair tossing across his forehead. It took Ren a moment to understand what he was thinking. She hadn't suggested this option because she'd never dreamed he would entertain such a thing. A boy in Theo Brood's position would never dare. . . .

"Bond magic," he said, breathing the impossible into the air between them. "I don't . . . I don't want to frighten you away. Normally, I'd never consider such a forward gesture. And if you want the bond removed when we get safely back to Kathor, I'll understand. I just don't see any other option, Ren. If we're going to survive, I need you." He looked up. "Vega. To me."

Ren didn't have to pretend to be shocked. This was as startling as Cora's possessing a devorium. An heir of one of the greatest houses in the world was suggesting *bond* magic with *her*. Ren was well versed in the history of House Brood. She'd studied their family, and all the others, hoping to find a foothold in the greater power structure that existed in Kathor. The only recorded instance of bond magic in the entire Brood lineage had happened nearly a century ago. The Broods had fought bloody battles with the northern rebels for decades. The family used notoriously brutal tactics. The only way to heal the decades-long divide was through an arranged marriage. Olivier Brood was bonded with Anni Graylantian—a daughter of the most powerful northern farming tribe. The Broods turned around and used that marriage as leverage against the rest of the rebels, dismantling them one by one. It wasn't the most promising precedent for Ren.

Of course, there were examples of bonded couples in the other houses. But it was the kind of magic that was reserved almost exclusively for marriage partners who existed on parallel levels of power. A second son would bond with a second daughter. A Shiverian might bond with a Brood, but they'd never stoop to bond with a Swift or even an Ockley. Power did not bind itself to weakness. It was already unthinkable enough that Theo could imagine a future like that between them so soon, but would he really ignore rules that had been in place for generations?

As she looked into Theo's eyes, understanding finally broke through her faulty logic. Of course. The answer was simple. Theo was falling in *love* with her. Certainly, the desperation of their circumstances played a role, but the truth was written in his patient and watchful expression. He looked like a fretful groom, waiting at a makeshift altar.

Ren struggled to form words as Vega landed on Theo's shoulder. He crossed the distance between them, biting his lip the way he always did when he was nervous. He set one hand on the bird's talons before offering his other hand to Ren. The gesture was an intentional one. He was linking the three of them through physical touch. Creating a bridge over which the bonding magic could course. Ren's hand trembled slightly as she reached out to him.

"I see a future between us," he whispered. "If we were back in Kathor, I would never ask this of you so soon. We could walk through the Giver's Gardens. We could go out together and spend time in each other's company. I would never want to . . . force your hand. But if we are going to survive this, let's survive together."

A slow-creeping dread filled Ren. This was what she'd wanted all along. A clear foothold. A path forward. House Brood had not been her original aim. She'd intended to work with literally any other house—intended to work *against* House Brood—but now she was being offered this? An opportunity to begin her dark task from within? She would be better positioned than she could have ever hoped, but her dread had a second source.

Bond magic was no trifling thing. It would knit the two of them together. Ren had no way of knowing how intimately. Most knowledge of the practice was anecdotal. There was too much variance, historically, for anyone to predict the consequences. Would she start to fall for Theo? Would he learn some of her carefully guarded secrets? Ren's stomach turned unpleasantly at those thoughts. She forced herself to speak, even though she was gripped by uncertainty.

"Binding myself to a Brood is no small decision," she said. "Before I do this, I need your word, Theo. I need to know that you meant what you said before."

He frowned. "About what?"

"What kind of Brood do you want to be? I cannot stand the thought of being bound to someone who doesn't have a care for others. I've . . . I've read all about the Canal Riots, Theo. I know the kind of men your father and your grandfather are. The kind of legacies they've left behind. I know how easy it would be for you to slip into their shoes and walk the same paths that they have. I need to know that you mean what you said about changing that legacy."

He shook his head, adamant. "I am not my father. I promise you that."

Ren wanted to point out that he could not truly promise her anything. It was likely that Landwin Brood would have the final say on who Theo became. It was even possible his father would demand they sever their bond when they returned to Kathor. A procedure like that was expensive—and dangerous—but not beyond the scope of House Brood's capabilities. Ren stood there, weighing her options, and realized her fears were small compared with all the potential rewards.

Theo was literally offering her the impossible. She had to take it.

"Yes," Ren whispered. "A hundred times, yes."

He tightened his grip on her hand.

"Breath to breath. What I have, I give you."

It was an old Tusk saying. The intentionality of his words wove into the magic. The spell curled briefly around her wrist like an invisible bracelet. Theo's fingers flexed beneath hers. She was standing there, wondering if it had worked, when Vega's existence poured through her mind. She could sense the deep pulse of magic. The brooding consciousness of the stone bird. On the other side of that consciousness Ren could feel Theo. It was like the first wafting scent of a garden that had been made just for her. She found herself frightened by how pleasant and alluring it was to her senses.

It was a relief—and a distraction—when the spells arrived. Everything Theo had stored inside of Vega over the years. Ren felt that knowledge clicking into place in her own mind. She looked up at him. It was such an intimate gesture. The hairs on Theo's arms had risen, and she knew just how vulnerable he must feel. He'd offered her something incredibly personal.

Ren tried to keep the mood light. "You know, they say the true test of a proper wizard's arsenal—"

"Is whether or not he has Evert's basic principles stored and stacked. You know you're not the only one who reads books, right? I've got all of those spells memorized. Trust me."

She laughed as Theo shouldered their pack.

"We need to keep moving."

He said those words as if the most significant thing in the world hadn't just occurred. Before he could turn, she caught him by the collar. Her hands took action before her mind could even confirm the thought. When he'd spoken of a future, this was the sort of thing he'd meant. Now she'd perform the expected steps. She drew him into a brief kiss. When she slid away, Theo's eyes were closed and his lips were still slightly parted.

"Priorities," she reminded him. "Let's go home."

Vega fluttered into the air before setting back down on Ren's shoulder. A little heavy, but the magic she felt waiting for her within the stone creature more than made up for that. Ren's plans were slowly altering course. Now she had several viable paths forward. Some more glittering than others. All she had to do was get back to Balmerick. As they walked, her mind honed to a fine point, focusing entirely on that goal—and that goal alone. The first step was to make a plan.

"If Clyde catches us, I have an idea," she said. "I've been thinking about our forced memories. The figure that was in my dreams—and Cora's dreams—but not in yours. I'm pretty sure I figured out why that would happen. And if I'm right, it means we can beat him."

And I'm always right, she thought.

39

The afternoon breathed a welcome warmth through the forest.

Ren and Theo took off their outerwear, tying it around their waists, as they walked. The hound's barking had stopped. Ren wished its absence made her feel any safer. If anything, it meant they had no way of calibrating how much of a lead they still had on Della's crew. And there was an odd stillness in the air too. As if the forest were holding its breath until they'd passed. Ren thought it was inevitable that they'd have to face someone when they made their final stand. She just wished she knew which hunter would reach them first.

Evening saw them halfway to the valley below. Theo wisely corrected their course, however, as the sun started to set.

"If we're porting to the Heights, we'll want to maintain a similar elevation."

Ren nodded. It was one of the few details that had slipped her mind.

"You're right. We're already asking the magic to send us a

long way in one direction. Forcing it to turn at a right angle, at the very last moment, poses a challenge."

Instead of down, they started hiking across. Watcher Mountain loomed on their right like a dark and solid shadow. Heavy cloud cover blotted out the light of the stars. In that darkness they were forced to slow their steady pace. At least there were proper trails on this side of the mountain. A good sign that they'd entered more settled territory. Ren wouldn't have minded crossing paths with a pioneer, though she'd felt the same hopefulness about spotting Della's farm. There was no guarantee anyone would help them this far away from proper civilization.

Exhaustion crept in as they trudged through the dark. Theo kept talking, an effort to distract them both from the lack of sleep. ". . . they have the best desserts there. It's down by the wharf on the corner. The building with that livestone pig out front. The pies are as big as your head. Nothing up in the Heights is even close to that quality."

"Mm-hmm," Ren mumbled.

"That pig is an odd statue. Did you know that no one knows who made him?"

"Oh?"

"Anonymous. Every other livestone statue traces back to a famous artist. Some are miscredited, of course, but every single one is *claimed*. No one ever claimed the pig. He's useful, though. Back during the War of Neighbors, he's the one who sniffed out an assassin that burrowed under the viceroy's house. Saved by a pig. They never publicize stories like that, though."

It was all Ren could do to keep stumbling on. They were on

a wide path with level footing, and if not for that, she'd have already asked Theo to stop and rest.

". . . but the first thing we'll do is visit the family estate. My mother will want to meet you. It's beautiful there. She'll want to show you the gardens. Her pride and joy. She's been curating them since they got married. The hounds will be there too. Fisk and Silver and Roland. They're all old as dirt. . . ."

Ren stopped walking. It took Theo a few seconds to notice. His boots kept crunching down the stone path, his voice barely loud enough to reach her. He was describing his favorite tree on the family estate. Like nothing strange had happened. Pretending that what he was saying was completely normal. Ren's mind kept turning over the same haunting detail. Like a stone that she knew a snake was hiding beneath. But she could not stop her hands from reaching out. Could not stop herself from lifting it up to see what horror would spring out. Theo had stopped to look back at her. There was an unexpected *presence* between them now. Ren sensed a distant nervousness.

I can feel his emotions, she realized. *Which means he can probably feel some of mine?*

"Ren? Do you need to stop for a rest?"

"What did you say your dog's name is?"

"Fisk?"

"The others."

"Silver and Roland."

She was thankful for the dark. It hid the murderous look on her face.

"Roland?"

He nodded at that. "Strange name for a dog. I don't know. My father picked it."

"Your father named him? When?"

Theo's head tilted. She could tell he thought these questions were strange. Ren did not care. She'd never needed to know something more in her entire life. "Well, I was pretty young. . . ."

"How old?"

Theo shrugged in the dark. "Nine or ten? He was my first pup. Not that our family really treat them like pets. More hunting hounds than anything. I'll never forget the time—"

"Stop talking, Theo. Please stop talking."

Her hands were shaking violently. All the years of anger coiled to life inside of her. It took every ounce of control to batter that forming monster back inside the gates, to slam the mental doors shut on its clawed fingers. She knew if she could not shut it out, someone was likely to get hurt. And that someone would be Theo.

Her tone had raised an alarm for him. He knew something was wrong and now he kept silent, wondering what misstep he'd made. The truth was that he didn't have any idea. He could not possibly fathom the depths of her fury. Ren breathed in and out until her hands steadied. She altered the course of her anger, channeling it in a more logical direction.

"I'm just . . . trying to understand. You're talking about your favorite bakeries. Restaurants down by the wharf. And now we're planning for me to meet your mother when we get home? Is that really the first thing that you think deserves your attention?"

Theo did not answer. He was smart enough to hold his tongue.

Roland. His father named a dog Roland. After my father's death . . . the heartless bastard . . .

"Because I imagined the first thing you'd want to do is walk into that teahouse," she said. "Help them clear away the wreckage. Take care of their expenses. Find out the names of everyone who was rushed into the hospital that night. Go and see if there's any help they need. Some of them will have been fired, if they're not in a union. It happens all the time. Maybe that's the first thing you should do, Theo. See if they need your help. If they want your help. And you could go talk to the three musicians that you stole the seventeen-string from. Maybe you could replace their instrument. If I were you, those would be the *first things* that I would be dreaming of doing."

Theo was nodding to himself as Ren's mind kept digging up other graves. She'd carefully redirected her anger, made it more logical sounding, but she couldn't get rid of the image in her mind. Some tongue-lolling hound on the Broods' family estate bearing the name Roland. *My father's name.* No doubt it was a slice of gallows humor. Something for Landwin Brood to privately smile about. A reminder that he'd won in the end. He'd crushed the fool who'd dared stand in his way.

The thought made Ren want to set the entire world on fire.

"You're right," Theo whispered. "Atonement first. I will make all of that right. And I will do that the moment I step foot in the city. You have my word."

For the first time Ren saw the road that was waiting for them. Their bond would secure her position—even if his father contested the decision. It would also complicate her angle of attack. Theo was both the bridge and the obstacle to all her plans now. She'd made a promise to herself. In those quiet and sleepless hours after her father's death, she'd vowed to punish the men and women who had his blood on their hands. She repeated that silent promise now. Twice. A third time. Until the thought had the unmistakable shape of prophecy to it.

Landwin Brood will die. His entire house will burn. And I will be the one who sets it aflame.

"Good," Ren said to Theo in a hollow voice. "I will hold you to your word."

They walked on in silence. Ren actually pitied him. He had no idea what she intended. No clue that he was now the key that would open the door and let the monster inside of his family's house. As their footsteps carried them down the darkling path, Ren's breathing steadied. Her future walked in step beside her—handsome and quiet and utterly unaware.

40

The bridge was perfect, unexpected.

Ren wasn't sure who'd built it, but she whispered her silent thanks to them. A single path wound around a jutting formation of rocks before curling back toward the mouth of the waiting bridge. It was wide enough for a very careful carriage driver. The sides of the bridge were shoulder high, designed with a pattern of hand-sized holes to keep the wood from taking on too much water. Beneath ran some kind of gorge. Ren didn't think the creeks could rise this high, but during a rainy season, she guessed the land would grow boggy enough to be unpassable without a bridge. It was possible Della's outfit had built it to transport their goods to the city. No matter its history, they couldn't have asked for a better place to make their final stand.

"You think it will work?" Theo asked.

"Narrow entry," she said. "Upper ground. No access from below. The only visible spot for someone to port to is that bare patch of grass. The path takes them directly through where we'd be setting up on the bridge. We can always cast a spell to ward against that. Which means there's no way to get behind us . . ."

He was nodding. "It's perfect. Light the candle."

Ren slipped the earring on one more time. She heard a brief strum from a three-string, a voice matching the rhythm easily, and it was a fine-sounding confirmation. "We're in range."

The two of them walked out to the heart of the bridge. Theo ferried a number of stones from the embankment to surround the candle, hoping to keep it upright even if movement jostled the bridge. Ren could tell the structure was old, but it was sturdy enough not to cause concern. Once the candle was firmly fixed in its makeshift keep, both of them summoned flame. With matching motions, they lit the waiting wick. The fire caught and Ren started her mental countdown.

"Now we set the wards," she said.

It was a bit strange to cycle through Theo's inventory. Not quite as expansive as her own, and arranged in a different order. It was like performing research in someone else's library and hoping the same books were all there. She'd have to get used to the feeling.

"Antiprojectile. Three layers. Let's put a fire resistance on the wood," she said. "Do you happen to have the momentum reduction charm?"

Theo shook his head.

"Maybe just a searing barrier, then? I don't want someone charging through and getting to us before we have a chance to hit them with a few spells. But let's make sure we avoid oversaturating the air with them. Staggering the layers a few paces should be enough."

It took time to cast spell after spell along the entryway of the bridge. Theo cast a movement charm farther down the path, promising that he'd adjusted the tolling to be quieter this time around. After they'd rehearsed the rest of the plan, there was nothing to do but set their pack out and lie down. The bridge's half-rotted wood wasn't the most comfortable bedding, but Ren was pretty sure she could have slept dangling from a wyvern's claws. Theo agreed to take the first watch.

"May it be boring and without consequence," she whispered, turning onto her side.

Sleep had been gently tugging at her tired limbs for two days now. She was swept into a dreamless state as soon as her head touched the satchel. It felt like she was awoken mere moments later, but when she looked up, dawn's quiet fingers were threading through the sky.

Theo was asleep beside her. Ren sat up in alarm. Her entire body protested. Her calves ached and her back was stiff. She shoved up to her feet. A glance into the valley showed no signs of their pursuers. Her mouth had gone dry. She realized she hadn't been drinking nearly enough water. Ren backtracked to Theo's side and did her best to slip out the canteen without waking him. He looked far more innocent in sleep. It was the eyes that made him a Brood. Cold and calculating. Eyes that had likely witnessed all his family's secrets. The details that the rest of the world might never know.

She was taking another swig when Theo's bell tolled. It was barely a whisper, not even loud enough to stir him from sleep. She tapped the toe of his boot before striding forward to get a look at what was coming. A glance showed the waxway candle had a little less than an hour left. Ren knew they could always extinguish the flame early—before it burned all the way down—but that risked exposing them in the waxways. They needed to buy as much time as possible.

"Wake up, Theo. Someone's here."

There was movement down on the path. The sides of the bridge were raised and slatted. Enough to catch glimpses of something but not enough to make out what. About a minute later the figure came around the corner: Della's hound.

"That's not good."

Ren had been hoping for Clyde. This complicated matters. They both watched as the dog's eyes caught up with his nose. He stared across the bridge, head tilting briefly, and then started to howl. Theo stood. He eyed the candle before looking at Ren.

"It's too soon. We need more time."

"I know."

The creature kept on like that, baying loud enough to wake up the entire mountain. It reminded Ren of the old hellhound myths. Dogs that could follow the scent of their prey even if their quarry traveled through the waxways. All the hairs on her arms stood on end when the hound fell silent. Ren's fingers tightened around her wand. Someone else was coming up the rise, led there by the noise.

The Mackie brothers.

Ren's real memories only featured them in jest. Both men had been mentioned a few times by Della and Holt. But the set of faded memories rattling around the back of her mind showed both of them scarfing down food at the table. She could also see the passive expressions on their faces as they dragged Ren to a shed to be tortured. They weren't nearly as muscled as Avy, but both of them were wide as doors, and there was a certain violence written in the way they walked. She and Theo took up their stances as the brothers strode to the very edge of their bridge.

One leaned down and picked up a rock. He threw it with a casual flick of his wrist, like a boy skipping a stone in a creek. They all watched as it caught in midair, spinning around, before falling harmlessly to the ground. The two of them exchanged a glance.

"Clever little spells."

The other one craned his neck. Ren tried to adjust, positioning herself so that she was blocking the way candle, but she moved a second too late. Their intentions were obvious.

"Looks like you've got half an hour left. Really think you can hold us off for that long?"

Ren's jaw tightened. "Why don't you try us?"

He reached his hand out, probing their defenses. There was a sharp sizzle and he pulled it back. He set the two fingers in his mouth like a child sucking a thumb, then smiled at her.

"Don't worry. We will put the two of you to the test. Hunt, go get Della."

The dog bolted back down the hillside. Ren and Theo could only watch as the creature went searching for his master. They'd return before long. It was one thing to hold off a pair of charging brutes like the Mackies. Quite another thing to hold them off while they were supported by the spellwork of other wizards. Besides, Ren had no idea how many people Della and Holt had recruited to their cause. It could just be their hired hands—or it could be neighbors from the surrounding region.

"What do we do?" Theo whispered. His eyes darted back to the candle. "We have to hold them off. For at least half an hour."

Ren watched the Mackie brothers settle in, leaning against the natural stone formations, every promise of violence in their eyes. It all depended on how soon Della arrived. If worst came to worst, they could destroy the bridge and keep running. That would mean leaving behind their way candle, though. Losing the one advantage they had in their possession.

"We could fight," Ren said, thinking out loud. "Before they have reinforcements."

Theo weighed that. "We'll be on the wrong side of our own wards."

"But they wouldn't expect it," she whispered. "And I doubt they know much magic."

Theo looked thoughtful, weighing all the risks, when the larger Mackie brother stood. Both boys straightened. It was like watching a hound catch a scent. The way the fur on the ridge of its back rises and its body goes perfectly still. Both of them stared down the length of the bridge.

"What are they doing?" Ren asked.

With no other warning, they started to advance. She couldn't believe what she was seeing. They picked up speed and hit the wards at a dead sprint. The magic shoved them back at first, but they kept sprinting against the grain of those spells, their shoulders lowered like battering rams into the magic. Ren could sense their wards starting to drain. She also smelled burning flesh. The magic was searing the skin along the brothers' knuckles and the bridges of their noses. It was inhuman for someone to resist that pain, but the Mackies didn't even react to it.

"How is this even possible? . . ."

Another shove back from the barrier. Still the two brothers came. Ren was watching in horror when the first Mackie brother broke through. He came tearing across, closing the distance fast. Ren saw that his eyes were half-closed.

"Drop him," she said.

Theo's blast hit first. A glancing blow to the shoulder that spun the boy around. Ren's bolt of concussive magic sent him right into the raised side of the bridge with a smack. The other brother broke through before they could turn. He learned from the first, ducking one shoulder to slip beneath Theo's spell. Ren took aim, but he was already there, jack-knifing through the air. He wrapped both arms around Theo's waist in some kind of wrestling move. The two of them went down hard, sliding dangerously close to their flickering way candle.

Vega swooped down. The stone bird struck true, one talon seizing an exposed earlobe. The Mackie brother screamed as half of his ear ripped clean away, spattering blood. It was just enough of an opening for Theo to scramble clear on his hands and knees. And that was enough of an opening for Ren to take aim.

At such a close range, her spell hit him like a strike of lightning. Her own feet slid back from the force of it. Ren's eyes widened as the magic launched him clear of the railing.

He went over the bridge with a scream.

She stared at the now-empty space, her heart pounding, and she noticed the one detail they'd missed. Something was scaling the grated side of the bridge. Carefully avoiding their wards. She saw its progress guided by a pair of blackened hands. Clyde was here.

The surviving brother was struggling back to his feet. His eyes fluttered open and shut in frightening sequence. Ren finally understood their bizarre charge. Clyde was controlling them the way that he'd controlled Cora. She'd said his power would keep growing, and clearly it had, if he could move these two around like pawns in battle.

Ren slid toward Theo as the monster appeared over the railing. Clyde looked more like the Clyde she remembered. Both of his eyes were bright blue. His lips had been restored to their rose red, and his skin had almost returned to a light tan color. Most of his hair shone brown, though there were a few burn marks running down the right half of his scalp. Dark bubbles of skin scaled his neck. Ren knew that all he needed now to complete his restoration was the two of them.

I am hungry. You are food.

He started to raise his hand toward them, but this time they had a plan.

"Now, Theo."

It all happened at once.

Vega landed on her shoulder. The remaining Mackie brother half stumbled to his feet. Ren slid forward so that she was positioned slightly in front of Theo. She needed to take the first wave of the chain magic for this to work. Theo wrapped both of his arms around her neck, making sure there was skin-to-skin contact. Ren could see the research as clear as day in the back of her mind.

Physical connection adds strength to bond magic. Often, it forces spells to amplify or merge. . . .

Clyde's spell hit her like a blast of death-woven air. She felt the bridge and the world rip out of her grasp as she was thrown once more into the memory. . . .

She found him by the bridge. It was a pretty thing, stretching halfway across to its intended partner on the other side of the canal. Her father was always busy, always moving, always talking. She loved the way he stopped dead in his tracks, though, the moment he spied her waiting. The way he set down everything in his arms to sweep her into a hug. She handed him the roll. He winked down at her. She saw the quiet pride that he felt in simply standing beside his daughter in front of all the other workers. Her final glimpse was of him walking across that bridge with the others. He held his head high. He kept his shoulders straight.

A king without a crown.

Ren sensed the dark passenger on her left. His clawed hand was set on her shoulder, drinking in her fear. Both of them watched the memory start to unravel. Her mind's effort to erase pain that it couldn't bear. Everything else came in ugly snapshots. Their screams tangling in the air. The sound of the earth breaking beneath them. Ren looked down and saw her father, bent wrongways in the belly of the canal. All the blood pouring out.

The shadowed figure was tightening his grip. Holding her there, until another voice sounded. It echoed in the memory unnaturally. Ren knew it sounded strange because it didn't belong either. She looked back. In the real memory it had always been Landwin Brood who walked forward at this point. Gilded and arrogant, his face full of faux horror. But this time Theo displaced him. Landwin's son strode forward, looking brighter than the rest of their surroundings. Golden hair the color of sunlight. Eyes like speckled forests. As he approached, the shadow at her shoulder fled.

"Come on, Ren."

Theo took her hand.

She felt herself being drawn away by his touch. The chain magic provided a path for them, as they'd known it would. And the bond magic that linked them meant they could travel it together. Ren was swept out of her worst memory and carried downstream into Theo's:

He strode out through the center of the gathered crowd. She could feel the anxiety dripping from his shoulders. The need to impress. The weight of everything he carried. Ren felt each of these emotions as if they were her own. Deep and nestled. It brought out an unexpected sympathy that she forced herself to set aside, something to be examined later, because until now she'd never felt this much empathy for him.

At his command the musicians departed from the instrument. She saw the way he grinned expectantly at the crowd. She didn't waste time watching him perform the magic again.

They had a plan. All she needed to do was execute that plan.

She broke free of Timmons's grasp on her arm. There was resistance. Moving against what had happened in the memory felt like trudging through the muck and mire of a swamp. Ren forged a path forward, though. She kept walking through the barely remembered crowd until Theo finally noticed her.

His drowning eyes lit with understanding. "Ren?"

"Come with me, Theo."

Both of them turned, looking around the sea of faces. Some were obscured. Not important enough to have carved a place in either of their memories of what had happened that night. Theo spotted their target first.

He sat on the railing, feet dangling. His collar was a little loose. A result of his time with Timmons, Ren knew. His eyes were wide and watchful. No doubt he was seeing more of the magic in the air around them, brightened by the breath he'd enjoyed earlier that night. Clyde Winters looked like he didn't have a care in the world.

She remembered what Timmons had said. That she'd been the last good thing for him. Watching him now, Ren saw that was true. He looked completely at ease. A boy who had no idea he was about to be burned from the inside out by his own magic the next day. They took up their stances and the memory flickered strangely.

This was the answer to the riddle that had been bothering Ren.

Theo couldn't recall a shadow in his vision. Not like the creeping presence in their dreams. It was such a strange inconsistency. Ren had finally realized that the revenant didn't visit this memory the way he'd visited Cora's or her own, because he already existed here. He was already invited. The creature—hiding in the depths of the real Clyde—watched them approach. Ren saw the eyes widen slightly. Clyde's hands rose in a defensive gesture.

It wasn't like changing the past. This was memory, wielded as a weapon. It was the paralytic that the revenant had been using to bind their physical bodies. Ren knew if they could be subjected to such magic, the reverse was true. The monstrous version of Clyde finally understood it had made a mistake. Predator became prey.

In the memory Clyde had no dark magic to fight back with.

In the memory he was just a boy at a party.

Ren and Theo both raised their wands.

The bridge blinked back into existence.

Only a few seconds of real time had passed.

Clyde was now frozen in place. He'd managed to leap from the railing and had approached them with every intention of sucking the marrow from their precious bones. Their combined magic had dropped him to a knee. He stared at the space between them with mindless dedication. It had worked. The chain spell's paralytic was reversed. Occupied in that other world, he was absent in this one.

Spells lit the tips of their wands.

"Now," Ren grunted. "Now we finish him."

Both of them unleashed fire spells at the same time. Their bright bolts struck his motionless chest. Ren cast another. Theo did too. By the time the pain shocked Clyde back to the present, it was already too late. Their magic bore down on him, burning away flesh, digging deeper and deeper until they could see the bright bones under his skin. Neither of them stopped casting until the creature's screams fell silent. The revenant who'd chased them across a mountain chain— who'd killed their friends—was reduced to ash and bone. Ren's chest heaved.

"We did it."

She was so relieved that she almost didn't see the other Mackie brother. He angled straight for Theo, who was turned slightly away, unaware of what was coming. No spells could work quickly enough. Ren met his lunge with one of her own. Her lowered shoulder struck the attacker's hip. It swung him off course slightly, and the knife that was about to plunge into Theo's chest bit down into his lower shoulder instead.

He let loose a scream as the surviving Mackie seized his collar, reared back, and plunged the knife toward Theo's stomach. Ren raised her horseshoe wand.

The Mackie brothers were not twins, but they died exactly the same way. Her spell spun him away from Theo with violent force. Up over the side of the bridge. There was a trailing scream and a distant crash, and then Ren dropped to her knees beside Theo. His skin looked like pale marble. Blood poured from two different wounds. A deep cut just under his right shoulder blade and a gut wound that looked slightly shallower. Her spell had kept Mackie from plunging his knife fully in, but the blood was still flowing far too fast for her to staunch it without magic. Tears streaked down Theo's dirt-smeared chin. He let out a pathetic moan.

"Ren. Help me. Ren, it hurts so much."

A string of images played through Ren's mind. One of the roads she'd imagined as they walked up to the bridge. The darkest possibility. It was second nature for Ren to prepare for every possibility. She knew if Theo died, she could still return home. They had bonded together. She could tell House Brood that the two of them had married in secret. The Broods would push back, but she could claim widowship—and eventually claim his inheritance. No witness would be able to counter her claim, because no one else had survived this journey through the woods. It would be the fastest route toward money and power. Far faster than any other path available to her . . .

But then Theo moaned again.

Some internal mechanism took control of her. The bond between them—that unfamiliar magic—flexed its newly forming muscles. She felt seized by something far larger than herself. A force that was equal parts pity and mercy and logic. She could not bear the thought of letting Theo die. Her mind shifted back into survival mode.

"Spells. I need to think. What spells?"

Blood was rushing through her splayed fingers. It soaked his entire front. His breathing was shallow and ragged. "Ren. Please. Con . . . Connery's binding. I have that one. From anatomy class."

His words set a missing piece of the puzzle down in front of her. Ideas formed around that thought. "No. Not Connery's binding. I need to use Ockley's cleansing spell first. Reduces infections. You . . . you probably have internal lacerations, so Connery's binding would just seal you up without healing what's bleeding inside. I . . . I need a sensory spell to find the torn tissue, then Hagland's quickening charm to get it regenerating. And then I'd use Connery's binding to close it all. . . ."

Theo's blood kept coloring the bridge beneath them. "All right. Do that, then. Do that."

Ren set to work. It was hard to maintain her composure, but she set aside the panic and fear that she could *feel* pulsing out from Theo—crossing their link—and focused instead on hunting for the right spells in his arsenal. She quietly found each one in the mental files, brought them to the forefront of her thoughts, and began casting. Theo was struggling to keep his eyes focused on her.

"Stay with me," she hissed. "Stay with me, Theo."

Ren knew it was not the last time that she would feel the weight of Cora's absence. Her own anatomical magic lacked nuance and skill. When Cora had used these spells, she had done so with all the touch and grace of an artist. Ren's attempts were elementary by comparison. Someone who knew the colors but not how to hold the brush or where to paint them. Her cleansing spell flashed out with such force that it briefly shook Theo's entire body. A large enough jolt that his teeth clacked together. He let loose another miserable groan.

"Sorry . . . sorry. Just stay with me, Theo."

She pressed on, knowing it would only get worse. The sensory magic was less invasive, but her first attempt at the spell yielded nothing. *Take a deep breath,* she coached herself. *Try again.* The second effort worked. The damaged tissue drew the magic's attention. Her spell tethered to those locations and she could feel them like invisible threads, stretching from her fingertips to the places inside of him that had been damaged.

"Now Hagland's quickening . . ."

Again her spell rushed forward with too much strength. Theo actually cried out, and she had to pin his good shoulder down with a knee to keep him from messing up the magic. He let out a guttural scream. She knew that his tissue was knitting together in quick and painful bursts. An accelerated healing that would feel a lot like someone's fingers were jammed inside his abdomen.

Theo breathed sharply in, and then his body went still. Too still. Ren saw that he was almost translucent. Halfway to becoming a ghost. "No. *Hold on*, Theo."

Her stitching was piss poor, but the wounds closed. The

tissue within was starting to regenerate. It took staggering to her feet to realize just how much blood Theo had lost. Seeing all of it slicking the wooden panels of the bridge, a new panic seized Ren. What if she'd been too slow? What if he actually died? Her eyes flicked back to the way candle.

The timing was nearly flawless. She could hear the sound of barking in the distance. Della and her crew were too late. It took grunting effort, but she sat Theo up and dragged him closer to the candle. His eyes blinked open once, only to close again. His lips were turning blue.

"Don't die, Theo. Please don't die."

It took all her effort to prop him up and position herself so she was sitting behind him. She let his head settle into the nest of her shoulder, reaching around to hold his gut wound with gentle pressure. Blood matted the front of his shirt. There was still one piece of magic to get right.

Ren reached into her pocket for the blades of grass. She set one of the blades over the flickering flame of the candle. It started to burn and smoke. The second blade was tucked in the very center of her palm. Ren held the image of Balmerick firmly in her mind.

Theo had stopped moving. Ren tightened her grip protectively around him. There was more barking. Closer and closer. Figures were moving up the road that led to the bridge. Ren sat there patiently until the magic of the waxways snatched them both.

41

The entire lower quad heard Ren's cries for help.

It was still break. The campus was mostly empty, but a few professors and doctoral students heard the noise and came thundering down the marble steps of nearby buildings. A search party had gone out for Theo Brood and Clyde Winters several days ago. It had taken a little longer to realize that Ren Monroe, Timmons Devine, Avy Williams, and Cora Marrin were also missing.

Witnesses and schedules and friends had corroborated the theory that they'd all been heading for the waxway room before vanishing. Investigators had arrived and known immediately that something had gone wrong. One of the deans had suggested combining their estimated distances and creating a search radius that way. The building had been temporarily boarded up.

Now figures rushed across the manicured lawns. Ren could only imagine how she looked clutching pale Theo in her blood-stained arms. "Get the medics, now!"

Theo was gently lifted from her. A professor led her into a waiting room as word of the incident spread. Investigators were quick to interview Ren. She walked them back through the entire story of what had happened. From the malfunctioning portal all the way to the standoff on the bridge. The emotional deaths of her friends. Discovering a farm that trafficked in the breath. She took great care to provide full details about Theo's affections for her, making sure to mention their new bond magic several times. She still didn't know if he would actually survive. If someone tried to deny the connection later, she wanted to get two steps ahead on countering those accusations. The investigators wrote down every single word in their official records.

Ren was permitted to take a bath after they left. She cleaned up, changed into new clothes, then stood vigil outside the operatory where Theo had been taken. Rumors were making their way around campus already. Whispers of what had happened. People were rightfully claiming that she had saved Theo's life. A chariot arrived outside the medical building. She'd been expecting her mother. It shouldn't have been a surprise to see Landwin Brood marching across the quad instead.

Theo's father was an older version of him. A little sharper at the chin, a little more lifeless around the eyes. He had not changed much since the first time Ren saw him. A decade-long hatred rumbled to life in Ren's chest. She saw a series of ugly little snapshots. Landwin at the canal railing, glorying in the sight of her father's broken body below. The smug smile he'd worn at the funeral the following week. She even imagined the dog, somewhere on his estate, bearing her father's name as some final insult. She took all that hatred and set it aside in a box. She would need it later to power her efforts. But this would be a long game. Her first move mattered.

Ren dipped into a respectable bow. A moment later she

straightened her shoulders. "A Monroe always stands tall," her father used to say. Her voice didn't tremble.

"You're Theo's father?"

He nodded. "I am."

"We have much to discuss, sir."

He looked at her with pure distaste. "You're the girl who was with him. The other survivor. Look, I'm grateful he's alive. I'm told you performed some basic magic to help him. But I hope you'll understand if my priority right now is my son. I do not have time for side discussions."

It was the kind of dismissal she'd expected from him. He offered a final look before circling around her, aiming for the hallway that led to where Theo was being treated. Ren considered letting him go, keeping her head down for now, but she'd waited too long for this moment to let it pass by.

"Not even a discussion with your future daughter-in-law?"

Those words wiped the smugness off his face. She enjoyed the unsettled expression that crept up instead. "Excuse me?"

"Oh. My sincerest apologies. I thought you already knew."

It was a pleasure to drink in his confusion. She could see him struggling to form a response. Ren held out one arm. There was a distant scrape of stone wings. Vega had nestled out of sight, up in the rafters of the great domed ceiling. She landed now with a flourish on Ren's wrist.

"Theo and I are bonded."

Landwin Brood seemed to see her for the first time. His eyes narrowed at the sight of Vega perched so comfortably there. She knew he was an intelligent man. Smart enough to see what his son had done, and all the implications it had on their future. Ren drove the dagger home.

"It will be such an honor to join your house."

He took a single, threatening step forward, but his words were cut off by the groan of a door. Down the hallway, one of the medics emerged. Ren saw an afterglow of golden light from whatever spells they were performing to keep Theo alive. A pair of surgeons followed. The witnesses forced Landwin to bite his tongue. The brief flash of anger in his expression was smoothed over by that same polish Theo had summoned so many times in the woods.

"Your son is awake," the medic called. "If you want to see him."

Landwin spared Ren a look. "I can't wait to learn more about you."

And then he was walking. The surgeons stepped aside. He entered that magic-brightened room and slammed the door shut behind him. The others took that as their cue to leave as well.

"Good work," the medic said to Ren. "It wasn't pretty magic, but it saved his life."

Ren nodded. She was still too shaken up by her first encounter with Landwin Brood to respond. She stood there, staring at the closed door to the operatory, until pain laced down her forearm. Vega's claws had dug into her skin. A spot of blood showed through the fabric. Ren watched the darkness spread in a circle.

It was a good reminder. There would be blood. She may have struck first, but Landwin Brood was well protected. His house was flush with assets. Destroying him would require great sacrifice. It already had. After a moment she shooed Vega into the air.

Carefully she rolled both sleeves.

"Learn everything you can about me, Landwin Brood. It won't save you."

42

R en was pacing her mother's apartment.

A letter had just arrived, bearing the Broods' family seal. Her mother had made tea. She'd returned to the corner of their living room and was sipping silently. Ren's own cup had stopped steaming some time ago. Her mother did not push her to open the letter, though Ren could see her peeking out from behind the book she was reading every few seconds.

It had been three days since they'd survived the fight on the bridge and ported back to Balmerick. Ren had been denied all access to Theo. Even if the explanation was reasonable— the Broods' house doctor ordered no visitors for the sake of proper rest—Ren knew the real reason they wanted Theo isolated. The Broods wanted time to convince him of his mistake. While their bond was fresh and new and relatively painless to have removed. They knew it would only grow stronger with time.

She'd allowed herself to believe they were failing, because she could *feel* Theo's mounting frustration. It was a sixth sense that her body was trying to process and accept as a normal, functioning piece of who she was. A sound just out of earshot. A flicker of movement at the corner of the eye that vanished if you turned to look directly at it. She'd felt brief flashes of impatience and exhaustion and heartache. But in the hours before the letter arrived, she'd felt a single emotion humming across their link: dread.

What did the letter say? What was Theo so fearful of that it dominated his every thought? Ren continued pacing until it became unbearable. She let out a breath, snatched the letter from the table, and ripped open the seal. The letter unfolded. Her eyes skipped down the page. It was an old study trick that allowed her to read faster than most students. Pinpointing key phrases and allowing her mind to fill in the rest with logical guesswork.

"And?" her mother asked. "What does it say?"

"It's an invitation."

Now Ren understood Theo's dread. She'd drawn first blood. Maybe she'd been too bold in her first meeting with Landwin Brood. Now he struck back. It was not the death blow she'd expected. He was not forcing his son to sever their bond. It was far more cunning. Ren knew that it was her fault. She'd made a mistake.

"They've scheduled Clyde's funeral."

"The Winters boy?"

"Yes. It's at the same time as Timmons' and the others'."

Her one request. She'd asked that the two funerals be scheduled at separate times, hoping to be present for both. Landwin must have learned of that request, and now he wielded it against her. Clyde's funeral would be in Safe Harbor's great monastery—located in the Upper Quarter—as befitted his station. It would also be the first event that Theo publicly attended since returning home. An event he was personally inviting her to attend. *I would have you at my side while I mourn my best friend*, the letter read.

"They thrive on cruelty," her mother noted.

"It is cruel," Ren agreed. "And rather clever."

The other funeral would be in honor of Avy Williams, Cora Marrin, and Timmons Devine. Having no bodies to bury, the families wished to scatter symbolic ashes at sea. The service would be in the Seaside Chapel, down on the beaches that were due south of their city's famed harbor. The two locations couldn't have been farther apart.

Landwin had arranged it this way deliberately, knowing Ren would not be able to attend both. If she attended the Seaside service, she would effectively be rejecting Theo's invitation. It was an effort by the Broods to plant doubt in Theo's mind. *Look at how she failed to support you in a time of need. She might be your priority, but you are not her priority, are you?* Even if Theo dismissed their claims, it would be a starting point for undermining their bond.

The alternative was to miss her best friend's funeral. As well as the funerals of Cora and Avy. Ren knew how much she owed them all. She was here because they were not. It would dishonor their lives, their sacrifices. Her presence at their funeral was the least she owed them.

Landwin was presenting Ren with a challenge, and there was nothing she liked more than a challenge. She set the letter aside and looked at her mother.

"I think I know what to do."

□ □ □

On the morning of the funerals, she stood before the mirror in her mother's room and began wrapping herself in the finest mourning dress she'd been able to find. It was a lot like the outfit Timmons had worn to Theo's party. Designed so that the shoulders looked more like armor than fabric. She'd also purchased a delicate black hat, from which a veil draped down to partially obscure her face. Ren slid her mother's bracelet over her wrist and adjusted the sleeves.

Her mother was waiting in the kitchen, fussing over a cup of tea. Ren halted at the sight of her. She wore the same black dress she'd worn all those years ago. It shouldn't have been a surprise. She was the same size and height, had maintained the same figure. But the image of her now—and the memory of her then—drew Ren across the room. She wrapped her mother in a hug from behind. She wanted to tell her that vengeance was coming. The man who'd ruined their lives was finally within reach. It would not be long now. Where the city's justice had failed them, Ren would not. Instead of speaking those prophecies aloud, she kissed her mother's cheek and handed her a candle.

"I'll see you in a few hours."

It was well before sunrise.

Ren set out for a funeral.

Ren knew she'd set foot in a much wealthier neighborhood when she spotted the livestone gargoyle prowling the roof of Safe Harbor's monastery. There was only enough light to make out the slumped shoulders and the pointed ears as the creature climbed the bell tower to get a better view of the city it had been charged to protect.

Except for the priests, Ren was the first one to arrive. Candles glinted beneath sprawling stained-glass windows. There was a rendering of a historical event in each one. She saw the first Delveans who'd sailed to this continent in search of the land where dragons lived. It was the only image that offered a nod to Old Delvea. Everything else centered on the founding of their pristine city. She spied the four famous ships that had sailed up the coast. Another window showed the discovery of the underground magical vein that had made Kathor such a powerhouse. There were depictions of crucial battles, duels, and inventions. Even the Broods' arranged marriage with the Graylantians—which effectively sealed the Accords—was rendered within the beautiful glass tapestry. Based on the stories they'd chosen—the grand scope of man-made heroism—Ren guessed this was where the wealthiest people in the city came to worship themselves on holy days.

It was such a massive building that she'd only managed to walk the left wing before a priest came forward to greet her. "May I help you, dear?"

"I'm here to pray," she said. "Before the funeral."

He nodded solemnly in return. "There are candles available in the front alcove, if you'd like to light one in honor of our dear Clyde. He was such a talented young man. Always left an impression on the people he met. How did you know him?"

Always left an impression, she thought. *Yes, I daresay I'll never forget him.*

"We were classmates. A candle. I think I would like that. If you'd excuse me."

He swept away. Ren followed his gesture to the glinting display, tucked in a room adjacent to the main hall. There were candles already lit by other parishioners, many that had burned through the night. Some to honor the lost. Others to mark new beginnings. Ren had never found any comfort in the practice, but it did provide the perfect cover for her own plan.

She waited until the nearest priest's back was turned, then removed a waxway candle from inside her dress. She tipped the wick to the nearest flame. It caught, dancing across in a brief slash of light. Ren moved deeper into the recess. Hidden in the very back corner was a looming door that led to the women's restroom.

Ren considered the space. There was a window with a deep sill. She eyed each of the stalls, every nook and corner, before deciding the window was the best location. She positioned the candle there, trying to make it look like an intentional decoration. When she was satisfied with her work, she returned to the entrance and carefully memorized the details of the room.

For visualization. If you cannot see yourself somewhere, you cannot possibly travel there.

Back in the main hall, attendees trickled through the front doors. It was still early. Ren took her seat, expression hidden behind her veil, and waited for the Broods to arrive. There was a gloomy shuffle near the front of the cathedral as a group of paladins ferried Clyde's casket to the front platform. Ren knew there was no body inside. She and Theo had left his corpse on the bridge. Burned beyond recognition. The thought still sent a shiver down her neck.

Some of the city's wealthiest citizens began making their way down the aisles. The Graylantians came first. Every single one of them went to light candles in the same alcove Ren had visited. She could hear them actually whispering mourning prayers as they passed where she sat. Ren knew they'd originated north of Kathor. They were one of the first Delvean families to heavily intermarry with the Tusk. But it was their pact with the Broods that had elevated them to royalty at the turn of the century. At least they hadn't completely abandoned the more religious side of their ancestry.

She spied the viceroy, flanked by guards, taking a seat in the front row. The grand emissary filed in after him. All the Shiverians came next—marked by their hawk insignias and disinterested expressions. Ren was watching another noble house make their entrance when she felt the slightest onrush of adrenaline. She knew she was not the source. It was pressing across her bond with Theo.

The Broods had arrived.

She spotted Landwin Brood leading them through the entrance. His gold hair verged on white. His suit was so crisp that it looked like it had been stitched together that day. Her vision of him at the back of the monastery briefly merged with memory. Ren remembered him at the back of her own father's funeral. She'd thought it was such a kindness that this stranger—the only stranger who'd called for help on the bridge—would attend her father's funeral. It had felt like such an honor when he stopped by her father's casket and whispered a quiet word.

Until he'd attempted to speak with her mother. She hissed a warning for him to stay back. Landwin Brood feigned surprise. He offered his sincerest condolences. Ren was so embarrassed.

Later that night her mother told her the truth. He was the man Ren's father had been fighting against. Roland Monroe's union had stifled *his* canals and *his* production. The bridge makers had visited them in the dead of night. Each one had sworn on the lives of their children: the bridge had been stable. Someone had tampered intentionally with its foundations. The collapse was no accident. Her father's death had been arranged.

Now Ren walked down the aisle of Safe Harbor's monastery and toward the man who'd authored that horrible event. He was surrounded by other Broods. His gilded wife glided alongside him, looking like she'd been summoned straight out of a painting. Theo's siblings and cousins prowled in their shadow, each one as golden as the next. Ren thought she was going to have to introduce herself to the whole family before spotting Theo.

He shouldered past the others, picking up his pace, and she felt a brief pulse across their bond. He wore a black doublet with brass buttons. It was an older fashion that might have made him look stiff if he weren't already smiling at her. Time in recovery had thinned him, drawing out the sharpness of his cheekbones and the point of his chin. Ren felt that strange pull again. Seeing his weakness drew on her strength. She wanted to throw her arms around him and tell him she was glad that he was alive, but she suspected that would be inappropriate at a funeral.

Theo apparently disagreed. He swept Ren into an unexpected hug. She let out a tight gasp before accepting the embrace, easing ever so slightly into him. Ren was just tall enough to get a glimpse over Theo's shoulder. The Brood family watched the interaction without humor. No exchanged smiles. No playful whispers about young love. She suspected it was more than just funeral decorum. Disapproval was written on each face. Ren pulled back, ignoring their glares.

"Well, that was *untoward*."

A brief grin split Theo's face. "It was a thank-you. For saving me."

"Oh that?" Ren asked. "Any sophomore student taking Introduction to Anatomy could have done the same. Not exactly rigorous spellwork."

A second grin surfaced before Theo remembered he was at a funeral. That serious demeanor settled back into his countenance. "You know that's not true. It was brilliant. The head healer was very clear in the report. I would have died if not for you. I owe you—"

A throat cleared. Landwin Brood had marched forward. He nodded once at Ren.

"I'm so glad you could join us. Theo, let's keep moving. This is a funeral *procession*, after all."

Ren noted the smugness in his voice. This had been a clear test of strength. Which funeral would she choose? Was she a pawn, to be moved on his game board, or something else? For now she let him think that he'd won by forcing her to come. She offered the expected curtsy to him and the others, then followed Theo down the main aisle. The Winters family was entering from a front vestibule. She found herself seated at the end of the third row, her shoulder pressed lightly to Theo's.

An elder cleric led the mass in singing a psalm. Ren mumbled her way through the liturgy, trying to ignore the way Landwin's voice dominated everyone else's. When they reached the time for prayer and reflection, Ren whispered to Theo, "I'll be right back. I want to light a candle."

He nodded once. She took the same path she'd taken earlier that morning, entered the same alcove, and ignored the normal prayer candles waiting there. Hidden from the main congregation, Ren walked into the prepared restroom. She glanced at the stalls, making sure there were no witnesses, then strode to the window. Her timing was nearly perfect. The way candle had burned hard and fast. Down to nearly nothing.

Ren reached out for the too-warm wax. She held an image in her mind, and when the flame died between her fingertips, she was drawn out of that monastery, across the city, and set down on a dune she'd chosen the day before. There were people gathering inside a humble chapel. Ocean waves clawed at the staggered shoreline. Ren adjusted her dress and followed the others inside. Ren's mother had saved her a seat in the second row. Ren took her place, quietly hooking an arm through her mother's, as the families of the deceased made their entrances. She'd missed the beginning of the ceremony, but not the part she cared about most.

It was strange to see their faces. Like potions that, when combined and stirred, had created the friends that Ren had lost. Avy's mother came down the aisle with her other son— Pree Williams—on her arm. She looked so thin compared with her boys, no more substantial than a whisper. Ren remembered Cora's confession, that Avy had bonded with his mother and allowed her to siphon his magic to stay alive. Rumor was that Pree had volunteered to take his brother's place. It was a taxing magic, but that didn't stop Pree from winking at Ren when he spied her at the end of the row.

Ren smiled back, but deep down she knew his life was no longer his own.

Cora's family came next. Her father had the same dark hair and olive skin as Cora. In an attempt to look dapper, he'd slicked it all back. The decision exposed a pale line at the top of his forehead, which Ren knew had been earned the same way farmers earned anything, through time and repetition. Her mother was slight of frame, hunched in on herself. Her eyes mirrored Cora's blade-sharp focus. Ren noticed she also bit her fingers in the same nervous way her daughter had. The two of them herded three children, all younger than Cora, down the row.

The next pair was the most painful to see. She'd met the Devines many times now. There was so much of Timmons in both of them. Her mother's silver-white hair was the same. Her father looked down their row with those familiar faded-blue eyes. She saw Timmons in the way that he gestured with his hand. In the way her mother leaned in to whisper something before raising the same challenging eyebrow that Timmons would have. It was like looking into a future that had been promised once and knowing the prophecy for a lie now.

"We are gathered here today to celebrate the lives of three brilliant young students. . . ."

All the same liturgy that was read for Clyde Winters was now read for them. Most Delveans did not know what to do with death. The Tusk had beliefs about the next life that offered far more comfort. Beliefs that were central tenets to how they lived in this world. Ren knew that wasn't the case for her—or for most Delveans. They'd left a lot of their religion in the old country, which meant their only comfort was in the other mourners standing in the aisles with them.

Ren cried two times during the funeral. First, when Mrs. Devine told the story of how they'd discovered their daughter's ability as an enhancer.

"My poor husband, bless him, cannot cook. He makes the effort, and that's about all he can make. Effort. And dishes, I suppose. One night, though, he made the most delicious soup I'd ever tasted. It was shocking. And then the next night, a fried fish beyond compare. It kept happening until Timmons spent the night at a friend's house. That night he served the most poorly salted rice I'd ever had the chance to meet." She laughed through her tears. "She'd been making the food taste better. Rather than hurt her father's feelings, she'd decided to help in her own way. And that was Timmons. Always lending her strength. Always making everyone else a little better."

Ren cried a second time when Cora's mother burst into tears before she could even speak her opening comments. Unable to summon eloquence, she reduced her speech to a single line.

"She was a good girl with steady hands."

Pree spoke on his brother's behalf. Telling wild stories that had the group laughing away some—but not all—of their tears. Ren looked around at that point and noted most of their peers at Balmerick weren't present. Also forced to choose by Landwin's decision, they'd gone to the monastery on the other side of town. A mark she intended to count against all of them. She settled back in her seat and followed the liturgy until her time had run out. She needed to get back.

She whispered a kiss onto her mother's cheek, then headed for the lonely alcove near the front right of the chapel. There was plenty of movement—small children ducking under pews and bored uncles pacing the back rows—so no one marked her departure. Ren found a second way candle waiting for her, set out as planned, lit that morning by her mother. An abandoned match sat beside it. Ren mimicked the motion of lighting it.

She fixed her mind on the image of that bathroom at Safe Harbor's monastery. After a long minute she closed her eyes and pressed both fingers to the waiting flame. There was a brief hiss, and then that power dragged her through space and time again.

A sharp scream shocked Ren back a few steps. It muffled quickly, but Ren spotted the source. A woman was sitting on a toilet with the door slightly ajar. She had one hand up to cover her mouth. Both of her eyes were wide as moons. She looked rather indecorous with her dress hiked up and her body twisting to keep everything covered.

"I thought I locked the door!" she exclaimed, half a whisper. "How the hell . . ."

And then she clapped the hand back over her mouth, embarrassed to have invoked the idea of hell in a place of worship. Ren averted her eyes and stifled laughter.

"My apologies," she whispered. "It was unlocked. I'll leave, though. Apologies, again."

And then she was gliding back through the alcove and into the main hall. Theo offered a look of concern. Landwin was watchful but not suspicious. She kept her head bowed, knowing there were dried tear tracks lining both cheeks. Landwin would notice she'd been crying. Theo would assume it was her reaction to what they'd endured in the mountains. It was not easy to mourn a boy who'd turned into a monster and hunted them. Ren sat there, patiently listening as Clyde's father spoke about his son's life. Her plan had worked. No one knew she'd left the monastery.

Ren's triumph was short lived. When the final speech ended, "The Winter Retreat" began to play. She felt Theo flinch to stillness at her side, clearly aware it was the song he'd played that night. The song that had started *everything*. Ren remembered dancing with Timmons before that moment. How alive she'd been. But now there were four empty caskets.

Grief finally struck. Ren wept. As the rest of the room began filing out, she stood with both hands hammered into the wooden back of the pew in front of her. Theo hovered at her side, his family waiting awkwardly at the end of the row for both of them. Ren couldn't force composure, though. She couldn't compartmentalize pain that was this large. She stood there and cried until Theo wrapped one arm around her shoulder.

"It's all my fault," she whispered. "It's all my fault. . . ."

Theo whispered reassurances, but even with their newly formed bond, he couldn't understand the weight of her grief. He did not know her secrets, could not fathom the guilt. She cried until the final note of the song stopped playing. Thankful to be able to hide behind her veil, she took Theo's hand and followed him down the row. The Broods had already turned heel and started following the city's other wealthy families into the outer courtyard.

Outside, the various houses stood in their separate groups. Ren had been studying all of them for so long now that she'd memorized family trees and faces. She knew who the first-born heirs were and what industries they would inherit. The more she'd read about their investments and holdings—at least those legally required to be viewable by the public—the more she'd come to think of these great houses as dragons. Ancient creatures who hoarded the wealth of their world all for themselves. Fire-breathing creatures, intent on leaving everyone else out in the cold. She looked around at them now and felt more confident of her plans than ever.

One day you will be extinct too.

43

The name of the teahouse was Spheres.

Ren had forgotten that detail, but not the scent or the sight. This was where she'd had her first date with Pree Williams. A small line had formed at the entrance. Unable to seat customers in their exposed interior, the shop had rolled tables out into the street and scattered a selection of mismatched chairs around them. It was a fine enough morning that most of the seats were taken and gossip was already being traded back and forth. Boiling teas filled the air with steam. Ren's eyes were inevitably drawn to the opposite side of the building.

Most of the debris had been cleared away, but that didn't make the damage look any less devastating. Half of the roof had caved in when the seventeen-string crashed from above. She remembered a run of stained-glass windows on that side of the building. Now their frames were empty and colorless. Ren was surprised to see the instrument was still sitting there, a nearly unrecognizable mass of twisted wood and snapped strings. It had landed a few tables down from where she and

Pree had sat on their date. Ren stared at that exposed section of the shop before turning to Theo.

"Stay here," she whispered. "Vega, with me."

He gave a silent nod as the bird fluttered to her shoulder. Heads turned as Ren made her way across the street. She was dressed this morning as befitted a future member of House Brood. It always helped to look the part. She wore a tailored plaid jacket that cost more than the rest of her wardrobe put together. Ren had chosen matching leather gloves and boots, both the same stormy gray color. Vega completed the look, talons clutched silently to Ren's padded shoulder. All were compliments of Theo's vast bank accounts.

She hated how quickly the folks in line shuffled to make way for her. Ren very deliberately took her place at the back of the line and waited for them to understand she had no intention of passing over anyone. There were some unsettled glances, but tea was being ordered, and the only sin at a teahouse was to dally before you had a drink in your hand. Slowly the line moved. Orders were taken until Ren reached the front. She saw customers at a serving table nearby, stirring honey too slowly into their tea, hoping to eavesdrop on the conversation. Ren smiled at a boy her age.

"I need to speak to the owner."

His throat bobbed. "Right. Of course. Um. Can you . . ."

"I can wait."

He ducked back inside. Several of the servers eyed her through a window. The boy returned a few moments later, escorting a woman Ren knew she'd seen before. She was tall and aproned. Her hair was in a tight braid, shot through with silver. She looked as if she'd lived a year or two in the last couple of days. Seeing someone like Ren was no comfort to her, but still she gestured warmly.

"Right this way."

Ren was led through the front entrance. The servers were busy inside, but she still caught glances from each of them as she passed. There was a sense of foreboding in the looks they exchanged. People dressed like she was dressed did not come to places like this with any sort of good news. Salt in the wound, no doubt. More empty promises, perhaps. Ren didn't speak until they reached a back office area. It was little more than an organized closet with a makeshift desk. She was offered a hard-backed chair. The woman's eyes flicked briefly to Vega before settling on Ren.

"My name is Marlow. My husband and I own the teahouse. We've already reported what happened to the constables. How can I help you?"

"That is the question I was going to ask you. My name is Ren Monroe. I'm here on behalf of the Brood family."

She watched for some sign of recognition. A curling lip or a tight fist. Anything at all. But after a moment Marlow shook her head. "The Broods who built the canal?"

It confirmed Ren's suspicion. No one had ever told Marlow any of what had actually happened. Likely the investigation was "ongoing." The city's warden and his loyal constables would chase down leads, interview witnesses, and report back some nebulous outcome. There was no telling who the guilty party was, they would say, even though hundreds of witnesses had been on hand that night.

There would be no official link to House Brood. Unless Ren delivered one.

"I know who was responsible for what happened to your teahouse," she said. "There was a party in the Brood family's villa in the Heights that night. It's located almost directly above where we are standing now. Theo Brood attempted a magic that failed. In doing so, he dropped that seventeen-string on your tea shop."

She saw a dark storm churning beneath Marlow's tidy expression. She had claimed to be here on behalf of the Broods. The easiest step in her mind would be to mark Ren as an enemy.

"Why are you here? Did you come to gloat about how you'd get away with it?"

"For atonement," Ren answered.

"Ah. I was wondering where this was going. Blood money."

Ren nodded at that. "Far better than no money at all. That's what will happen, by the way. The investigation will turn up no suspects. It will be framed as a mystery. One that you cannot investigate because you have no access to the Heights. No contacts that could inform you otherwise. You'll be left to pick up the remnants of this store on your own. Justice is not waiting around the corner. It's already been decided. You will lose."

"So, what, you think you can just buy your way out of this?"

Ren couldn't help admiring Marlow's resolve. It was a proper woman, raised in the Lower Quarter, who would spit at such an offer. She tried a different approach.

"Do you know the name Roland Monroe?"

Marlow's eyes narrowed. "He was one of the men who organized the Canal Riots."

Ren nodded. "I am his daughter. House Brood was responsible

for his death. I've spent most of my life trying to access the power that killed him. I am not truly a Brood. There's no gold running through these veins. Only the same iron that's in yours. I have, however, been afforded a rare opportunity. I am inside their pretty little house now. I have every intention of burning it to the ground, but before I do that, I would use the resources at my disposal to do some good."

She reached into her jacket pocket and held up a fresh money slip from the bank.

"Name your price."

Marlow looked like she still wasn't sure whether or not to believe any of this. When Ren maintained her serious expression, she snorted. "Sure. Twenty thousand mids should do the trick."

"That's just for repairs?"

Marlow nodded. "Yes."

"You mistake me. This is not an invitation to make ends meet. Dream bigger. I don't want the number that will restore the teahouse to what it was. I want the number that would help you make it what you've always thought it might be. Once you have that number, write it down."

Ren slid the blank money slip across the table. Marlow chewed on her lip for a moment. She reached out, picked up a writing utensil, and scribbled a figure. Ren didn't even look at the number. She turned the slip around and nodded once.

"I'll make sure this money arrives in your account. Before I go, I have one more question for you. If you wouldn't mind . . ."

Ren found Theo waiting in the alleyway. Marlow had written a list for Ren. She slid that piece of paper into his waiting palm. "Names and addresses," she said. "Those are the victims. Everyone who got hurt that night. Marlow marked the ones who would appreciate a visit. She also marked the ones who would prefer a faceless deposit in their account." Ren drew a little closer to him. "I know some of those names, Theo. Aunts who played cards with my mother. Friends I went to school with. If you want to be a different kind of Brood, it starts right now. It starts with them."

Resolve flowed across their bond. She didn't need to look him in the eye to know that he fully intended to make all of this right, or at least as right as it could be made with deep pockets and a few apologies. She knew it was better than what any other Brood would have done.

"I have an appointment at Balmerick," Ren said. "Agora's waiting for me."

He nodded. "Take Vega with you."

The stone bird fluttered slightly before settling once more on Ren's shoulder. She tapped one of the stone talons before nodding in return. "You're doing the right thing, Theo."

"Because of you."

A final look, and then they both headed their separate ways.

44

Ren strode across a desolate campus. Classes had been canceled to give students time to mourn and recover. She saw overly dedicated students perched here and there, but for the most part it was a ghost town. Ren wanted to confirm her new position with the Broods to Agora and hoped to alter her course load accordingly.

Before she visited, however, she silently returned to where it had all begun. There was the familiar grove of trees. Ren envisioned the ghost of Cora Marrin walking past, waving briefly before ducking inside that waiting building. The doors had been bent by the force of their wayward magic. There were ropes signaling the whole building was off-limits. Ren glanced back, and when she was certain that no one was watching, she ducked under the rope and went inside.

All the braziers had been doused. Only morning light, slightly diffused by the bone-thick windows, offered a view of the damage. Scorch marks on the walls. All their lit wicks had burned holes down through the wax display. Ren walked in a slow circle. She passed the seats where Theo and Clyde had been. She could still see Theo's boot heel pressed into the wax canal, a taunting smile curling his lips. Ren continued around the circle.

Here was the spot where Avy had taken his feet. All the veins in his neck flexed in anger. His voice like a warning. She passed the seat where Cora had nervously hissed for Avy to stop, biting her fingernails the whole time. Finally, Ren arrived where she and Timmons had been seated.

The room was empty. The chairs vacant. Except for their ghosts. She glimpsed her friend seated there with perfect posture, silver-white hair glittering in the light of the candles.

"Timmons . . ."

The scene played out in her mind. Clyde's blast of magic and Theo's raised wand. *The unsuspecting wizard is most susceptible to spellwork.* Ren had already calculated their fates at that point. The brawl had simply provided a better cover for her own plans.

In fact, she'd decided what would happen as soon as she saw Theo and Clyde pass by her in the courtyard outside. Her mind had traced the cause and effect, how point A might lead to point B, and she'd reached down. Ren had plucked the blades of grass and hidden them in her pocket. Inside the room she'd counted down the seconds, keeping track of the room's warnings of incoming magic. Just before the spell drew them to their separate locations, Ren had raised her own wand.

"Vega. Leave me."

The bird took flight, winging back through the dark entrance. She didn't want the statue to witness her words or her magic. She had no idea what Theo might be able to learn through the vessel, which existed at the very core of their bond. When the scrape of stone wings faded, Ren began explaining herself to the dead.

"I used my altered coil spell, Timmons. Remember that one? I worked on the mechanics senior year. You . . . studied with me. In the library. Well, you sat with me as I worked on it. But we were together when I did the research for it. Always the two of us . . ."

Her dead friend didn't respond. Ren's plan had seemed so simple. Coil spells bound things briefly together. She'd intended to use the magic to briefly link her destination with Clyde's and Theo's. She very specifically guided their route toward the mountains, thinking the three of them would end up a little lost. Ren would have valuable time to display her abilities to two of the most powerful heirs in the city. It would be a crucial chance to earn a spot in one of their houses.

"But I got it wrong, Timmons. I . . . I don't know how I got it so wrong."

She still wasn't sure why Avy, Cora, and Timmons had been drawn in by her spell. She'd created specific barriers during her casting. She'd aimed her magic at Clyde and Theo. She had taken every imaginable caution to avoid having that magic impact the others.

Why had it gone wrong? Had the coil magic been more powerful than she'd originally calculated? Or was there something about the waxways that had overpowered her spell's carefully summoned boundaries? All she knew for sure was that the magic she'd cast had worked. Too well. It had coiled around *all six* of them. It had bound *all* their locations. And then Timmons had unintentionally amplified the distances.

All while Clyde was being devoured by his own active magic.

"You weren't supposed to be there. In the forest. It should have just been me, Clyde, and Theo. None of you . . . none of this was supposed to happen."

It's all my fault.

Theo assumed she was blaming herself for not protecting them, for not being clever enough with her magic to keep everyone alive. He didn't know—could never know—that Ren had caused all of it in the first place. Her magic had gotten them lost. Her magic had resulted in their deaths.

The ghost of her best friend watched with those bright, unblinking eyes. Across the room, Cora's and Avy's specters had taken their feet as well. She knew they were all dead, but that didn't take away the guilt of their imagined glares. She screamed back at them.

"I'm sorry! I didn't mean for this to happen! This isn't what I wanted!"

Her chest pumped up and down. Ren had no tears left to give them. She'd already mourned. No, she'd come back to this place to complete a necessary task. It was important to stand in the exact place as before. She set her feet the same way and held her wand at a matching height. Her body was oriented just so. When Ren felt certain about the positioning, she performed the coil spell a second time. It wasn't functional magic. Not this time. There were no sources to which she could link herself. But that didn't matter. All that mattered was the performance.

Ren knew investigators would return once the residues had fully settled. They'd run traces to determine what had happened to cause the accident. Her coil spell would undoubtedly leave a mark. Every magic did. Now she'd have a reasonable excuse if they ever asked her. Coil magic? Yes, of course. She'd returned after the funerals, hoping to hold on to that final memory of her best friend. Before they were lost. Before they were hunted through the wilderness by one of their classmates. That was the source of the magic they'd sensed. Just a sad girl attempting a spell that might link her to the memories of her dead friends one last time.

She took a final look around the room.

The ghosts flickered and faded.

"I will not waste it," Ren whispered. "I promise I will not waste this chance."

The dead said nothing to absolve her. The silent echo of that empty room forced her to turn around. She tried to ignore the chill that ran down her spine as she walked back through the dark doorway. Vega fluttered out from a nearby tree. The bird landed on her shoulder with a sharp dig of claws. Ren gritted her teeth but kept walking. Her eyes fixed on the distant buildings. She saw the way Balmerick's coal-black spires pierced the clouds like spears. It was a reminder of what she was facing. All that power and wealth, the boundless ambition.

Ren could not afford to dwell on the past.

Not if she wanted to win.

"Come, Vega. Let's hunt."

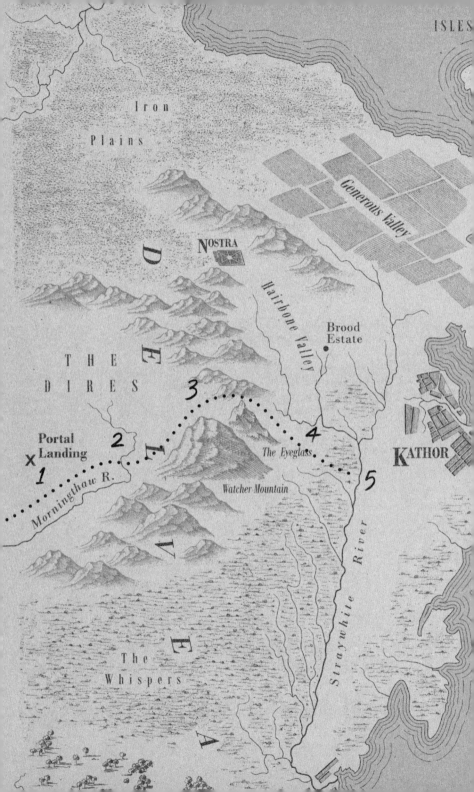

The Waxway Landing - This is the precise location that the six of us were dropped by the errant portal spell. Clyde was dead on arrival.

The Bridge of Light - Our group crossed the Morningthaw River using a spell that solidified sunlight into a bridge. This is also where we discovered Clyde was pursuing us, in the form of a revenant.

The Taming Path - This path led to a wyvern's nest. Theo attempted a mating dance that appears to be hoarded knowledge by the city's elite. I have found no reference to it in any textbook.

The Breath Farm - Our first human contact was with a farm that existed as a front for dragon's breath production. After some research, I believe the farmers were working with the corpse of a dragon called Providence.

The Final Bridge - Theo and I made our final stand against the revenant at this location, narrowly defeating him and two mind-controlled field hands.

ACKNOWLEDGMENTS

The very first book I ever finished was titled *Greyglance*. I'd written short stories for creative writing classes and for publication. I'd started several ambitious projects. But that book was the first full-length novel that I actually *completed*. After spending time polishing it with my writing group, I sent it out to agents. It quietly gathered up a rather large stack of rejection letters. There was interest from agents in certain facets of my work, but the truth was obvious: I wasn't ready. My writing just wasn't quite there yet.

This book—printed, bound, and in your hands—is a very distant, grown-up cousin to that first one. When I started working on it with my writing group, one long-time member said, "This is *Greyglance*! You realize that, right? Do you realize how far you've come?!" And honestly, I'd forgotten. There were a few of the same names. A plot line here or there. The occasional bit of magic. But I hadn't set out with any great intention to revisit that old story. Some ideas just come back to find you—again and again.

I want to begin by thanking my wife, Katie. You've heard every version of this story. Different character names. Altered magics. All of it. You believed in that first version—and you believed in this one. Thank you for always listening, even though I'm sure it feels like I'm dragging you through the waxways and into a different world each time.

I am so grateful to my fantastic editor—Kate Prosswimmer— for seeing me through on this one. You snatched this story out of thin air, found all the places where it could be improved, and gave me the politest shove in the direction of writing the best possible version of this story. Thank you for believing in this book from the very first page.

No editor works alone, just as no author works alone. My thanks to Justin Chanda and Karen Wojtyla at McElderry. I'm grateful to Eugene Lee for keeping this all organized and Greg Stadnyk for the genius concepts that led to the cover for this book. A huge thank-you to Nicole Fiorica for so much hands-on work on world building, edits, and more. I have Erica Stahler and Gary Sunshine to thank for cleaning up every nook and cranny in this manuscript. Thank you for leaving no stone unturned. I'm also indebted to the Bose Collins studio and their artists for producing the cover that stole my heart and is undoubtedly the reason many folks picked this up in the first place.

Of all my books, I think this might be the one that has me most indebted to my writing group and my beta readers. There were a few times where I felt lost during the writing process—or even during the submission process—and you all were like guiding lights back to shore. I'm especially indebted to Caitlin and Jen for their early reads. Your advice completely changed the last third of the story and likely guided the entirety of this series. Thank you.

A well-earned shout out to my agent, Kristin Nelson, and

the entire crew at Nelson Literary Agency. When I think of this book, I think of several long phone discussions we had. We debated so many things on this particular story, but what strikes me most is that you took the time to dig into those conversations with me. Thanks for never being too busy to chat it out.

Finally, thank you dear reader. I'm glad you get to read this version—and not that first one. Some of our stories are like stones. Rough and edged. We have to set them down in the river of time and let them take shape in our absence. I would have handed you something dull and difficult with that first version. Instead, I hope that as you read this version, you felt like I'd set a fine, polished stone in your outstretched hands. Something with a shine to it. Something worth turning over and showing to others. Thank you so much for picking this one up.

Turn the page for a sneak peek at

A WHISPER IN THE WALLS

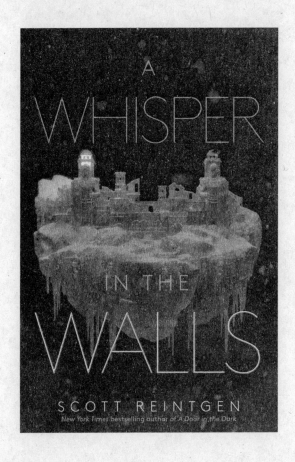

REN MONROE

It was hard to feel like an honored guest when no one would speak to her.

Ren Monroe found herself at yet another party in the Heights. Tonight she was a guest of the Grand Emissary of Kathor. His handwritten invitation had possessed more warmth than all the conversations she'd attempted thus far. She'd arrived an hour ago. Theo had been stolen away to a private room for an arranged meeting with the viceroy himself. The other Broods sought out their own comfortable circles, leaving her completely alone.

Ren tried not to feel bitter about Theo's absence. She knew tonight was important. The warden had announced his retirement. There were one hundred livestone statues scattered around the city, eagerly awaiting the command of a new master. It was possible the viceroy would even go as far as assigning Theo the post tonight. She remembered sitting by a fire, when they were lost in the mountains, and listening to Theo talk about this dream of his. He'd secretly been working toward it for years. And then she remembered who else had been sitting around that fire. Cora had been asleep. Timmons had been sitting close enough to Ren that their knees had been touching.

Before I let both of them die . . .

Ren shoved that thought back into a shadowed cage in the corner of her mind. She took a deep breath and tried once more to join the nearest conversation. Music danced in and out of their words. As she approached, however, the group fell silent. She received a polite nod, a quiet compliment on her dress, and then suddenly they had somewhere else to be. It was hard not to feel like this was an echo of the past. A year ago Timmons had forced Ren to attend another party in the Heights. A slightly wilder one. That night, Theo had been their host. Ren remembered sitting alone on a couch, sipping her drink and watching all the other students who'd already secured their bright futures. That version of her felt a world away. She'd gone through so much. Surviving in the wilderness. Escaping from a revenant. Bonding to a scion of a great house.

And yet here she was—alone once more.

As she watched the group depart, Ren spotted Landwin Brood. He was seated near the fireplace in the study across the hall. He caught her eye, raised his glass, and offered a satisfied smirk. Her social status was undoubtedly his doing. Similar obstacles had risen time and time again over the last few months. As she finished classes at Balmerick, she'd quietly probed for potential alliances. Classmates, teachers, anyone. But even the Broods' staunchest rivals—the Shiverians— refused her offers to meet. It wasn't exactly a problem that she could bring to Theo, either. After all, how would she explain the *why* behind her desire to make those new connections?

Well, I need someone powerful, who hates your family, to help me destroy your house. Any ideas?

It was already difficult enough for Ren to veil her feelings from him. Their bond offered emotional insight into each other. Brief slashes of raw *feeling*. Ren had gotten quite skillful at summoning new explanations whenever he sensed that slumbering rage that lived inside her.

Almost on cue, Theo came thundering up the steps. He nodded once to his father before turning to Ren, concern written on his face. "Everything all right?"

He can feel my frustration. "Yes, of course. I just got the wrong name for one of the Jamison sisters. It's nothing. I was just embarrassed. What about you? How was your meeting?"

"Confidential," he replied, then winced at how haughty that sounded. "For now. I'm sorry. It was just a preemptive conversation. He wanted to know about . . . what happened to us."

"In the mountains?"

It was a foolish question. That was all anyone wanted to know about her and Theo. The rumors surrounding their time in the mountains were many, a culmination of stories that were starting to edge into myth.

"Yes. More out of curiosity than anything. I . . . I think he might have been vetting my handling of Vega. Making sure I'd demonstrated clear skill . . ." He shook his head. "I don't know."

Theo was biting his lip. She did her best to focus—ignoring his father looming in the background—and set her eyes on the uncertain boy she'd bonded with. The boy to whom her entire future was now tethered. "Who else would they consider for the role?"

Theo's eyes darted nervously about the room. "The retiring warden has a nephew serving in the guard. He's not from a major house, but he's got plenty of actual experience. The Carrowynd family has a daughter—Zell—who has livestone training like me, but I'm not sure if they had the same intentions that I had when we commissioned Vega. Traditionally, the crown wants someone young who can fill the post for several decades. But what if they ignore tradition? There are generals from the War of Neighbors who would be very sensible choices. . . ."

"But you're the best fit?"

He blushed slightly. "Yes, I am the best fit."

That was good. Theo was already powerful, but she'd learned about the structure of his family over the past few months. He was a generation away from proper influence. If Ren wanted to destroy House Brood, she still had a lot of careful planning and waiting ahead of her. Being engaged to the new warden, however, would usher in a measure of influence that was not directly tied to House Brood. That might provide opportunities for Ren as well. She found herself nodding.

"Worrying won't help," she said. "Why don't you refill my drink instead?"

That earned an unceremonious snort from him. But Theo accepted the invitation, leading her into the next room, where an open bar was waiting. Ren caught a final glimpse of Landwin Brood. He was deep in conversation, but that didn't stop his eyes from flicking up as they passed. It was good to know that he at least thought she was worthy of his attention.

Theo procured a new drink for her. The weight of that cold glass in her hand brought on another echo of memory. Last year, she'd set down a glass just like it as Timmons drew her out to dance on the balcony. The revelry had paused when Theo took the stage. He'd performed his fateful party trick, which sent a massive instrument crashing recklessly down into the city. His worst hour had been an opportunity for Ren. A door opening in the dark. She had been brave enough to walk through it—and now she felt there was no turning back. She could only press on deeper into the shadows and hope there was some light waiting for her in the distance.

A dinner bell rang before they could take their first sips. Theo led them through the crowd, heading for the sprawling banquet table in the far corner. Ren paused at the threshold, eyeing the available seats, and was surprised when Theo tugged her on toward the staircase.

". . . what are you doing?" she asked.

"We were asked to sit up here tonight."

She raised a curious eyebrow. Theo grinned at her reaction. Clearly, he knew something was afoot. Ren felt a pulse of adrenaline. The upper floor was always reserved for the lords and ladies that ruled their city. At these obnoxious dinner parties, the heirs normally sat at a separate table, almost always a floor below. Ren and Theo had found themselves positioned that way at any number of parties this summer, fraternizing with the other young men and women who would one day be handed empires.

Now she allowed herself to be drawn up the stairs into the presence of true power. She had to remind herself that there was nothing special about the people in the room. No blood or magic that ran through their veins that made them any different—any better—than her father and mother. Still, it was hard not to feel the weight of their collective meaning to the city. Like entries from a history book that were stepping out of the pages, taking on flesh and bone before her.

There was Able Ockley, the most dangerous duelist in the city. He was lost in conversation with Ethel Shiverian—she and her sister had practically invented the levitation magic that was keeping them all afloat right now in the Heights. Not to mention a hundred other spells. Balmerick's headmaster—Priory Woods—looked red-faced and drunk, though that did not stop the grand emissary from sweeping over to pour more wine in her cup. Other members of the ruling houses were present: the Graylantians, the Proctors, and the Winterses. At the head of the table, the viceroy sat like a golden seal confirming their power. All of them chatted amicably as servants glided ghostlike in the background.

Theo guided Ren to where the other Broods were sitting. Landwin sat in gilded silence. His wife—Marquette—always seemed positioned slightly behind him, even when seated next to each other at the table. She kept her hair short, beautifully shaved on one side, and appeared to be uninterested in the conversations around them.

Ren's attention was drawn by obnoxious laughter to the eldest son and heir to their house: Thugar Brood. She'd learned that his great vice was the flesh, which meant he rarely took notice of Ren. He kept himself in prime physical condition, nothing wasted, and his wife looked like she'd walked right out of a drunk's fantasy. Ren thought if a single thread of her dress unraveled, she might come pouring out onto the table.

Beside them sat Tessa Brood. The girl waited, straight-backed with her hands folded neatly in front of her. Ren thought she was the most dangerous of the group. Quiet and intelligent. Tessa was a famous singer who had earned a permanent role in the city's finest acting troupe. Ren had initially believed it the result of nepotism. Most of their positions were the result of nepotism. But then she'd heard Tessa sing. Her voice was threaded through with gold. It might have been more moving if she hadn't heard Tessa use that same voice to skewer servants for even the slightest errors. She was tilted ever so slightly toward her mother, quietly commenting on something.

Theo and Ren took the two remaining seats. She felt a blush creep down her neck as their movement became some unspoken, final piece to the puzzle. As they sat—completing the table—the other conversations in the room fell quiet. Servants tucked away neatly into the corners of the room, nearly blending in with the wallpaper behind them.

The viceroy stood, tapping his glass with a spoon.

Delvean fairy tales were full of bumbling kings. They failed to do their duties and any number of wizards would arrive to save the day. The viceroy didn't fit into those old stories. His ability with magic had been unrivaled at Balmerick—Ren knew some of his records there had endured the test of time. That felt like an important foundation for the man who existed as the primary check on the influence and power of the five major houses. His gray hair was thick and long, brushed back artfully. He had high cheekbones and a narrow jaw, covered over by a neat gray beard. He'd risen through the government—a second son from one of the minor houses—and Ren marveled at his calm as he addressed the wealthiest members of their society.

"Good evening," he began. "I have several announcements that deserve your undivided attention—and then we will get back to the business of growing fat and happy. First, we've negotiated a new position with Ravinia. The recent sanctions against the free-port have been lifted. All of you may resume whatever trading you pretended to cease over the past three months. Everything can be out in the open again. Business as usual."

There were a few nods, a few raised glasses.

"Next, I would ask Theo Brood to stand."

A shiver ran down Ren's spine. It felt like her name had been called too. She watched as her bond-mate took his feet. There was a lesson for her there, written in his posture. Power in the way he lifted his chin, set his shoulders, and stood before the closest thing they had to a king.

"As many of you know, the defense of our city—and its interests—is paramount. For all the petty rivalries that exist between the great houses, we have always been unified by that common interest. If war knocks on our door, we all answer. If a plague comes, we all share the antidote. It has always been this way between us. In peace, the best are allowed to thrive and survive. But in times of trial, the city's livelihood is our greatest priority. Kathor comes first.

"As such, we take any appointment to the city's defenses very seriously. It is no small task to be one of the shields that stands between Kathor and its enemies. After all, there are many who would take joy in seeing us fall. Any person appointed to such a role walks out into the world bearing *our* seal on behalf of *our* people. Theo Brood, do you think yourself worthy of such a calling?"

Ren could sense the emotions that question stirred in him. This was a moment that he'd patiently approached for many years. Now that it was here, he showed no signs of nervousness.

"I am ready and willing. My worth will be proven in time, Viceroy."

She saw the viceroy's eyes flick briefly to the right. When Ren followed his gaze, she caught the most subtle of nods from Landwin Brood. A silent confirmation between them. Then the viceroy's attention swung back to Theo.

"Well spoken," the viceroy said. "It is my honor then, on behalf of House Brood, to approve you as the next watcher of the valley. I am sure you're familiar with this position. After all, a Brood has held the post—or a version of it—for nearly a century. . . ."

Ren might have missed what had happened if she didn't feel pain sear a path across their bond. Her stomach turned and it took all her self-control to *not* react to that sudden rush of emotion. Theo's pain dripped into her. His disappointment flooded her mind. She finally saw the error. He was not being named warden. The viceroy had used some other term.

". . . the watcher might be a family title—and the mountain castle might belong to the Broods—but it also acts as a functional piece in the armor that Kathor wears. Thus, it falls to me to give final approval for the man or woman who should claim one of the most time-honored posts in our city's long history. . . ."

She noted the others' reactions just as Theo's emotions honed into a fine-pointed shame. All around the table, smiles like daggers. The worst were offered by his own family. Thugar looked like he was barely keeping himself from laughing. His sister wore a condemning smirk. His mother's eyes were downcast. Landwin Brood did not bother with the effort it took to smile. He simply watched his son take in the weight of what was happening. Ren could not help admiring the way Theo kept his face neutral. Even as the entire table enjoyed some joke at his expense, he stood his ground and pretended indifference. Ren felt a fierce sense of loyalty to him at that moment. Completely separate from their bond. Her fingers itched to reach for her wand and wipe the smiles off their faces. She'd never heard of that specific title, but the expressions around the table made it clear: this was no desirable fate.

". . . you will take a few days, gather your possessions, and make your way to Nostra. You go with the full commendation of this city, the full support of your house, as well as the faith of your people. Everyone, raise a glass to Kathor's newest watcher of the valley."

A raucous cheer rang out, followed by the clinking of glasses. Those sounds could not fully hide the curious whispers around the room. Theo didn't react the way Ren might have. He simply bowed his head, rather than thundering angrily out of the room. She felt that pitted dread in his stomach begin to roil. It was burning a path toward something Ren found far more useful: anger.

Theo took his seat and refused to look at any of his other family members. She waited to ask him until the servants hustled out the first course, distracting those seated nearby.

"What just happened, Theo? Where is Nostra?"

She had a vague inkling of an idea. A memory from some corner of a map.

"Exile," he whispered back. "My father has exiled me."

As a plate appeared in front of her, Ren heard the unspoken words at the end of that sentence. Words Theo would never say aloud, because he cared too much for her, even if they were true.

My father has exiled me . . . because of you.

Ren didn't understand all the implications. She lacked context. Was it a true exile? Something else? For a while, the two of them sat there in silence, hating Landwin Brood in equal measure. They ate their food without a word, chewing like it was their only duty left in the world.

Topics that normally would have fascinated Ren made their way around the table. Magical theory and state secrets, all of it tangled with the light tinkling of silverware and glasses and laughter. Landwin Brood caught Ren's eye as the entrées were served. He raised his glass, ever so slightly. A clear taunt. She'd imagined her bond with Theo would open an entirely new world. A rush of resources and power and influence. Her chance to begin setting an empire on fire.

But now Theo was leaving. Would Ren be expected to go with him? Or would she be abandoned here—as she was earlier tonight—in this glittering circle of wolves? She could only imagine the strain of being separated in that way from someone she was bonded to. Maybe that was the point: to break them. Rather than show weakness, Ren met Landwin Brood's appraising stare. She lifted her own glass and offered a lifeless smile.

It turned out to be one of the best meals she'd ever eaten.

THERE IS NOTHING MORE DANGEROUS THAN A FAERIE TALE.

In the magical underworld of Toronto, four queer teens race to stop a serial killer whose crimes could expose the hidden faerie world to humans. . . .

Wish them luck. They're going to need it.

"Beautifully written and deliciously complex . . . I couldn't get enough."—Nicki Pau Preto, author of the Crown of Feathers series

A *New York Times* and Indie Bestseller

"One of the freshest YA fantasies I've read in years."
–NATASHA NGAN,
New York Times bestselling author of *Girls of Paper and Fire*

"A richly woven standalone fantasy that's as beautiful as it is fierce . . .
Rebecca Mix has solidified her place as YA fantasy's new auto-buy author."
–ADALYN GRACE,
New York Times bestselling author of *Belladonna*

"Feral and tender at once."
–CHLOE GONG,
New York Times bestselling author of *These Violent Delights*

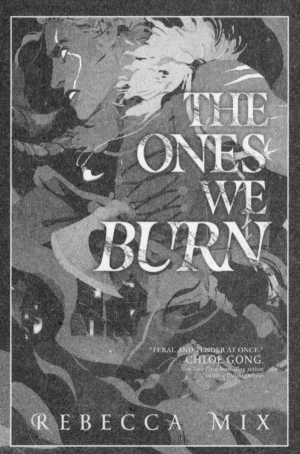

PRINT AND EBOOK EDITIONS AVAILABLE
Margaret K. McElderry Books
simonandschuster.com/teen